The
Temptation
of Gentry

Published by Karen G. Berry.

Available through Amazon.com and other bookstores and online stores.

Cover design and artwork by Mark Ferrari.

Original photos from pixabay.com are CC0 Public Domain.

The
Temptation
of Gentry

Karen G. Berry

Other Works by Karen G. Berry

The Gentry Books, one through three –
The Temptation of Gentry
The Confession of Gentry
The Reconciliation of Gentry

Other novels –
Love and Mayhem at the Francie June Memorial Trailer Park
The Iris Files: Notes from a Desperate Housewife

With Shannon Page as Laura Gayle –
Orcas Intrigue
Orcas Intruder

For every English teacher I have ever had.
Thank you all, every day, for the difference you make in the world.

There are only two stories.
One is, someone went on a long journey.
The other is, a stranger came to town.

John Gardner

SEPTEMBER 1996

Kathryn

Kathryn concluded that, despite sharing parents, her daughters were of different breeds.

Marci had arrived squalling like a summer storm seventeen years earlier, demanding the breast. She'd spent her chubby grade school years with crossed arms, glaring when denied anything. At some point, she'd quietly transformed herself into a petite, slim teenager who always got what she wanted.

Gretchen, Kathryn's second daughter, had arrived long, limp, and silent, asking little of the world other than to observe it. She observed, catalogued, compared. At age ten, she'd exhibited no drive to acquire anything but knowledge. She'd approached Kathryn at age six with a question about amniotic fluid. "Is it like the ocean, Mom? It should be, since . . ." She thought for a moment, ordering her ideas. "Life came from the ocean and we come out of amniotic fluid."

Kathryn had studied her daughter's eyes. "Is the ocean the womb of the world?"

Excitement dilated Gretchen's pupils, black against the brilliant blue of her irises, holes in the Arctic ice. "Maybe." Kathryn had driven Gretchen to the library because that's what one did with a child like Gretchen, pointed her toward the reference shelves. Go forth, child. Go forth and shine.

Five minutes with an encyclopedia sent her to lean against Kathryn, downcast. "Electrolytes, carbohydrates, proteins and urea."

Kathryn had stroked back her daughter's white-blonde hair. "Can you put that in layman's terms for your mother?"

"Like that stuff I have to drink when I'm sick."

"Pedialyte?"

"Yes. Pedialyte with pee in it. It isn't high in saline at all. I thought it would be. Because human beings are very high in salt."

"So are potato chips."

A gentle shake of Gretchen's head cleared it for the next batch of deep thinking. She gave her mother a look of patient disappointment before they went home.

So, it appeared that humans didn't start out as bitter. Life kept adding salt until they all pickled in their own brine. Those who lived at the coast were especially salty. For Kathryn, each day started with licking salt from her lips, and each day ended with a thorough washing of her skin in an attempt to forestall the effects of salt and age. Kathryn was weathering just fine, but the siding on her home was weathering poorly. The longer boards on the big house in particular. Something about the span they encompassed made them permeable to peeling and swelling. Fixing it was going to be expensive. She would have to tap into the divorce settlement that she had (so far) refused to touch.

Kathryn hated to think about money. She felt it was a point of pride. She never had when she was married and she hadn't intended to ever start. So much for intention.

While she mulled over matters financial at her kitchen table, she sipped coffee and worked on the crossword. Her scientific observer lurked nearby on the narrow back stairs, her nightgown tucked around her hips, her bare feet braced on the black grip mat nailed to the risers.

The phone's ring made Kathryn drop her pen. This was an old phone with a real bell, and there was no way to turn it down. "Mumford residence, this is Kathryn." Daytime calls were usually from the grade school, asking Kathryn to come fetch her youngest from the nurse's office. Gretchen was already home feigning illness.

"Kathryn. It's Rob. We have a situation, here."

"A situation?" Her voice was polite, but archly so. "Is it Marci?" Had her older girl created a situation at the high school? This would have been so unlike her. Kathryn was almost excited at the prospect, a little variety in their lives.

Rob let out a burst of the nervous laughter that punctuated most of his conversations. "No, of course not. The new computer teacher will be here in a few days and has nowhere to live."

"I see." But she didn't.

The local housing shortage was acute, as most of the homes at the Oregon coast belonged to people from Portland who only visited them a few times a month. The people who actually had to live at the coast in order to work couldn't afford to live in the towns that offered employment. "That's too bad. How does this concern me, Rob?"

"Well . . ."

Oh lord. Did Rob think she'd converted her home into a bed and breakfast?

Cottage roses? Chintz? Of course, just what she wanted, to fill up her rooms with firm young couples who kept her up all night with their athletic marital bliss while she slept fitfully, then rose at dawn to make scones for them. Or maybe he envisioned more of a rooming house, Kathryn in a frayed robe with a cigarette dangling from her lip, telling people lights out at ten and a dollar extra for breakfast. "I'm sure there's something in Wheeler."

"I was hoping to find something closer. Is your little house furnished?"

Gretchen kept inching farther down the stairwell. Kathryn put a hand over the receiver and let out a hiss. "Go upstairs and do a better job of pretending to be sick."

"Kathryn? Did I lose you?"

"I'm here. But I don't think my little house is an option. It's basically a shed with a bathroom."

"You should be a real estate agent. You're really selling it."

"I'm being honest."

"Well I'm sure it's not *that* bad. Doesn't it have a helluva view?"

Her head fell forward. "Yes. It has a helluva view."

"A view makes up for almost anything. Could I look at it?"

Kathryn considered. There was a small amount of mental math, rent versus the portion of child support that would go directly to her older daughter once she started college the following year. She imagined the rent money accumulating in an envelope labeled "*siding*." When the siding was fixed, she could kick out this tenant. The warped siding would disappear, replaced by cedar shingles and clean white trim. And all this would happen without cracking the divorce settlement, which for reasons both personal and perverse she never wanted to use.

She would win.

The steps creaked under the weight of Gretchen's surveillance.

"Give me an hour."

 ∽

And so, instead of wondering about a twelve-letter word for falsehood, Kathryn filled a bucket, splashed in some vinegar, and attacked the window that gave onto the beautiful view. Gretchen industriously applied a broom to corner and cobweb. The sun shone through Gretchen's nightgown to reveal legs longer than her mother's and not much thicker than the broom handle. "We could start a house-cleaning business, Mom. We'd be rich."

"Honey, professional housekeepers aren't particularly wealthy." The walls were tracked with nicotine drips. Kathryn didn't remember ever smoking in there. But there were some evenings she didn't recall. "Can you kill that spider?"

"It's a house spider. They're harmless, Mom. And they . . ."

Kathryn took the broom and mashed the insect onto the ceiling before the plea for mercy could become any more impassioned. "Here's your broom. Get back to work. We need to wash down these walls before we paint them."

Gretchen frowned. "Mom. Who is going to live here?"

"A high school teacher. Maybe."

"Is it a boy or a girl?" She sounded like she was anticipating a baby, and needed to knit a little pink or blue cap.

"A teacher, Gretchen, not a newborn."

"Okay, a man or a woman?"

What a perfectly sensible question.

The last person they'd hired for the position was a woman. She'd fled almost immediately. Perhaps the football coach had asked her out. "I think it's a man."

Gretchen narrowed her eyes. "Will he be Marci's teacher, then?"

Kathryn leaned her forehead against the spotted glass, imagining Marci's eruption. She managed not to say *I need a drink* before she returned to washing the windows. "Gretchen, go fetch me some coffee."

"Coffee leeches your adrenal gland. Adrenaline is your 'high-octane' fuel. You use it when you get mad or scared. Excited, too."

"How do you know these things? And why?"

Gretchen stared back with her eyes of Arctic blue. "I just do."

The crunch of wheels on gravel announced Rob's sedan. Early as always. Gretchen flew off to the house so she wouldn't be caught out in her nightgown. Kathryn waited, staring out the window at the view. Stunning. And she so rarely noticed it anymore.

When Kathryn bought the house, she thought she'd never look at anything else.

She'd first seen this house on her honeymoon when she was twenty-one. In 1971, anyone could buy a second home at the Oregon coast, including people like Kathryn and her new husband. They were two capitulating hippies, cleaning up, settling down, joining the Establishment. They were still renting back in Portland, but Kathryn bought their house at the coast outright with cash from a life insurance settlement. The big house had an unimpeded view and direct beach access, a bad foundation, carpenter ants, mildewed bathroom fixtures and warping window frames. But it was the little house that sold her. It sat just north of the big house, right at the top of the bluff, promising solitude with a view.

Repair money went to shoring up the structural problems of the big house, instead of fixing up the little house. She'd wanted to convert it to a studio for some as-yet undefined creative pursuit. Her ex wanted to free up the garage and park the mower in here, put up a pegboard for the tools he didn't use, install a workbench. She didn't let him do that, but she didn't do a thing with it, either.

Rob's wide and sagging face appeared at the window that comprised half the door. He looked hopeful, as always. "Kathryn. I've missed you at the meetings."

"Well." She drew herself up, mouth tight. She didn't want to talk about AA meetings. "We're just talking about the little house today. All right?"

Rob nodded.

"All right then. Here's the master suite." The marital bed, banished from the main house ten years before, took up most of the square footage. "Over here we have the formal dining room." Kathryn rested her hand on the red vinyl of her parents' dinette set. "And here's our state-of-the-art kitchen." The kitchen lined up along the north wall, a tiny fridge, the bathroom door, a two-burner stove, the closet door, a rusty sink with a tattered calico curtain on a piece of clothesline hanging below it. Thankfully, Gretchen had already removed the mousetraps.

Rob stuck his head through each door in a show of interest. The closet wasn't too terrible. The bathroom was dominated by a gargantuan claw-foot tub that reclined, voluptuous and welcoming, like a circus fat lady in a tiny tent. Over it, some rigged-up arrangement of nickel pipes, bars and faucets created a shower.

"I think he'll want it." He rapped his knuckles gently along on the wall as if locating a stud. "How much?" When she named a ridiculous sum adequate to the sacrifice of her privacy and the eventual acquisition of new siding, Rob chuckled in relief. "I'll call him and tell him about it. He'll probably need a phone line for his computer."

She shrugged. "I can have one installed." Why did computers need phone lines?

"I'll have him call you." Rob's face was round and open, greyish and pocked. It reminded her of a bowl of oatmeal. But a very *kind* bowl of oatmeal. "You know where we are, Kathryn. When you want to start coming back."

Her voice, when she spoke, was hard. "The rental, Rob. Just the rental. Have the renter call me." He nodded and left.

The renter? What the hell had she just done to herself?

And it came clear in one of those humiliating bursts of illumination that overcame her like the occasional hot flash. Rob was offering her this renter in the same spirit in which he'd taken her to the basement of the Catholic church across the highway, the same spirit in which he sat patiently beside her at meeting after meeting.

He thought she needed help.

Gretchen emerged, elated at having evaded yet another day of school. She wore a grubby red sweatshirt and too-short jeans that showed off her bony ankles and large red clogs, her platinum hair twisted into braids. She casually handed Kathryn her purse and car keys.

Kathryn frowned. "Where are we going?"

"We're going to get paint. You said."

"You're sick, remember?"

Gretchen shrugged. "You need help."

Kathryn didn't want any damn help.

⁓

At the hardware store, Gretchen held out a chip. "It's called 'Yolk.'"

"It's quite . . . intense."

"It's sunny! And look at this, Mom." She held out a bottle. "It takes rust out of sinks. I checked the ingredients and it should work!" The little housekeeping scientist, excited about rust-free sinks. Kathryn was excited the paint was marked down. "Can we get ice cream?"

"You're sick, remember?"

Gretchen blinked her white lashes. "Ice cream would make me feel better."

They waited to cross the traffic on the drag. Mostly local, more trucks and fewer Suburbans. Her friends' Land Rovers would be back for weekends. They would drop by, sit at her dining room table, drink wine and tell her about the old neighborhood, who'd moved up the hill, who'd moved down, who had done the unthinkable and moved to the other side of the river. A few of them would confess to affairs. Kathryn operated under a clear double standard when it came to infidelity. When women cheated, it was a matter of identity and affirmation. When men cheated, they were scum. Kathryn forgave whichever friend was bedding a soccer coach, but perhaps she would dodge her friends until the next spring. She did that some years.

They always forgave her, too.

Gretchen had a hint of a frown on her brow. "Mom? What are you thinking about?"

She forced a smile. "Summer is over."

"Will you miss your friends?"

"A little. But I have you." And then she sang. "*I know . . .*"

"*I know . . .*" Gretchen sang back, smiling. She knew her cues.

"*. . . you belong to somebody new . . .*"

"*But tonight . . .*"

"*. . . but tonight, you belong to me.*" They held hands and crossed the street, singing.

⌒

Gretchen's face floated over the glass case, relying on visual analysis rather than asking for a taste. "It's hard to pick."

"Then have two scoops."

"I can't *eat* two scoops." Sometimes Kathryn missed Marci's childhood. As a child, her older girl had practiced no moderation. Gretchen was too troubled by waste. She also had a little trouble with choices. After every tub was inspected and she'd finally made her selection (Marionberry Pie), Gretchen pulled her cold blue gaze from all that frozen sweetness to her mother. "What do you want?"

"Nothing."

Gretchen's shoulders folded in defeat, then squared in defiance.

They sat outside, Kathryn's back to the wind so her lighter wouldn't blow out. Gretchen lapped at her cone long enough to reassure herself that she'd made a good choice. She held out the cone. "Have some."

"No thank you."

"You never want anything, Mom."

"I live on air."

Gretchen wrinkled her nose. "You live on smoke." She looked up at the sound of a familiar rumble. That rumble was perhaps Kathryn's least favorite sound in the world. The source of it sat too high and went too fast, and her daughter Marci's furious face filled the passenger window. Such a lovely face when it wasn't rolling its eyes. How could her older daughter squander her beauty on all that petulant face-making? More to the point, how could her daughter squander *anything* on that *boy*?

Gretchen muttered, "We're busted."

Marci swung herself down from the ridiculous truck and stomped over, radiating accusation. "Mom?"

Kathryn put out her cigarette, smiled. "Yes, sweet Marcialin?"

This was a cue. Her daughters had been raised on cues, hitting their marks every time. But Marci didn't want to play. She looked from her mother to her sister and back. "What's *Gretchen* doing sitting down here on *Main Street* eating *ice cream* when she's supposed to be in *school*?"

Kathryn raised her eyebrows. "What are you doing down here in that . . . *vehicle*, when you're supposed to be in school?" The truck in question rumbled away, and Marci gave the taillights a betrayed glance. Kathryn loved it when that truck left. The limited but potent charms of what drove it would never outweigh the dangers.

Marci dropped herself into a chair. "Hey, Short Bus. Can I have your ice cream?"

"No way, Fatty." Gretchen kicked a red clog against the leg of her plastic chair.

"Pig. What's with the Heidi braids?"

"They're a celebration of my cultural heritage."

Marci snorted. Such charming children. Marci had her father's coloring: bottle-green eyes, rosy cheeks, a mass of brandy-colored hair she was forever pushing out of her face with the exact same gesture he'd used back when he'd had that much hair. But her body was Kathryn's: short and wiry, with narrow shoulders and a trim waist that spread into capable hips and a round bottom. Her arms and legs were slightly curved and tight with muscle, as if she'd need to land a hard blow or launch into a sprint at a moment's notice. The tipped-up eyes and squared little nose also came from Kathryn, but from whence came that pouty little mouth? Those breasts?

Gretchen was built on her father's basic plan, but without any discernible muscle or girth, just twiggy arms and legs that stretched to absurd lengths. The only curve on her body was her hard little rump. She had Kathryn's coloring; platinum hair, blue eyes, white skin that turned tawny in the sun. The aquiline perfection of her nose came from her father, the wide Scandinavian mouth from Kathryn. Like Marci, her eyes also tipped up at the corners over the angled planes of her emerging cheekbones. While the effect was kittenish on the older girl, on Gretchen, the angle lent something wolfen to her gaze. If these dramatic attributes ever came together in the beauty they foretold, it might be dangerous. For now, she was just an awkward, bony girl with features far too large for her face.

"Guess what, Marci?" Gretchen smiled, lightly bouncing in her plastic chair.

Kathryn studied Marci's outfit, a pair of flared brown cords and an orange sweater. "I wore that same outfit when I was in college. Did you get that out of one of my trunks?"

Gretchen bounced harder. "Marci! Guess what! You'll never guess."

Marci rolled her eyes, of course. "No, Mother, I did not get it out of your *trunk.*"

"Yes you did. You're supposed to *ask.*"

"Marci!" Gretchen bounced higher. "Come on, listen, guess what?"

Kathryn frowned. "Those are my boots."

"No they're not your boots." But they were Kathryn's boots. Such gleaners, these daughters.

"Marci, GUESS WHAT?"

Marci shuddered with impatience. "*What?*"

Gretchen beamed with joy, her smile a beacon. "Mom's renting the little house to one of your teachers!"

⤖

Kathryn had tucked up under a throw with a book, a cigarette and a drink. She and Gretchen had washed down the walls and painted them "Yolk." They'd buffed the weathered wood of the floors and applied the rust remover to the kitchen sink and bathtub. It had amazed Kathryn what Gretchen could accomplish, considering how sick she was. A miraculous girl, that Gretchen.

Everything was ready for the tenant. Or, as Marci referred to him, *the Tenant.*

Kathryn stretched out her aching legs on the low sofa. She loved it; the invincible Swedish red leather, resilient padding and clean lines. The best part didn't even show, a kiln-dried hardwood frame that would last a lifetime. It had belonged to her parents.

She sighed in contentment.

"I'm so excited about having a tenant. Just think, I'll have a teacher living in my driveway." Marci was in the kitchen on the phone to Vu, the only friend she seemed to have in this town. Her voice rolled in exaggerated pitch, up and down. "Maybe he can drive me to *school* and help me with my *homework*." She stopped in the doorway to give her mother a furious smile.

Kathryn had filled in some of the more alarming gaps in her knowledge. "He's an award-winning computer science teacher."

"Wow. Did you hear that?" She listened. "Vu says he sounds like a real pussy-magnet."

"Tell Vu to come for dinner. We'll have soap."

"Stop laughing, Vu. This is not funny." Marci hung up the phone and stared at it. "I hate this phone. Why can't we have a normal phone like normal people? Oh wait. I forgot."

The wall phone she referred to was mustard yellow and had an absurdly long curly cord. Kathryn spent most of her phone calls trying to get the kinks and twists out of it. But she intended to leave it right by the back door. It went with the rest of her kitchen, which resembled the set from "The Honeymooners."

She'd found all these flaws forgivable because this was supposed to be a "second home," a "beach house," a "place at the coast." A certain level of dilapidation was allowable in a secondary property. It was meant to offer a charming counterpoint to the first home. But Kathryn's former home in Portland had suffered from its own level of dilapidation.

That Portland house was a true Craftsman with a huge porch, a massive front door that led into an entry tiled in tiny ceramic hexagons. The oak floors were too dark and too worn. The lath and plaster walls crumbled every time she drove a nail to hang a picture. Like the floors, the wainscoting desperately needed refinishing, as did the wooden sills for banks of many-paned windows, all fitted with the original wavy, bubbled glass. The old kitchen was all original and problematic; more of that hexagonal tile on the counters, high ceilings, glass-doored cabinetry that wouldn't stay closed. Rooms opened into each other, parlors and hallways and pantries, creaking wooden stairs, a landing the size of a bedroom, the drafty attic.

Kathryn had loved everything about that house, including the husband who lived there with her. The husband who, one evening, walked into the living room and started to pace. Michael's eyes were a little wild, like he was in the grip of a fever. She asked him what on earth was wrong.

"I have a son, Kathy."

When he told her that, she'd kept her composure. Kathryn excelled at the keeping of composure. She considered Michael's years at the commune before they met, the possibility that one of his free-love adventures had resulted in a recently discovered son. She imagined a tall blond boy, a teenager with his father's tawny skin and jade green eyes. A love child from the summer of love. She'd actually smiled. "How old is he?"

Michael had checked his watch. "Seven hours."

She was sitting in a rocking chair, nursing a drink and a six-month-old baby girl. The baby was ten years old now, Gretchen. Kathryn was still nursing the drink.

In her position, people would have understood if she'd forgiven Michael. She'd graduated with a major in art history and a minor in voice. For heaven's sake, she couldn't earn a *living*. But she'd packed up her girls and driven to their place at coast, and she'd never returned. As far as she was concerned, the Portland house no longer existed. Perhaps it was invisible.

The phone rang, jarring her from this familiar reverie. Marci's voice rang clear and sharp as its bell. "Mumford residence, Marci speaking." She listened. "One moment, please." She carried in the receiver, holding it away from her body as if it were a dead mouse she'd found under the sink. "I think it's *the Tenant*."

Kathryn smiled. "Hello?" On the line, no one spoke. But she heard sounds; city traffic, a dog's high whine, a quiet intake of air as an unknown man gathered his breath.

"Hey. This is um, Gentry. Rob Renton gave me this number?"

Gentry. It sounded like "gently." His voice was low and hesitant. She spoke in her most modulated tones. "This is Kathryn Mumford. And I guess you're interested in renting from me?"

Marci spun on her heel and left the room. Kathryn wanted to applaud her, and wished there were roses to throw.

Another pause, another intake of breath. "I'd like to. But, um, I wondered if there was furniture?"

"A bed, a kitchen table and two chairs."

"Is the table sturdy?"

"The table is indestructible."

"And Rob said I could park, um, nearby?"

"Right outside the door."

He made a little involuntary "huh" of excitement. "It sounds perfect. But I have a dog."

"A dog?" Dogs dug and stunk and shed and drooled. They were eager. They *panted*. "Is it a *big* dog?"

"I think he weighs, um. Maybe about the same as I do."

Unless this was an extremely small man, they were in trouble. "No."

A long pause. "No?"

"No. A dog won't be a problem."

"Okay. Great." She could hear his smile. She gave him directions, which took a little time. He was worried about his mail, so she gave him her post office box until he could get his own. He gave her his estimated time of arrival, so they made plans to meet at Back to School Night so he could follow her home if needed.

"I'll see you there, then." He coughed, as if releasing something trapped his throat. "I, um, have to go. Bye." He hung up.

Kathryn stared at the fire, considering his small concerns. The sturdiness of the table. The proximity of his parking spot. Could life be that small for anyone?

"Was that him?" Gretchen held out her hand for the receiver. "How did he sound?"

"He sounded . . . safe."

"Safe? *Safe*?" Marci paused in the kitchen doorway, making of it a small proscenium. "Oh Mom. *Please* don't do this to me. *Please*?" Her hands performed a theatrical gesture of supplication. "I'm *begging*. Don't get me a teacher!"

"Would you rather have a pony?"

"*Mother*!"

Kathryn raised her brows. "Watch your tone."

Gretchen carried the receiver to the kitchen and Marci took it and slammed it down before dialing another number. Kathryn could hear Marci complaining away again, probably to Vu. Eventually she slammed down the receiver again. She was determined to break that old phone. Kathryn adjusted the things that kept her muffled, the blanket, the smoke, the drink. She only needed to call out for a copy of Sonnets from the Portuguese to complete the picture. Maybe she could have a spaniel delivered. She made the worst fires. A hearth like this deserved better. "Could one of you girls poke the fire for me?"

No one appeared.

The phone rang. And rang. And rang again.

"Could someone get that?"

No one did.

Kathryn sighed, set down her drink, unwrapped herself and went to the kitchen.

"Kathy? It's Michael. Marci called a minute ago."

She opened her mouth. Nothing came out.

"Kathy? Are you there? You're renting out the tool shed? To who, Kathy? I need a name."

She couldn't speak. She couldn't move. After ten years, his voice still entered her like a shaft dropped from a great height, piercing her with a transparent column of anger, grief, longing. Then, mercifully, the shaft moved through. She closed at the point of entry, she closed at the point of departure.

She was able to move again.

Marci

Marci was searching for a word. A word for Back to School Night. One word, that was the rule, and it had to sum up the entirety of Back to School Night in a coastal town, where the school's band played old songs that got the coastal parents up on their feet, clapping and shaking their fists to that old time rock and roll. The booster club sold reheated popcorn by the bag, pizza by the slice and soda by the can. Everyone lined up for their starring moment at the podium. It was as exciting as the old bumper cars on Main Street.

The word was "lame."

This was a night to see what everyone else's parents looked like. No matter how mad she was over the stupid *tenant*, looking at everyone else's mothers made Marci grateful for her own, who had taken up a station by one of the gym doors. Kathryn would never get a perm or stomp around the gym in men's trainers. Her shoes were always impeccable. She smoked too much to be fat. There was a tattoo, but it didn't show, so Marci pretended it wasn't there.

Marci couldn't believe the tattoos on those other parents.

With studied indifference, she pretended not to watch her mother. Kathryn had come to meet the new teacher and show him the way to the house because he sounded "a bit wayward." Marci closed her eyes and imagined a wayward computer teacher living in her driveway. The glasses. The footwear choices. So much to savor.

"I love my life."

"Of course you do. You're rich." Vu, the student body president, sat next to her, wiggling his pinkie around in his ear.

"Would you *stop* that? It's *revolting.*"

He licked the pinkie in question and pretended to test the wind, then dragged it down her arm. She hit him in the shoulder with a fist. Next to her sister Gretchen, Vu was the most intelligent person Marci knew. "And by the way, I'm not rich."

"Riiiight." Vu rolled his eyes. He'd lived in America since he was four. When they first got to the States, his family stayed in Portland with relatives. Vu never stopped talking, but would not talk about what had happened to his father. Vu's mother and grandmother were housekeepers in a motel where Vu worked the front desk at night, one of his approximately fifteen part-time jobs. He scanned the crowd with his large brown eyes. "Jesus. Did someone leave the barn door open?"

"That's rude, Vu." But he had a point. The gym was full, mostly because of The New Computer Lab. The teachers were so excited about The New Computer Lab. They said "The New Computer Lab" in every sentence. In health class: "As soon as The New Computer Lab is set up, you can do your herpes research at any online library in the country." In newspaper class: "As soon as The New Computer Lab opens, you can format your articles on the computer." In English class: "Of course, once we have The New Computer Lab, we can join the Emily Dickinson message board!"

Wow. *Exciting.*

Marci understood that it was 1996, and the computer lab was supposed to get her backwards high school rolling down that information superhighway. Thanks to the new technology department, all the graduates in her class would be computer-literate fishermen, waitresses, cannery workers, hotel maids and retail clerks. Or maybe instead of cannery workers, they could churn out data entry clerks? Every student would graduate with a proficiency certificate in "Oregon Trail" (able to trade oxen for axles and ford rivers).

Her father had bought a computer for her, and it just sat there in her room. She didn't know what to do with it. Vu also had a computer. He'd bought his own. Vu was going to PSU to study business and Marci was going to Colby to study journalism. They were getting out, with or without some computer lab. Everyone was going on about what a great teacher they were supposed to be getting, and all she could think was, why would any great teacher come to *her* school?

But it was Back to School Night and Marci was head of the yearbook staff and it was her job to be enthusiastic. She sat on a folding chair in a row behind the podium with every other person who had something to talk about. The principal, Mr. Renton, droned away about the new heating and cooling system. He was so earnest, so sincere, chuckling away as he went on about the wonders of HVAC. Fans, condensers, ductwork . . .

Vu hung his head back over his chair and pretended to snore. Marci bumped him with her leg, then remembered she had on a skirt. She'd possibly just flashed the entire auditorium. She yanked down her hem. "What a great night."

"Sarcasm is passive-aggressive, do you know that?"

"I didn't know that." She studied the goose bumps on her thighs, pressing her knees together. Renton continued to talk long after he had anything to say, while the great herd of parents shifted nervously in the bleachers. She listened to all the smoker's hacks and tried to pick out her mother's.

A boy walked into the gym. A boy, a man, a guy. She couldn't tell. He was tall and shaggy and hopelessly beautiful, tired eyes and sharp cheekbones and a mouth that looked tender and cruel at the same time and she hated his hair and his clothes were hopeless and he had a stupid *wallet chain* but she panicked because *yes*, that's what she *wanted*, she wanted *that*. She wanted that so much more than what she already had.

She had to stay calm.

Ms. DeGroff was touching his arm, smiling, shouting something at him, pointing towards Marci. Marci hoped she was saying, *See that girl over there? She's your soul mate.* Not likely, but he did walk over. He had this amazing walk, like he owned the world, no, like he was *creating* the world with each footfall.

Okay, she was getting a little carried away.

He sat down next to Vu. He was obviously a new student, but not the kind who sat behind the podium on Back To School Night. That was an honor reserved for the overachievers like her and Vu. This new guy was not an overachiever. He was the same type of guy as her current boyfriend, the type who lurked by the door waiting for Coach Gilroy to thunder over and confiscate his knife, tell him to take off his hat, pull up his pants, lose the chew, Goddamnit, and have some sonofa-bitching respect.

Marci had decided the year before this was her new type.

She thought of them as members of the FCWA (Future Cannery Workers of America). They were mean, cute, and fun. But this new guy didn't look fun. He looked like a poet who could fix your car. What would be the first words he'd say to her? Her heart beat with the possibilities. What had Garret's first words to her been? *You talk too fuckin' much.* She shivered a little, remembering it, and gave a look around for Garret.

She didn't see him.

The new guy had a face her mother would call pretty. *Now who is that?* she would ask, trying to get Marci to look at anyone besides Garret. *What a pretty young man.* Her mother meant that as a compliment. Most of Marci's male class-mates would have to immediately start hitting each other if they heard her moth-er call them pretty. This new guy wasn't pretty, he was beautiful, even with that stupid hair. It was definitely time to get his attention. She stretched out her legs, which were not long, but boys still looked at them.

The new guy didn't look.

That was weird.

Vu's eyebrows went up. "Damn, Marci."

"Oh shut up." She pulled in her legs, hoping Garret hadn't seen her. She scanned the crowd, found him lurking by the exit, expecting Coach to thunder over, etc. But Coach Gilroy wasn't in attendance, for some reason. Garret was probably go-ing to light up a joint and crack a beer in the gym to celebrate. Marci glanced back at the new guy.

Hello, beautiful loser boy. Look at me.

He didn't. Instead, he took in the gym, blinking his brown eyes.

What would someone new think, walking into that little high school? The green walls, ancient bleachers, kids standing in the upper gym dropping things on those below, the tacky homemade banners all over, "The Pirates," "The Fighting Fishermen," "The Cheesemakers." There was actually a team in their conference called the Cheesemakers. They'll kick your ass all the whey. They'll cream you! Get it?

You probably had to live there.

On the few occasions Marci's father had forced himself to step inside the doors of her school, he looked around in disgust. He was particularly horrified by the gym. It was just a gym. A dirty gym, because with the wind and the salt and the sand and the dirt, everything there was always dirty. She'd been able to tell exactly what her father had thought of it by how gingerly he'd set down his Italian driving loafer on the floor.

What was this new guy thinking? He kept yawning and rubbing his eyes while Renton stunned everyone to sleep with his heating and cooling detail. She decided that he looked like a model who lived in a van. That happened, the living-in-the-van part, because the other big failed industry was logging. She decided he could also be a member of the FDTW (Future Displaced Timber Workers).

He'd fit right in.

He still hadn't looked her way. Fine, she'd make him look at her. She openly stared until he turned her way. He cocked his head a little, as if he were trying to place her. It was the perfect expression to go with an opening line of, say, "Do I know you from someplace?" But he didn't say that. He didn't say anything. He just smiled. His smile started shy and crooked, then opened up in the sweetest, most sincere way, showing his straight white teeth.

Marci turned away, blushing. She'd meant to embarrass *him*.

In lieu of anything else to think about, she began to plan their future together. First, she'd get him to cut his hair. She was sure she could do that. She'd convinced Garret to give up Skoal but he still had those faint white circles in the back pockets of his jeans. When she left, he would take it up again, and she wouldn't care because she'd never see him again.

She forgot sometimes that she wasn't supposed to care about that.

She searched out Garret's face in the crowd. He was sitting by Trent Barthel, pretending not to watch her. His profile belonged on an ancient Roman sculpture of a young god. She would miss him, once she got things right with this new stranger.

She went back to her plans.

After the haircut, they could begin dating openly. Garret would want to fight him, but she decided the new beautiful guy was a lover, not a fighter. He'd disarm Garret with his beautiful smile, and Garret would accept that she was with the new guy. They'd be the school's favorite couple. She'd only been a Homecoming princess, but maybe with this beautiful stranger by her side, she could take Prom.

Principal Renton's voice cut in. "And now . . . I want your student body president to talk to you about some exciting new things happening for our school."

Vu leapt to his feet. Finally, the moment they'd all been waiting for.

Principal Renton handed over the microphone and Vu swung it around by the cord for a moment, and began to exhort the gym. "HELLO everyone and WELCOME TO BACK TO SCHOOL NIGHT!" Everyone jumped because after Renton, Vu sounded like a combination televangelist and game show host. "We, as students, want to thank ALL YOU PARENTS for approving the HISTORIC LEVY and USHERING OUR SCHOOL INTO THE FUTURE!!!!"

The historic levy. Marci began to snicker.

Vu ran back and forth, throwing his fists in the air, and it would have been corny if the whole crowd hadn't joined in and jumped to its feet and started cheering! But they did! Vu had them all going strong! Rah Rah Rah. He was more exciting than the tenth graders playing their band class version of "Takin' Care of Business." Awesome.

Vu ended his spiel by CALLING OUT. "I want to hear it now for our NEW TECHNOLOGY TEACHER, MR. GENTRY!" The gym went silent with anticipation. Everyone looked around, waiting for some balding guy with glasses and baggy Dockers to come out and start mumbling about computers.

The beautiful guy lurched to his feet. He took off his cap and stuck it in his back pocket, which, Marci noted, had no faint white circle from a Skoal can. He dragged an arm across his eyes, stepped up and took the microphone from Vu. Marci sat there staring at the ponytail snaking down his back to his waist.

Marci knew this was the single most embarrassing moment of her life.

He squared his shoulders and looked around. "Um, thank you. I'm glad to be here." His voice was very low. Kind of humble. Sexy, really. For a teacher.

Vu turned around and gave her a look with one raised eyebrow. He mouthed "Um?"

Marci wanted to die.

"It was, um, a long drive from Detroit, and I'm dead on my feet, but I'm excited to be here. Trust me, we're going to build a great program together." She could hear the smile in his voice when he said that. "I'm excited to have this chance."

A soft sound rose up from the crowd. She decided it was a collective female sigh. The teacher stood there, tall and sleepy and silent, and all the women were waiting, and, well, sighing? And cooing? And murmuring? Going all Elizabeth

Bennett on Mr. Darcy? Everyone was clearly worked up about all the exciting program building they'd be doing together.

He spoke again in that low, halting voice. "A computer lab is . . . more than the machines. It's more than the hardware and software. It's the information we gather there, and what we can do with it. I'm excited to be able to work on this with you. Thank you all for this opportunity."

There was some polite, surprised applause, and then it built. People were actually clapping for him. A lot.

Well, Marci thought. I guess he's Jesus.

He dropped the microphone into Vu's waiting hand. He walked back and sat down so hard that it made the other chairs jump. Then it was Marci's turn to stand up, pull down her skirt, take her place at the podium and smile, smile, smile while she told the broke parents, the motel maids and cannery workers and fishermen why thirty-five dollars was a terrific price for all the precious memories held in the yearbook. After she finished, the enthusiastic throng started throwing thirty-five dollar checks at her, chanting, "Give us yearbooks! Give us yearbooks!"

She sat back down.

Just one more quick look, that's all she'd allow herself.

He'd pulled his cap over his face, stretched out his legs and folded his hands on his chest. He was napping. Vu snickered, twisting in his chair like he had to pee. Something small could keep Vu going for hours, and there was the new computer teacher, not small at all, snoring softly in front of the entire assembly. Sleeping in public places explained that chained-up wallet.

Tiffany Green got up to speak in her uniform, which she wore *every single day*. Tiffany was the head cheerleader even though she was only a junior. This was an unheard-of accomplishment at the school, which awarded positions by year rather than merit because no one there had all that much merit. Tiffany never got tired of saying, *You guys, I'm only a junior, but . . .* or, *Well, you guys, speaking as a junior . . .* or *What do I know, you guys, I'm only a junior!* Marci was appointed editor of the school newspaper when she was only a junior, also an unheard-of accomplishment, but did she ever say that? Out loud?

Tiffany's boyfriend, Creepy Alex, was clapping for her, as was her mother, Jeannie Green. Jeannie drove one of the buses, and gave home permanents and applied acrylic nail tips in her living room to make extra money. She was the definition of an embarrassing mother, but she was at every game, watching Tiffany cheer.

Tiffany stood up on her tiptoes to talk into the microphone. Whoever Tiffany's dad was, he must have been short. Or maybe she was just small because her mother smoked a lot while she was pregnant. Marci did know she was premature, because Jeannie Green liked to talk about Tiffany's time in the "Isolette."

Vu turned a rapturous face to the backs of her thighs, possibly hoping she'd drop something. She didn't, so he jumped up and took the microphone out of the holder and handed it to her because something like that was too technically challenging for Tiffany. She smiled at him, and he beamed.

While everyone's attention was riveted by the Charlie Chaplin love story at the podium, Marci took the opportunity to reach over and give the teacher a poke in the shoulder. He woke up with a jump. Vu sat back down and started muttering in Vietnamese. He could be saying anything at all. When the two Oanhs started laughing, Marci knew she was missing something good. Once, the librarian asked Vu how to say "Good morning" in Vietnamese. He coached her carefully, and she spent the morning proudly greeting everyone with the phrase "Please lick the dog's penis." One of the Oanhs finally translated.

God only knew what he was saying about Tiffany.

The new teacher looked at Vu with narrowed eyes. He leaned over and let out a string of something low and fierce in Vietnamese. It was Vu's turn to jump. He blinked behind his silly glasses and laughed, nervous. The teacher stood up and walked to the door. The eyes of every female in the gym followed him out.

Vu was respectful and quiet for the rest of Tiffany's spirit club pep talk.

⌒

They stood up and folded chairs to help out the janitor.

"By the way, I hate your new glasses."

"They're cool in Portland, Marci."

"They're not. Trust me." They started for the door. "What did that guy say to you, anyway? Did he tell you to please lick the dog's penis?"

"Actually, no. It had to do with respect." Vu shook his head. "I think he's a psychopath. He's a nice psycho, and apparently a deeply religious psycho, but he's a psycho. I'd keep all Bibles and knives away from him."

Hmm. The word was "intriguing."

Marci needed to find her mother, who always waited by a door so she could slip out for a cigarette. She had that in common with Garret, smoking and the way it always kept them hovering near exits. Kathryn looked like she was just about to do the slip. Marci gave her a meaningful look, intended to let her know just how strange and embarrassing and weird this teacher appeared to be. Kathryn smiled back and shrugged as if to say, "Oh well. What can I do about it?"

The answer was, nothing. There was nothing her mother could do much of anything about, apparently. Marci didn't want to say the word for Kathryn. But there it was.

"Useless."

Gentry

It was 2,500 miles from Detroit to the Pacific Ocean, and most of that was Montana.

My mileage calculations were right on target. I was set to arrive on time until I found myself battling my way through the last mountain pass, where it rained like someone had trained a hose on the windshield. I usually enjoyed this kind of driving challenge, but it was already dark and my eyes burned, my hand ached from the gearshift, my jaw hurt from clenching my teeth and I hadn't slept since somewhere back in the Rockies. I was afraid if I pulled over to relieve myself I'd fall asleep by the side of the road. Normally that would be fine, but I'd promised to be there for Back to School Night, and I try to keep my promises.

The rain stopped when the altitude dropped. The air smelled wonderful, but I was probably overreacting to the olfactory stimulation, preparatory to hallucinating due to lack of sleep. I had good directions from Rob Renton, and I drove right to the school. "Hey Bosco?" He took a break from drooling on the plastic window to stare at me, ever alert. "We're here." Bosco wagged and I parked and tried to find an entrance. Was this really the whole school? It seemed incomplete, unprotected.

Right there, things got a little hazy.

I found the door to the gym, and a small white woman with dark hair and a big smile appeared to be expecting me. She took my arm, told me her name which I couldn't hear because there was an amplified speech about a new boiler blasting out of a loudspeaker right over our heads. She made some sweeping, scooping movements towards the podium with her entire body. Did she want me to lift the podium? Find a shovel? I finally understood the point of all her gesticulation. The empty chair up there was for me. I walked over and sat down and looked up at an auditorium full of white people. They were all strangers, and they were all staring at me.

Things got more hazy. People zoomed in and out of my perception. A fox-faced girl with a sly smile and hair the color of good whisky. A chuckling man talking about ductwork, his back so pillowy in his white dress shirt that I longed to lay my head down on it. A very short red, white and blue dress. Vietnamese profanity. Nothing made sense. At some point I had to stand at the podium and say something to the crowd. I have no idea what came out of my mouth; Romantic poetry, the Cyrillic alphabet, De Profundis, I'm not sure.

All of a sudden, everyone was clapping.

I remember stumbling back outside to the Jeep. I needed to find my landlady. I sat down by Bosco, put a hand on his fur and closed my eyes.

Oblivion.

⌒

I don't like to wake up not knowing where I am.

It was light out, and someone was banging on the side of my Jeep, yelling. Bosco barked, protective. "Good dog, Bosco." Everything we owned was in there. It wasn't much, but I appreciated his watching out for it. I sat up and licked my lips. Salty. I needed a drink of water. "Let's go, boy." And he did, immediately, on the tire of the Jeep. As much as I would have liked to join him, I worked there and knew it would set a bad example to the students.

The air still smelled wonderful.

I entered the school without checking in at the office, found a sign that said "Boys" and burst through like I was conducting a raid. The urinal looked clean. The sink did not, but after I washed my hands, I opened the tap and drank until my stomach complained. It was the best-tasting water I'd ever had in my mouth. I stood up and let out a belch. "Excuse me," I said to no one. I patted my pockets until I found a toothbrush.

I was supposed to go find the principal and have a meeting, but when I saw myself in a mirror after 2,500 miles of driving, living on rest stop coffee and cookies, sleeping in the Jeep and speaking only to my dog, I realized how far I'd strayed from the accepted standards of civilization. I stank. With Bosco, it was okay to stink. As far as Bosco was concerned, it was preferable. But I preferred to meet my new employer when I didn't.

A kid came in, looked me up and down. "Rough night, huh, dude?"

Kids said "dude" here. No one said "dude" in Detroit. I was on the West Coast, even if I couldn't see the ocean in the dark. He shook his head. "Morning is not a happening thing."

"Not this morning."

"So you're new? What homeroom?"

I let it pass, because life is a series of small humiliations, with an occasional large one thrown in for variety's sake. Being mistaken for a student was a small one.

I found the school secretaries, who were as kind and helpful as school secretaries always are. I met with the principal, who was as placid and even-tempered as he seemed to be on the phone when I interviewed. We talked about what had gone wrong and how I would fix it. "A challenge," he told me as he handed over the keys. "I hope you're up for a challenge." I accepted the keys and I left without even looking at the lab because I love a challenge, and I love to fix things, but I wanted a shower even more.

It wasn't cold outside, but the fog sat on my skin and made me feel cold. "Bosco, are you cold? No? Good. Hey Bosco? Let's go find the house."

The Pacific Ocean was somewhere to my right, covered over in a bank of fog. I'd waited all these years to see it, and I saw nothing but fog. As we tried to follow the directions, I wondered how to explain not showing up the night before. "I decided to sleep in my Jeep." Hm. There was no decision-making, so that would be a lie. I didn't lie. "I passed out in my Jeep." Definitely not, no, no use of "passing out," no. I could "end up." "I ended up sleeping in the Jeep." That worked.

I could also blame these directions. I knew I was getting bad directions when I wrote them down, but Mrs. Mumford sounded so nice that I didn't want to interrupt her. Every so often I could hear her strike a match, draw, inhale, exhale. And then she would begin again, her voice relaxed and musical. I was in a phone booth when I wrote these down. Maybe something important was lost while I plugged in more quarters.

"Bosco, can you figure out these directions?" Bosco couldn't. I didn't think he was trying hard enough. Bosco barked. "Hey Bosco? Are you trying to direct me? Let's try one more time. Let's concentrate on solving the puzzle."

Mrs. Mumford told these bad directions like a story. *Once upon a time, you drove down the coast highway and you came upon a giant Sitka.* I thought a Sitka was a tree? I wished I had some good directions. Good directions mentioned highway numbers, mile markers, names of streets, tenths of miles on the odometer. Good directions told you to go north or east on roads, as if you had a built-in compass, an inborn ability to navigate by the stars. Bad directions mentioned things like stores and gas stations and restaurants, embellished mailboxes.

I was looking for a "kind of a curve." Which kind of curve? I'd had plenty of geometry, try me. "*When you see water through the trees, go toward it.*" So I would hit the ocean, and turn . . . left. I needed to go "*a little way, but not too far.*" This was not a precise directive.

I thought I'd found the turnoff. I wrestled my Jeep off the highway onto a gravel drive that ran along the top of a cliff that fell away into the ocean. The sun chose that moment to break through the clouds. It streamed across the sky, raining gold on the horizon, the Pacific Ocean shining like Heaven before me. My mouth fell open, my eyes filled, and I stomped on the brakes to keep from driving right into the glory of it. The Jeep shuddered to a stop.

I wanted to fall on my knees and pray.

Amen.

I would have lived in a tent to be near that ocean. But I didn't have to. I found the kind-of-a-curve, there was the mailbox that resembled a salmon, the houses were right where Mrs. Mumford said they would be and there was plenty of parking, just as she promised. The little house balanced near the edge of the bluff, over the beach. I'm not a bold man, I think before I speak, and usually decide not to speak after thinking. This little house was as close to living on the edge as I would ever get. It was perfect.

Thank You.

Amen.

I stepped out into the roar of the ocean, running my tongue over my lips to savor the taste of this new place. The wind whipped my hair out behind me, blew up the tail of my baggy shirt and made it fill and snap like a pillowcase on a clothesline. I laughed out loud. Bosco stood facing it down, his tail streaming magnificently behind him.

I glanced at the big white house, which was big. And white. That house could wait, because it wasn't mine. I opened the door to the little house and stepped inside.

Hey, House.

I was not alone. A kid sat cross-legged on the bed. Ten, I guessed. She looked at me like I was going to bite her, but I don't bite. Bosco doesn't either, but he really worked her over with the sniffing. "Bosco, *sit*. Good dog. Hey. I'm Gentry and I think I live here."

She turned a bright red, stood up and ran off, arms and legs and blonde braids flying out every which way. Okay, that must have been the wrong thing to say. But she was a kid, kids are curious, she'd be back.

I took a look around. One door out to the driveway, one to the bathroom, four walls, plenty of windows, the ocean in three of them. The walls were the color of an egg yolk. My stomach growled.

I inspected the plumbing. A tub for Bosco with a shower for me. A toilet I immediately put to use, with a small window right over it at eye level. I would have to go extra, just to enjoy the view. I washed my hands. "Good water pressure, Bosco. I wonder where the hot water heater is and how many gallons it holds." Bosco didn't actually care about things like that, but he was patient about the fact that I did. I found it in the closet, which was ridiculously big considering what I'd be putting in there. But at least I had the answers to my important water heater questions.

Bosco sniffed around the fridge while I did a quick outlet count. Definitely a power strip, no telling about the circuit breaker situation. And we had a phone jack.

"We're all set, Bosco."

He smiled, panted, wagged his tail. And scratched at the door. When I opened it, he ran right for the steps like he'd lived here all his life. He bounded effortlessly down to the water. I thought about following him, but I knew that bounding effortlessly was not within my physical limits, not after too many nights asleep in the Jeep. Under optimum circumstances, I could still bound effortlessly, but I'd fall down if I tried at that point.

I needed to get the computer out of the Jeep.

I needed a shower.

I needed to go to the main house to introduce myself and apologize for last night.

I needed to go over to the first bed I'd encountered in, well, I couldn't think how long. I needed to lie down on it for a minute.

Just a minute.

⤳

When I woke up, it was dark. Very dark. I didn't know where I was.

Okay, I was in Oregon. But where was Bosco?

I opened the door. "Bosco!" He barked back. A calm bark, an "I'm here" bark. We know all each other's barks. But he didn't want to come in, so I closed the door. I'd slept through my first opportunity to see a sunset over the Pacific Ocean. Ah, well, I forgave myself.

When I tried to turn on the overhead light in the main room, the bulb stayed dark. Very dark. It was never dark in Detroit. Enough neon shone in my window at night to read by. A shower sounded good, but the bathroom had no light bulb. I opened the refrigerator to make sure I didn't live in a fuse box nightmare. The fridge light came on so I left it open.

I showered and dressed by the light of the fridge.

⤳

Light bulbs.

Outside, no moon and a black ocean. I watched a barn burn down one night in North Dakota, working as part of a bucket brigade trying to keep it contained. The ocean roared like that fire, but it gave off no light.

Bosco let out a bark of hello from under the Jeep. "Are you coming with, Bosco? No? What do you have under there? Do I want to know?" I could have investigated, but the lights from the big house beckoned, as did the aroma of roasting meat wafting out an open door. But this was a back door. The house actually seemed to be on the lot backwards. I would have had to walk around the house to find a hypothetical front door and what if they saw me through the windows?

I decided I was being weird. I do a lot of that. Being weird. Just go in, already.

The open door stood there waiting, and there was more than meat on the air, there were potatoes and onions cooked to sweetness and something else, something green because there's always something green on a plate whether you want it or not, and it smelled so good, Dear God, I wanted that food in my mouth. I counted the hours that stretched into days since I last ate lunch in a school cafeteria.

Please, I have to eat.

Amen.

I walked into a kitchen. That seemed like a safe way to enter, through the kitchen. The food wasn't there, though, it was in the dining room, where they sat at a long table. No one noticed me.

The little girl. "He seems nice."

"Then where was he last *night*? After the *assembly*?" Another girl, older. "Vu says he's a psychopath. He thinks we should hide the knives."

The mother. "Then he's a psychopath with excellent rental references."

"Like you even checked them *out*."

"They were thoroughly checked out."

"He fell asleep at the *assembly*. Garret saw him asleep in his *car* this morning."

"He drove from Detroit, Marci. He must have driven straight through. Of course he fell asleep."

"At the school? That's not a good sign, Mom. He'll sleep in class. He has an *earring*. And he looks way too young to be a teacher."

I've had my share of embarrassing moments in my life. I may be the Grand Prize Winner in the Embarrassing Moment Sweepstakes. But this was a new one, for me, walking into a room to find myself the topic of conversation. It felt like one of those dreams where you look down and you're not wearing pants.

"He doesn't look that young."

"He looks about ten years old."

"He looks older than *me*, Marci."

"It's going to be like having an adult foster child. They'll annihilate him."

They still hadn't seen me. My mouth was dry, no phlegm available to clear my throat. My "Ahem" sounded a little forced, so I followed it up with an "Um." I threw in a "Hey." And they all turned to stare at me with startled eyes. Incoherent babble about the door was open and where's a store and needing light bulbs and sorry about not knocking flowed freely from my mouth, my mouth filling with saliva and need and lust for the food on that table.

"Welcome to Oregon." The mother said the magic words. "Are you hungry?"

"I'm starving."

Invisible hands guided me to my seat. Dishes appeared. I gave thanks. And I ate.

~

The Lord gives, and the Lord takes away.

The older girl was probably sixteen or seventeen. I had a dim memory of her from the night before. The yearbook? Was she speaking in Vietnamese? About lifting some cheerleader's skirt?

What?

She would be my student. When she reached for my empty plate, she rolled her eyes. "I noticed you pray before you eat. You must be praying not to choke to death." She turned on her heel and walked out of the room.

Ah, I could tell, I'd made a fine first impression.

"Marcialin!" The mother was upset enough to put out her cigarette. Almost immediately, she lit another. "I'm sorry."

"I'm, um, used to teenagers, Mrs. Mumford." That made her smile.

The little girl stared. Mrs. Mumford was the source of her white-blonde hair. "Were you really praying?"

"I was saying grace." I tried to sneak it in unnoticed, but someone always noticed. What made people more uncomfortable, public prayer or public masturbation? I thought it was a draw, but in truth had never attempted the latter.

She wasn't staring. She was studying. "Why do you do that?"

"You say grace to say thanks. I'm always grateful to eat." I smiled, but she turned red and stared down at her plate. I was glad she looked away. Kids younger than eleven were hard for me to deal with, not because of how they acted or thought or bounced around all the time, but because when I met the eyes of a young one, I almost remembered. And I do not remember.

I shook my head to clear it.

"You're Catholic?" inquired Mrs. Mumford.

"I am." She recoiled, recovered. I was familiar with that reaction to my archaic faith. Admitting you have religion is shameful. It isn't that people are uncomfortable with you, it's that people actually pity you. They just don't know the right things to say in this situation. Some are also a little afraid of contagion. God germs.

She smiled politely. "There's a Catholic church right across the highway."

"Here's some *light* bulbs." The older girl smacked them on the table with a filament-shattering thump. She sat down and scowled at her plate. This was the girl who was fearing my annihilation minutes before. When she looked up, I smiled. She didn't smile back. I did have a nice smile, I knew that. It was one of the things people said about me. *Gentry, you have the nicest smile*, or, *You're such a good listener, Gentry.* What a fascinating man I was, with all my smiling and listening.

"Thank you. What was your name?"

She rolled her eyes. "Marci."

That's not what her mother called her. "What's that short for?"

"Something stupid."

Her mother spoke with restraint. "Her name is Marcialin. It's a variation on an operatic role. I was trying to be creative. Of course, Marci hates it."

Marci shrugged. "Who wouldn't? But it's better than Gudrun."

Her mother put out her cigarette. "Gretchen's name is a variation on Gudrun."

"Gudrun? Norse, right?" She nodded. "Is that another operatic role? Or from Lawrence?"

"No." Her eyes flashed a little, interest or surprise, I couldn't tell which. Her eyes were a pale blue that I knew from the Dakotas. "I just like the name Gudrun."

"And you like opera."

"She used to *sing* it." The older girl pushed her food to the sides of the plate with an empty fork. "What's *your* name again?"

"Gentry."

"I thought maybe it was Gudrun. Do you always sleep in your car?"

"I guess it depends on the circumstance."

"Really." She tried not to smile. "And *how* long have you been teaching?"

"Five years."

"Five *years*? No *way*."

The mother spoke up. "So you like it?"

"It's delicious."

She smiled. "The work. Teaching."

"Oh. Teaching? Yes. I like it." It was my vocation, but I'd learned not to use such a Catholic term out in the regular world. "It's the only thing I've ever wanted to do."

"Being a *teacher*?" Marci snorted.

Gretchen rose up, pale and silent, to float off into the kitchen. She returned bearing a large glass of milk and an empty plate, onto which she ladled a magnificent pile of food before setting it in front of me. Did she read my mind? "Thank you."

Her voice was barely audible. "You're welcome."

While I sated myself with seconds, Mrs. Mumford made rapid-fire inquiries as to my reasons for coming to Oregon, my whereabouts during the years when normal people have a childhood. Unfortunately, since my mouth was crammed full, I was unable to answer her questions. I chewed each bite thoroughly. I shrugged, smiled, chewed, and when I absolutely couldn't avoid it, offered the most oblique and general of replies.

This was the worst part of meeting people. The give and take of facts.

"Where's your family?"

"I don't have one. Thank you for feeding me. The food was fantastic." I took the light bulbs and helped myself to some roast beef and three rolls for Bosco.

Dogs need to be fed.

Gretchen

Gretchen walked up the drive. Slow. Slower. Slowest.

The bus's taillights winked around the curve up the highway. She'd missed it. Missing the bus gave her a head start on staying home. Still, her mother was home. She looked down the drive towards her mother's station wagon.

She started down the forty-four steps to the beach.

She scanned the sand. There weren't a lot of people that morning. There were usually people and dogs on the beach. All kinds of people, all kinds of dogs. She'd asked for a dog when she was six, and received a breed book instead. That was her dad's idea, to study all her options. She'd never been able to decide. She could recognize most breeds, though. She would verify the breed by asking, *Is that a Portuguese water dog?* or whatever. She was almost always right, and most people liked to talk about their dogs.

The beach was always interesting. Rocks, driftwood. Shells, oysters and mussels, mostly, clams, some sand dollars. They were scoured and usually broken. But Gretchen liked broken things. All the stuff that used to be alive, different kinds of kelp, fish, birds. All kinds of dead stuff. Sometimes, there was a purple tide, and whole entire beach was covered with little lavender jellyfish. They got very dry and felt like paper. You could smell it for miles.

There were more bugs than most people noticed, and birds. During certain seasons, there were nests she checked on. It was a kind of a job. She saved the broken shells, certain feathers. She'd looked up the gestation of the eggs, and if there were any that didn't hatch at the right time, she took those, too. She let them dry, and whatever was inside attached to the side and made the egg wobble when she spun it, like a Weeble. Occasionally she found an abandoned nest that was small enough to take home.

There was a little river near their house. In the summer, the river water ran warm. If stupid little kids didn't scare them away, she could look at minnows. Minnows weren't all that interesting. The truly interesting things were all in tide pools, animals that looked and acted like plants, plants that looked and acted like animals. But to look at the tide pools, she had to go pretty far down the beach.

Sometimes, other people on the beach were interested in tide pools.

At the beginning of that summer, when she was looking at one, an old man had stopped and talked to her. She'd been hoping he'd shared her interest in mollusks, but he'd asked boring questions, like, how old are you, where do you live, do you like school. Gretchen was disappointed but polite.

He'd pulled down his running shorts. *Ever see anything like this before?*

Gretchen had kept her eyes on his face, pretending she couldn't see it going up, going down. She wasn't going to say one word.

Cool little customer, aren't you.

He'd pulled up his shorts and walked down the beach. When he was gone, she'd started to shiver.

She wanted to tell someone, but if she told Marci she'd make fun of her, and if she told Mom she wouldn't let Gretchen go down on the beach by herself. So she'd pretended the wind made her eyes water, and wiped them dry.

Men were gross, she'd decided. Gross, but interesting.

The beach was too empty to go down to the tide pools and feel safe. She went back up the forty-four steps to face her mother. She decided on step eighteen that she had a sore throat.

She had sore throats as often as her mom would let her.

Her mom was in one of her moods where all she wanted to do was stare out the window. "If you're sick, you need to go to your room. And stay there."

Gretchen never minded being sent to her room. She loved her room, every part of it, not just the specimens and collections, but the yellow walls and white curtains and duvet, the row of framed pictures on the wall, pages from a book of fairytales her mother had when she was a little girl. She'd recently taken all the books out of her bookshelf to make room for her shells, specimens and birding materials. Her books were in stacks in the closet. She liked to read in the window-seat. Gretchen loved her windowseat. She could sit there and watch the ocean when she didn't go to school, or at night when she couldn't sleep. She could keep an eye on everything.

Especially the little house.

The little house sat between Gretchen and the water. Gretchen could see the front door very easily. She'd seen her sister come and go through the front door late at night, meeting her boyfriend when their mother was asleep. She'd never been seen, spying from the second floor.

That meant Gretchen could watch the teacher.

She'd started watching him the night before in the high school parking lot, waiting for her mom to finish a cigarette. A Jeep with Michigan license plates had driven up, and a man and a dog got out. The dog was huge, maybe a Newfoundland, and the man was kind of tall. She heard him say *Good Bosco*! and *Back in the Jeep*. He'd walked into the gym.

Her mom had never even noticed any of it. People never noticed interesting things.

After he'd come over and eaten all that food, she'd turned on the outside light so she could sit in her windowseat and watch him move in. It didn't take very long. He gave the dog stuff to carry in its mouth, and he called it, Good dog, Bosco. Good dog. The dog got excited and almost knocked him down a few times. The teacher didn't seem to mind. But he didn't take the dog with him when he got into the Jeep and drove to school that morning.

Except for the dog, the little house was empty.

She'd always wanted to live out there. When she opened the windows and the door, the air moved through so fast she felt like she was out on a boat. The little house felt brave to her, on the other side of the driveway, all alone on the edge of the world. Gretchen wasn't sure which came first, being brave or being alone, but she knew you had to be one to be the other.

Gretchen had helped clean the little house. She'd painted the walls so it was white on the outside and yellow on the inside, like an egg. If Gretchen lived out there, her sister wouldn't be able to meet her boyfriend in the little house when their mother was asleep. And Gretchen wouldn't have to wake up when Marci came in late, and she wouldn't have to hear her mom get mad and start yelling at people who weren't even there. But then she couldn't hear her mom if she fell down or something else.

Still, it wasn't fair that some stranger got to live there, was it?

She stepped inside.

The big dog lay on the bed on top of a sleeping bag. It rolled over and showed her that it was a he. She gave him a nice long belly rub. She decided that human males should have something like that to hide their ugly penises.

Her hand smelled *terrible*.

He let her see his teeth. He was probably very old. Bosco rolled over and lay on the bed with his nose between his paws and watched her, his eyes the only part that moved besides his tail.

The teacher had moved the bed from under the window into the corner, and he'd hung a metal cross with a dead Jesus on the wall over it. She stood there for a minute, staring at the nails in the hands and feet, the mouth hanging open. Horrible. As bad as a penis. There was one of those prayer necklaces looped on one side of the cross.

He'd put a chair next to the bed like a nightstand, clamped a little light to the back and put a Bible there. She didn't really want to touch any of this religious stuff, it gave her the creeps. She switched off the lamp. Generating electricity destroyed salmon runs, but maybe the teacher didn't know about dams and fish ladders because maybe there weren't any in Michigan.

She would look that up.

He'd put the kitchen table against the wall under the big window. A computer covered most of the table. Gretchen wasn't sure about computers. Her dad had bought one for Marci for her last birthday. He bought Gretchen a bike for hers. She didn't know how to ride a bike and no one would ever teach her, but anyway, this computer was hooked up to all this other junk with cords. Leaning against the part that looked like a television was a photograph of him with an old man. Gentry's hair was short, and he looked happy. So did the old man.

He had a big box with more cords and junk in it stuck under the table. He also had a CD player and the same CDs Marci listened to.

Gretchen knew she was a little snoopy. She'd snooped through all Marci's stuff, but she kept her mouth shut about the interesting things she'd found. She'd snooped through her mom's stuff, too. Jewelry. Trunks full of old clothes. Old sketchbooks. Her mom could really draw. Gretchen drew, too, but nothing was finished, and only small parts were detailed. She drew to remember the characteristics of what she watched. Gretchen wished her mom still liked to draw, because she could teach Gretchen how to do it better.

The dog's bowls were very clean. The kitchen cabinet was empty. He'd left the seat up in the bathroom. She put it down. His soap smelled nice. So did his "deep hydration" shampoo. His deodorant smelled like nothing. He had one open and two unopened medium bristle toothbrushes, three packages of waxed mint dental floss, and toothpaste for sensitive teeth. A razor, disposable, also wasteful. A bunch of black terrycloth hair band things. A wooden hairbrush with black bristles. She cleaned the hair out of there and threw it out the window so birds could use it for nesting. A big brown robe hung on the hook on the back of the door. It smelled nice, too.

Gretchen smelled a lot of things. Marci said that was probably why Gretchen didn't have any friends, but that's how animals got information and her sister forgot that people were animals, too.

She'd put hangers in the closet for him. Everything was hung up except for T-shirts and socks and underwear, which were on a shelf. His dirty stuff was in his bag on the floor, next to sandals that looked like they were made out of brown tires. She didn't smell his dirty laundry. He had a couple of caps and a fishing rod, and a whole entire box of books. She thought it was nice that he kept his books in his closet, like she did. Some of them were about computers, and some of them looked like poetry books. She picked up one. It was full of little notes in pencil, "prototype of Rb. Caru., marooned 1704," or "poss. Emersonian?," "Prof clms. Irony but I disagree," "Art func of Society or vice versa?," "TRITE." Sometimes just some words underlined and a line over to the side, where there would be a "?" or a "!" or a "B." There were a lot of "B"s. Sometimes a little list. One said "Ocean.

Tide. Lunar. Cycle. If this obvious then why am I in this class because even I can figure this out."

Gretchen thought the poems were boring, but his notes were interesting.

He had some God-sounding books, like *The Confessions of St. Augustine, On The Imitation of Christ*. More Bibles, two, no three, no, four Bibles. She made herself pick one up and look. It was full of notes in different colors of ink, the pages like tissue paper.

Computers and Bibles. No sheets on the bed, no food in the fridge, no towels even. She looked around, her arms crossed.

She needed to get to work.

Lorrie Gilroy

You know, as a football coach, it really pisses me off how the principal gets all on my ass about lesson plans and curriculum requirements and such and then some sonofabitching computer geek can waltz in here two weeks late and everybody bows down to him like he's the goddamn second coming of Jesus Go Dancing Christ himself.

See, this is a rough town. It only gets rougher in the fall, once the Willamette Valley summer folks decide they're done with it for the year. They pack up their Land Rovers and Expeditions and go back to Portland to listen to opera and drink their five-dollar cups of coffee and we're glad to see the back of them.

Fishing and crabbing and drinking can start in earnest, once we get our town back. This is a fishermen's town full of fishermen's kids. This isn't a summer resort for those Willamette Valley sports fishermen. We've got the highest VD rate and the most participants in the free lunch program in the state. That's right, we're number one. And what the hell we're doing with a computer science program, I have not one clue. These kids don't need any sonofabitching computers. These kids need a good ass-kicking.

I argue about this stuff with Jeannie. She should be on my side, see, since she drives a school bus. I teach the kids, she drives them home, and the kids drive us both crazy. She knows what we're up against. "So what the hell is it with these computers?"

"It's 1996. We need to get with the times. It'll give the kids more options," she says, switching from a game show to a talk show.

"Options for what?"

"Options for what they want to do in life, Lorrie."

Kids don't need options. Kids need discipline. You have to have it, see. It's what makes you a teacher. Any asswipe can sit in front of a classroom and say shit, but a teacher makes you listen to whatever shit he's saying, that's the difference. I can make my kids shut up and listen.

I wish my team would listen. The football season's going like hell. Have I mentioned that? Have I mentioned how tired I am of watching my players wander around the field like each and every one of them has his head up an ass instead of a helmet? Friday nights are like open season on my players.

Jeannie says, "Stop talking about football and pay attention to me." She says, "You want something to eat, Lorrie?"

Not if she cooks it, I don't.

So the new computer room is directly next to my classroom, and I had to listen to the hammering and drilling and crap every time I came by this summer. Drove me nuts, and I have enough to worry about this fall, with this team I have. I've got enough worries, one goddamn player with a speck of ability and the rest nothing but asswipes, without having to hear about the computer teacher. That's all anybody's been talking about around here, the new computer god. The other one stayed a whole week. I wondered how long this one would last, but I didn't even catch his entrance last night because I was having a talk with an asshole about a knife. But I heard about him from Jeannie. He made quite an impression with the ladies.

And so, today, see, this kid comes staggering down the hall with I-don't-have-a-sonofabitching-clue written all over his face. I don't know this kid so I figure he's new. Maybe he's been up in Alaska fishing with his dad, because he looks like a fisherman's son, baggy jeans and long hair and a cap, everybody's gotta wear a cap indoors.

But what was this box of cords and whatnot, and what was he doing outside the new computer room, standing there at the door and dropping shit out of this box? You've got to help a kid like this. It'd be criminal not to. It's just a question of how you help him. You can carry things for him, or you can just shoot the poor clumsy loser and put him out of his misery. So, I tell him, "If you're looking for the new computer geek, he's not here yet. He doesn't start till tomorrow, see."

And he says, "I'm the new computer geek."

Well, shoot me dead. All that sonofabitching hair. He looks like a hybrid, like a combination sissy and stoner, right down to the earring. I hate earrings. I don't even like them on women, see, and if one of my players shows up with an earring, he has two choices, Goddamnit, take it out for the season, or get it ripped out by me, because I hate earrings on men. It's like tits on men. What's the point?

But I've got to be careful what I say to the players this year, because a couple of parents said I was "too harsh," like, and now I've got to treat my players like a bunch of little delicate babies. This nice-to-babies policy probably applies to this computer teacher, too, so I hold the guy's box and show him how the classroom keys work, see, and he studies the procedure like he's never even seen a key before. Yeah. Put it in here. Turn it. Look, the door opens. Useless, I tell you.

What are guys like this for, anyway?

I put out my hand and introduce myself. "Lawrence Gilroy. Friends call me Lorrie." He sets down the box and gives my hand a shake. "Gentry." That's a pussy name, but he hasn't got too pussy of a grip to go with it, big, square hands, long arms, probably basketball, he's tall enough. Looks like he could maybe be Indian. Feather, not dot. Just clarifying. They've got a natural gift for team sports. In the blood, see, leftover from the hunting days. Just saying, historically speaking and shit.

I give him one week.

Gentry

Lorrie Gilroy wanted to know the price of everything before he broke it.

"What the hell's all this stuff for? How the hell much does something like this cost, anyway? More than new uniforms, I bet. How the hell's a team supposed to have a motivated, winning spirit when they look like they got their sonofabitching uniforms out of Ma and Pa Kettle's closet, I ask you? Why don't I just slap some goddamn water buckets on their heads and send them out there, I ask you?"

I took these questions as rhetorical.

At one point he turned to me and demanded, "What the hell kind of a name's Gentry, anyway? Just one name, like Fabio or Cher?"

Lorrie and I lacked common cultural touch points.

He careened around, bumping a printer that needed delicate calibration. He tripped on a cord and yanked a network card out of a CPU. He slammed the lid of the scanner. I had to get this man away from the equipment. "Copies!" I shouted. "I need to make copies! Take me to the copy machine!" My duplication fervor startled Lorrie, but he took me back to the copy machine and talked me through the complex process of using it ("there's a code for every classroom, see, so I just use 1000. I have no clue who it belongs to, but then my copies don't come out of my budget.").

As soon as he left, I went back to the lab for the rest of the day and part of the night. When a janitor came in and started rattling around in that way that says "I have important janitor things to do in this room," I made myself go home.

I was excited about the equipment. I begged and borrowed in Detroit, though I never stole. I was proud of what I patched together, but this new lab was full of everything I could ever want. I just needed to take it all apart and put it back together the right way.

⟋

"You don't look like a computer geek." That's what Lorrie Gilroy said to me before he almost knocked over the server. "You don't look like a teacher, either. But you really don't look like a computer geek, let me tell you."

I have never known what this means.

I graduated from college five years ago. Whenever I took a class in computer science, everyone in there looked like me. Right around my age, jeans and T-shirt, male. Of course, things might have changed since 1991. Maybe there was a new breed out there, because in the world of computer technology, everything kept changing. Probably I wasn't even qualified to teach anymore, but no one had figured that out yet.

My friends from graduate school couldn't believe I taught, not with all the "big bucks" out there in "private industry" for "computer geeks." I had a deep and personal aversion to the term "computer geek," but I forgave my friends, because I owed them. They were instrumental in the development of my capacity to sin. The church had a complex organizational system for sin, from petty through mortal. My sinning fell mainly into a category of my own devising, "recreational sin." Just about everything fun fit in that category.

I arrived at college very young and completely innocent. With the help of my friends, I moved from vicarious sin, another term of mine which means the experiencing of life through the exploits of more mature, more fortunate young men, into recreational sin, meaning I was finally able to experience some of what made me feel so guilty. Friends helped me through this transition with great tact, strategically administered alcohol and much laughter. I was indebted to my college friends, even though they thought I should sell my soul to private industry to finance their poetry careers.

⟳

I had missed the sunset again. I forgave myself again.

Bosco was happy. He'd been rolling in an assortment of washed-up marine life. "Bosco, you smell worse than I did last night." He gave me a putrefaction-flavored lick on the hand, because as far as Bosco was concerned, this was a compliment.

He took me on a tour of the house. All of a sudden we had stuff. In general, I hate stuff, but some of this was welcome. Needed, even. A little red teakettle on the stove. A plate, a bowl, a coffee cup. A knife, a fork and two spoons. Extra light bulbs. A stack of towels. Toilet paper. Flowered sheets, a wool blanket and two pillows.

I felt like the shoemaker, and I had no idea who the elf was.

"Bosco, I get both pillows." Bosco ignored me and curled up in front of the refrigerator where the condenser made a warm spot. I folded up the wool blanket and put it on a chair, spread my sleeping bag over the bed, stripped off my clothes and slid into the cold, clammy sheets. Not exactly the sensation I was hoping for. But they warmed around me, and they were so smooth, like skin.

Hey, now. Don't think about skin. Just go to sleep. Sleep, in a bed, not in a bunk in a dorm or a cot in a cell or a futon on the floor, but a bed.

I slept.

⟳

A door slammed. I sat up in a panic. "Bosco? Bosco!" Why didn't he bark? My face was wet. I dragged the sheet across my eyes, wiping away whatever had fallen. I was in Oregon, I reminded myself. It was Saturday morning, and this was Oregon. The sound of the ocean, the smell of something good. Coffee?

A cup of coffee sat next to the bed. A note stuck to the bottom of the cup.

Come over to my house. I'll make you breakfast.

Judging by the handwriting, my elf was Gretchen.

I picked up the cup and carried it to the window. Down on the beach, my dog ran for all he was worth, his stiff legs churning up sand, his ears and tail streaming in the wind. Beside him ran Gretchen.

She bounded, effortlessly.

Kathryn

Kathryn heard the knock on the back door. He stood on the stoop, framed in the window like an Italian masterpiece. A young Christ perhaps, or a tutor from the corner of a Botticelli canvas.

Or, perhaps just the *tenant*.

She opened the door and smiled. "Good morning."

"Hey." He handed over her father's favorite coffee cup and Gretchen's note by way of presenting his invitation. "Mrs. Mumford? If this is, um . . ."

"Come in. Knock the sand off your shoes first, please. My entire life is a war with this sand. And you need to call me Kathryn, unless of course I'm too old to address by first name, in which case you have to do it anyway."

He smiled. "Okay, Kathryn."

She smiled back. "And I'm to call you Gentry. First or last name?"

"Only."

Oh, the intrigue. It would be quite a mystery until he wrote the rent check. "Please, have a seat." He did. Very good. She poured him some coffee. He lifted the cup to his mouth like something sacramental, pausing to breathe it in before he sipped.

The rapture on that face.

"Hey Kathryn? Can you tell me why the, um, coffee out here is so good? Even the coffee up at the teacher's lounge was, um, wonderful."

"Well," and she suppressed an urge to say "um," "We have great water. Great water makes great coffee. How was the water in Detroit?"

"Wet."

She laughed a little, and he smiled. What a sweet and bashful smile.

They sat and sipped at the table for a few moments, listening to the ocean. He looked rested and mild. When his dark eyes rested on Kathryn, she didn't feel stared at, challenged or invited. Just seen.

He spoke so softly. "I wasn't prepared for how beautiful your face is."

"Excuse me?" A blush poured up her neck.

He cleared his throat. "I wasn't prepared for how beautiful your place is."

Through the flames of her embarrassment, she managed a reply. "It is beautiful here, yes."

"Oh. Um." He reached into his pocket and pulled out a wad of cash. "There's first and last." She found this act of commerce as embarrassing as her mishearing a few moments ago, and tucked the money into her jeans without counting it. He blinked. "There's no lock on my door?"

"Oh, I meant to have one put on there. This week, I promise, I'll . . ."

"I can do it."

"No, I want to have a professional install it."

He frowned and smiled. At the same time. "I've installed plenty of locks."

"No, you shouldn't have to." Gretchen came in with the gigantic dog. "The sand . . ." she protested, but, too late. The big shaggy thing started to shake.

"Hey Gretchen? Maybe next time let him shake before he comes inside." He said it so kindly, but Gretchen still blushed. Her white hair flew out behind her as she hurried to dip bread in her special French toast batter. The bacon she'd cooked earlier warmed in the oven.

The dog went immediately to sit at Gentry's feet. "Hey, Bosco. Did you have a good walk?" He rolled the big, wet, tracking, smelly, panting mutt around on the floor for a moment. The reek was intense. "May I wash up?"

"Of course." He scrubbed thoroughly at the kitchen sink before rejoining Kathryn at the table. She decided to eat some breakfast herself. She had an uncharacteristic appetite.

Gretchen set a plate before him. "Would you like some syrup?" He shuddered. Kathryn understood, because this was her reaction to syrup. Gretchen took off a lid and extended a jar. "Peanut butter?" He clapped a hand over his mouth and gagged. Gretchen slapped the lid back on and looked at her mother. Gentry looked at his plate.

Well, then.

"Gentry? Would you care for more coffee?" What a distracting little hubbub they raised as she poured him another cup of coffee and Gretchen put away the peanut butter and put some jam on the table and that odd little moment of shuddering and gagging passed. They all managed their condiments without any further embarrassment, though Kathryn found herself transfixed by his huge hands on her flatware, which was itself large and heavily patterned in an old-Norse way. She'd been using these utensils for most of her life, but she understood after seeing him wield a spoon that this cutlery was meant for the hands of Vikings.

He spread his jam thickly, arranged his plate carefully, then set his utensils aside and clasped his hands under the table. He dipped his head and closed his eyes. Gretchen's cool blue eyes watched the movement of his lips, the pulse in his eyelids, the sign of the cross. She looked mildly revolted but undeniably interested.

He opened his eyes and saw her staring. He smiled.

Gretchen didn't smile. "Why do you do that again?"

"So I can eat." He took a bite, and his chewing slowed. Savoring. "This is great jam. Is it crabapple?"

"Quince. Gretchen and I made it last summer."

Gretchen blushed. "We made huckleberry, too," she mumbled. She gave him a large glass of milk, which he drained off in two gulps, so she got him another.

How many years had it been since Kathryn drank a glass of milk?

He ate with appreciation and enjoyment, but not the alarming hurry of his previous visit. The dog watched every bite he put in his mouth, and when the occasional scrap fell, quite by accident, it was clear the dog liked quince just as much as Gentry did. Just when she thought she'd have to badger him into small talk, Gentry wiped his mouth. "Hey Gretchen? I appreciate what you've done out there. It's very nice. Thank you." Addressing a child, there were no "ums" from Gentry.

Gretchen's mouth clamped tight to stop a smile of delight.

"He said thank you, Gretchen."

She recovered enough composure to speak. "You're welcome." She was going up like a flare that morning. "I think it's interesting that you don't have a TV."

"I don't have too much time for television."

"Don't you miss cartoons?"

"I've never actually watched cartoons."

Gretchen raised her white eyebrows. "In your whole entire *life*?" He shook his head. "Well, you *should*."

"Why?"

"Because they're interesting. I mean, funny, you know, and fun." She sat up straight. "Even though some of them are . . . trite. And some of them are really," and she paused for a moment, ". . . derivative." She pronounced it, dee-rive-ative.

"Every story is derivative, Gretchen." He pronounced it correctly. "Have you ever read what John Gardner wrote about it?" She shook her head no, but there was something artful in the way he gave her the benefit of the doubt. Because then, of course, she couldn't wait to hear what John Gardner wrote about it. He went on about two stories that were actually one, "depending on your point of view."

Her "Oh!" was a little burst of delight. "I get it. That's true." She thought. "Cartoons just have one story. Someone has something and someone else wants it."

"Ah," he said, "the triangulation of desire."

"What's that?"

"It relates to focus. Do you know how your eyes create depth perception?"

"It happens when two different points of vision converge on a single point. When the images meld in your brain it creates a perception of depth. I mean, I don't know exactly how the brain does it but that's the mechanism."

He smiled. "If you understand that three points are necessary for perception of an object's position, then the concept of triangulation of desire is easy to follow." This explanation went on and involved the salt shaker, the pepper mill and the jam jar. Kathryn picked at her food and listened to a computer teacher discuss literary theory with a ten-year-old. They did a nice job of it, actually. Then he turned to Kathryn. "I meant to ask. Der Rosenkavalier?"

Again, heat poured up her neck. "Oh. Yes. That's it exactly. Are you an opera fan?"

"A friend is."

A friend. What kind of friend? She felt her color rise yet again, absurd, all this blushing. "Do you want more bacon? There's more French toast."

"That would be great."

Marci thundered down the kitchen steps, wearing far too little. "Gretchen, why don't you ever put on a new roll, I'm sick of dripping dry because you . . ." She stopped, crossed her arms over her camisole to hide the breasts she certainly hadn't inherited from her mother. "Wow." She gave the room a look of general betrayal, then thundered back upstairs.

Gentry's eyes stayed firmly fixed on his plate.

Marci was back down in a moment, wearing a tattered paisley robe from her mother's closet. She poured herself a cup of coffee and made a sour face over it. "Why are you in my house?"

He lifted a fork full of French toast in her direction as an answer. And smiled.

Gretchen returned to the topic. "Anyway, there's one you might really like. Everything happens inside a computer." She told him the name.

"Hm. I haven't watched that, but I think I saw a link. There's probably a website." A link? A website? Kathryn decided she wasn't in this conversation in any form or fashion. "Do you like computers, Gretchen?"

"Computers?" She shrugged. "Kind of. Well, no. I mean, I don't know anything about computers."

"Neither did I when I was ten."

Marci gave her little snort. "Was that like, two years ago?"

"Marci." But Kathryn shouldn't have bothered to scold her, because Gentry ignored her. Marci was so rarely ignored that Kathryn wondered how she could stand it. Had Marci ever felt the pall of her younger sister's shadow falling across her in all her seventeen years of life? Gretchen was hardly substantial enough to throw a shadow. She was a little sandpiper, digging away at sand shrimp, busy all the time, gray and slightly damp. Gentry really looked at her while they talked, with those gentle, appreciative eyes. Good. She needed to be seen for the rare and precious creature she was, and no one at her school . . . enough. If Kathryn continued to think along those lines, she'd need to spike her coffee. That was no way to start a perfect September day.

"Well, thank you for breakfast. I need to go put the lab together."

Kathryn winced, thinking of parent meetings about this particular debacle. "I don't know anything about computers, or what they're for, or why we need them. But from what I understand, the lab is already somewhat . . . assembled. You'll have to take it apart and do it over."

"That's okay. I prefer to handle the equipment myself."

"I could help you." Gretchen ducked her head. "I mean. If you, you know. Wanted me to." She waited.

"Hey Gretchen? Would you like to come with? I mean, if your mom says it's okay."

He had asked her out of politeness, and he politely waited for Kathryn to say no. He couldn't know, of course. He could not look at that rare and beautiful child, and see a social failure who had never before received an invitation. Not once in her young life.

Still, he was unknown.

Gretchen's eyes widened. "Can I go? *Please*, Mom?"

Kathryn's heart strained, pulled in two directions. "That's fine. Be home for dinner. Both of you."

Gretchen rushed out the door before Kathryn could change her mind. She waited in the Jeep, toying with a set of dog tags that hung from the rearview mirror, while he took the beast of a dog inside his little house. He emerged with an armful of cords. As he closed the door, he looked at the knob, worried.

Kathryn needed to get him a lock.

～

There was nothing like September at the coast. The summer people left, the tourists stayed away, and the town lost its economic base. Businesses hanging on for one more summer closed, never to reopen. The high school kids gave up their jobs. Those who didn't fish lost the only money they would see all year. Kathryn lost something dear, too. She lost the summer companionship of her Portland friends.

And yet, she never grieved September. Those who chose to live at the edge of the world would have this month of perfection all to themselves.

Time to plant tears, says the almanac.

Marci was grumpy and bored. Her, oh, Kathryn didn't know what to call him, her dangerous distraction wasn't lurking around, leaving fish scales on Kathryn's furniture and mumbling incoherent responses to whatever Kathryn might say to him. Marci was at loose ends. "I have nothing to do, Mom."

"How can you have nothing to do?"

"Garret's on the boat and Vu's at work." Marci put on her most proper voice. "Mother. I am lacking sufficient diversion."

Kathryn answered in kind. "Good heavens. This will never do."

Marci gave her head a theatrical toss. "Mother dear. I wonder if you have any idea at all how dull it is here in the provinces for a young woman of my social standing."

"I'm intimately familiar with boredom, my precious, precious Marcialin. And if you're lacking in acceptable pastimes, I could use some help in the conservatory. No, you don't have to thank me. It's my pleasure to ruin your nails."

Marci laughed as she went to find the garden gloves.

∽

Kathryn planned to pass the time on a chaise with a tall drink and a slim book of Mary Oliver. A slim book was all she could take, as the poems left Kathryn emotionally exhausted.

Marci worked rose food into the soil. "Why do you like roses so much?"

"Because they're temperamental and thorny, but beautiful as they bloom. Like certain daughters."

"Mom?" Marci sat back on her heels, watching the water. "It's weird not to have Gretchen here. Are you sure that teacher is okay?"

"I'm sure."

"How do you know?"

Kathryn considered his meek appearance at the door, the morning's shared breakfast. "I know a lion from a lamb, and that's a lamb."

"If you say so." Marci wiped at sweat, streaking her forehead with soil. "So what's Garret?"

Kathryn forced a smile. "He's going to be a lion. But not yet. He's just a surly cub."

A broken cloud drifted across the sun, which reached through with brilliant pink fingers. "Mom? What's it called when the sun does that?"

"A Jacob's ladder. You climb that ladder to get to Heaven."

"And what if you don't believe in Heaven?"

"Then you just enjoy it."

"That's what I'll do, then." Marci settled back. "You should, too."

"All right." With a lift of her jaw, Kathryn took it all in. The cliff that bounded her property fell away before them, and the beach stretched out along the roaring ocean below. The green water, sun-streaked sky, ridges of tall grass that waved behind the sand as if telling it good-bye, since it was doomed to be pulled away by the tide. But the tide always brought it back. The rocks and cliffs backed it all with their clinging trees, branches beaten back by the wind.

Those trees. Every writer, every poet compared them to scorned women who offered themselves up, reaching out for what rejected them so completely that their arms broke from the force of it. And yet they stood. Proud of being broken.

"Whenever Garret talks about staying here, I think he's crazy. But when it's like this, I completely understand why someone would want to stay."

Oh, no.

The stretch of coast was violently beautiful. And so was her daughter. She was another view Kathryn took for granted, hair streaked like the sky, eyes green as the sea. Kathryn had words to share with her. You're so young, she wanted to say, too young to take root here. You wait for love rather than life, mistakenly believing they're one and the same. Keep your arms by your sides. Don't reach for what breaks you.

She kept her silence.

⌒

A ten-year-old and a seventeen-year-old required solid food, but Kathryn had stopped participating in dinner. Kathryn preferred meals she could smoke or drink. She actually kept a cut crystal ashtray on her dining room table. It matched her wineglass. "I think we'd better double what we usually make for dinner."

Marci didn't complain about it directly, preferring to call Vu. "Apparently we've adopted the *tenant*, and he's going to eat here every night. I really don't think I can stand that. Because you should see how he eats. He shoves it in like he's starving." She listened, started to laugh. "You're making that up. No, you're making it up. There's no such thing as a Japanese competitive eating contest. Vu, you're so weird." Silence. "They dip their food in water first? Gross." While she laughed and complained, Kathryn commenced her cocktail hour. She'd made it all the way to five o'clock. That was acceptable, wasn't it? She had it under control.

He came in after knocking the sand from his boots, and washed up thoroughly. Kathryn watched with trepidation while he loaded his plate. Gretchen stared and Marci smirked while he prayed. How profoundly difficult that would be, to pray in front of nonbelievers at every meal.

He ate slowly, normally, while Gretchen asked him question after question about computers. He answered every query, he never spoke with his mouth full, he snuck food to the dog waiting under the table, and he ignored Marci.

Oh, he did speak to her, once. Only once. He nodded at his plate. "Hey Marci? This, um, what's this?"

"A seafood cassoulet."

"It tastes . . . I can't even find a word for it." Marci snorted, but he shook his head, refusing to be dismissed. "No, seriously. It's ambrosial."

"Ambrosial? Seriously?" Not that Marci cared what adjective he used to describe her forty-five dollars worth of seafood in a cream sauce. He ate half of it.

After dinner, Gretchen and Gentry ran down the steps to the beach with the dog. They made a fire. Kathryn could see them silhouetted against it, the dog between them, as the sun went down.

She knew her Gretchen would sing to the setting sun.

Gentry

I stared at the fire, glad for the warmth. Gretchen was singing. A Beatles song. Where did she learn that?

Bosco stared at her, his head cocked. "Don't sing along, Bosco."

Two small white dogs with brown spots approached. Back ends up, front ends down, eyes bright. A little barking, a lot of wagging. Bosco began to roll them around with his giant paws. Gretchen stopped singing. "I can't figure out if those are Rat Terriers or Jack Russells. What breed is Bosco?"

"He's a mutt."

She started to sing again.

Today, Gretchen learned how to add RAM to a computer, install a network card, change a toner cartridge and clean a keyboard. These are necessary life skills. In exchange, Gretchen offered to teach me to cook. She claimed cooking was also a necessary life skill. I warned her that she'd have to start with the very basics.

The most basic step would be deciding what to eat. I never learned how, so restaurants don't work for me. It takes too long to make up my mind and I'm haunted by the dish not chosen. After I call the waitress back and change my order a few times, I'm sometimes invited to leave. I have to leave huge tips.

I've learned to completely avoid the menu and order the special, or let the waitress decide. They like to do that. If I'm with a friend, I can wait for him to order and say, "The same for me." I've eaten some unusual things doing this, like fried cheese, which tastes okay but the idea of it. With a few friends, I confess my inability and let them take over.

Taking women out to dinner never worked. They sometimes thought my ordering system was a form of flirting with the waitress. One asked me, "Is this one of those shows? Is there a hidden camera somewhere?" Another insisted I order for her. My panic was blind. I excused myself and left. When I saw her at work the next day, she refused to speak to me, and I've never asked a woman out to dinner again.

I know this is weird. I don't have any answers, here. I'm messed up.

Gretchen stopped singing. "Will you come over for breakfast tomorrow?"

How did she know I was thinking about food again?

"I don't eat before church because I take communion."

"What's communion?"

I considered telling her that communion was my personal favorite of the seven sacraments. The highlight of my week was kneeling at the rail, the body of Christ melting on my tongue in a miraculous physical and spiritual union with God. I imagined the horror that would cross her innocent face if I told her this.

"It's a Catholic thing."

She shrugged. Went back to singing.

The sun was setting on Saturday. I should have found the church and made a confession. What would I confess?

My face broadcasts guilt. This was a liability in grade school. Me and my guilty face. I envied the Native American kids who made their faces into masks when the inevitable question came up, *Who started this*? I studied that mask. I wanted it.

When I was six years old, an old Vietnamese couple moved in next door. Educated Vietnamese people, doctors and professors, came to this country as refugees, but my neighbors were farmers who washed clothes in the toilet and started fires in the oven. Canned goods and telephones were completely mysterious. I was only six, but I did know where to wash clothes and what a can opener was for, how to turn on the oven. I translated for them, made their phone calls on the phone in my house, which I was forbidden to touch but for them, I'd do it. I went with them to government offices and the bank and anywhere else they needed me to go. I struggled with the language they fed me along with my dinner. They served everything in bowls, and used their fingers as much as their chopsticks.

These illiterate farmers were passionately Catholic. They took me back to church. I found out about Holy Days of Obligation, Catechism, Stations of the Cross, Venerations, and Eucharistic Adorations. If I wasn't at their home, I was at church with them. I went to Religious Ed, First Communion class, Masses of Reconciliation. The priest looked out over the congregation, and I thought he looked with the eyes of God. Everyone there called him Father Mel.

He stopped me one day outside the church. *We're happy to have you back.* I stared at him. *I wonder if your father will join you one day. We hope he'll return. Would you tell him that?*

He watched a long shudder make its way down my body, and frowned. *You know, I've wondered if you could speak, because you're so quiet. Why do you never speak to me?*

He smiled. *Call me Father.*

I remember what I said. *I hate that word. I won't even say it when I pray.*

He spoke very softly, then. *Just call me Mel.* His small hand reached toward my hair, then pulled back, like it was hot to the touch. *The Lord appreciates that you help your neighbors.*

God had nothing to do with it. I helped them because I loved them.

The word they called me meant "grandson."

One afternoon I came in their door into a crowd of people I had never seen before, calling out in the musical sounds of their language, crying, hugging. My neighbors grabbed me by my shoulders and pushed me face to face with a shy, brown-eyed boy somewhere near my own age, and said, *Meet your cousin.* They had reunited their family, and though they were more than happy to include me, I hated that little boy. I wanted to kill him. I could feel it in me.

I needed more, then, from the Church. I found the priest with the small hands and the soft voice. I was furious, inchoate, but he waited until I could spit it all out, my rage and envy and murderous urges. He listened. He let me know I was forgiven.

God is infinite, and I hope His patience is as well.

There was a patch of woods near us, trees into bracken into bushes, trailing down the bluff to the beach like something spilled. There were grasses here I'd never seen, some close and green, some growing up and curving back down. I eyed a clump of berries near us, wondering about Bosco and poison. If I asked Gretchen about anything in her landscape, she would be able to name it.

"Hey Gretchen? What kind of berry is that?" I pointed. "Over there."

"There are two." She jumped up and busied herself at the bushes.

I wanted to explain my blindness, to tell her that I grew up with weeds poking through cracks in the pavement, stunted trees that struggled for a while and gave up in the air pollution. I didn't understand that anything green had a name beyond "tree" or "grass" or "weed."

Mel tried. He took me to a city park, where oak and maple trees arched over my head. Like Adam, he gave names to the tiny songbirds that startled and scattered as we approached. Thrush. Warbler. Vireo. Shrike. I remember smiling at the name of the Yellow Bellied Sapsucker, but remained silent as the birds flitted in and out of sight. I was mostly silent that year, but Mel kept trying. He is a Franciscan, a lay order devoted to the goal of service. He took me camping and taught me to dig a worm, bait a hook and clean a fish. As a fearful tourist in this natural landscape, I pretended not to care. Still, I was privately shamed by my ignorance of all flora and fauna.

When I was twelve, Mel sent me to a school run by the Jesuits, devoted to the goal of churning out educated young men who understood everything and questioned nothing. Those brothers filled me with a faith so strong that I am helpless before it every day of my life. But I never took botany there. The brothers felt I had no aptitude for the natural sciences.

The brothers thought they understood my guilty face. It was not my own sin written there, but the abhorrence and pain of a Christ-inspired boy. The nuns also thought I was a soul in torture, and I was, but it wasn't sin that hurt me. Nuns scared me. I mean, they really scared me.

My teachers awakened my mind as well as my soul. I graduated at fifteen with scholarship offers based on my outstanding academic record and extreme poverty. I chose a little teaching college in Georgia because it offered a master's in education and was driving distance to Athens. Interesting things we base our decisions on when we're fifteen and listening to a lot of R.E.M. and don't even own a car yet. My college was church-affiliated so the Jesuits were happy, not as happy as they would have been had I chosen a Catholic school, but at least it wasn't run by the Baptists. I was happy, it was a fine decision.

But this haunted face of mine, especially in college.

I was sixteen pretending to be eighteen and accountable to no one but God. I found a system. The week was spent doing whatever I wanted with a girl named Rebecca. The weekend was spent begging God's forgiveness for everything I was doing. Rebecca was my every waking moment, my every night's dream. My every confession.

Confessional styles vary in the Church. The older the order, the more likely one is to kneel in a booth beside a screen, delivering a list in archaic language to a dozing priest. At college, I went to the oldest church I could find and mumbled my confession. I would have preferred to say it in Latin. And I could have.

Of course, the Franciscans don't do confession like that.

Mel wrote a lot of letters the first year I was in college. He talked about learning, faith. He recommended Martin Buber and asked after my oral hygiene. I don't know if he thought I was too young, too shy, or what, but he didn't ask me any questions about girls. When I came back to him that summer, I was almost dead from heartbreak and still he asked me nothing. I couldn't eat, I couldn't sleep. If he'd asked me about girls it might have done me in.

In my sophomore year, I found a way to feel better. It involved an astonishing variety of women, each body a complex and beautiful mystery. I craved the oblivion of sex without love, how it could erase pain, at least while you were doing it.

Somehow, Mel caught on.

When I came home for Christmas break, I found myself face to face with Mel, sitting down as we had so many times before for a nice conversational confession. He was calm. *Talk to me, Gentry. Tell me about girls.*

I wasn't going to tell him a thing. Not one thing. I had done my Catholic duty. I had received absolution, performed my trifling acts of penance. To be on the safe side, I hadn't touched anyone for a week because I was coming home. I hadn't even touched myself. But that guilty face of mine, it gave me away.

Gentry. Look at that face. My boy, I know you. Talk to me. He looked calm, almost amused. He wanted to hear about my little college adventures, to remind me that God loved me, had plans for me, had died for me, and it was not so that I could mess around all week and say I was sorry on Saturday. The sacrifice of Christ is ultimate, infinite. I knew I was cheapening it.

Tell me about girls.

I told him about girls.

I told him about how smooth the skin of a girl is, and how soft, and how she smells on the back of her neck, how a girl's shampoo is the sweetest smell I know. I talked about kissing, kissing that goes on for hours, never sure if it will ever be anything more and not caring, because you're having her mouth and she's having yours and you learn a new kind of communion, then, the communion of a kiss. I talked about the sweet miracle of breasts, round and soft and white, about nipples that start out soft and pink and rise into raisins under your fingertips, under your tongue. I talked about what it feels like to put your hand between a girl's thighs and feel the heat radiating out until you think you'll be scorched, unable to stop until you find the soft source of that heat. The softest place there is. What a girl sounds like when you hold her and touch her and put your fingers in her, what she says in your ear, whispering, what you can ask her, what she will tell you, everything, all the mysteries she'll breathe in your ear if you only ask. What a girl smells like, tastes like, what sounds she makes when you kiss and suck her, trembling and whimpering and panting until she's helpless, you can make her helpless, and that's when she's yours and you know you'll die unless you're in her, pushing into the heat and the wet and the tightness, moving and feeling her move with you, rocking in such an agony, making her cry out, waiting there, balancing on the edge, holding back until she demands it, until she works her hips and makes you, she takes yours, and that falling clenching fire, behind your eyes and in your hips and down your thighs. The drumbeats that sound through you both when you're lying there after, holding her, kissing her, loving her, wet and spent.

And then you can do it again.

We were silent for a few moments. I forced myself to look in his eyes. *You asked me to tell you about girls.*

Mel sighed. *And so you did, my boy. So you did.*

Inspired in part by this conversation, I finally learned how to make that mask. I learned it during my years of teaching. No one had more to lose by looking weak than my students in Detroit, except maybe me, the man trying to teach them. I can harden my face, but it's an effort of will. I have to concentrate. If I could have done it as a child maybe life would have been different. Maybe. Maybe not. Maybe nothing would have made any difference.

My face no longer broadcast my guilt, but my guilt remained.

I knew where my church was. I should have gone for reconciliation, but I was reconciled, God, to the fact that my recreational sinning seemed to be over since college. I was reconciled, almost relieved.

Almost.

❧

Gretchen returned, her shirt held before her like an apron full of berries. "Open your mouth." She placed one on my tongue. Tangy. "Salmonberry, *rubus spectabilis*." The other had hardly any taste at all. "Thimbleberry, *rubus parviflorus*." After this small rite, she sat down and we ate the rest of the berries, Bosco at our feet. I threw him one after another. No poison.

As the sun reached the horizon and sank like molten stone, I bowed my head.

God, You made me, with all my failings, all my hope. You must have had a reason for botching the job so badly. But You also made this luminous child. This rugged Oregon beach. This strange and beautiful world of nature, for which I have no names.

Good work, God.

Amen.

With a voice like silver bells, Gretchen sang down the sun.

Marci

Marci sat in the school cafeteria, trying to eat. She wasn't anorexic, she was just grossed out by cafeteria food. Garret would take her somewhere else if she asked him to, but he could only afford bad restaurants and she was sick of clam chowder and clam strips and corndogs. They ate at school, where they also served clam chowder and clam strips and corndogs.

No wonder she couldn't eat.

Most kids ate in the cafeteria so they could have their free lunch. Marci didn't qualify, which along with her GPA made her a social outcast. Life was so unfair when your dad paid his child support. Garret was there, perseverating on his favorite subject: why Marci had to go to school "so far away." "Babe, Maine. I mean, come on. So far away. Do you know where it is, even?" He had a mouth full of clam strips. It wasn't his fault he ate like an animal. Everyone there did.

"Yes, I know where Maine is. I can read maps. Sort of."

Garret was a genius with a map, so this almost made him smile. "They've got a Portland there."

"I'm aware." She looked around the cafeteria in a quiet panic. "Where's Vu?"

"Yeah. We need some Vu delivered and have'em put in chopsticks."

"Oh, nice, very nice. Racism for lunch." Vu settled across from her with his tray and his great big smile. "Hey Marci. Tell me again what you think of my new glasses."

"I hate your new glasses."

He gestured towards her chowder. "I can't believe you order that. They make it with big cans of nondairy creamer. My auntie told me."

"I wish she didn't work here. I hate being a cafeteria insider." She picked up her cheap cafeteria spoon to try again with the nondairy chowder, and mentally saw her mother's expression whenever she picked up a cheap spoon. Her mother only liked nice things. That's why she hated Garret.

"Vu?"

"Hm?" Vu was plowing through his gross lunch, perfectly happy.

"Never mind." Vu might be the only person at the school she would miss.

There were entire lunch hours she spent imagining her life differently. If her parents hadn't divorced, they would have stayed in the big old house in Portland. She'd have gone to Lincoln because her mother hated private schools. But maybe her mother would have let Gretchen go to Catlin Gabel with all the other sensitive oddballs.

Her dad would work seventy hours a week, and part of that time he'd be "at work," with quotation marks, but her mother would ignore that. Mom would keep herself busy by sitting on the boards of nonprofits. She'd always be working on an auction. They'd be a normal family with one weird kid, one of the thousands of Portland families that came to the coast for weekends and summers.

She would never, ever have known Garret.

Garret's GPA was just high enough to make graduating a possibility. His mother was incarcerated for something unexplained that involved drugs. After she went to prison, Garret went to live with his dad, Garreth Blount Senior, who owned a fishing boat. Garret liked living with his father. "My dad keeps it all so clean. The house is just like the boat." After graduation, Garret would join his dad on the boat full time. They were both excited about this.

"Hey. Wake up, babe." He grabbed her under the table and pulled her closer on the bench.

"You guys? Hi?" This was Tiffany, standing by the senior table. She was a junior, by the way, so Marci didn't know why she was there.

"Where's Alex? Tiffany, where's your boyfriend?" Creepy Alex was also a junior.

Tiffany stood so straight, that cheerleader smile pasted on her face. "Hi, Garret."

Garret's eyes were small and a very deep blue, almost purple, like the huckleberries her sister and mother used for jam each summer. He kept those eyes on Marci, winking in reference to what he was doing under the table. "Stop." Marci shoved his arm. But Garret only stopped when he wanted to.

Next year, when she factored in the time zones, she'd be waking up at just about the same time he did. When she left her dorm room (and the idea of a dorm made her shudder), Garret would already be miles out in all kinds of weather, pulling up lines, icing fish. While she was going to classes, Garret would be selling his catch to the canneries. She would be at the library trying to study, which was going to be hard because she'd never actually had to study, and he'd be heading in, his huckleberry eyes narrowed against the wind.

She once said that in front of her mother, the huckleberry eyes thing, and Kathryn was proud of the metaphor, even though she couldn't stand Garret.

"You guys?" When Tiffany spoke, Marci shuddered. "The new teacher? He's *cute.*"

Marci rolled her eyes.

Vu spoke with a full mouth. "I'm telling you, that guy is whacked."

Sometimes Vu was just annoying. "He's not whacked."

"Believe me, I know a psycho when I see one. He's a time bomb. See that ponytail? It's a fuse."

"Ugh on the hair."

"Faggot." This was Garret's contribution. His hand on her thigh tightened enough to leave bruises. Marci watched Gentry going through the line behind Coach Gilroy. He looked lost and reluctant and appealing in a strictly puppy dog sense. She didn't care. She still didn't want a teacher living in her driveway. She'd even called her father to ask him if he could please send her mother more money every month. He laughed and said, *Right, honey.*

Marci sat there, trying to come up with something mean to say about Gentry because that was her job at the table, to be mean. Her heart was not really in it. "Gentry looks like the guy who throws up at keggers."

"Hey!" Vu sounded insulted. "*I* throw up at keggers!"

The class was fine, whatever. Gentry believed in a metaphorical approach. Everything was like something else. "This program is like a notebook. You open it up, write something, save it, close it." Silly, but it worked. "What's the one step that's different than paper?"

"Saving," someone mumbled.

"Exactly." All the cannery kids opened up Word, put stuff in there, saved it, closed it. Everyone but Garret. "Garreth, are you getting all this?" He kept calling Garret "Garreth," which was actually his name, but you didn't call him that unless you wanted a fist in your face.

There wasn't much verbal class participation, but Marci could tell by their sideways glances and uncomfortable smirks that her fellow students were interested. Well, she wasn't, because she knew most of this. So did Vu, who raised his hand and said, "Is it okay if I take a nap, Mr. Gentry?"

"Sure. I'll wake you up at snack time."

Everyone laughed, especially Vu. And that was it. He'd won them all over with one lame slam. Hands started to go up, kids started asking questions. Garret didn't. He was too angry, his bowed legs vibrating. Why didn't Garret just tell him to drop the 'h,' instead of sitting there silent and furious? She watched him getting worked up, his cold purple eyes, corded arms, the working in his clenched jaw, all that raw anger circulating through his body, aching to explode out of him. He was almost as angry as Marci.

That was why she stayed with him.

Gentry

I like rules. I like puzzles. Math is all puzzles, with the rules for solving included. Learn it once and it will never change. Poetry is a different sort of a puzzle. How beautiful can a puzzle be? My earliest poems were prayers. In college I sat in poetry classes, grimly fixed on the instructor, desperate to understand. One professor misinterpreted my baffled gaze. She referred me to Student Mental Health Resources.

Computers combine the math and the poetry in a way I can't explain.

On the first day of class, I wrote my rules on the board.

GENTRY'S RULES
1. No food, drink, or chewable substances are allowed in the computer lab at any time. Ever.
2. Respect the equipment.
3. When I ask you to talk, talk.
4. When I ask you to shut up, shut up.

These are straightforward rules. Easily understood by all. Reasonable. Important. I follow them myself.

I follow some other rules. I never curse, I keep my promises, and I don't tell secrets. I also follow some vocabulary rules. I never say "you guys," as in "What are you guys doing?" I try never to use the word "indicate," especially as in "You'd indicated that you'd be here to take your make-up exam." How was this indicated? Semaphores? Flares? What's an "indication"? Isn't that a medical term?

But there's always some student who "indicates" to me that he doesn't plan to follow my rules. On my first day of class, this student appeared to be Marci's boyfriend. His name was Garreth Keith Blount Junior.

What an ugly name.

I had a girl named LaShonda in this class, my first white LaShonda. There were no black kids in this class. None. As a matter of fact, I'd seen no black kids in the school. I did have a couple of Oanhs, and a Hoan-Vu Nguyen. I stared at the name, trying not to feel emotion of any kind. It was a common name, Hoan-Vu. Almost as common as Nguyen. I taught at least two boys a year with this name in Detroit. But one of them was extraordinary.

I breathed in and out through my nose, wiped my eyes, prayed a little.

I looked up to find him. He was not the Hoan-Vu Nguyen I knew in Detroit. He was a well-dressed young man in objectionably fashionable eyewear, and he'd sat next to me behind the podium on the night I arrived. An achiever. The school police would not pat this young man down, searching and finding weapons, cigarettes or worse. He was not going to get himself killed.

"Are you Hoan-Vu?"

His smile seemed eight inches across. "How did you guess?"

"Call it a hunch. Do you go by one or both?"

"Vu."

"Okay, Vu." I was not ready for another Hoan yet.

I heard a string of something foul from the back of the classroom, some garble pushed out around a wad of chewing tobacco. It sounded like "thefuckvu, yougottanewgirlfren'rsumthin?" But it was half-mumbled and buried under the spit he was not brave enough to eject in my classroom, so I wasn't a hundred percent sure.

It was convenient that Garreth Keith Blount Junior made a point of being the last to leave the classroom. I preferred to confront kids alone. They were more likely to back down if they didn't have an audience. He headed for the door, where I blocked his way, looking down on him. The kid was short.

"Hey Garreth? Did you have something you needed to talk about with me?"

He gave me a look of suspicion. "No."

"Okay, great." I stared down at him. "I wanted to remind you this class is required. You can pass it now or keep taking it until you do."

"Idonfuckineedit."

"You need it to graduate. Computers are a fact of life. Everywhere you go, every bank machine, every cash register, that's a computer. Navigation equipment, scales. They even have computers in prison, Garreth."

He shouldered me against the chalkboard, right into my rules.

My fists tightened and my jaw set. I worked in a school with armed guards and metal detectors. The halls seethed with gangs. I went to seven funerals my second year teaching there. I've never had a student touch me. Ever. I wanted to hit this Garreth more than I'd ever wanted to hit anything in my life. I moved right up on top of him.

"Hit me so I can have you expelled, or get out of here. One or the other."

He pulled back and tried to smile. His teeth were yellow from tobacco. "Sorry. I tripped." He spoke clearly when he lied.

"What's going on?" Marci stood in the doorway, looking from one to the other of us. "You're a moron, Garret." I reminded myself about breathing. "Gentry, I'm making lasagna and Gretchen told me to make sure you knew, so you'd come over for dinner, not that I care but she wants you to, so will you?" I nodded. He spat in the trash can and she shot him a look. "Gross. You said you quit."

He mumbled, "Jusstrynastaywake." After they left, I turned back to the chalkboard, where my impact had rubbed away my rules.

I erased, and carefully wrote again.

⌢

If I'd been able to walk along an ocean in Detroit, I might have been able to stay there.

The best place to walk is a strip of wet sand just out of the water's reach. In dry sand, it's like trying to run in a dream. There are places where the sand is ridged like the old washboard my neighbor used before I showed her how to use the washing machine.

Bosco brought me a perfect throwing stick. I angled it up and away, and he took off running before it left my fingertips. He leapt over a log, startled a bird, chased the bird, forgot the bird, found the stick and got to work burying it.

I laughed. "Bosco, I thought you were old, but a school counselor would say you need Ritalin." He smiled and ran off. Good dog. Forget the Ritalin.

I sat down on the log and rubbed away the salt on my face, which sent me back to a week on the Georgia coast with a girl named Jillian. I wondered if every time I went down to the beach, I'd be lost in a sexual reverie.

Bosco dropped the stick and stared at it, then looked up at me in happy expectation.

"Yes, look there. A stick."

He nudged it with his nose.

"I see it. But I don't want to throw it anymore."

He woofed.

"Stop woofing at me, Bosco, okay?"

He wagged and smiled.

"You'd be a fine coach, Bosco. I can't disappoint you."

I threw the stick. But he didn't bring it back to me, he ran happily to greet . . . ah, Gretchen. She trotted up, pulling wind-whipped strands of white hair out of her mouth. "How was your first day of school?"

"It was fine, just fine."

She studied my face. "But did you actually like it?"

"I think I will."

She seemed relieved. "Marci says you're coming over for dinner?"

"Someone invited me, I hear." She ducked her head and blushed. "Hey Gretchen? Would you throw that stick for Bosco?" She threw a stick and Bosco ran for it. The sun was warm, the wind strong, but the air was mild. I wanted to take off my clothes and swim, but I could tell by the water that Bosco shook on me, and the surfers in wetsuits, that I would never swim in this ocean. "I thought it always rained here."

"Not in September. This is the prettiest month of the year. Just wait. The rain comes. Do you want to see a tide pool?"

"Sure."

She ran ahead, leaving tracks for me to follow to the pools full of things with wavy edges and transparent sections. She named every animal, every plant. Most of these creatures seemed to be some of both. She told me what they lived on, their life spans, going so far as to detail their reproductive systems.

"Hey Gretchen? This is amazing."

"It's just stuff from books. I want to discover something new." She shaded her eyes and marked the sun's position in the sky. "It's time to go in for dinner."

I called Bosco. I was a happy man, knowing that I'd be fed.

Kathryn

She accused Gretchen of ghostliness, but it was Kathryn who haunted the halls in the night, opening closed doors, standing over her sleeping daughters who often slept curled around each other like kittens in Marci's bed.

On the last night of September, hunger drove Kathryn down to the kitchen to stand at the fridge, picking through leftovers, eating with her hands. As she stuffed her mouth with cold food, she wondered what kind of a beast she'd let inside. Not the dog. The man who entered her back door without an invitation.

That man was starving.

She closed her eyes and remembered the night he arrived. He ate with a ferocious, canine rapture. His teeth ripped and tore and chewed. His Adam's apple bobbed with the struggle to keep swallowing in time to his intake. Kathryn was surprised he didn't chew and swallow his own tongue. Never before had she seen anyone eat like that. While Gretchen watched, her fists flexing in readiness for the Heimlich maneuver, Kathryn let herself be hypnotized by the tearing of the flesh, the gluttonous slavering of the young wolf seated at her table. What would it feel like to want anything as much as that man wanted to eat?

She sat at the table to have a cigarette. Or three.

The ocean was finest at night. When lit by the moon, waves danced like tiny shards of broken glass, silver, sifting and shining. But the new moon ocean thrilled her most, that void full of violent sound. A weak yellow light shone out the window in the door of the little house. He must have been reading, but this late? And what did he read? Because that beautiful head was full, even though he said next to nothing.

She considered with admiration his effortless evasions of her questions, his deliberate opacity. It was nicely done. What kind of creature was he? Like a beast wandering into a settled area to hypnotize the villagers with his savage perfection, he let his feral beauty and overwhelming appetite speak for him. Let me feed here and leave me alone, ma'am. You may stare as I eviscerate what you give me, you may shiver as I lick my chops, and you may watch the flick of my chestnut tail as I leave your fire's warmth. But leave it I will.

She wondered if he could be domesticated, but it was Gentry who had trained her family. Within a week, they'd learned to wait to take their first bites until his grace was finished, because somehow, whether or not they wanted the blessings of the Lord on their meal, he said it for all of them. And they were trained in other particulars. His quiet "Excuse me," his gentle "Um, I have to do something" made it clear. Only the present would be discussed. Because she enjoyed his presence at her table, Kathryn denied her curiosity so that he would remain.

He earned his meals. It had been so long since she had a man around to do what men do. Tend to the car. Clean the gutters. Hammer new boards onto the steps down to the beach. Make the kitchen windows open and close, finally, after all these years. Help her plant things. Cut exactly where she pointed on the gnarled apple trees over by the garage. Mow the absurd patch of grass. Repair the mower. And the dishes, every night he and Gretchen did the dishes.

And the dead animal patrol. He didn't need mousetraps in the little house because Bosco kept it clear. But in the big house, Gentry emptied traps and re-set the wires and dispatched the corpses without compunction while Gretchen sobbed over the fate of the "poor little mice." Out in the yard, he cleared away the husks of baby birds, throwing them over the bluff into the brush, forbidding his dog to follow. He and Bosco actually caught a live mole that had continuously unsettled the lace top hydrangeas. Gretchen studied the eyeless creature, its sleek black fur, its pink, fingered nose. She made him let it go.

He didn't like Marci's computer. But when she complained about the speed, he disassembled it and added something and put it all back together again. He taught Gretchen how to use his, because she needed to learn on a "real" computer. He helped both girls with homework. He did all this without being asked. He made himself indispensable.

He gave Gretchen rides to school every morning. They went out for lunch on the weekends, and came back scented with barbecue sauce. He took her to every soccer game, every football game, every basketball game, explaining the rules patiently, inspiring her to care about sports. They got up early to dig clams. They went to the arcade, they took drives in the hills in that rattletrap Jeep. They constantly talked about kites, watched them being flown, referred to certain people who "had it down," that kite flying.

He took her to the library every week. He never took her to church, even though Gretchen asked him to. He made polite excuses. Gretchen tracked his religious schedule and openly resented his church time. His faith was almost unbearable to her, because God was kept like all his secrets, below his skin, in his blood.

Kathryn inhaled her smoke and studied the dark. Yes, she'd made a grave miscalculation, feeding this fine young beast. If only she would have remembered the problem with feeding the strays of the world. She once fed a classroom lizard over Christmas break and conceived an affection for a hopping green creature that ate living crickets. If she fed it, she came to care about it. How did she forget this?

He was the only friend Gretchen had.

OCTOBER

Lorrie Gilroy

Tourist season's over, finally. I always say, if it's tourist season, then why the hell can't we shoot'em?

I know these kids are going to eat this Gentry guy for breakfast. "I'm worried about the guy. He's some goddamn after-school special victim or some shit."

Jeannie's waving around a potholder like she's putting out a fire. "I'm thinking about inviting him over for dinner with Bobbi."

"Bobbi?"

"You know. Bobbi that works at the Doubletree. She's head of housekeeping."

She wants to fix him up with one of her buddies. Biddies is what they are, bunch of skinny hens, not one good for much besides scalding and plucking, and when they get to cackling and fussing you want to tear your hair out, believe you me.

I rate women by boobs and boats. Jeannie has neither so don't ask what I'm doing over here because I don't have a clue myself most of the time. Especially when she's cooking up dinner or trying to fix up one of her friends with some poor helpless sonofabitch who can't even run a door key.

I tell her no, don't do that. "He's probably a fairy."

"That man is not queer, Lorrie Gilroy. A woman knows."

"Okay, maybe he's not queer, but he's something. Do you think he's Indian? I think he's Indian."

"Whatever he is, it's cute."

Men are not cute. Gentry's also not much of a teacher, I don't think. He needs to quiet down that classroom of his. Today it was so loud in there that I stuck my head in the door and told his kids to shut up. "SHUT UP!" That's all I said, see, and Jesus on the Cross Christ, the look he gave me. A person could hold a grudge over that kind of look.

But when lunch comes, I sit down next to him at that beat-up old table in the teacher's lounge, you know, no hard feelings and all that. "Well hey there." He doesn't look up from his tray. And it's not like he was still praying over it, which he does, did I mention, this guy prays over his lunch tray every day before he eats. A praying computer geek, how about that?

I'm looking at the tray, trying to figure out what's on there and losing my appetite while I'm at it. He's putting it away. I watch him eat for a minute. "Must taste better than it looks. Or smells." He drinks his milk, says nothing. His classroom is loud but he's so damn quiet. I can't get the guy in a conversation to save my life. But I try with a joke. "So, this car's going down the road. And in the car, there's a Mexican, an Indian, and a Black guy. Who's driving?"

He swallows.

"Guess. Come on."

He stares at his tray.

"The sheriff, that's who's driving." He turns and stares at me like he can't have heard me right. I start to eat. "You better do something about that classroom of yours," I tell him. "It's a zoo. Kids can't learn in a zoo. How the hell are they supposed to learn anything?"

He finally says something. "Hey Lorrie? My kids learn."

"Bullshit. You need discipline, see, kids can't learn without discipline."

"I have discipline."

"Sure doesn't sound like it to me."

That's when he stands up, picks up his lunch tray and walks out.

See what I mean about quiet? Won't joke, won't argue, won't even talk about football. Also, I'd like to figure out what he is. Indian or Mexican is my best bet.

I'm eating my lunch, which turns out to be tuna something or other, and I think about the team. I've got exactly one kid that doesn't play with his head up his ass and that's Alex Fournier. He's a junior and I play him at quarterback but he was born to be a wide receiver, see, cause this kid's afraid of a hit and not one of the shit-for-brains I've got guarding him can save him from a clip, not one, so he should be catching pretty passes and running for his life because pure fear of taking a hit would power this kid past the goal line every time. It's hard when you've got a quarterback who flinches.

You've got to be prepared to take a hit.

I'm sitting there minding my own tray, and then here comes Rob Renton, our principal. He's got one of those big round faces where it looks like all his features got scared and decided to huddle up together in the middle for protection. Rob's supposed to kick ass around here, and instead he's the guy who walks around being nice to everyone. What the hell is that about?

He wants to talk to me.

He tells me we're supposed to be posting our syllabus, now, we're supposed to have a web page for each class so the kids can check in and make sure they have all the assignments, which wouldn't be necessary if the kids paid some goddamned attention in the class where they're supposed to, but this is the way it's gotta be, now, thanks to the goddamned computer network and all that.

Rob tells me to have Gentry help me with it.

That's it right there. That's the hit.

⌒

So I have to cancel a practice and stay after school and go to the computer lab. Oh, this chaps my ass, let me tell you, I been teaching for fifteen years and I have to sit down and learn about the whatever you call it from this quiet guy with the earring and the hair. But at least when it comes to computers, he has something to say.

Like this. "You can edit the text first if that's easier and then paste it in your planner. Or do you set your planners up in tables? Because you can paste the whole table. This program will convert it to html."

I look at the screen, quiet-like.

"I can show you if you, you know, if you, um, have them stored on the network."

I don't say anything.

"You used the network drive, right, not your local drive? I mentioned that in the manual."

I stare at the wall.

"You know, Lorrie, this is the easiest Web tool I could find. It's what they used to call WYSIWYG."

That's nice, wizzy-whatever the hell that means.

He talks some more Computer Greek to me, maybe another five minutes or so, showing me everything. And then he looks at me. In fact, the little sonofabitch sorta stares at me. And then he says, "Hey Lorrie? Do you have any idea what I'm talking about?"

I stare back.

"Have you even turned on your computer?"

"I've got a great idea," I say.

He shrugs. "I'm open to any ideas at this point."

"Good, because I've got a great one. Why don't you do this for me?"

"What?"

"Yeah. Just paste all this all up on the Internet table for me. Put some silverware beside it and call it supper. Whatever."

He's quiet for a minute. "I don't accept that you're hopeless."

"What?"

"I don't accept that any student is hopeless."

"Look here, I'm NOT your student."

"I have to teach you something. Correct?"

"I guess."

"So if I'm the teacher, then what are you?" He looks at me hard, and I think, well what do you know. This little asshole might have some discipline in him yet.

I look back at him for a minute. A long one. "If I let you show me how to do this, will you let me buy you a beer?" He's thinking, he's really thinking about this one. And then he nods.

I turn to the computer. "Just pretend I'm hopeless," I say. "Like I don't know jack shit. Just start at the beginning, like you're dealing with an idiot, see. Just do it that way."

Which is exactly what he does.

⁓

So it's a while later. He showed me all that crap and it's done now, and I think maybe if you put a gun to my head and said it was a matter of posting my syllabus on the Internet or blasting my brains on the wall, I could maybe do it again by myself.

Maybe.

We're driving along in my truck. He had plenty to say when he was showing me how that computer crap works. Now he's quiet again. "You got your ID with you, right? How old are you, anyway?"

He thinks for a second. Like he has to remember. "I'm twenty-seven."

"You look seventeen." He stares out the window. "You should comb your hair, or better yet, cut it off." He blows a little air out his mouth. I guess he's wondering why he agreed to let me buy him a drink. I remember a joke I heard. "Hey, how's a woman like a postage stamp?"

He sighs. "How."

"You lick'em, and stick'em, and send them on their way."

He doesn't even laugh. "Hey Lorrie? What year is this, '67 or '68?"

"68." I've got a Custom Cab Ford, all original. Robin's egg blue. A classic, not some piece of shit Jeep that sounds like he's torturing it when he tries to get it into gear. "What year's the Jeep?"

"68."

"Hah. Go figure. You have that for hunting?"

"No. I don't hunt."

"Why the hell don't you hunt?"

"I, um, hate guns."

Pussy.

He starts dicking around with the push-button Philco. "Leave it alone, you aren't going to find NPR or whatever the hell you're looking for on it."

"Um. Lorrie? Where are we going?" I don't know. Where do you take a guy who prays in the teacher's lunchroom for some fun?

I pay attention when he's talking to Tom Seidenberg in the lunchroom. Tom will say "How was your weekend?" and he'll go on about clamming with that littlest Mumford kid, taking her to the miserable games, the arcade, all that shit downtown. Then there's church, which he doesn't talk about but I know he goes there because I see his Jeep in the lot when Jeannie's driven me off my rocker and I'm driving up to Astoria to get away. Oh, and I see that Jeep at the library. I wouldn't want to forget the sonofabitching library. I mean, when I was his age, I got laid on the weekends. Jesus on the Barrelhead Christ. I still get laid on the weekends.

I don't think Gentry would know a good time if it sat on his face.

I think about taking him to Uptown Annie's, that's a funny idea, a guy like this in a tit bar. I could use it tonight, watching his eyes pop out of his head, I could use a laugh. But I don't want to scare him. "Here's where we're going." I pull up and park.

He looks at the sign, reads it out loud like a kid reading billboards on a Sunday drive. "The Wet Dog."

"Let's roll, Gentry. You, me, and that stupid earring."

I like the Wet Dog. Country bands, cheap whisky, and a lady bartender with thighs that could crack a man's head open like a walnut. It doesn't get much better than this, I tell you. But I have to warn him about something before we go in. "Listen, if you root for the Pistons, just keep quiet about it in here. I mean it. That could get real ugly real quick in here."

He gives me a sideways look. "Okay."

We take a table, and then I go over and talk to the bartender. This woman hurts me. There's just something about a woman big enough to knock the shit out of you if she wants to, I dunno, I can't leave her alone and I can't get her to give me the time of day. She dances around behind the bar and shakes her big ass and leaves with the biggest, ugliest, meanest looking fishermen you ever saw. I figure I have to get lucky at some point.

"Helloooo Faye," I say.

"Go away, Lorrie," she says.

"I love it when you talk sexy to me," I say.

"The usual?"

"Times two."

"Oh." She looks over at Gentry. "You brought your girlfriend."

"I'm gonna turn you over my knee, Faye."

"Promises, promises." She gives me two shots and two beers, and I take them over to Gentry. He knocks back that shot, and then he drinks the beer, fast.

"How about some video poker?"

"Gambling with a computer?" He shakes his head. "Just light your money on fire instead." He does know something about computers. Maybe he knows something I don't.

He looks over at the pinball machines, starts digging in his pockets. "Want some quarters?" I ask him. He holds out his hand and I put a few on his palm. Reminds me of my nephew. I go back over to get him another drink and bother Faye. "Set me up, woman."

"Who's your pretty friend?"

"Oh, he's not your type. He has all his fingers and teeth, and he takes a bath more than once a year. Now, ME on the other hand . . ."

She rolls her eyes, walks that big ass down to flirt with some bikers.

Someday.

I go find Gentry, give him his beer. "Okay, can you play pool?"

He nods, and he's right. He can. He personally kicks my ass at pool, and then at foosball. And then we do some darts, and he's good at darts, too. Damn good. Well, shoot me dead. I'm crap at darts. "What are you, the pinball wizard?"

He smiles a little. "There has to be a twist."

And that makes me smile. Finally.

Well that's fine, he can kick my ass at pinball and darts. It's not like these are the games that matter. And because it's what's on my mind, I talk about my two crap seasons in a row. We might do okay in wrestling, but you know, I can't stand wrestling, and I don't give a good goddamn how we do in wrestling, but we better do okay because I don't want to get fired because I don't want to have to move, and the frustration, I tell you, the frustration of a season . . .

He clears the board again. Rolf Handry wants to play Gentry a game for money, so I go back to see if maybe Faye would like to screw till the cows come home. She's batting her eyes at some merchant seaman with tattoos leaking out of his shirtsleeves.

I hit the bar with my fist. "What have I got to do, Faye? Tattoos? Leather? Tell me, Faye, because I'll do it, I mean it, you look like the screw of a lifetime, you look like you could kill a man, but I bet he'd die happy."

She says, "If you were the last man on earth, Lorrie Gilroy, I'd switch to women."

I think she wants me.

And I look over, and Gentry's having a different kind of fun, now. He's got his hands full with Darlene from the lunch line. She looks better without the hairnet. She's got her hands all over him, and he doesn't look too unhappy with the idea.

I make my way over to where they're sitting. "Are you ever gonna buy me a drink?"

"Yes." But first, Gentry introduces me to Darlene, like I don't know her. Everyone in town knows her. You know, I've got a rule about women, see. And this is it. If I wouldn't ask her out sober, I won't mess around with her drunk. Gentry's seen Darlene every day since school started, and she's been dishing him up double helpings and moon-eyes, every day. As far as I know, he never says more than "thank you" to her. She's not what he needs, she's cute and all but she's a double helping of small town trouble because she's banged every young guy around here she isn't related to, and who knows, maybe a few she is.

But hell, what the hell do I know, I date Jeannie so it's not like I have standards.

He brings back a round for all of us, and it's quite a round with maybe ten shots of whiskey on a tray, and six beers. "Jesus Christ. How the hell did you get her to serve that up?"

"I don't know. It was on the house, too."

"She did that just to piss me off."

He laughs, and then he shoots two just like that. This kid can knock it back. "Hey Lorrie?"

"Yeah?"

"That bartender said to give you a message. But I, um, don't swear so I can't." That makes us all laugh. And he takes Darlene out on the floor and she's as happy as punch to be swinging Gentry around by his baggy Levi's. I'll be goddamned if she isn't teaching him how to do a line dance. I'm a two-step man, myself. She puts his hair back in a ponytail and trades hats with him, see, so he has on her straw kicker hat, and she has on his trucker cap.

Aw, that's awful cute, Gentry. Might as well go for it, everybody else has.

A few more targets of the split tail variety come in, and I try to talk to a few of them and I get shot down a few times and I figure, screw it. If I want rejection I can go talk to Faye, which I do. I sit down on a stool. "What's a man have to do to get a drink around here?" I holler.

Faye rolls her eyes, starts down my way. "What do you want?"

"There's what I want, and what I *need*."

She starts to laugh. "What you *need*?"

"You. I need you more than I need a *team*, this season."

She throws back her head and laughs, man, look at that neck on her, she looks like she could tow a barge with that thing, and then she gives me a look and says, "You want it *that bad*, Lorrie?"

"I do."

And she's leaning toward me, she's close enough that I can smell her, she smells like Marlboros and coffee and draft beer, and I can look right down her black T-shirt at her knockers, fluffy and white like two loaves of Wonderbread, a little gold cross on a chain hanging right between, and she's smiling some wicked smile like she'll tear my throat out, and I think this might be it, this might be the night, the night I've waited for, and . . . Goddamnit, what the hell?

Some big-as-a-mountain Pacific Islander has Gentry by the neck, holding him about a foot off the ground. Darlene is pulling at the guy, yelling, swearing. I'm thinking, I better go kill Tojo, but then Gentry, who is just kinda hanging there by the neck, limp-like, stiffens up and kicks out and catches that sucker in the balls real hard with one of those Danner boots he wears. Ouch. I figure I got about forty-five seconds before the big guy stops holding his balls and starts breaking Gentry's ribs. "Gotta go," I say.

"You," she says, "are a first class idiot."

Darlene is tending to her man, but he's making a move like he's getting off the floor. I get the hell over there and pick Gentry up by the back of the shirt and drag him to the truck.

———

He's slouching over by the window. "So much for the Wet Dog," I say. "You fight there, you don't get back in for a while."

"That's probably for the best."

I was almost in Faye's pants, I just know it. I'm pissed. "Kicking a guy in the nuts is a faggot way to fight, Gentry. Not that I blame you. You were a little out of your weight class, there."

"I never even *mentioned* the Pistons."

"Well, with him you wouldn't have to."

"Who was that?"

"Darlene's boyfriend. Commercial fisherman. Name of King or Prince or Duke or something like that. Earl? He shows up, all the rest of you have to clear out for a while, but eventually he goes back to Alaska and Darlene reopens for her own season. Say, you up for another drink?"

He moans a little. "I lost my hat." He looks out the window. "Oh no. Pull over."

Oh Jesus-in-a-toilet-bowl Christ. Could this guy be any more of a disappointment?

I pull over and he gets out fast. I get out and walk around, and it's like I thought. I hold his ponytail out of the way. "Aw, isn't this sweet," I say. "I have to do this with Jeannie sometimes."

He spits a little more and stands up. "I bet you do." And then he smiles. That's right. He's smiling at me. Why, insulting my woman like that, I'd clock him, if he wasn't smiling. I put him back in the truck and we drive for a while.

Well, this didn't do such a great job taking my mind off my troubles, see. Nailing Faye, now, that would have taken my mind off things for sure, for at least an hour, I bet. Okay, maybe half an hour. But with Faye, maybe an hour.

Goddamnit.

Now the team is all I can think about.

So I'm telling Gentry about how disappointed I am in each and every one of my players, what sorry sons of bitches they are, every last one of them. And don't think I didn't tell the little shitheads that, forget that "harshness" crap, I told them, I was harsh as hell. I told them what a bunch of losers and assholes and pussies and faggots they were. Forget those parents. I mean look at it, every sonofabitching one with his head up his sonofabitching ass, what a bunch of pussies, the whole outfit's worse than useless, see, the cheerleaders could play better offense, the mothers could play better defense. I'm so goddamn sick of treating them like sonofabitching fairies all the time . . .

"Hey Lorrie? Did you ever try telling your players that you're proud of them?"

"Proud? You saw them play Friday night. Did you see one sonofabitching thing to be proud of?"

"I did."

"You did?

"I did. I saw plenty to be proud of."

I never thought about being proud of losing. I drive along, and I think about that a minute. About being proud of those boys. How they go out there, knowing they are worthless sacks of shit, but how they go out and play anyway. And he thinks I should be proud of that.

And maybe I should.

∽

I have to find his turnoff, he's renting some little shack by the water from her grand ladyship Kathryn Mumford, and of course there's no good lighting here, her royal highness probably wants to let the stars light her way home or some such garbage like that, snooty little Portland bitch that she is. "Where's your turn?"

"Up there about thirty feet."

I pull into his driveway on the gravel someone needs to rake, and I sit there for a minute, letting the truck idle. "You have fun tonight, kid?"

He thinks. "Except for the choking part, and the throwing up, and I lost my hat, yes, I did."

"That's good. You never know with you religious types."

And that makes him laugh. "Thank you."

"You're welcome. So, how about some fishing?"

"Fishing?"

"Yeah. That thing where you dip a line in some water and hope something bites? I know you're too much of a pussy to hunt seeing as how you're afraid of guns and all, but maybe you fish?"

He takes a minute, like maybe he's never heard of fishing before, or maybe he's figuring out if he can stand to do it with me. Finally, he says, all serious-like, "I fish."

"Got gear?"

"Yes."

"Okay, then. This coming Wednesday? Oh-dark thirty." We sit there for another minute. I guess I'm waiting for him to get out, but he doesn't seem to be going anywhere. It's almost like, well, see, it's like he's a little shaky from that big Samoan pushing him around, see. And maybe he's not quite ready to be alone.

Or hell, maybe he's just too drunk to walk.

He turns on the radio, and he starts dicking around with the Philco's buttons again. I open my mouth, but this time, I close it. I don't tell him to leave it alone. I let him play with the radio. He finds the country station and leaves it there, which is right where I like it.

"Hey Lorrie? Can I get something clear with you?"

"Sure, fire away."

He raises up his hands like he's confused. "You keep asking me out, and I'm sorry, but I like girls. So if you're gay . . ."

"Goddamn. GOD DAMN. Sonofabitch. You think I like your earring? Is that it? You think I think it's pretty, that I want a matching one? You little . . ." And he's laughing, he's laughing so hard and I start to laugh, too, and before you know it the whole truck is shaking with how hard we're laughing. "You're *determined* to get your ass kicked tonight, aren't you." And that just keeps us going. But we settle down eventually, even though he has the hiccups.

Finally I wipe the tears out of my eyes, wipe my nose on my shirt. I roll down the window. The air smells like the ocean. Living here, being next to it every day of my life, I sometimes stop smelling it, like you get used to the smell of a woman and don't miss it until she's gone. I look out at the water, churning away like it does. The moon shines down and makes a silver line down middle of all that black like the blade of a knife.

Maybe his landlady has the right idea.

"I dunno, this moonlight sure is romantic." I'm thinking that's going to get him laughing again, but I look over and he's leaned up against the window, sound asleep. Jesus, he looks young. I go back to looking off the edge of America.

He's just a kid, you know.

Just a kid.

Marci

At some point in the night, Marci woke up sweaty and panicked. Gretchen wasn't in bed with her, and she wasn't in her room. When Marci opened her mother's bedroom door, the smell of booze rolled out. She could have lit the air on fire. Her sister wouldn't go in there when it was like that.

She found Gretchen downstairs, asleep on the couch with the Discovery Channel playing silently, her arm bent over her eyes like a wing. Marci straightened Gretchen's arm and tucked the afghan around her cold and bony feet. She sat down, just barely hearing Gretchen's breathing over the sound of the ocean.

Oh, little sister. Where would she fit in? In the third grade, Marci had read a book about a group of people who lived on rafts, forever circling on an underground river. Maybe her sister would fit in there, wearing fish skins and diving in the darkness.

Gretchen was always embarrassing in one way or another. Her pants were too short, her hair in tangles, her mouth chapped around the edges from licking her lips while she rooted around on the beach. The coast rat boys in her class were horrible to her and the coast rat girls ignored her. And there wasn't anything Marci could do about it except tell Gretchen not to be so weird.

But Portland was full of schools where she wouldn't be an outcast for having the kind of brain she had. Their father could afford to send Gretchen to any of them. Their little brothers went to a good school. If Gretchen lived with them, she could actually learn how to get along with boys. And Eve would get Gretchen straightened out as far as clothes and going to a salon to repair the wind and sun damage to her fine platinum hair.

And Marci would die of loneliness without her little sister.

The moon shone in the window and lit Gretchen, her hair white, her skin silver. Marci could almost see through her. She searched her mind for the word.

Ethereal? Diaphanous? Spectral? All of these, she decided.

All of these, and "weird."

∽

The phone rang at five. She ran to the kitchen to get it. "I hate you. Did you *just* get home?"

"Yeah." His voice was sleepy. "What're you doin' babe?"

"Being pissed."

"How 'bout you come off it."

"How about I hang up on you."

"Oh trust me, you wanna hear this, babe." She heard him drag on a cigarette, imagined him lying on his back in his bed, naked and smoking, the phone wedged to his ear, a cigarette in on one hand and his penis in the other, getting hard over telling her whatever stupid thing he was going to tell her. Her thighs felt warm and weak.

He told her he'd been at the bar with Brian Barthel, testing out their fake IDs. Gentry was there with the coach, and he was falling all over Trent's older sister, Darlene. "He was shitfaced. And then we had to leave but I'm pretty sure they hooked up."

"With Darlene Peck? The lunch lady? Wow. He must have been really drunk."

"He was hosed."

"Fascinating." She hung up on him, and returned to the couch to consider the idea of Gentry having drunk sex with the slutty lunch lady. Sickening. She fell back asleep so she wouldn't have to think about it anymore.

∽

She woke up to Gretchen kicking her. "Get off the couch. You take up all the room."

"Get your dirty feet off me. Do you see how dirty they are?"

"I'm not dirty! You're just fat!"

Their mother spoke from the kitchen. "I wish you dirty, fat children would be quiet."

They both started to laugh, Gretchen's arpeggio giggle falling down the scales. It was officially Saturday morning.

Marci enjoyed Saturday mornings. Gretchen loved any day that she didn't have to go to school, so she was in a good mood. The paper was thin enough to read with two cups of coffee. Saturday was the day Gentry slept in, so he hadn't already filled in the crossword puzzle.

Her mother stirred sugar and cream into her coffee and started to sing. "*Michelle, ma belle . . .*" Her mother had the corniest taste in music, but she could sing anything, even with all the cigarettes. If she hit a bad note, she ran the phrase without realizing she was doing it, that same phrase over and over until she figured out how to sing it right. This, Marci had figured out, was a leftover from her days as a voice major. Gretchen had inherited Kathryn's voice. When they sang together it was sweet enough to make Marci cry. They clowned, vamping around the kitchen table with socks on their arms singing "Hello Dolly." Another time Marci found them on the arms of the sofa, pretending to ride horses and singing "Happy Trails." Whenever she came into the room, they stopped, because Marci couldn't sing.

Gretchen found her favorite cartoon, then ran for the back door, stopping when Kathryn raised a hand. "It's too early."

"But he made me promise!"

"Gretchen, be considerate."

"But he *told* me to wake him up! To watch cartoons!"

Kathryn peered across the drive for signs of life. "Are you sure?"

"He made me promise to get him before another week went by!"

"Mother, he might have a hangover." Marci thought that would win. Her mother always respected a hangover.

But Kathryn waved it away. "Oh, I've never seen him drink."

Gretchen flew out the door, across the drive and banged into the little house. Marci wondered if Darlene was still in there. Did she do it with her hairnet on? Were seconds allowed?

There was no word for something that ridiculous.

She made her voice high and formal. "Mother? Mother dear?"

Kathryn looked up from the editorial section. "Yes, my precious, precious Marcialin?"

"What if our comely young tenant is entertaining a lady friend?"

"A *lady* friend?"

"Yes." Marci resumed her real voice. "Because he was up at the Wet Dog last night getting drunk and making out with the lunch lady."

"Oh dear." They watched out the window. They were both relieved when Gentry staggered out of his house wearing nothing but enormous yellow sweatpants and his sleeping bag draped over his head. Gretchen popped out behind him, put her hands on his back and pushed him across the drive. His pants snapped and billowed in the morning wind, barely hanging on a set of hipbones so sharply carved, they looked dangerous. Only the embarrassingly large bulge just below his waistband kept them from falling off.

"My God," muttered Kathryn.

"I'm going to throw up," said Marci.

Gentry limped into the kitchen and stood there looking so miserable and confused that Kathryn handed him her coffee cup. He took a sip and quickly spat the coffee back in the cup, then handed it back to her. Gretchen steered him into the living room where he hit the sofa hard.

Kathryn gave her one of those "Mom" looks. "Why don't you take him some coffee without sugar in it."

"Why don't you, when you pour out that cup."

Kathryn met her eyes, and coolly took a sip.

"Oh. My god. I'm seriously going to throw up." Marci snatched the cup from her mother's hand and dumped it in the sink.

"Thank you for pouring me a fresh cup while you're at it, dear."

Marci ignored the coffee pot and peered into the living room. He sat on the couch, staring at the TV like he couldn't understand what was happening there, which was understandable because it was a stupid cartoon. Gretchen sat beside him, utterly transfixed. Marci kept her voice low. "Mom? So, you really need to think about this. Gretchen walks in there all the time. He needs a lock. And, I don't know, probably better curtains. And maybe a do-not-disturb sign?"

Kathryn nodded. "Of course. I just . . . *forget* that about him."

"You forget what? That he's a guy?" Marci was again subjected to the grotesque

mental image of Gentry and Darlene going at it. It was nastier than something
dead on the beach, so she made herself pick it up with her mental hands and put it
in a special mental box and shut the lid and throw it into the mental ocean. Done.
Totally.

She would start over. Gentry was the teacher who lived in her driveway. He
liked computers, coffee, Jesus, crossword puzzles, washing his hands, and her little
sister. That was as much as she knew about him, and as much as she wanted to
know about him.

"Take him some coffee."

"Mom."

"Do it."

"No." His head had fallen back, and he was snoring. *Really* snoring. "Isn't that
snoring bothering you?" She walked in and waved her hand between Gretchen
and the screen. "Hello? Gretchen?"

It took a minute for her little sister to pull those blue eyes away. TV hypnotized her like that. When she finally looked up, she was as far away as if she were
underwater. "What."

"I said, isn't that snoring bothering you?"

"What snoring?"

"*That* snoring."

Gretchen frowned. "That's nothing compared to yours." She turned back to
the TV and slid to the floor to be even closer to the stupidity. Gentry toppled over
on his back. He put an arm up over his head and started to snore again. There was
something so ugly and male about the snoring. Those sweatpants were disgusting.
And why didn't he have on a *shirt*? She didn't want to see his six-pack.

"Mom. He's passed out."

"Are you telling on your teacher, now?" Kathryn materialized with arms
crossed, looking suspicious or maybe just repelled by visible male armpit hair. She
gave her head a little shake, her wide mouth looking oddly serious. "I don't like
this."

Kathryn was vigilant about other people's drinking. Her own drinking varied,
and was therefore impossible to trust. Marci never knew which stage she was in.
At the current moment, her mother was in the "I drink, but I rarely get drunk"
stage. Next came the "Yes, I'm drunk, make something of it" stage. This was followed by the falling down, throwing things out the windows, pissing on herself

stage. This stage was almost a relief, because after that she went back to meetings. The only hard part about the AA stage was knowing it would end, and they would all be back to the "I have it under control" stage again.

"All right. Get him out of here."

Marci gave him a good jab in the arm. He flinched and flew up to his feet, breathing hard through his nose. He glared, but saw nothing.

"Gentry? Hello. It's just us."

He kept his fists clenched at his sides. The man was ready to *fight*.

Kathryn frowned. "Gentry, are you all right?" She sounded so mom-like that Marci expected her mother to rush across the room to lay a hand on his head, checking for a fever.

He didn't answer. His flashing eyes finally landed on Gretchen. Something went out of him, then. His face collapsed into something unbearable and sad.

He picked up his sleeping bag and left.

⌒

Kathryn and Marci spent the entire afternoon cutting up clams. There were three buckets. "Can't Gentry cut these up? Whoever dug them should have to eat them."

Kathryn shook her head. "He's in no shape."

"That's not *my* fault. Who's going to *eat* all these?"

"He'll recover." Kathryn shoved a wisp of white-blonde hair back behind her ear. "Take him the aspirin."

"Can't Gretchen take him the aspirin? Isn't she in charge of him?" But Gretchen was sitting on the living room floor, lost in the TV world of nature, learning and information. Marci wished her mother could see how strange Gretchen was.

"I hope he doesn't make a habit of this."

The word was "hypocrite."

⌒

She pushed open the door. "Knock, knock." She flipped on the light. He winced. He lay flat on his back, wrapped up in a brown terrycloth robe and staring up at a spot on the ceiling over the bed. Marci's attention was caught by a metal cross on the wall over his head.

"What's that for, vampires?" Not even a smile. "It's creepy in here. It looks like the Rotary Club's Halloween haunted house." She ventured in, her first visit to the little house since he'd arrived. So strange to have someone else's stuff all over it. Not that he had much stuff. He had embraced a minimalist lifestyle. "Gentry, where are your personal belongings? Did everything fall out of the Jeep on the way here? You should probably keep the top on your Jeep when you're moving."

He didn't respond.

"Oh come on, it's almost dinnertime, shouldn't you be recovered by now?" She shook the aspirin. "Here. A present from Mom." She put the bottle on the table and sat down on the bed.

Gentry sprang up fast.

"Wow, you move fast for a person who's dying of a hangover."

He said nothing, just went to the kitchen sink, where he shook aspirin directly into his mouth and drank from the tap. Swallow, repeat.

"Gentry, you can take too much, you know."

He stood with his hands on the edge of the sink, looking down. Something flickered in her mind, a line from a story. "You look like someone in a story I read. I can't remember where it's from, but a man's standing at the sink and he looks like he's going to push it through the floor. Oh, and by the way, Garret said he saw you last night. At the Wet Dog."

He hung his head, as if shamed.

"He said you looked like you were really having a good time."

His hung his head lower.

"A very good time. With Darlene Peck."

His head was hanging so far down, she couldn't even see it. Just his hair, still with that pink scrunchy hanging off it. Then he straightened up and went into the bathroom. He didn't shut the door, so she walked over to watch him brush his teeth. He kept gagging, but he kept brushing. He splashed water on his face but it stayed green. He ran his wet hands through his hair and when that pink hair thing came off in his hand, he looked at it, confused. He dropped the scrunchy in the garbage, grabbed the door and shut it in her face.

She sat down at his table and waited.

You know, this was awkward, listening to her teacher pee. When he finally emerged, he looked mostly human again. He got busy with making coffee. "What was Garret doing at the Wet Dog?" His voice was full of snot and gravel. "He hasn't been in high school that long, has he?"

"He has a fake ID. And he was out having fun, just like you. You two have so much in common."

The look on his face, like a sickly prince accused of being a commoner. "I have nothing in common with Garret."

"I disagree. You both like to go to the Wet Dog. You both hate your first names. And look at your rigs. You both have winches and KC Daylighters. I know why you have those, Gentry. I know we're going to find you out some night, drinking beer, looping, mud running."

He looked like he wanted to run outside and remove his winch, right then. She wanted to tell him not to worry, Garret was planning to replace his winch with a brush guard. But she didn't.

"I have fog lamps, not Daylighters. And I would never drive a short box."

"All the bad boys drive short boxes, Gentry. I bet you secretly dream of a short box with forty-inch Groundhogs and an eight-inch lift kit."

He cracked up. And then he winced. "Salinger."

"Salinger?"

"Yes. *Franny and Zooey*. The sink thing."

Yes, of course it was Salinger. Something inside her sparked and sizzled in an unfamiliar and not entirely unpleasant way. She wondered if he felt it, too. Marci stared at his pale and suffering face, but he just looked like he wanted to puke.

Gretchen opened the door and peered in, suspicious. "What's *taking* so long? The *chowder* is ready. And your *friends* are here."

"Which friends?"

"Come see for yourself," Gretchen huffed out, slamming the door.

He put his face in his hands and moaned.

Kathryn

Kathryn had seen the impossible. Gentry was too miserable to eat.

Marci had guests at dinner that night. Garret, Vu, and another boy Kathryn didn't know named Brian Barthel. He was part of the huge Barthel clan that permeated the coast. When she went to meetings, about half the attendees were named Barthel, though of course she was not supposed to know their last names.

They'd stopped by as she was carrying the food to the table, as boys so often did. Food radar or something of the sort. She had a pot of chowder big enough for a family reunion. It only seemed polite to extend an invitation. But Kathryn hadn't been following the conversation since Vu asked her what she thought of his new glasses. Vu was busy showing off for Brian, who was confounding community expectation by actually attending college. But she had no idea what he was talking about and didn't care enough to ask. The focus of her attention was Gentry, who sat in an uncustomary spot at the other end of the table studying his bowl with an expression of exquisite suffering. Apparently it was a very painful bowl of chowder.

Brian sounded disgusted. "They pay fifty bucks a shot. My roommate, he does it once a week. You can't do it more often, it makes it less . . ."

"Not as much bang for the buck?" offered Vu. "That's stupid, it's not like we all don't do it every day, anyway."

"Do I need to know that?" asked Marci. "And why are you talking about this in front of my little sister?"

"Ethics are a big part of biology, Marci," Gretchen informed her.

Vu glanced Kathryn's way. "So, Brian, are you going to do it? I would, but they probably don't want any from Charlie."

"No way. No way." Brian was adamant. "Who knows what they do with it."

Garret snorted. "Who cares what they do with it? It's just . . . stuff."

Marci frowned. "It's not just *stuff*."

Brian insisted, "It's *important* stuff!"

Garret scoffed. "It's *stuff*. Who cares."

Gretchen sounded vaguely insulted when she spoke. "You guys don't have to call it 'stuff.' I know what it's *called*."

Kathryn frowned. What on Earth was this stuff they were talking about?

Marci looked appalled. "You wouldn't seriously do it, would you, Garret? I can't believe you'd seriously do it."

"For fifty bucks? Damn straight I would. Gettin' paid to . . ." He shrugged and smiled.

Brian shook his head. "It's no way to make money."

Garret said, "I'd take it."

"Listen, guys, we live in a market economy!" Vu gave in to one of his fits of gesticulation, arms waving, voice rising. "In a capitalist society, *everything* is for sale!"

Brian was nearly shouting. "It's not a cash crop!"

"Why not?" Garret sounded honestly baffled. "Roe's a cash crop."

"It's not *roe*, I don't *believe* you, Garret." Marci was upset. "I can't believe you. How about *you*, Gentry? Would *you* do it?"

"Hm?" He looked up, blank.

"We're talking about selling your semen," offered Vu.

Kathryn almost dropped her cigarette. "You *are*?"

"You know, when sperm banks pay their donors. That's the topic at hand, as it were. You get fifty bucks a pop and Garret thinks it's fine and Brian thinks it's immoral and I think it's a reflection of the cold, hard economic realities of the . . ."

"Shut up, Vu. Well, Gentry? Would you sell it?"

"Me? Would I?" He shuddered a little. "I'm Catholic."

The table erupted.

"I'm Catholic too and I call bullshit! That's a COP OUT!"

"It's just STUFF!"

"It's important STUFF!"

Marci banged on the table to gain everyone's attention. "I don't care what your CHURCH says, Gentry, I want to know that YOU think. You can't just vomit out what your church says, you have to have an OPINION!"

Gentry raised a hand like he was going to bless them all. "Could you all . . . please . . . stop *shouting*?"

Magically, everyone did. They all sat there quietly while he turned over the idea in his head. "I think a man's relationship to his, um, seed seems transitory, but it contains the future. And he needs to treat it with respect. It shouldn't be sold."

"His *seed*? Did you just call it *seed*?"

Vu said, "Okay, that's really pretty, all that talk about respect and the future and your 'um seed' and everything. But seriously, Gentry. At fifty bucks a shot, think how much money you've mopped up with dirty socks. I'd already have college paid for."

Gentry covered his face with his hands.

"All right, that's *enough*. This is my table, and I declare this conversation over."

The boys all looked at their chowder, stifling snorts of laughter. Gretchen appeared to be completely unfazed. But Gentry kept his face covered, and his shoulders started to shake. He threw back his head and howled with laughter. And, of course, that did it. Everyone joined in, even Kathryn, even Gretchen.

"Too loud . . ." Gentry buried his head in his arms, moaning very softly.

For a man suffering to this extent, there was only one cure. Marci left with her friends. Gretchen went up to bed.

Kathryn cracked the hard stuff.

⌒

The ice in her drink clinked as she waved it for emphasis. "Why *Whitman*?"

"Why *not* Whitman?"

"Whitman is so . . . *predictable* for you. When I was in college, every boy who looked like you carried around 'Leaves of Grass' under his arm. Every single one."

He smiled. "Hey Kathryn? What did you carry around under your arm?"

"A sketchbook. Because the only way to get those boys to sit still and stop spouting anti-war rhetoric and Dylan lyrics and poetry of the Kosmos was to draw them. Youth is so vain."

"I don't know that I agree." His speech was a lovely patois of formal and slurred. He took another thoughtful pull on his glass of whisky, which held no ice at all. "Youth might be vain, but it deserves to be vain. Whitman knew it."

"Whitman was *old*. Why do young men love him so much?"

"Because he loved them. He worshipped youth. He made it holy." He stared at the fire. "Divine I am inside and out, and I make holy whatever I touch or am touch'd from, The scent of these arm-pits aroma finer than prayer . . .'" He dissolved into snickers. Such a boy. "I think this is the first time I've been warm this month." He stared at the flames, a sweet, tipsy smile playing across his dry lips. His head dipped, dipped again. He fought to keep his eyes open, but the heat and the hour and the whisky conspired against him.

She didn't want this conversation to be over. "A penny for your thoughts."

"They're not worth a cent." That was a mumble. He set his glass on the table so as not to spill, careful even as his head fell against the back of the sofa. And though it meant he wouldn't talk poetry with her any more that night, Kathryn was glad he'd slipped into oblivion. She could feast on the sight of him without fear of embarrassing herself, unlike this morning when she'd come in to find him half naked and sleeping on this same sofa.

She just wanted to study his youthful perfection.

She stroked his silky hair away from his sublime face, moved it so it fell down over the back of the sofa, a shining curtain that had absorbed the heat from the fireplace. She pulled her hand back from that fine, heartbreaking mane before her hand burst into flames. She remembered hair like this on the boys of her youth, young men who protested the war, burned their draft cards, ran away to Canada. A few of them went away to war. An angel-faced boy named Christian had never come back.

His face was unmarked, unlined. Where was his beard? She wanted more than anything to kiss his cupid's mouth, but despised the thought of her own, the reek of tobacco on her tongue. So she leaned to his ear, cooed in a voice made low by drink and cigarettes. "*It seems to me the beautiful uncut hair of graves.*"

His eyes flickered open. "It's too hot." His lips were dry, cracking. "I'm burning up." He grabbed his shirt. With a violent tug he popped open the snaps and bared his chest. "Open a window," he groaned. "Please."

"Sh." She lay one of her hands, always cold, across his forehead and put the other over the thud of his heart. "Sh. It's okay." The comfort was instant. He stopped his thrashing and passed out again.

She sat beside him, yearning.

Who was it that decided that women were not as moved by physical beauty as men? That was a lie invented by someone ugly and old. There was no hair on his chest, but there were his hard nipples, the tautness of his belly. Those hipbones like knives.

Other lines came to mind. *It is for my mouth forever, I am in love with it, I will go to the bank and become undisguised and naked, I am mad for it to be in contact with me.* The taste of a man, his tender skin, the hard column of his neck like iron under that soft covering. The smell of a man, like moss and wood and the sweet rising rivers that flow below the bark. The sound of a man, the sighs, the low moans at the touch of her tongue.

She moved lower, slowly, finally, following a trail down from his navel to find the hair she sought, hair from which sprang such beauty, so straight, so ready, so sweet, tasting of salt and smelling of pennies, rising to her, begging, filling her mouth like it belonged to her mouth and her mouth alone.

This was what her mouth was for, to hold that beauty, so she could hear those sounds he made, and know that it was her, her mouth, on him, for him, giving that to him, taking him.

He was hers.

Remorse. Hers, not his. What had she done?

He was drunk, disoriented, but his eyes were so grateful. He reached for her, and *no*, she hissed, *please, don't try, NO, I mean it, don't try. Please don't touch me.* But he gathered her onto his lap and held her as she sobbed. He stroked her hair, he hushed her.

I can't stand it, she cried against his naked chest. *I can't.*

Marci

"A place at the coast." That's what her Portland friends called a beach home. And they all had them. Marci had understood this about homes as she grew up; every family had two. Your mother was with you at both places, though she was almost a different person in each one. Your father was usually at work.

Your real home was where you lived most of your life, with school, piano lessons, healthy snacks and carefully traded play dates. There were rules at your real home, and a babysitter and a housekeeper who came in now and then. It was expected that you would brush your teeth twice a day, and change out of dirty clothes, take a bath every night, put away all your toys. Your beach home was for the summer, when you ate whatever you wanted whenever you wanted it, screaming and playing in your yard with friends after dark while your mothers sat in lawn chairs drinking wine and laughing. The coast was sleeping in too late or getting up at dawn to dig clams, picking your nose because the salt air dried it, tangles in your hair, forgetting about real shoes and baths.

You were not supposed to live like that all year round.

Her mother hardly ever went to Portland anymore. But her friends stopped by the house all summer long on Sundays, putting off the drive back, complaining about eventual traffic. They sat around comparing. Her mother's friends talked about who bought which house in what year, how much they paid, what kind of a deal it turned out to be. What work was being done on which house, who was doing it, how much it cost, what they all thought of it. Whose place was up for sale and why, maybe so they could move closer to the water or get a better view or finally make the move into Cannon Beach, the town they all criticized for the cost and the covenants and the traffic. It was like a big game of cards, everyone laying down their bids. Kathryn had bought the most interesting house on the largest lot with the best view in the quietest, nicest town at the most unbelievable price and she hadn't ever had one thing done to it.

Kathryn won.

But their house was terrible. They didn't even have a deck. When the weather was nice, her mother's friends parked their cars further up the drive so they could sit outside on the parking area. They wheeled around the cheap plastic chaises and opened up the ancient aluminum folding chairs until it was all arranged just so, and they sat out there on the gravel and gossiped and drank red wine and passed around a bottle of high SPF sunscreen and complained about the elasticity of their skin and hot flashes and private school tuition. They could do that for hours, drinking and complaining and sniffing their hands and forgetting to even *look* at her mom's view of the water.

Really, Marci hoped someone would shoot her if she turned out like that.

At some point in the conversation, someone always said it. "You don't know how I envy you, Kathryn, being able to stay here all year round." And her mother would look around at the peeling paint and the moss on everything and the way some of the windows wouldn't shut, that old phone, no dishwasher, the linoleum on the kitchen floor, the washer that smelled like mildew, and Marci could tell that her mother was thinking about December when it got dark at 4:30 and the rain and the wind never stopped.

Her lucky mother just smiled and poured another glass full.

Every single one of those families had one kid around Marci's age, and another a year or two older or younger. When she was little, these kids were Marci's Roxaboxen friends. They spent their summer days trying things. Trying to make themselves swim in water so cold, it made them shriek. Trying to divert tiny streams that ran to the sea. Trying to find shells that weren't broken. Trying to get each other to touch the dead gulls/fish/jellyfish. Trying to build something out of piles of burnt and soggy driftwood. Trying.

They loved it back then, but kids Marci's age didn't show up anymore. They only came to the beach for one or two token weekends over the summer because they had lives. Still, her mother always let Marci know if someone was coming. "Anney says Kirsten's coming this weekend. You girls should *do* something." Lauren or Devon or Morgan or Kirsten would show up. Marci would sit in the living room with whichever one it was, analyzing what she wore, being as funny as she could. Both would try to pretend they still had things in common.

The word was "awkward."

If it was a boy, Evan or Cameron or Jordan or Dustin (all the boy names also ended with "n"), it was even more awkward. Marci could remember when they were sandy kids running around naked on the beach. Now the boys had shoulders and whiskers and driver's licenses and deep, polite voices. Marci had to get even more sarcastic than usual to deal with it.

The word was "excruciating."

Evan hadn't been by in a long time. She'd known him since she was born. His mom's name was Sally. He was extremely intelligent. He could also occasionally be funny. "Why don't you ever call Evan?" her mother liked to ask her. "I thought the two of you got along so well." Why didn't she just say, "Evan is not Garret!" Marci wondered how her mother made her dating choices when she was seventeen. Maybe she lined up the attributes, like a foul mouth and a big truck and breathtaking muscle definition versus nice manners and a goofy sense of humor and an overwhelming interest in botany, and chose appropriately.

At least coast boys were careful about birth control.

Sometimes when she visited her dad, Marci did go out with Portland boys. That's what they were, boys. Their mothers were in Junior League, not prison. Their cars were quiet. Their hands were clean. Their kisses tasted like Altoids. Portland boys took her to expensive places, but just for dessert. They talked about their teams (soccer, lacrosse), their parents (married but in counseling), and their college plans (expensive and private). Marci wasn't on any teams and her parents were divorced. She made these boys nervous, so they talked too much while she smiled and nodded and occasionally let herself lick her fork. While they paid, she excused herself to throw up the little bit she had eaten, because they made her nervous, too.

Garret never made her nervous. He took her to Pig-n-Pancake or Mo's. He said, "You better eat or those tits will go away." Sometimes they drove up to Warrenton because he wanted a Grand Slam. He drank and smoked and swore. He smelled like fish and sweat and his mouth tasted like cigarettes, and sometimes his hands were filthy.

Garret would kill for her.

Her mother wondered what she and Garret *did*. "What in the world do you find to *do* in this town, Marci?"

They drove around. Garret's truck was fast and it got bad gas mileage, but as he said proudly, "It's paid for." They roared up and down the same ten blocks getting whiplash while he talked about his dad's boat and nets and lines and pots and poundage and knots and what was running where. Sometimes they met Garret's Astoria friends up at Young's River Falls, or out at Simmons field. There was beer. Cheap beer. Someone was looking for pot, buying pot, selling pot. They called it "weed" and "reefer." Garret's friends thought she was funny because she insulted them to their faces. She hated all of them. Garret couldn't wait to move up to Astoria. "I'll party all the time," he said, even though as far as Marci could see, he was already partying all the time.

But every few weeks, he wasn't in the mood to party. He came by to get her and wanted her to sit right next to him. No music. He stared at the road as he drove, his jaw as hard as iron. On those nights, Marci knew he'd been to visit his mother.

Her mother hated him. "He's so . . . limited. Marci, honestly. What is it that you want from a boy like that? What?" Marci couldn't explain that she hated most of what she did with Garret. But after they cruised the gut a few hundred times or partied with his brain-damaged friends, they found a place to park. And there was something about the way it felt when he curved his hand around the back of her neck and pulled her to him, giving her no choice.

That's what she wanted from Garret. What she was getting at that exact moment. His face in her neck, his hands in her hair, relentless until the end, when he clamped his hands on her shoulders, "Hold still, hold *still*," keeping her motionless while he fought for control.

He always lost the battle, shuddered and moaned and collapsed against her.

The dashboard lights reflected on his sweaty shoulders. His heart hammered against her chest, knocking to get in. Her hand brushed the muscle and tendon of his neck. She felt so close to him, and so alone. "I need to go home."

Garret sat up, pulled off the condom and threw it out the window. He tenderly folded his penis back into his jeans and pulled down his shirt while she found her jeans, put them on, zipped her hoodie. He fit himself back under the steering wheel and made a show of finding and lighting a cigarette. "Garret, I mean it. I really need to go home."

He stared out the window, slowly exhaling. "I'm finishing my smoke."

"Fine, I'll walk."

"Suit yourself."

"Don't be an asshole."

He took one last long drag, looking out at the ocean, and flicked his cigarette out the window.

Finally, he started the truck.

⌇

In the driveway, he cut the engine and stared at the door of the little house. "It sucks he's in there. I hate that guy."

She missed those long nights on that big bed, too, when there was no such thing as a hurry because as far as her mother knew, Marci was asleep in her room. "I can't do anything about it. Believe me, I've tried."

"That sucks. You know what else sucks? That you have to go all the way to fuckin' Maine."

"Whatever. I'm not having this conversation again." She made for the door but he took hold of her arm with a fisherman's grip she couldn't break. "Let go."

"I'll let go when I want to let go." He stared at her for a moment, his mouth working. He dropped her arm. "Now get outta my truck."

She slammed the truck door, hard, and watched as he roared up the driveway in reverse. Stupid, dangerous and loud. Her arm throbbed. There would be bruises.

The outside lights were off and the house was dark, but the door wasn't locked. Her house was never locked. Marci turned on the kitchen light. Her little sister sat at the kitchen table, head on arms, sound asleep. Gretchen had gone from crawling into bed with people to randomly falling asleep all over the house.

"Wake up, creeper." Marci grabbed her bony shoulder and gave it a shake. "Come on, wake up." Gretchen's head lifted, slow and graceful. It reminded Marci of a tulip straightening when you put a penny in the water. Marci gave her shoulder a gentle push. "Go up to bed. Go on." Gretchen sleepwalked up the kitchen stairs. Marci felt a stab of guilt for not taking her up and tucking her in. But a glance through the dining room to the living room showed the silhouette of a head lolling back on the sofa. She could smell the booze from the kitchen.

Someone else needed putting to bed even more than Gretchen.

"Come on, Mom."

But it wasn't her mom. It was Gentry, his hair hanging over the back of the couch like a blanket. A bottle on the table, two glasses. And her mother, passed out across Gentry's lap.

Maybe if she stood there long enough, if she stared at it hard enough, this wouldn't be what it looked like. Because this was too much. Her mother had dented fenders in parking lots. She'd run her cart into shelves at the grocery store. She'd smashed several sets of dishes. She'd fallen asleep at the dinner table, yelled at Marci and not remembered what she said, and probably done other things Marci didn't want to know about.

But this was Marci's *teacher*. Did her *teacher* have to see her mother drunk?

She stepped closer and poked his shoulder with her finger. "Gentry, wake up." Nothing. "Open your eyes. Open your eyes." He blinked. "What are you *doing* here?"

"Hey Marci." He dragged a hand across his eyes. "I'm not exactly sure." He looked down, as surprised as Marci to see Kathryn sprawled across his lap.

"My mom passed out on you."

He brought one of his huge hands up to touch her hair, then pulled it back. "I think she was, um, really tired."

"That bottle looks like you were both really tired." She put her hands under Kathryn's armpits and pulled, but Kathryn was dead weight. And also drooling. Tears pressed against her eyelids and that was as much as Marci could stand, to have him see her cry on top of everything else. She gave another yank.

"Marci." His voice was so soft. "Let me help, okay?" He put his hands on Kathryn's waist and lifted her to her feet. He rose up behind, her partner in this drunken dance. Her mother hung there, bowed at the waist like a dancer, her silvery hair cascading down. She looked as strange and graceful as Gretchen.

A sound startled them both. Marci knew that sound. It was the thump of a belt buckle hitting the floor, muffled by the jeans that had fallen down with it.

For one long, ghastly moment, Gentry looked down.

Her mother landed in her arms and he stumbled out of the room, yanking up his jeans.

There was no word for this. None.

⁓

She banged open his door and landed a fist to his gut. "How *dare* you touch my mother." She hit him again and he put a hand to his stomach, but he didn't stop her. She kept hitting him, and he kept *letting* her. She had to hit him *harder*. He finally grabbed her wrist to stop the blows, how *dare* he stop her from hitting him, she had a *right* to hit him. She sank her teeth into his shoulder. A hand in her hair jerked her back.

"You can't bite me." He said it gently, firmly, like it was a rule she didn't know.

"I will kill you."

"No one is going to *kill* anyone."

He held her by her hair. He turned her around and pinned her arms to her waist, pressing her so close that she could barely kick him. She moved across the room like a little girl dancing on her father's feet. At the door he put her down and she grabbed the frame, but it took barely a shove to break her hold.

He closed the door behind her and held it shut.

She rattled the doorknob and pounded on the window. "I HATE YOU!"

Nothing. She put her hand on the doorknob and heard it. The mounting thunder of a dog's growl. Bosco sat over by the Jeep, his eyes shining in the light from back door of the big house.

She looked at the big dog, and back to her own house, where the kitchen door hung open. Beyond it, her mother slept on the couch like a sated little spider. Above it, her pale sister fluttered at her window like a moth. And what was she? A bee banging at the door, that couldn't get in.

This wasn't fair.

Marci pressed her forehead against the cold glass of his window. He was just on the other side, holding the door shut. She could hear his ragged breathing. For one long moment, she imagined smashing her head through the glass, the blood and commotion when it all fell apart.

Bosco growled.

Gentry

Tiffany Green was in academic distress. I thought she could make it through, even though the best way to describe her progress was what my track coach called "sucking wind." Lorrie had warned me not to, but I'd let Tiffany come by the lab after hours. Tiffany and I were working on a spreadsheet. It was my first cheerleading spreadsheet. We were working on tabbing from cell to cell in Excel. I kept checking the time. Vu was supposed to be there.

"So anyways, Gentry? I was thinking?"

That was terrific, that she was thinking. To be honest, I was surprised that Tiffany was thinking. God, forgive me, I am tired. Too tired to be nice. "Hey Tiffany? What were you thinking?"

She giggled. "I probably shouldn't say."

Certain tactics had probably worked for Tiffany. She tried those tactics with me. Cocking her head. Batting her eyes. A little "tsk" noise. She cast her eyes sideways to see if any of it had been effective. I needed to teach Tiffany to use the online dictionary to look up the word "simper." And tell her to stop it.

I closed my eyes. Outside this classroom, there were driving beaches where I could test the limits of the Jeep. There were dunes. There were sticks to throw for Bosco. There were gulls, with their piercing calls that hurt my heart. Inside this classroom, there was only Tiffany in her red, white and blue cheerleading getup, unable to understand what the arrows meant.

There were so many ways to be an idiot, weren't there.

I knew I had to get my attitude together. It was not right to regard a student as an idiot. I rarely thought anything like that about the kids in Detroit. They were so well-defended, it was almost a miracle to get some knowledge through their studied indifference, but they were parched for it. I went slowly, and waited. Parched areas catch fire. The flames of their learning were bright and beautiful.

In Oregon, I had to go slowly, very slowly, so slowly. I wasn't going slowly enough for Tiffany. I also wasn't going slowly enough for Alex Fournier. But I'd *tried*.

Alex was too busy with practice and training to come in to the lab during any school hours I could arrange, so I'd arranged to tutor him at my house. He sat at my table, physically present and completely absent. I asked him, was there something he was interested in? Because if you find something the student enjoys and you draw a line to it with software and hardware, before he knows it, he pays attention. I thought, well, football, correct? I've helped kids build spreadsheets to sort and tally data about every sport there is, even archery. Even bowling. Even, and I'm serious, curling. So I asked him what interested him the most.

And he looked at me, and somehow I knew that the only thing on the Internet that interested this kid was exactly what I never looked at.

Lorrie wanted greatness for that young man.

It was my job to find at least one thing to like about every student. Including Alex. Including the girl sitting next to me in the lab. I needed to find something to like about her. Maybe, I didn't know, the way she smelled? I breathed it in a little, and sneezed. I really shouldn't smell the students, anyway.

"Gentry? I was wondering. Did they even *have* cheerleaders at your last school?"

"Yes."

I glanced over at her, her hands stilled on the keys, her face frozen in that same mask of panic. At the games, she was one of six pale girls who stood in a line and called weakly to the crowd. Tiffany was precise and controlled as she led their routines. "Were they good?"

I remembered the cheerleaders in Detroit, boys and girls both. They smiled, called, answered, clapped, stomped. They built complex human structures higher than the backboards. They launched one another to the rafters. And they lined the halls and led the students in chanting me out the door of that school, celebrating one of the most painful moments of my life.

"They were fantastic."

She ducked her head. Something in my answer stung her.

My nose hummed and itched, and I let out another volley of sneezes that covered the monitor in spit. I wiped it with a sleeve.

"Hey, Gentry, do you have allergies?"

"Oh, hey, Vu. You decided to show up." He was my TA, and I could list fifty things I liked about him. "Hey Vu, do you have a half hour? For some peer tutoring?"

He drew himself up, smiling. "It would be my immense, and I mean, *immense* pleasure to help Tiffany." Vu took my seat beside Tiffany. He could help her with her directional challenge and I could sit at my desk for a few minutes, just a few, to study the insides of my eyelids.

I reached a decision, listening to Vu guide her with more patience than I could summon, listening to her take it in. I decided that I would let Alex drop this class, a requirement for juniors called Introduction to Fundamentals of Computing. I'd based it on a curriculum I developed and guest-taught to fourth-graders all over Detroit. Fourth-graders could pass it, and Alex couldn't. I would let him drop it as a favor to Lorrie Gilroy. My decision would allow Alex to enter his senior year without an F, and spare me one of Lorrie's tripartite rants about Alex, potential, and frustration.

But the truth was, I was only letting him drop because I didn't want him in my lab, and I never wanted him up at the house again.

I heard Vu. "How about it, Tiffany? You and me? You've got this figured out, and Gentry said we had a half hour." She giggled. He continued. "Actually, I don't need a half hour. More like five minutes. Maybe three, actually, and that's if you're lucky."

She giggled again. "If I'm *lucky*?"

"Yeah, you know us Asian guys. We may not be the biggest, but we're the fastest."

"If you're done, then you can take this elsewhere." My voice echoed, rough and angry.

They looked up at me. Vu blinked behind his odd little lenses. "Gentry? Not to be vulgar or anything, and I mean this in the most respectful way possible, but what's up your ass?"

I shook my head at their scolded, silent faces. "It's been a long day. You should both go." They lifted their bags and filed out.

I closed my eyes and tried to go back to beaches, Bosco, the cries of gulls. But Gretchen was in these thoughts. Gretchen, with her white-blonde hair, her icy blue eyes that always seemed to be fixed on me.

She was always watching me.

At night when I looked out my window to the east, I could see her silhouetted in her window, watching. I might be alone in my house, typing notes, correcting assignments, playing Ruin. I'd catch a movement from the corner of my eye and there she was, perched on my bed, looking at me. Sometimes I sat down alone at Kathryn's kitchen table and when I looked up, she sat across from me. This should have startled me, as used to being alone as I was. But she was so quiet, so sylphlike, blown in like a whisper. She never startled me.

I remembered the first time I got in my Jeep to drive to school. I looked out at the ocean as I buckled my seatbelt, and when I looked back, she was beside me, staring straight ahead, her face pained. She expected to be told to go away. I drove her to school, and watched to make sure she made it safely inside the doors. I decided the sight of her walking into the school, her shoulders back, her almost white hair falling down, her books pressed against her chest like a shield, that was the bravest sight I'd ever seen.

When I was a kid, I liked school. It was safe there. I kept jumping up grades, so

I was rarely bored. Best of all, they fed me. I even slept there, eyes closing during a slide show or a movie. Teachers usually let me sleep. But kids liked to jar me to wakefulness as painfully as possible, because I woke up swinging, ready to defend myself.

They thought that was funny.

And I found myself once again falling asleep in a classroom, but the classroom was mine. It was empty and still and safe, and if I put my head on my desk, I could sleep.

God, please let me sleep without dreams. Amen.

⌒

I woke up in the dark, the pale face of a girl floating above me. I sat up, looked around to locate myself. The lab.

"You stay away from my *mother*, you *hypocrite*."

"Marci. None of this is your business. You need to leave it alone."

"Leave it *alone*? Like you fucking left my *mother* alone?"

"You can't swear in here."

"What, is that your *rule*? Your stupid *rule*? Why don't you make a new rule about staying away from women when they're *drunk*?" We degenerated. She was yelling about how someone so *effete* could be such a predator, and I said I guess I'm an *effete* predator, then, and she kept slamming her hand down on my desktop and I stood up and told her to get out, get out, just get *out* of the classroom and in the middle of all this the lights came on, stunning me with their brightness.

"Everything under control in here, little buddy?"

I looked at Lorrie. I'd been shouting. I had never raised my voice once in Detroit, not even when Primus made me leave the classroom, but I'd been standing in a darkened classroom shouting at a student. At Marci.

I sat back down. "Everything in here is fine, just fine."

He watched Marci stomp her way out the door. "Under control, huh?" He sniffed, loudly. "Doesn't look like it to me, but see, I'm pretty stupid about those things. I'm pretty stupid about most things, so maybe you better explain something to me." He smiled. "Did Marci say you were boning her mom?"

He ducked out. I put my head on my desk.

God, spare me this. Please. Amen. I'm an idiot. I thought I was past this drunken, reckless falling. I thought I'd left it behind in college where it belonged. But

God? I still wasn't sure what happened. Well, I knew what had happened, I just wasn't so sure how.

You forgive all, even the stupidest of sinners. Even me.

The morning after that night, I'd scraped my hungover self out of bed and gone to early Mass at the small wooden church. While my stomach churned, beautiful Vietnamese girls broke my heart with the purity of their voices. I stood, sang, offered my responses. I prayed. I took communion. I lit the candle as I always do, and I left.

And that was all taken care of. But what exactly had happened?

I didn't remember asking, and I didn't remember being asked. I remembered being drunk. Laughing about Whitman. Putting my glass on the table because I was close to dropping it. Waking to her mouth on me, the hunger and the mercy and winding my hands in her hair and oh God, she worked me over.

The shock and the white hot fire of it.

If this is a sin, then why do You make it feel like that?

Why did she cry? Please, God, I don't remember. Ah, but the Marci part, that I remember, and God, if You had to make me remember a part of this, why that part? Am I never humiliated enough for You?

God, please. Don't make me leave.

Gretchen

Gretchen was secretly jealous of her sister's birthday. Her mom said Marci was five years old before she realized that all the kids in the world weren't trick-or-treating just to celebrate her birthday. Gretchen's birth date was February 15th. It was somehow worse, being so close to a really good birthday. "If you poach it for too long, it's going to be dry, dry, dry."

"It's my birthday and I'm doing the cooking."

"You're doing the ruining. If I can't cook the fish, can I at least clean the lettuce?"

Marci whirled and glared. "If you want to clean something, go clean your *room*."

"My room is clean."

"It stinks. It's full of garbage. You're making the whole upstairs reek with your trash."

"Marcialin," their mother called from the living room. "Everyone in this house is allowed to have her room just the way she wants it. Which includes you."

"Fine, keep your rotten litter, you little weirdo. But get out of here and let me cook."

Gretchen trudged up the back stairs. She stopped at the door to her mother's room and looked in. Everything in that room was the color of old eggshells, the walls, the comforter, the pillows stacked up on the sleigh bed, which was also painted that color. The only color in the room was an orangey-red painting over the headboard. It was, as her mother explained, an "abstract," meaning it wasn't actually a painting of anything.

Her mother called the room her "sanctuary." She liked to sit right in the middle of the bed under that painting with her knees pulled up, leaning back against the pillows, reading books of poetry. She wore reading glasses, and if Gretchen went in, she would look at Gretchen over the top of them. Gretchen liked that. But if she stayed too long, her mother would read her a poem. Gretchen hated poetry.

She walked over and smelled her mother's bed. The bed smelled like her mother's bubble bath. It was a little bed, really, only a double, but they all fit, including Marci when she came in and lay down, too. All three of them could still fit in the nest. But that wouldn't last. Gretchen had done the research at the library and knew she would probably be far taller than both her mother and sister. She hoped that curling up against her mother would always make her feel safe.

She stopped at the door of Marci's room, which was closed, and the hinges squeaked so Marci would know if she opened the door to see if whatever Marci was smelling could actually be coming from her own room.

Gretchen gave up and went to her own bedroom. She stood in the door and took a small sniff. Nothing. She decided to sniff her way around the room's perimeter, so if anything did smell funny, she could localize it. On her way past the bookshelf, she did smell something a little sour. It might have been a bird's nest, because after all, those had a lot of spit in them. Or maybe it was the shoe. For years, shoes washed up because a freighter lost a container of them. She had one, all covered with barnacles, a men's size thirteen. She took it in her hand and gave it a sniff. Just saltwater, which was the cleanest smell she knew.

The cleanest, next to the way Gentry smelled.

He liked showers. She could sit under his bathroom window, the one that looked northwest, and listen to him sing in the shower. Sometimes he sang church songs. The smell of his soap poured out the window with the steam.

When Gentry came in to eat dinner, he went to the kitchen sink and washed carefully, dragging his fingernails in the kitchen soap to leave little grooves. He rinsed for a long time and used a clean towel to dry his hands, then put that towel out in the laundry room. Marci called it "the surgical scrub."

Gretchen knew that Gentry was clean. He brushed his teeth all the time. He never wore the same socks twice. He changed his sheets every week. He even gave Bosco lots of baths. All of these things told her that Gentry liked to be clean. But no matter how clean someone kept his penis, he still urinated with it.

So why would her mother do that?

The answer was simple. The only reason a woman would ever do that to a man was because he liked it.

It was disgusting. It was more disgusting than her brothers having booger flinging contests, more disgusting than that old man in the running shorts on the beach.

She'd observed enough about men to know that they were all disgusting.

She sat in her windowseat and stared at his door. He hadn't come to dinner all week, but they'd made plans to do all the Halloween stuff together before the *thing* happened.

She decided to go out and get him.

⌒

She was supposed to knock.

Marci had a big talk with her after the cartoon morning, all about how Gretchen might find a girlfriend in there with him and it could be "weird." Okay. Gretchen didn't know what she could see that would be any weirder than what she saw on the couch.

She walked in without knocking.

Bosco thumped his tail and went back to sleep by the refrigerator. Gentry was asleep at his table, his head down on his arm beside the keyboard. That looked uncomfortable. It reminded her of the boys who had to put their heads on their desks as punishment at school. One of them always fell asleep. He had his prayer necklace, which she'd learned wasn't a necklace at all but something called a "rosary," wrapped up in his right hand. She moved his mouse around a little to see what was on his screen.

> Mel, not Thanksgiving, sorry. The break is too short. Christmas, though, I
> will definitely be there. Nowhere on this earth I would rather be at midnight
> 12-24. Tell Loren I said to please start baking now.
>
> I wish you were signed on. If you would sign on when you get this and see
> if I'm on that would be great. I wanted to talk to you about something, I
> need some help with a

Mel? Was that short for Melanie, or Melinda, or Melissa? Gretchen felt hot things pounding behind her skin. Be with her at midnight on Christmas? He said he didn't have a family, so it wasn't a sister. He didn't have a family so she thought he'd be with her family on Christmas.

And who was this Loren girl who baked for him?

She felt stupid, she was so stupid, so stupid. Gentry had a girlfriend.

He'd never marry her mother.

He sat up fast. Gentry always looked scared when he woke up. He looked around, eyes blind to what was really there, until he found her face.

He looked relieved until she started yelling at him.

"Where are you going at *Christmas*? I thought you'd be *here*! I want you to be *here*! Who's *Mel*? *Tell* me! Is Mel your *girlfriend*?"

"Stop. Hush." Gentry put down his beads, took her hands and looked in her eyes. "Mel is short for Melvin. He's my uncle."

"But you said you don't *have* a family."

"I have Mel. I'm going to see him at Christmas. Okay? All right?" He pointed to the picture of him and the old man. "This is Mel."

"Well who's *Loren*?"

"A friend of my uncle's."

"Loren is a *man*?" She felt so stupid that she started to cry.

He held out his arms. "Come here."

She sat on his lap, she was too old for that but it felt so nice that it made her cry even more, she was crying so much that she had to wipe her nose on his shoulder but she didn't think he cared about that. His arms were around her and he put his face in her hair. He breathed in through his nose, inhaling. She could hear the churn of the ocean, the hum of his monitor, the squeak of the wooden floor as he rocked a little. He kept smoothing her hair with his big hand. Nothing had ever made her feel so safe. But she still remembered. She started to cry all over again because how could he do that with her mother, how could he *be* like that?

"Hey, now. What's this about?" He said that into the top of her head. How could she tell him? She hated what her mother did to him, it made her scared and sick and the only way she could stand it was if they got married. And she wished he hated it too. But he didn't, she could tell. He hadn't hated it at all. And if she said any of this out loud, he'd be so embarrassed that he'd never talk to her again. He'd go away.

Marci would love that.

"I *hate* Marci. She'll make you go away."

"No she won't."

"She *will*, I don't know *how* but she *will*. I *hate* her."

"No one will make me go away." He kept his face in her hair.

But he didn't know Marci, he didn't understand her. She could make him go away. Gretchen didn't know how, but she could.

"Will you please come in for dinner? Please?"

"I think," he whispered into her hair. "I think I shouldn't."

Kathryn

Kathryn had let Marci cook her own birthday dinner. Marci had roasted the Brussels sprouts, made the salad and poached the lovely salmon that Garret had brought by. Kathryn had baked the cake. The table was set, the cake frosted, the suitcase wrapped, the card signed. Kathryn had things under control, didn't she? Yes, under control.

Gretchen came to the table and sat down, eyes red-rimmed under the white eyelashes. "Gentry won't come to dinner." Her lips trembled. "He hasn't been here all week. I don't think he's going to eat here anymore."

"Well happy birthday to me, then." Marci stared at the fish. She actually looked sad. Garret sat there, silent and glowering.

"Of course you're happy. You're happy because you're always so *mean* to him."

"I'm not *mean* to him, I just . . ."

"Girls. Enough." Kathryn pushed her chair back and threw her napkin on the table. She stepped out the back door, lit a cigarette, and considered her best course of action. It had been four days. Both her daughters were miserable and it was all her fault.

It was also ridiculous.

Kathryn had liked it better in the dim, primeval past, when she was a front line soldier in the sexual revolution. She had fun, she caught diseases, she went to the clinic and she moved on. But that was twenty-five, almost thirty years ago. Gentry wouldn't remember those days, because Gentry was only twenty-seven years old. He was supposed to be an adult, and adults dealt with things like this, murky, drunken encounters that were best forgotten.

She opened the door to the little house without knocking. He sat at his table, fingering a rosary. When he saw her, he pretended to be contemplating the computer screen before him. His face. He looked so guilty and haunted. She looked from his face to the beads on the table to the crucifix on the wall. He was so terribly Catholic. Oh my god, was he?

Was Gentry still a virgin?

She felt sick. How was she supposed fix this?

"Gentry, I think I must owe you some kind of apology."

"No, don't apologize." He kept his eyes on the screen. "I, um, don't know what to say."

She brightened her tone. "You could say, 'Kathryn, you really shouldn't drink like that.' Because I know I was drunk. Or you could say 'Do you have any idea what you said to me, Kathryn?' Because I must have said something horrible to you, because you haven't been over for dinner all week. So you could spare me the details, and say I'm forgiven for whatever it was I said or did. I'll have to take your word for it, because I don't remember."

"You don't remember?" He no longer looked tormented, he looked incredulous and a little insulted.

"I remember nothing past the Whitman." She feigned concern. "My God, what did I *say*?"

"Nothing. I mean, you were nice." He looked down at his lap.

She tried to avoid looking at his lap.

"Well, thank goodness." She resisted an overwhelming urge to stroke his hair.

"Are you going to come over for dinner? It's Marci's birthday, there's a nice fish, and we all want you there. There's cake."

He looked trapped. "Um, sure. Give me a second."

She closed his door. She thought about his hair.

She went to find herself a drink.

Gretchen

Gretchen stared at the fish. "You shouldn't be allowed to cook anymore."

"Shut up."

Gentry pushed his food around on his plate. Probably he wasn't very excited about roasted Brussels sprouts with too much garlic, poached fish that was dry, and salad with too many green pepper strips in it. This was a terrible dinner.

"Well." Her mother stubbed out a cigarette. "What are you being for Halloween?"

"A traditional witch."

Her mother lifted an eyebrow. "What makes a witch traditional?"

"A traditional witch is like in the Wizard of Oz." Gretchen chased a reeking, greasy sprout around her plate. "Some girls in my class are being sexy witches in fishnets."

"Ick." Marci's nostrils flared. "I can hardly wait to see for myself at the school carnival."

"You don't have to go this year. Gentry's taking me."

"I see. Are you two trick-or-treating first?" Why did Marci sound so mad? She hated having to do that on her birthday every year.

Gretchen shrugged. "If we have time."

"Well, watch out for Gentry. He's not eating dinner, so he'll probably steal all your candy."

"I don't like candy." Gentry sounded insulted.

"You like all food."

"Candy isn't *food*. You can't call candy food."

"Of course it is."

"Hey Marci? In which of the four basic food groups would you put it?"

Garret actually spoke up. "He's right, babe. Candy's not food. Food's like, meat, or something." Gentry and Garret stared at each other. They were surprised to agree.

"Well, this fish is food, and Garret's feelings will be hurt if we don't eat more of it. So let's . . . dig in." Her mother was trying to get control of the conversation. Everyone took a bite except Gentry. He pushed his fish around and sighed.

"I'm surprised that you participate in Halloween, Gentry." Marci still sounded angry. "Isn't it, I don't know, too creepy or something?"

"Catholics are used to creepy. Relic worship and all that."

"What's relic worship?"

"It's veneration of a holy relic. Praying to bones, vials of blood, mummified body parts, that kind of thing."

Gretchen was glad that someone finally mentioned something interesting. "You do that? You pray to bones?"

"I don't personally, no. I don't venerate anything but God. I don't even venerate Christ as much as . . ." He stopped, pressed his lips together in a flat line.

"What's 'venerate'?"

"Another time, Gretchen."

Marci shrugged. "Who cares if it's a cross or a bone or your little prayer abacus? When you think about it, it's all the same bunch of superstitious garbage."

"Marci, you might be my sister but you're a horrible person and I hate you."

The table was very, very quiet.

"I'm afraid that Gretchen won't be going anywhere with you tonight, Gentry." Her mother's face was set and stony.

"Excuse me." Gentry stood up. He took his plate into the kitchen and let the door slam behind him.

They didn't even carry in the cake to cut it. Marci just went into the kitchen and carried out slices on the little white dessert plates. She used the wrong size forks on purpose. Gretchen's stomach hurt. She couldn't eat, she just moved her cake around. Garret ate his in two bites and ducked out the back door.

"I'm glad we're alone, now. What a perfectly lovely display, girls. I'm so proud of you both. Really. This was exceptional." Her eyes were like ice, and her voice was just as cold. "Gentry will be here for dinner, Marci, and he will be treated with courtesy and respect instead of this endless baiting. And Gretchen, I never want to hear you say anything like that to your sister again. Now please go do the dishes cooperatively, without any more bickering."

Gretchen didn't say one word to Marci while she dried the dishes, not one single word.

So, that was it. That was her Halloween with Gentry. They'd carved a pumpkin and that was all they were going to do. Her mother hadn't bought any candy because no one ever came to their door, and they wouldn't be trick-or-treating. Gretchen wasn't even going to the stupid school carnival. She'd thought a lot about going to the carnival with Gentry. There was a chance that someone might even have asked her, *Who is that guy?* She'd had her answer planned out. *Just a friend.* She wanted to say that about someone. Out loud.

That she had a friend.

NOVEMBER

Kathryn

November was the advent of winter, and the beginning of the rotating holiday schedule. This year Kathryn had the girls for Thanksgiving, and the selfish bastard who'd ruined his daughters' lives with his careless infidelity had them for Christmas. No hanging out suet for the birds for the Animals' Christmas. No roast pork. No daughters on Christmas morning.

The unfairness of it was a ravenous little beast lodged in her stomach, eating its way out. It was only tamed with alcohol.

The girls left for school in darkness, and returned when it was nearly dark. It seemed all their time together was spent at the table with meals eaten after the sun had gone down. She felt as if she were living in a cave. The girls spent too much time in front of the television. She tried to sit with them, but the noise of the commercials drove Kathryn off the sofa and to the kitchen table, where she sipped and stared at the darkness outside. Why not go to bed early, why not sleep until it was light, in a month like November? It made no sense that in a month she associated with everlasting darkness, Kathryn woke long before dawn.

She'd decided it was because she was getting old. As a child back in the fifties, she was puzzled when her grandmother called her parents at six in the morning, shocked that they were still in bed. There was a time change, Central to Pacific, but even so, her grandmother had been up for hours. When you get old, you need less of everything, including sleep.

Gentry was not old. So what woke him? Because he was awake just as early.

She heard him before she saw him. The crunch of gravel as he walked up the drive to get the paper, his dog beside him. The opening of her back door, the brushy sweep of his feet on the cocoa mat before he stepped in, mindful of her fretting about sand on the ancient, indestructible linoleum. Michael had always hated that flooring, but she wouldn't replace it. What was that joke she told him? *Linoleum is like a man. You lay it right the first time, and you can walk on it forever.* Shows what she knew.

She tracked him by the creak of the door, the click of his dog's toenails, the tread of his boots. He usually ran his laundry before he went to bed. Morning brought the tumble of the dryer as it began turning his clothing round and round. She waited for the running of water into the carafe, the grinder, the gurgle of the coffeemaker.

Only coffee could lure her from the warmth of her bed in November.

She rose up and yanked on cotton leggings. Over her nightgown she pulled on an enormous sweater with snowflakes across the chest. It had belonged to a tall grandfather who died long before she was born. She pushed her cold feet into shearling slippers and went to her bathroom. She finger-combed her hair away from her bare face. No one could accuse her of vanity in the morning.

He looked up from the paper and smiled. Bosco sprawled at his feet, taking up most of the room under the table. "Hey."

"Good morning. Did you sleep well?"

"Hm."

Her cigarettes and matches were stashed in the pocket of her sweater. It was time for cream in her cup, then sugar, then coffee, and she watched it turn the perfect shade of light brown as she lit her first, finest cigarette of the day. She leaned against the sink and took first her sip. Bliss, smoke mingled with coffee and morning breath. She couldn't imagine how disgusting this would taste to someone else, but there was no finer taste in the world to Kathryn.

He was doing the "across." Tapping that old mechanical pencil on the table while he thought. He never asked for help, but he would occasionally sigh, set it down, let her pick it up, watch her while she filled in a few words. She knew the opera answers, and he knew his Bible, but they had to wait for Marci for names of pop stars.

He sat back, the puzzle half-blank, the chair complaining under him. All that sculpted muscle, hidden by those ragged, baggy clothes. He was . . . no, she told herself. Drop that.

"A penny for your thoughts."

He made a face, part smile, part frown. "Not worth a cent."

"I doubt that."

"Okay. I was thinking about oil filters."

That made her laugh a little.

When she sat down, Gentry steadied the table. "I should fix this."

"It's always wobbled. Even back when it was my nana's."

"Your nana?"

"Yes. My mother's mother was Nana. This was her table. After her funeral, I tied it to the top of the Volvo and drove it home from Minnesota."

"That's a drive."

"Yes, especially under an upside-down kitchen table. I had to re-tie it more times than I could count." She was so angry with Michael for staying home with Marci, for not being along to tie the damn thing properly. She had hated him for it.

Overhead, she heard the thump of bare feet, the flush of a toilet. "Gretchen will be down in a minute. Are you hungry?"

"I'm starving."

Why, she wondered, as he filled in another answer. Why did he starve himself? Kathryn had a reason to deny herself. She was divorced and angry and she drank too much, but she was determined not to be that divorced mother who dragged men home to the horror of her children. But why did he do it? He had that artless masculine beauty that could have filled every night with a willing partner. Why didn't he take advantage? Why, when what she remembered of him was so . . . no. She would not allow herself to do that.

She studied Gentry's face. There was mystery there, a secret told by dark eyes and high cheekbones. "So, I called my grandmother Nana. What did you call your grandmother?"

"Bà."

"Bà? That's what Vu calls his grandmother. So you're part Vietnamese?"

"No."

"Then what are you?"

He swallowed, opened his mouth. The dryer alarm went off, making them both jump. He bolted to the laundry room. Everything he took out of that dryer was sturdy, dark, and cotton. Even his towels. She watched him pull out a tattered plaid shirt and shake it with a practiced snap. Male ironing. He stopped, frowned. With thumb and forefinger, he carefully pulled a tiny piece of peach lace away from the flannel, something feminine that had clung to the side of the dryer, stealthy as a spider. He removed it as delicately as if he were trying to keep a cobweb intact and dropped it back in their basket before he finished making his small, precisely folded stack. There was something touching about the way he took care of himself. It was so obvious he always had.

Kathryn turned her attention to the window. The sky lightened, but there was no real sunrise. The day would be nothing but murk.

He sat back down. "I should clean the gutters."

She fought an urge to push his hair out of his face. "The rain will do that for us."

Bosco shifted and groaned, dreaming his old dog dreams. She sipped her coffee. He filled in another answer.

They worked on their puzzle.

Lorrie Gilroy

This guy's got the most embarrassing gear I've ever seen.

He's got a twenty year-old yellow Berkeley ugly stick with a Zebco reel, some piece of shit his uncle gave him for his eleventh birthday, he's had the same stick since 1979 and he won't even tolerate you laughing at it because his uncle's some kind of god on earth, I guess. But that isn't the worst part, no. The worst part is, the little asshole catches more fish with it than I do with my G Loomis.

He's always ready at Oh-dark-thirty. He doesn't own waders so I take him out in the boat. Weekday mornings I usually take him to the jetty or to Social Security beach, and he's always good to go, with his corny little box of hooks, his baseball cap, and that sonofabitching joke of a rod he has. He's usually pretty quiet. I like quiet, but I think it's about time he gave up stonewalling me and gave out a little information, see.

It's a Wednesday and we're sitting in the boat because I'm tired of the jetty. Too many Vus down there. I'm trying to get him to tell me about that Mumford woman, but I'm being sneaky-like. I'm talking about the weekend, telling him about this little wildcat from Warrenton I met this last weekend, hoping that will get him talking.

He listens to more details than I thought he would. And then he smiles a little. "Hey Lorrie? Do you have, um, a waterbed, by any chance?" Like that. And then he cracks up and what really pisses me off is that I've got a waterbed, see, a California King, and I don't get the goddamn joke I guess.

Okay, no more talking about women.

"So, you're originally from Detroit?" I wait, and he doesn't say anything. "Is that where you're from?" Not a lot of Indians in Detroit, I don't think.

"No. I went there with Teach For America."

"Are you shitting me? You taught in, what, some Detroit slum? You did that?"

"Yes. Yes, I did."

I move my line a little bit. I figure that's as much as he's going to say, because he's not exactly what you'd call the talkative kind and this is the most information I've managed to get out of the guy. I give the line a flick. "I can't imagine having to teach kids like that."

He gives me some bleeding heart look. "I was trying too hard at first. The idealistic teacher who was going to fix everything by making computers meaningful to kids who lived in a war zone. Once I gave that up, the kids figured out how computers could help them."

I sit there for a minute, because that's the longest I've heard the man speak. I kind of feel like I should take my hat off and put it over my heart to mark the moment. But I decide to move the line a little more. "Like how?"

He shrugs. "One kid was a dealer. He wrote a program to help manage his business."

"Goddamn drug dealing trash using taxpayer money like that. Pisses me off just to hear something like that. Did you make him stop? Is he in prison?"

"No, Lorrie." He's talking patient-like, like I'm a goddamned student and he has to explain it all to me. "I helped him figure out other uses for the software. Now he's a systems consultant for minority-owned small businesses."

"No shit?"

He nods. "Another kid almost dropped out her senior year. Danaia. Brilliant girl, so bored with school that she decided to leave. She came in the lab to say good-bye and caught me sitting at my desk playing a game, so she looked it over. She said she'd never seen such a pile of sick, violent, misogynistic garbage in all her life. 'Only white people would make up this trash.' I said, 'Do you think you could do better?' She said, 'I know I could.' I taught her some code, I mean, basic Basic because that's all I can do, and it was amazing. She was like a savant. She pushed me out of the way and sat down and cracked in and completely rewrote it."

"Why the hell did she do that?"

"To clean it up. She lives in Silicon Valley, now, designing games for girls with a positive slant. She sends me prototypes to test. I tell her if they get too didactic."

"What the hell is didactic?"

He just smiles. "So, no, Lorrie, I never had any trouble teaching kids like that."

Well, Jesus Get a Haircut Christ. I feel ashamed just looking at him, I sincerely shit you not, I feel like an asshole. "They sound like good kids."

He nods. "I miss them. But they either graduate or die."

"Die?" That raises the hair on my neck. "Jesus Christ. I never had a kid die."

"Never?"

"Not one."

"That makes me glad I moved here." He looks out over the water. "That and the fishing."

I smile a little. "If they were still logging around here, we'd have a dead kid every year. But we don't log anymore. Put most of my relatives out of business when that happened."

He frowns. "Isn't this where *Sometimes a Great Notion* was set?"

"What's that, a book?"

"A great book. About Oregon loggers. You might like it, Lorrie."

"Forget it. I've never liked a book."

He cracks up.

We sit in the boat and he keeps pulling in those fish, one after another. Pulling them in with that ugly stick. If you didn't know anything about fishing, it might look like he wasn't doing anything special. But he looks out over the water and his hands and wrists move in a way I could never get the hang of, subtle-like in a way that makes the bait alive to the fish. He isn't thinking about it. You can't think about it. It's the hardest thing in the world to do and it looks like it's the easiest.

That's how he fishes.

⌇

Later, we're at work, and he comes in my room all panicked. "The office scheduled all these conferences."

"So?"

"I've never done conferences."

"Didn't they have conferences where you used to teach?"

"I scheduled them but no one ever showed up."

"Didn't you ever see the parents?"

"Mostly at funerals."

Again with the dead kids. Gives me the sonofabitching creeps. "They're just parents. Jesus, I'm smarter than the parents nine times out of ten. If I've got'em beat, you sure don't have to worry about it." I'm pretty good at conferences. Mostly, I meet with the parents of the wrestlers trying to convince them that wrestling's a whole hell of a lot less of a pussy sport than basketball, I lose so goddamn many kids to basketball, and this soccer deal, don't get me started on soccer, but back to Gentry. "Show me one of those portfolios you make the kids put together."

"But it's all elementary at this point. Look." He opens up one of the kids' portfolios as he calls it, that's a nice sissy word, portfolio, and he shows me these spreadsheets and charts and tables and presentations and newsletters and process papers, and manuals and transparencies and covers and all this shit he has them doing, you name it, he's got everybody doing it, every fisherman's son. All stored on the network, no paper involved, but it's all there. "Hey Lorrie, you understand that this is all basic stuff, right?"

"Sure, I understand." I understand that I'm stupid but I'm not that stupid. I can tell that he's been teaching them a whole hell of a lot more than how to turn on a sonofabitching computer, which is about all he's been able to teach me. When I walk past his classroom, all I hear is kids talking and music playing and once in a while, him saying "Listen, now, I want you to listen. Shut up, please." And this is what he gets out of them. Eight weeks, he's been here for eight weeks. Unbelievable.

I guess he teaches like he fishes.

I tell him to show the parents this stuff, show them all the pretty portfolios, and they'll be very, very happy, and he seems like he'll be okay now. Jesus.

He might be teaching them plenty, but he needs to have more control, more discipline with his classes. I coach, see, I believe in authority, and if those little shits smell fear on you, you're through, so I do some martial arts in my spare time because it helps me to keep authority with the kids. There's nothing like kicking the shit out of a bag when you're thinking about the waste of it, the absolute sonofabitching waste of the potential of a kid like Alex Fournier, if that kid with those legs and those lungs and those hands just had a little more confidence, where he could go in this world . . .

But anyway, Gentry lets his students get away with shit I can't believe.

This Garret kid, now there's an overdue ass-kicking if I ever saw one. "Can I see Garret Blount's portfolio?" He pulls it up, there's a cover sheet with the term assignments and the grades, and it's complete and his work is passing. "How do you manage to get work out of this kid? Because I can't get him to do shit in Careers. Tells me he doesn't need it. Dad's boat. That's the career."

And Gentry scratches at his jaw like he has a flea. Nervous-like. "I let him leave the minute his work's in. He does it so he can walk out of my classroom."

That's all wrong. You don't treat a kid like Garret this way, you don't let him out of anything, you put him in his place, that's how you handle him. His little bitch of a girlfriend's going to grow up to be just like her mother, and the thought of that should make any man's balls crawl up in his gut and hide out, I tell you. How does Gentry live up there? And that Vu kid, if I was a violent man but I'm not but if I was, I tell you, that kid would be driven into the ground feet-first like a railroad spike.

And then there's Tiffany. You know, I see her walk in there so short and straight and serious like she is, finding a way to be in Gentry's face every day for one reason or another and the only reason is that she's trouble. I've known that quiet little girl her whole life and she's making a first class idiot of herself. He acts like it isn't happening and you can't be stupid about this shit, not in high school. I want to talk to Jeannie about it, to tell her that her daughter's about to jump the track, big time. But Jeannie and I aren't getting along so hot these days.

"You're watching out for that little Tiffany, right? You don't need to be alone with that one. It could be some first-class underage trouble of the split-tail variety, if you get my drift."

That face of his clouds up fast. I think with a face like that he can't exactly be a stranger to the idea of a student and what it feels like when a pretty one gets it in her head to push things. Jesus Christ, it's even happened to me. But now my little buddy is pissed at me. What the hell. Gentry can be as moody as a woman.

It might cheer the guy up to see me make an asshole of myself trying to learn how to do something new. "Hey, you know what you need to teach me? The Internet." Oh, and he perks right up. He tries to show me how to get to some deal the kids made up, and I'm trying but Goddamnit I hate feeling stupid, you know?

"Lorrie, you make it harder than it has to be."

"It isn't hard, it's just STUPID."

"Just relax a little."

"I told you, I HATE this shit."

"Lorrie, I have an idea. Go back."

"What?"

"Get out of this."

"How the HELL do you do that?"

He has to show me how the hell to do that, of course. "Just keep clicking forward through the prompts."

"The what?"

He shows me, and I do it, and he has me do some more shit. "Pick a password." I type "profootball" because no way do the pros have to dick around with computers I bet, and then he tells me to type in "Betty Page." Whatever, I feel like a sonofabitching secretary, but if it makes him happy. "You're surfing the net, Lorrie."

"No shit?"

He says all patient-like, "Click there."

It's like a dream, watching it come into focus, line by line, watching that woman take shape right before my eyes. "I'll be goddamned." Betty Page. This is her. This is the woman of my dreams. This is the woman I been looking for all my whole, sorry, sonofabitching life, I tell you. "This is it, little buddy, this is her."

He smiles. "I thought you'd like her."

"Is she still available?"

"Let's find out." He clicks a little, reads. "Hm. This is interesting. She was born in 1923."

"So you're telling me she's seventy-some years old."

"Yes. But she's currently single." He's laughing at me, the little sonofabitch. The kids start to come in, so I leave.

I can feel stupid in my own classroom just fine.

⁓

I've got a girlfriend right now, anyway. I Dream of Jeannie, as I call her. Gentry asked me, what, after the song? And I say no, after the TV show. "I've never seen that."

Jeannie's not a dream, I'll tell you that much. She's bony and whiny. Between the sheets, she's something like a sack of antlers. I need a game plan for getting rid of her. Believe you me, I've tried. I've screwed around on her and ignored her and refused to meet her sister. She still won't tell me to go away. I need a plan.

And I'm trying to think of the plan there in my classroom. I decide to show the kids some video so I can think. I need to think. This is Careers, I think.

"Vu, start that tape."

He looks at the cover. "Sir, Mr. Gilroy, Coach, I fail to see the relevance of this video to my possible future, to any possible career choice I might make."

"Shut up and start the tape. And I'm going to quiz you on it, so somebody take notes so I know what the hell it's about."

"Yes, sir." He starts the tape.

I leave the classroom and go to the lab. He always has music playing in here in the mornings, he lets the kids bring in their own stuff, he'll play whatever they want. I don't run my classroom like that, no sir. Some of those kids are just sitting in there playing computer games. I hear him helping somebody with math and there's no computer at the table where this kid sits. That's Gentry, he's a good guy, that's why I'm there, for help.

"Little buddy, can I see you out in the hall?"

"Is it important?"

"Get out here in the hall."

He gets mad but he gets. "What is it?"

I tell Gentry my game plan. See, I need Gentry to come with me to Jeannie's for Thanksgiving. I mean, there he'd be, all sensitive and complimentary and shit, see, and I'll look like such an asshole by comparison that Jeannie will have to dump me. That's my game plan. I think it's a good one.

Gentry isn't so sure. "Will, um, her daughter be there?"

Well, my little buddy is not quite the blind bonehead I thought. "Nope. She's going over to Alex's house for dinner. His aunt's a good cook."

He looks a little sideways at me. "Are you cooking?"

"Hell no, buddy, Jeannie will cook and it's football for you and me!"

"Good."

"Good? You like pro football?"

"No, I mean, good, you aren't cooking."

Well screw you very much, little buddy.

                             ⌒

I should've cooked, the truth be told. Because it's a week later, it's Thanksgiving, the big day, and Jeannie's opening the door. I hate this place, I hate the way women have their houses, all blue and white and fussy and dead flowers and shit, and everywhere you look there's Tiffany in some goddamn shiny getup with too much makeup, every wall full of those eight by ten nightmares from gymnastics and dance and those damn cheer camps that take every penny Jeannie makes, which isn't much.

"Oh you MADE it!" Jeannie says and throws her arms around him like he's a long-lost nephew. Gentry gives me a panicked look.

"Just go look at the TV," I tell him. Jeannie gets busy in the kitchen getting together some mess for us to eat. Our job is to watch football. Pretty soon we're called to the table. And there's the rub. There's food on it, food that she cooked.

Jeannie scampers off to the kitchen like a deer on meth to get more food, and I tell Gentry to try an appetizer. "Go on, try it. Don't pray over it, that won't help, believe me."

He puts something in his mouth, chews, gets a look on his face like you wouldn't believe, and spits it out, and my little buddy's not a picky eater. He looks at all that food and shakes his head. "I can't do it."

I whisper, "Let's get out of here. Pretend to be sick."

He hisses back, "I'm terrible at lying. *You* pretend to be sick."

Jeannie walks in smiling and sets a big glass of purple Kool-Aid by his plate. He stares at it and right on cue, he gags.

Time to make it happen.

I pull him up and put my hand over his mouth, almost like a head lock, see, drag Gentry to the door. "Come on, little buddy, don't barf on the rug . . . He's sick, gotta go, sorry . . . that's the ticket, fella." And I'm getting out the door, on the way to truck, Gentry's laughing so hard in my hand I think I might accidentally smother him, and Jeannie's standing in her doorway, all sad-like.

"What am I gonna do with all this food?" she wails.

I throw Gentry in the Ford. "Flush it down the goddamn toilet, I guess." He's howling, I gotta get him out of here.

I need to get a big woman. They always know how to cook.

⌒

So, the Wet Dog it is. I'm here to talk to Faye about a cheeseburger and a little action. She gives me the cheeseburger but she's sitting tight on that action and nothing I say will change her mind.

Darlene is another story. She's up here in the bar wet-eyed over some family Thanksgiving bullshit she's spilling over to Gentry, her stepdad was a sawyer who got laid off temporarily fifteen years ago and never got called back and apparently he's home today making her mom's life hell on turkey day, which is bad enough but for love of Jesus does she have to sit in here and moan about it because who the hell in this town doesn't know that story. That's the story of this whole county.

But Gentry's drinking and he's listening, oh yeah, the sensitive guy, and then they're dancing slow and shit, and hell. They're leaving. That's the other story of this county, isn't it, getting drunk and screwing someone you don't like. "Don't do it in her CAR, little buddy," I say, "Jesus, have you SEEN her car? Let me give you my house keys, try out the waterbed . . ." but they're out the door and it's too late. So I turn my attention back to Faye.

Who is ignoring me in favor of some social disease down the bar.

I don't know what the hell's wrong with my little buddy, but a little bit later he comes running into the bar like he saw a ghost. "Take me to my Jeep." He's almost shouting at me and my little buddy doesn't shout. So I get take him back to the Jeep.

I'm trying to ask him what happened, is Darlene a vampire? Was her boyfriend hiding in the back seat? What? But he isn't saying a goddamn word, not one goddamn peep.

Nobody can be quieter than that sonofabitch.

Marci

M arci could tell her little sister was sad that Gentry hadn't come over for Thanksgiving dinner. All that cooking and no one to eat it.

He didn't come over the rest of the weekend, either. Gretchen took him heaping plates covered with gravy. The plates came back empty, so Marci doubted Gentry was sick. Unless he gave it all to the dog. But he stayed away, which Marci enjoyed. Just her, her mother, and her strange little sister.

All right, it got a tiny bit boring.

On Monday morning before school, Gretchen hung around the kitchen with her hairbrush. "You're pathetic."

"And you're mean." The door opened, and Gretchen leapt up, eyes shining, only to fall back into her chair when it was just Garret.

"You ready, babe?" Garret's eyes were usually tight on Mondays from a weekend of squinting out over the sea from under a cap, because he hated sunglasses.

"Almost." Marci rinsed her coffee cup.

"No hurry." He was almost smiling. Gretchen gave him a look of utter loathing and took herself out the back door to wait in the Jeep.

Garret couldn't stop smiling. He hardly ever smiled. And he didn't usually come into the house anymore in the morning. He didn't like to see Gentry sitting at the kitchen table with their mother, drinking coffee and looking at the paper while Gretchen brushed out his hair. Lately, whenever Garret was over and he got close to Marci, Bosco sauntered over and sat on her feet, smiling his big slobbery smile. Or he'd lean his big hairy body against her and pant, and blow dog breath all over Garret.

No Bosco, no Gentry, though, this morning.

Kathryn waltzed through the dining room, singing to herself. Thank you very much, Mother, Marci was sure Garret enjoyed the concert. "Where is Gretchen?" Kathryn cocked her head, studying Garret's face. "My, Garret. You certainly are in fine fettle this morning."

"Huh." Garret looked away, because he didn't know what "fettle" was. "Babe. Let's go. I got somethin' to tell you." Whatever it was, it was making him ridiculously happy. He put his arm around Marci as they left, and she ducked away. If he touched her in front of her mother it might prompt that mother/daughter talk that they'd never managed to have.

They were out in the driveway when Gentry slammed out his door and into the Jeep. He drove out so fast that he kicked up gravel. "I hope my sister is wearing her seatbelt."

"You're not gonna believe this."

"Okay, spill it. Why are you so happy?" He opened his mouth and told her.

For some reason, she'd been sure that he was going to tell her Gentry's name. It wasn't Gentry's name. Marci felt her mouth hanging open in horror. She hated phrases like "dawning recognition," but it applied. Because this explained it all. This explained why Gentry didn't date or have girlfriends or hook-ups. Because he *couldn't*.

As relieved as Marci was to get that news, she was still horrified. "Darlene actually *told* you that? She told you something that *private* about someone? Because decent people don't talk about things like this, Garret."

"She told Trent and he told me." Garret's smile was beginning to lose power around the edges. "I thought you'd think it was funny."

"You thought I'd laugh because Gentry is *impotent*? Well, I'm not laughing. And you can't tell anyone else about this."

His hands clenched the wheel and his face was stark. "You can't tell me what to say."

"Fine. Do what you want. Just know if you *do* talk about it, I'll never speak to you again for as long as I live."

She lit down from the truck and pushed in the back door, startling her mother, who sat perched over the paper like a small white bird. Marci took a moment just to see her, her full mouth and blue eyes, the airy platinum of her long hair, her severe collarbones and dry little hands, the faintest smudges of newsprint on her fingertips.

Like the sun coming through a cloud, Marci was pierced with a radiant clarity. That awful night, that horrible night, Gentry hadn't done anything with her mother. He wasn't *able* to.

"Mom? Will you give me a ride to school?"

"Of course, but . . ." Kathryn threw her hands up in frustration. "What is the *problem*, Marcialin? The tension around here is enough to drive me to . . . well, I know you don't enjoy having a teacher living here, but I thought it was working out. I really did, and this is *completely* unacceptable. And I can't just kick him out."

"It's fine. You don't have to . . ." Marci shook her head. "It's just . . . just . . . the weirdness of it. But I promise, I'm over it."

"Are you?"

"Yes."

"Are you going to apologize to him?"

"Mother Dear. Must it be engraved?"

"I think not." When her mother smiled, the papery little wrinkles around her eyes were the most beautiful thing Marci had ever seen in her life.

Gretchen

"Can I help you carry anything in?" Gretchen was stirring the stew while Gentry washed his hands. Hands, Towel, Porch. "Bosco, stay in the kitchen."

"Will you carry the stew? Mom cooked it." She told him so he didn't have to ask. Bosco followed them into the dining room and hid under the table.

Her mother and Marci were already there. "Ready? I'll serve up." Her mother looked so happy, ladling stew into bowls, passing the rolls.

Gentry smiled at his bowl. "It smells great, Kathryn."

He was happy about the food. It was time to ask. "Where does Mel live?"

"*Mel*?" Marci blinked. "Who is *Mel*?"

"His uncle. He's going to visit him at Christmas. But I don't know where he lives."

Marci frowned. "So, you have an uncle?"

Gentry nodded, chewed a big piece of beef. He took his time before he finally swallowed. "The Midwest." He opened his mouth, put in another piece of meat.

"Exactly where in the Midwest does your uncle live?" Her mother sounded a little interested. "I thought you didn't have any family?"

Chew, chew, chew. No one else was eating. He swallowed.

"Just an uncle who lives in this small, um, community." Gentry put another big bite of stew in his mouth. He chewed so much, Gretchen's teeth hurt from watching him. He looked down at his bowl. Empty. He made a move for seconds, but her mother grabbed the ladle.

He started on his salad, stuffed in a roll. Chewing, chewing. Marci rolled her eyes. She moved the roll basket and the salad bowl, trying to get everything out of his reach. She waited for the salad to go down.

"Where exactly is this community?"

Finally, he took the last bite. He reached for more rolls, and his arms were long, but Marci threatened him with a fork. He put his hand in his lap. He had no more food and he wasn't getting any. He swallowed, and swallowed again.

Marci took a big sip of water, maybe to help Gentry wash down all that food.

"My uncle lives in a monastery in North Dakota."

Marci sprayed out her mouthful of water all over the salad bowl.

"That was just vile, Marcialin." Her mother began swabbing it up with a napkin.

Marci was laughing, choking. "So you're from North Dakota? And you were raised in a monastery? Like Quasimodo?"

He shook his head. "Hey Marci? Quasimodo was raised in a cathedral."

Her mother stared at him, blinking. "Your uncle is a . . . monk? So you're actually going to a *monastery* for Christmas."

"He's a retired priest. I set the brothers up as Internet providers when I got out of college, and I have to make sure everything's working right."

"Wait, wait. Let me get this all straight." Marci waved her hands. "You're spending Christmas with . . . your uncle priest in a . . . North Dakota Internet monastery."

"It's not an Internet monastery, it's a real monastery."

"It just gets better and better."

"You see why I don't bring it up."

"I do."

"Thanks for understanding. And Gretchen said you're going to your dad's for Christmas? Where does he live?"

Just that quickly, her mother was up and in the kitchen. Marci and Gretchen looked at each other, sober and quiet.

"In Portland." Marci almost whispered. "With his wife Eve, and our little brothers."

It was Gentry's turn to look confused. "You have *brothers?*"

She nodded. "Yes. Graham and Spencer. But never mention my dad around my mother, okay? Or our brothers. Never. Okay?"

When her mother came back, she had a drink in her hand.

Gentry

God, thank You for Oregon.

I think Bosco likes it here. Not that he ever complained about anywhere else. I just think this is a good place for a dog. Especially a big dog like Bosco. He's one of the biggest dogs I've ever seen. *What kind of dog is he?* I'm asked this, and I don't know, of course. Like me, Bosco has no history.

When I was about to turn fourteen, Mel said, *My boy, it's time you asked for something.* I liked it when he guessed what I wanted. When he *knew.* But the time had come for me to ask for something. So what do you want for your birthday?

I want a dog.

There was Bosco on the morning of my birthday. He was supposed to be a full-grown mutt, but he kept growing. Most of the time, he's lived with Mel, but Bosco has always been my dog. He's thirteen years old. He's never had a leash. Gretchen takes him down to the beach, throws sticks for him. She pets him even though he smells like whatever he finds down there to roll in. Bosco likes dead things. So does Gretchen.

Gretchen is a miracle.

She folds my laundry when I forget and leave it in the dryer. She inventories my clothing, decides what needs replacing. Am I embarrassed? Of course I'm embarrassed. But she's a master of tact. She reads the tags inside my shorts and throws what I need into the cart when we're at Fred Meyer together. You have to admire a girl like that.

She wants to teach me to cook. She understands, somehow, that it's a complicated thing to undertake. I drive her to the store. She watches me stock up on cereal. She suggests I might need sugar. When I explain that sugar would make the milk sweet, she accepts that I can't drink anything sweet. She doesn't comment on my weirdness. She studies my reactions carefully while we shop, hoping to divine my preferences, even though I don't recognize the raw ingredients of my favorite dishes. She hopes I'll ask her for something.

I wish she could tell me how to fall asleep.

⌒

I still wasn't sleeping. Different thoughts kept me awake, scenes replayed in my mind. I kept trying to find the exact moment when I first messed up. Maybe at birth. I thought God definitely had a sense of humor, and that lately, my joke of a name was in His punch lines.

The finest moment was Monday in the lunch line, with Lorrie. I stopped at the main course and Darlene just stared at me. So then Ethel, one of what Lorrie refers to as the "hairnet lifers," gave me two corndogs and smiled. "It's okay, Gentry, honey, it happens to everybody now and then." Darlene took one of the corndogs and bent it in half and set it back on the plate.

Lorrie nearly choked.

We sat down at the table. Lorrie thumped my shoulder. "Look, little buddy. You had five shots in less than an hour. That's all it was." He laughed again.

But that's not what it was.

At first I kept thinking, what am I doing in this car with her, I don't know her. But I kissed her, smelled her, felt her breath in my neck and the sweet, strange softness of her woman's body under my hands. I stopped caring that I'd have to face her at work. The mind steps back, the body moves forward, and the body wants another body. Just to touch her, to feel her writhe, to feel her hands on me. I let out a groan when she pulled at my belt, but the memory of Kathryn flooded me.

Kathryn crying.

I put my hand on her shoulder. "Hey, wait." She ignored that and kept working on the buttons. I took hold of her wrist. "Really, knock it off."

She sat up. "What's your problem?"

"Hey Darlene? I can't, I don't . . . how about we go out to breakfast instead?" That didn't go over so well. When she started to yell, I got out of that car.

❧

If I believed in that sort of a thing, I'd believe that she put a curse on me to make me go dead. Corndog voodoo. I don't want to be dead. God, listen. My sad acts of self-abuse were all I had left and I didn't want to give them up. But what was safe to think about?

These things were not safe. Darlene and her anger in the back of her car, her furious eyes over the corndogs. Kathryn, her mouth, and then her tears. When I thought about my girl in the Gulf of Mexico, all I saw was the barrel of a gun.

I needed to think harder.

So I returned, as always, to Becca.

She was perfect. Her red hair, the color of those Oregon sunsets she told me about. I remember my astonishment that all her hair was that color, red shot through with gold. The color of daybreak, but it smelled like a night-blooming vine. And her breasts, almost golden, like peaches. And when we made love, the faint line of sweat on her upper lip, the salt I kissed away, oh, Becca. My perfect Becca. The taste of you.

My door creaked open. "Knock, knock. Sorry, I know it's late but your light's on."

My light was on all night, every night. I sat up fast, glad it was cold enough that I'd been under the covers, furious at the interruption of what promised to be a profoundly successful event. And in my outrage, one thought stood out.

Why was there still no lock on the door?

"Can I talk to you?"

As soon as possible, I would stand. Standing would be good. Chairs would be good, a desk, maybe. An entire classroom, even. With other students in it. She came in and shut the door like I'd asked her to, and sat down next to me on the bed, causing the springs to squeak and the hair on the back of my neck to rise. A female student, seated on my bed.

I couldn't panic. "Marci, get out."

"I have to ask you something." She looked at the chair beside my bed and retrieved a Bible. She grabbed my hand, yes, that hand, and put it on the book. Fantastic. "Swear. Swear on this Bible that you didn't touch my mother."

"I swear to God that I didn't touch your mother."

The look on her face and my shame made it possible for me to get up and walk over to open the door. Bosco, who'd been sleeping soundly in the warm spot in front of the fridge, dutifully lumbered to his feet and went out.

You didn't have to leave, Bosco.

"Hey Marci? You need to leave."

"Okay." Her voice was soft. Almost humble. But she didn't move.

I stood in the doorway, watching Bosco sniff and stretch. The weather was clear. The rain had arrived, just like Gretchen said it would, but that night, everything was mild, the breeze soft as kisses. "I don't understand Oregon weather."

"No one does. Gentry?" Her voice was the voice of a child. "Do you think my mother is beautiful?"

"Yes. Your mother is beautiful." Very beautiful. Painfully beautiful, and I had thought about it, every morning and almost every night and at least once an hour in between, and I dreamt about it and prayed about it and Please God, make me stop thinking about it.

I expected the Bible to sail through the air, hitting my back, but it didn't. Marci wasn't biting me, there were no blows. I turned around to face her.

"Good. I'm glad." She sat on the bed, hugging her knees. "There's this line that people cross over when they drink too much. I've seen it at keggers, you know, some girl gets mad at her boyfriend and tries to hitchhike home, some loser decides to play firewalker and burns up his shoes. It's this line, and once people cross it, they become . . . grotesque."

"Your mother is not grotesque." She nodded. I waited by the open door. "You need to go." But still, she sat there.

"That night when you put me in that hold. Where did you learn to do that? I thought maybe it was part of your teacher training in Detroit."

That almost made me laugh. "No. I've never laid a hand on a student." I realized that what I'd said was no longer true. I'd put my hands on Marci and wrestled her out my door. I had touched her. I closed my eyes, remembered the shock of her teeth on my skin. And my stomach hurt. "Except for you, Marci."

"What were you supposed to do?" Her voice was soft, so soft, a voice I'd never heard from this girl. "I'm so sorry, Gentry." She dashed a hand under her eyes. And then she rose up like smoke from a fire and brushed past me and out the door, airy and quick, nothing left behind but the scent of her hair.

Bosco watched her go. He was an old dog, but he was huge and wild, his coat washed silver by the light of the moon. My beautiful beast. He lifted his head and let out a strange, stifled keening. It hurt to hear him try. "Bosco. Stop that. You're not a wolf." He ignored me. He looked up and found the moon. The moon unlocked his voice.

He opened his throat, and let the full howl pour out.

DECEMBER

Marci

On the first of December, Gentry looked up at his empty classroom and frowned. One of the Oanhs spoke up. "It's the first day of crabbing, Gentry."

"Ah. I see."

Marci was sure he didn't.

⌒

December meant crabbing. Vu was out working with Garret and his dad. Garret was exhausted at night. He couldn't even give her a ride to school.

Marci had three choices. Her mother behind the wheel of that embarrassing Volvo. The school bus.

Or Gentry.

⌒

The first morning, Gretchen staked her claim. "Get in the back." That left Marci sitting on a jump seat the size of a hardback book, watching the dog tags swing from the rearview mirror while her sister and Gentry chatted away about her school, his classes, what to do on the weekend.

The word was "dull."

He had a bunch of church to attend this month. "Feast days." No eating, just praying at these feasts and apparently this affected how many of the basketball games they'd watch. Fascinating, just fascinating. They talked all the way to the elementary school, which was partly built from a Quonset hut and not nearly good enough for a kid as smart as Gretchen, not that anyone seemed to care about that but Marci. She stared at the crooked part in her sister's dirty hair.

Gentry had stolen her little sister, and Marci missed her.

They rolled up to the curb and Gentry yanked on an emergency brake that Marci doubted would actually work. Gretchen clambered down and Marci slid between the seats to get in the front, aware that her crotch was almost touching Gentry's shoulder. But he didn't notice, of course. He was watching Gretchen cross the street and make her way to the door. Marci watched, too. All those kids milling around, and no one even acknowledged Gretchen's existence. It would be different for her in Portland.

"Buckle up, please."

Not necessary, that warning. She always remembered her seatbelt when Gentry drove.

Marci had learned to drive her stepmother's Lexus because that was the cheap car. Her dad cautioned her about the overly polite Oregonian driver. *You have to watch out, honey, because everyone in this state is so courteous that the whole traffic pattern freezes up at a four way stop, everyone saying, "No, you first, I insist, please."* Obviously, her father had never ridden with Gentry.

When Gentry drove, he kept his eyes on the road, carefully watching for all possible hazards because Gentry *liked* hazards. He hit potholes hard. He took corners fast enough to make his tires scream. He *accelerated* whenever he saw a speed bump. He rolled through stop signs. He ran yellow lights. He failed to use turn signals. He ignored detours. Really, by the way he drove, Marci should have guessed he was impotent and making up for it behind the wheel.

"Gentry? Do you drive like a lunatic on purpose?"

"As a matter of fact, I do." And he laughed, his hair whipping around in the ice-cold wind that leaked through the cloth top. Occasionally, it whipped over and hit her in the face and she could taste his shampoo.

He would never drive like that with Gretchen in the car.

When they got to the high school, she grabbed her backpack and saw the crumpled paper bag on the floor. "Gretchen forgot her lunch again. She probably did it on purpose."

"I'll take it over to her."

"You're so stupidly nice."

"Thank you." Marci decided that his smile was pretty sweet.

She walked into her school alone. She'd been living at the coast for ten years, and just like her sister, she had no friends. She had a place at the school, a role she played. The sarcastic girl at the lunch table who was smarter than most of her teachers, so they were all a little afraid of her. The rich girl who dated the poor boy, a romance right out of an S. E. Hinton book. The Portland girl who'd never belonged at this school. No one there had a clue who she really was, including Marci.

She'd numbered the days until she would leave. Her father would fly first class with her because her father always flew first class. He'd told her to pack light. "I'll get you whatever you need when you get there," he said. "We'll shop in New York." This was supposed to excite Marci. But she wasn't Eve. And no matter how much money he spent on her, no matter how helpful the salesgirls were, no matter how many dollars filled her Colby closet, she would still be a girl from a dirty school on the Oregon coast.

She'd walk in, and no one would acknowledge her existence.

Just like home.

Gretchen

"Hey Gretchen?" She looked up from her book to see him standing across the lunch table holding out her lunch. "You forgot this."

People were looking. Especially the girls. "I'm not really hungry."

He set it down and lay his hand flat on the table. "Is anyone sitting here?" No one ever sat by her, across from her, even at the same table as her if they could help it. She managed a shrug. "Will you save it for me?"

"Yes." She slid her book across the table to save his place. Just in case. All around her, she felt the eyes of the other kids on her. She really, really wished they'd all just die or something.

He was back with a tray, loaded with a lot more food than usual. He used the tray to slide the book back over to her. "That's a good one. Do you want one of these milks? She gave me four." He slid one over.

Gretchen decided she was maybe a little thirsty. But she couldn't see how he could stand to eat the food on that tray. "Do teachers get free lunch?"

"We do."

"I'm glad. I'd feel bad if you had to pay to eat that." He smiled, but she was serious. He started to eat so she opened the bag and got out her sandwich. It was a bagel, actually. A whole wheat bagel with cream cheese, cucumber and tomato, with a black olive stuck in the hole. Her sister was a pain, but she made nice bagels.

A boy she hated stood by Gentry's shoulder, hopping from foot to foot like he had to pee, waiting to be noticed. The kid finally poked him in the shoulder. "Hi."

Gentry swallowed. "Hey."

"Uh, hey, is that your Jeep in the parking lot? My uncle has one just like that. It rides really bumpy. Does yours?"

Gentry sounded confused. "Does mine what?"

"Does yours ride bumpy?"

Gentry frowned. "I'm used to it." Was there something wrong with this stupid boy? Who cared if his uncle's Jeep was bumpy? Gretchen stared at the table, waiting for them to start talking about cars, which she didn't find interesting. But Gentry talked to her, instead. He had a hand on the cover of her book. "How old were you when you first read them?"

"Nine."

"So last year?" She nodded. "I was ten. Mel gave them to me. I think of all of them, I like *The Magician's Nephew* best."

She rolled her eyes. "*That's* a surprise."

"You sound like your sister." They both started to laugh, and everyone turned to look.

The kid Gretchen hated gave up and went away.

"So Gretchen, you have a *visitor*?" Her teacher was there, smiling with too many teeth. All women smiled like that around Gentry. They smiled like sturgeons.

With a sigh, Gretchen said it the way her mother had taught her, the oldest person first. "Miss Lanahan, this is Gentry. Gentry, this is Miss Lanahan."

Gentry stood up, always polite, and extended his hand. "Hey."

"Oh, I've *heard* of you. You teach at the *high* school?" She sounded way too excited.

"I do, and I have to get back there in a few minutes so I hope you will, um, excuse us?" He sat back down.

"Well." Miss Lanahan blinked. "Certainly. Enjoy your *lunch*." She walked away too quickly.

"Hey Gretchen? You've read those Lloyd Alexander books, right?"

"With Taran? Yes."

"I wonder if they hold up."

"What do you mean, hold up?"

He was chewing, so she had to wait for him to swallow. "Some books hold up to rereading, and some don't. The Narnia books hold up."

"Yes, they do. They really hold up."

He smiled. "As much as we go to the library, we've never talked about what we read." At the library, he read all the computer magazines, then loaded up with poetry books and novels by people with Spanish names to take home. Gretchen had no idea he'd ever liked the same books she liked.

Some girls she hated stood by the table. They looked everywhere but at Gentry and laughed at nothing. The girl closest to his shoulder kept moving her hair around, using her hand to arrange it in front, then behind her own shoulder, as if it would be interesting to him where she put her stupid hair. This girl was rude to Gretchen, but Gretchen felt sorry for her whenever she smiled because she had teeth like broken windows in an abandoned building. And that boy she hated was back, jumping around and asking for a ride in the Jeep.

"I have to go." Gentry took his tray and stood up. "Gretchen? I'll see you at 3:45?"

She nodded. And then he was gone.

Everyone was staring at her. That boy she hated was still standing there. "You ride to school in that old Jeep every day? My uncle has one just like that. It rides bumpy."

Gretchen shrugged. "I'm used to it."

The girl with the bad teeth smiled. "Who is that guy?"

Gretchen lifted her shoulder in a shrug. "Just a friend."

She picked up her book and went back to reading.

Marci

Marci knew that standing in the driveway wouldn't get her father's car to arrive any sooner. But she couldn't help herself. For as long as she could remember, she'd waited alone outside for her father's car to prowl down the driveway. But for the first time in her life, she had company while she waited. Bosco leaned on her legs, trying to get her to pat him, which she wouldn't because her hand would smell. Gentry was making important last-minute Jeep adjustments for his trip to see his uncle priest, and Gretchen was getting in his way.

"Leave him alone, weirdo."

"I just want to see it in his ear." "It" being a tiger's-eye earring from the gem shop in Seaside. He straightened so that Gretchen could tenderly inspect his earlobe. "It matches your eyes." Gretchen sniffed a little. The word was "melodramatic." "Do you like it?"

"I do. I like it so, so much."

"You two make me barf."

"Shut up." While Gretchen shoved her, Gentry went to get his bag.

Her father's Saab came rolling down the drive. He pulled in alongside the Jeep and rolled down the window. "So, is this your mom's new ride?" He gave her a smile, and Marci's heart tightened a little. She loved and hated everything about her father's face; his square jaw, his artificially white teeth, the wrinkles beside his eyes the exact color of her own. She loved his thick hair that never quite calmed down, his golf tan, the slim gold wristwatch he wore all the time, even while he slept. And she hated it.

The word for her dad was "successful."

"Are my favorite girls ready to go?" He was about seven feet tall, so his hugs were like being picked up by a force of nature. Thrilling, but she was always happy to be set down unhurt. Gretchen stood there with her arms wrapped around herself, looking miserable and windblown. "Hi honey. Are you ready?" She looked at him out of the corners of her eyes and gave a little tip of her head. "Okay. I'm going to say hi to your mom, okay?" She gave another miniscule nod.

Marci got in the front seat. Her dad was ridiculously careful with Gretchen. Like she'd startle and fly away. Gretchen climbed in the back seat, big old muddy Bosco right behind her, smiling and panting. "His *breath*, get him *out*."

"I want him to come with us." Gretchen clutched his smelly fur.

"Oh grow up, you little alien. It's one *week*." Marci rolled down the window to let out the dog breath. "The word is 'fetid,' Gretchen."

Her mother stood on the back step, blinking up at her towering father, telling him to come in the house, she had gifts for him to put in his car. Her mother expected men to carry things for her. Her father shook his head. "These girls will be knee deep in presents. Eve's been shopping since August. Save them until they get back."

Her mother stood there with that destroyed look on her face.

Nice job, Dad. Way to devastate Mom. He did things like that and then asked, *What? What did I do now?*

Gretchen sighed. So did Bosco. Ugh.

Gentry came out of his house with his duffel bag. Marci supposed it took all of a tenth of a second to take it in; Marci and Gretchen in their father's car, her dad's politely impatient expression, her mother standing there about to cry, her hair blowing around her face like snow in the wind.

Gentry walked over and put his arm around her mother's shoulder.

Her dad's head shot back like he'd been hit in the face. Gentry stared back at him, jaw set, eyes cold, and slid his hand down Kathryn's side to her hip. Gentry pulled her mother up close to him like he owned her. And her father looked at her mother like he'd never seen her before. Like he'd forgotten how small and cold and beautiful she was.

Marci didn't want her father to be mad. She just wanted it to be a little more even between him and her mother. And this lie certainly did it. This lie made her mother look like a woman who had moved on with a man twenty years younger than her. It had the side benefit of making her father look old. It was perfect, she thought, watching the ocean through the car window. Perfect, and completely embarrassing.

Marci watched her father's eyes turn so hard and narrow that they looked like little bits of green glass embedded in his face. Their mother smiled like there was something bitter in her mouth she wanted to spit out. "Michael? This is Gentry."

"Is it, now."

"Oh, Michael. Enough." Her mother pulled away and went into the house.

Marci usually hated pissing matches, but she was fascinated by the way her father clenched his right hand into a fist, the working of the muscles in Gentry's jaw, how tall he stood, how wide her father's shoulders spread. Gretchen watched, too. "They need some antlers," she muttered. "Or horns."

Her father stuck out his hand. "I'm Michael Mumford. You're the *tenant*?" He said "tenant" the way another person might say "tapeworm." Gentry didn't seem too impressed by her father. This must have confused Michael, because everyone was impressed by her father.

Her father finally put his hand down after it hung there for about twenty seconds.

No, Gentry was not impressed at all.

Gentry was not short, but her dad loomed over him. "Well, kiddo, are you keeping my girls safe?" Gentry gave him a look of utter disbelief, then said something in a lower voice than Marci could hear. Her father drew back, turned on the heel of his expensive Italian driving moccasin and walked to the car. His face was red when he got behind the wheel. "Like it's any of his goddamned affair how often . . . *what* is that . . . *Jesus!*" He jumped out and opened the back door. "Out. OUT! Look at the *floor mats.*" Bosco lumbered out, his toenails leaving white scratches in the leather of the back seat. "Goddamned sand and hair . . ." Bosco trotted off, his tail wagging, and went to sit at his master's feet. His work was done.

Michael Mumford executed a tight three-point turn to show off his car's handling. As he drove away, Gentry stood by the house like the lord of the manor, his faithful, stinking beast by his side. Her father barely said a word all the way back to Portland.

Marci couldn't believe it. Gentry had won.

Lorrie Gilroy

Well, I pull up to the house and I figure, Hell, I'm in luck after all, because I want to give Gentry his Christmas present and his Jeep's still parked here, so I guess he hasn't left for wherever the hell it is he's going.

I got him a book on martial arts because the way I see it, guys like Gentry are natural born for martial arts. I've explained all this to Gentry, but I hope the book does a better job. It all boils down to the fact that guys like him looked about twelve years old through high school, and guys like me couldn't stand those little geeks, because I mean, they were like girls but without the good parts, right? So what the hell are guys like that for, anyway? So, we stuffed them into lockers and trashcans, shit like that, until they went off to MIT to become engineers or computer geniuses, and guys like me, we went off and managed gas stations or coached football, and that's why Gentry would be so good at martial arts. They've got all this repressed anger from the shit they took from guys like me and when they get into martial arts, they build up their little muscles and then they let it go and really kick ass, but of course, they fight in a weight class, so they mostly end up kicking the shit out of each other, but that's okay.

I told all this to Gentry, and he laughed at me. He says he can fight, he claims he can take care of himself. This I don't believe, so I got Gentry a book, because guys like him read.

So I park, it's kind of early so I go up to his house quiet, and there's nobody home but Bosco, and he takes me right up to the back door of the main house. I look through the window and there they are drinking coffee at the table, cozy as a pair of bran muffins, Gentry and her royal highness, Dame Mumford. No big deal, right? He's in there every morning. Only, get this, Gentry has on her robe, and she has on his. I'm standing there like a bass mouth and they're looking right back at me with the same sonofabitching expression.

Well, Gentry gets up and comes out closing the door behind him, and he's got on this pink fuzzy robe that won't shut, and I'll be damned. You just never know about those quiet ones. "Merry Christmas, little buddy!" I'm trying hard not to laugh. "What, did your robe shrink?"

He makes a noise like something strangling. "Please leave."

"Well, don't go hissing at me, I just brought you a present, little buddy, but it looks like you got one already today." I don't know why I call him my little buddy, he isn't that short, and all of a sudden I'm thinking that really isn't the best nickname for him after all.

"Thank you." He doesn't sound like he means that, somehow, he takes the present but he doesn't even look at it, and it took the sales girl fifteen minutes to wrap it all pretty like that. "Merry Christmas and go away." He tries to get the robe adjusted, and I can't stop laughing, and I should stop, this is too easy, and too goddamn funny.

"Same to you, kid. Damn, an older woman. You got your starter fixed, I guess?" He looks at me like he'd like to kill me.

"My hot water was out. I just borrowed her shower."

"You were right when you told me you were bad at lying. Real bad."

"Shut up, Lorrie."

"You're real tough there in your pink bathrobe telling me to shut up."

"I mean it."

"Oh, I'm scared. I'm shaking in my boots. Merry Christmas, little buddy." I have to leave, I'm laughing too damn hard, and he's going to pop me and I've never been hit by a man in a pink fuzzy bathrobe before. "Hell, I should've gotten you slippers to match." And then I get out of there. When I leave, he's knocking on the back door, trying not to be too obvious that she locked him out.

Goddamn.

⌒

So, I get home and the phone rings and it's Duchess Mumford, and I've never heard a woman swear like that. She swears worse than Faye. I tell her not to worry about it, nobody in this town gives a good goddamn what she does, and nobody would believe he did it with her, anyway. That pisses her off a little.

I tell her, see, I don't care, if she wants to do the horizontal tango with somebody young enough to be her son, it's none of my goddamn business, if this whole Mrs. Robinson deal works for her then I won't tell anybody, not because of her but because of the kid, he's a teacher and he's got a reputation to protect unlike, say, her. That pisses her off a lot.

She's threatening me if I so much as breathe a word of this to one soul, dead or living. This kind of shit. The bitch is crazy. All about her kids, she will not have her kids subjected to this kind of such and such and so on. She's pouring this shit in my ear, frantic-like, and in walks Gentry, and he's white as a ghost, and she's yelling in one ear and he's begging in the other, and I finally hang up on the lunatic and take Gentry by the shoulders and I swear, I swear to God, who I don't even believe in anymore but I know he does, that so help me God, I won't tell one single solitary soul what's going on between him and that drunk old bitch.

And I'll be goddamned if he doesn't haul back and paste me one.

Well Merry Goddamn Christmas Eve. Maybe the little sonofabitch can fight after all, because he can hit, that's for sure. He can hit hard. Of course, I sit him down, and I get him settled, it takes a minute, and the goddamn phone keeps ringing, and finally I go to find some ice for my face and ask him could he maybe get that before I have to tear it out of the wall and he picks it up, and I swear, I can hear that woman across the room.

"If she screws like she fights, this is all worth it."

Okay, he looks like he's going to drop the phone and hit me again or maybe bash in my head with the receiver, but he keeps reassuring the crazy woman. "No, he won't tell anyone. He won't. Hey Lorrie? You won't tell anyone, will you?"

"Why does she think anyone CARES?"

"He won't tell anyone. Kathryn, please. Please calm down."

Uh-oh, he told her to calm down. I could've told him that won't work. "Tell her to have a drink." That doesn't seem to go over too well with Gentry. He gives me a look.

He's talking real soft to her, now, he's getting a little mushy now, and maybe this mushy shit will work. "No. I mean . . . it was . . . you're wonderful."

Christ. I might hurl.

"I promise, Kathryn." Oh, no. He's promising shit, and I could've told him not

The Temptation of Gentry

to promise anything to an angry woman because you'll promise anything just to get her to shut the hell up and then you're stuck with whatever you promised. "No. I will. I have Bosco, I'm packed, I'm getting gas and heading out."

He looks a little embarrassed. "Um. Okay. So Burl is open. Thank you."

Oh, Mommy told him where to get gas on Christmas Eve. Nice.

His face gets all weak, like he's having one right there on the goddamn phone. "Okay. As soon as I get back." Now he's all embarrassed, turning away from me. Now he's whispering. "I, um, have to go. Bye." He's hanging up.

Gentry's seeing something in this Mumford woman that I can't. I don't like her, see. I don't know, maybe it's the ringing in my ears from her shouting or that shriveled feeling I get in my package when a women talks about ripping it off with her teeth, hell, who knows, maybe I'm just funny that way.

I'm icing my jaw, and he's going, driving off to North Dakota, for Christ's sake, all smiley and happy, Goddamnit. I tell him to get the hell out of Dodge. No way's he gonna stay happy.

Not with a bitch like that.

Gentry

The Lord insists that I love my fellow man. I fail, at times. I fail miserably.

This man barely looked at Kathryn when he spoke to her. Her beautiful face was destroyed. This man had the power to do this. He had the power to take Gretchen away. And he had a sixty-thousand-dollar car.

I was unsure which of those facts made me want to hit him the most.

Kathryn looked ready to cry. Gretchen did, too. The only person who didn't was Marci. I saw whose daughter she was, then. I saw. I was rude, I know that. I have manners. I was supposed to shake hands like a good dog. I couldn't.

Pompous. That's the word. This man believed himself important. I could see the universe through this man's eyes, and he sat squarely in the center of it. How could any mere man feel important at the edge of the ocean, in the presence of God? Why did he feel important? Was it because he could put Gretchen in his car and drive away with her? Did he have any idea what a privilege it was to have Gretchen in his car? What if he got in an accident? What then?

This man would not get in an accident. He drove a sixty thousand dollar car with leather seats, an incredible sound system, a sunroof, and tiny wipers on the headlamps. I assumed he had one of those security systems that shouted at you, the kind where you were just trying to get into your own rig and you accidentally bumped the car next to you and the whole thing started to whoop and blink and holler "MOVE AWAY FROM THE VEHICLE!" I'd bet money on it.

Bosco tracked sand all over his leather upholstery. Go, Bosco. Good dog.

Kathryn drove a Volvo wagon. She shared it with Marci. I changed the oil last week, put in some winter weight. Kathryn's car had one hundred and ninety-two thousand miles on it. Kathryn deserved a sixty thousand dollar car. But according to the Consumer Reports website, Gretchen was much safer in Kathryn's wagon than she was in this man's car. I tried not to think about this as Gretchen went down the driveway.

My CJ5 was safe, whatever Consumer Reports had to say on the subject. Besides the seatbelts, it had fog lamps, a roll bar and a winch in case I got stuck. My Jeep had never failed me, never let me down. It was almost paid off. I assumed that Saab was paid off. I assumed everything in that man's life was paid off.

I wanted to hit him in the mouth.

I had to get out of there. I was packed and ready to go to my uncle's, Bosco in the copilot's seat, wagging and waiting, but I couldn't leave Kathryn without making sure she was all right. I don't know why I thought she might be. She was not. Not at all.

I couldn't leave her alone.

God, consider that phrase, please. That phrase had meaning. 'I couldn't leave her alone.'

It could mean, I couldn't leave her alone at the edge of the world, curling up around her bottle. I couldn't leave Kathryn alone.

It could mean something else, too. I couldn't leave her alone. I couldn't leave her be. I tried for ten weeks to forget what had happened between us and my failure was spectacular and humiliating. I watched everything she put to her lips and silently cried out, me.

She was in her kitchen crying. I wanted to be the one she cried for.

I found her in the kitchen, I held out my arms. "Come here."

She came to me.

I couldn't leave her alone.

God, forgive me.

⌒

I wasn't happy leaving Kathryn's house. I left without my robe. My uncle lived in a monastery, plenty of robes there. I hung that pink one on her doorknob. But Kathryn promised on the phone that we'd talk when I returned, and that was enough to give me hope. Because, God, it was over. Over, after five years.

Five years of celibacy, finally over.

It was the Friday before Dead Week. Her name was Jillian.

I'd watched the back of her head for weeks. Sitting in class, taking notes, wondering what her hair smelled like. This last class, like all the classes for my master's, was mired in hypothetical models and representative samples. *Of course you'll all find this out in the fall, won't you*, the professor threatened, shooting out a look so bitter it reminded me of the first time I bit into a kumquat, that shock of sour, chewing through the pips to the sweet, sweet skin.

The girl shook her head, the instructor ranted, I waited. Sweet skin.

As I left the classroom, her hand was on my arm. *I'd say hello to you but I don't know your name.*

Gentry.

She rolled her eyes. *I mean your first name. Listen.* She came too near my face. *I'm running away. Care to join me?* Her breath was warm. *Come on. Let's run away.*

I could smell her hair.

Only if I get to drive.

She threw me the keys.

She told me to drive until she said to stop.

Everyone says you have some ridiculous hippie name and that's why you don't use it. They say you were raised on a commune. Where are you from again? Vermont?

Always, this conjecture. I let them do it, I never contradicted or corrected.

Was your dad an organic farmer? Did he have long hair too? Someone had to be a poet, since you are. Was your mother a feminist poet who wrote odes to her orgasms and had lesbian love affairs? Or did she, you know, weave things? Parents are awful enough without all that pot smoking and Birkenstock-wearing and talking about the March on Washington. Oh my god. The ponchos. The braids. Just the fashion alone, I couldn't bear it.

She was the kind of funny that frightened me, because it hurt. I needed her to be quiet and I couldn't stop her mouth with a kiss. But I could drive with one hand. Her eyes closed, her mouth opened, but she made no words. Just sounds.

Oh yes, beautiful girl with the sharp tongue. Not so sharp now.

I looked over at her color rising, hair blowing in the eighty-mile-per-hour wind. To combine this and driving? Perfection.

She turned her attention and mouth to me. I tried not to moan, prayed not to die but knew there were worse ways to go. I thought about some of those ways, trying to take my mind off what she did, trying to remember steering, braking, the mechanics of keeping the car on the road. Because being killed, no, I was too young, I hadn't even had a teaching job yet.

After a bad swerve, I put one hand in her hair, tightened my fingers. *Hey now. Stop.*

She sat up and frowned at the countryside. *We're almost there.*

I swung the car, guessing, prompting, *Here? Left? This one? That way?*

No. Go on. This one! We shuddered and slid to a gravelly stop, raising dust.

I smelled the water, licked my lips and tasted salt. Like the great lake where I'd camped with Mel that first summer, the ocean reminded me of acreage, the fields of early corn, ruffling in the dry wind of the Dakota prairie.

I uncoupled from the machine, stretched my arms, legs. Rubbed my neck. Relieved myself near the car's back tire.

When I turned around, she was leaning against the car, staring at the water. *Well? What do you think?*

Beautiful.

Beautiful? Is that the best you can do at your first sight of the ocean? You're supposed to be poetic and mysterious.

And organic.

Yes, that too. She pointed. *There's the cabin.* She disappeared around the side.

Cabins, to me, were small, rustic, and usually on the shore of a lake. This was more of a house. I approached this so-called cabin with a fair degree of suspicion, and waited at the front door until it opened. Naked, she was pared to the bone, too much bone, all pelvis and collarbones and knees. But the upward tilt of her breasts was soft, exquisite, vulnerable.

I put my mouth on hers and tasted the ocean.

∾

The moon shone in an open window. Her breath blew softly across my chest. I traced her with my fingertips, the veins of her wrists, the ridges that crossed her forearms. She murmured and pulled her hands to her shoulders, crossing her heart, hoping to die. Or not.

The scars of others hide my own.

I put my face to her hair and inhaled. Honey and milk and salt. An Old Testament banquet laid out for me in a stranger's bed.

Outside, unfamiliar water churned. It had to be almost morning.

Wake up, I whispered. *Let's go swim in the ocean.*

⌐

Her wince. *You kind of tore me up. This salt stings.*

I'm sorry.

I'm not. You're as good as they say.

Who were "they"?

The sun rose, a luminous head raised from some bloody feast devoured below the horizon. A Blake engraving come to life. She wrapped her legs around my waist and fell back in a float, her hair a dark corona around her pale face. I dipped her out of the water like fisherman with his catch. She came up streaming, smiling.

Our hair wound together in salty ropes.

We burned in our net of sin.

⌐

I sat down at the table without drying off.

Is that a hint? She laughed, fastened an apron around her waist. It stuck to her wet hips, pearls of water on her breasts. *What if I don't feed you?*

Then I'll leave.

You'll only stay put if you're fed. Hm. She frowned and opened the fridge. *Bacon is so full of nitrates that it doesn't matter if the power's been out, right?*

I have no idea.

Well, if you die, I'll blame the bacon. She perked coffee in a little white perco-lator. I listened to the burble while she flipped the bacon. My stomach clenched at the smell.

Patience, I reminded myself.

She finally set a plate before me. I gave thanks and shoved everything in my ravenous mouth. Women were miracles, I decided, the way they found a box and a package and made a meal. She nibbled the edge of a biscuit and watched me. *You eat like a pig.* I smiled at her with full cheeks, pointed to my empty cup. *Pig!* She poured the coffee.

I swallowed. *Thank you.*

That's better. Do you want the rest of it?

Yes please.

She refilled my plate. *You're a cannibal, too, because bacon comes from pigs and you're a pig. Eating your own kind. But all you Catholics are cannibals.*

I took my plate and coffee cup to the sink and ran some dishwater. She walked behind me, took off her apron and tied it around my waist. *Nice view.* Her hands brushed the backs of my legs. The hair on my neck rose and prickled. *You look pretty in a skirt. It's a pity you aren't Scotch.*

Scottish. And a kilt has a back to it. I carefully turned the apron around.

She shrieked a little. *Keep that thing out of the dishwater!*

I turned to slip a hand around her neck. *Why don't you.*

Gently pushing her to her knees.

⁓

I needed a shave. I never needed a shave, so I found that surprising. I had another sip of coffee. *Do you have any fours?*

She sighed. *Go fish.*

I drew the four of hearts, lay it down with the four of spades. She immediately lay down the four of clubs. *You seem to be cheating.*

She shrugged. *I'm a terrible person. Do you have any twos?*

Go fish.

She drew a card, made a face.

Do you have any kings?

Go fish.

I drew a card, lay down a pair of kings.

I swear, you're the luckiest person ever.

Luck? I'm employing strategy. And now I want a jack.

Right. She handed over a jack, and I lay down another pair. *After this, do you want to play strip poker?*

What, will we put clothes on?

Yes, she said, laughing. *We'll play get-dressed poker.*
I'll have to find my clothes.
She lay down her hand, spoiling the game. *I'm bored. I miss the TV.*
Hm. I shrugged, and gathered the cards.
I heard you don't watch TV. I heard you don't have one in your room, and you won't watch in the lounge. Why?
I started to shuffle. *There was no TV where I grew up.*
Oh my god. I was right. Her eyes looked slightly wild, like she was getting sick. *I knew you were raised by pacifist vegetarians who didn't believe in TV. And you were homeschooled. Were you? Tell me!*
She laughed like a wild woman and I laughed too.
It ended in bed.

~

Wake up right now. Wake UP!
The dark room, my hammering heart, that waning moon.
You had a bad dream.
I never dream.
Everyone dreams. We just don't remember. She raked her fingers through the mess of my hair. *Your hair is longer than mine. Another part of your hippie childhood. Your parents never cut your hair, and you grew up barefoot with no TV. Only . . .* She thought. *Catholic doesn't fit that story. Shouldn't you be Buddhist or Wiccan or something?*
It was time to distract her. I knew one way to do that.
It burned.

~

Night swimming.
I'd done this with Becca at her grandparents' farm. We snuck out to swim in a pond, small fish tickling my feet. I swam and Becca floated, her body white against the green surface.
Different girl, different water.
Jillian moved her arms a little, arched her back to stay up. She was too thin to be buoyant. *I think this is probably how it is in the womb. I remember it. I do. Do you?*

I don't remember anything.

She ducked her head back to try to stay afloat. *Are you burning too? It's all that damn salt.* I couldn't decide if it was the salt, what we were doing, or if I'd finally caught something. I'd ask Sandy what to do, of course, that was how I handled any question like this. I'd ask Sandy and he'd tell me what to do.

Jillian? Why did you ask me?

Ask you what?

To come with?

She almost sounded angry. *I've watched you for two years and you haven't given me a glance. It was my last chance to see if what they said was true.*

She was baiting me. *What do they say?*

She kept her silence.

Well? What? Is it true? What they say?

I hate you, Gentry. She kicked out for shore. I knew she wanted me to follow. But I didn't care where she went to, what she believed about me, what they said, whoever they were.

I lay in the moonlight on top of the ocean's water, dreaming of Becca, and how I could taste the singular familiarity of her skin under the sulfur of that green pond water.

⁓

Two pounds of bacon. A box of biscuit mix. Six cans of soup, one can of chili. Two boxes of macaroni and cheese prepared with canned evaporated milk, which lent it a sweet flavor. Three bags of marshmallows consumed on three consecutive nights after being toasted over fires I built by the water.

The coffee was running out, too.

She frowned into the open refrigerator. *You eat too much.*

I'm still starving. I was finishing a supper of canned vegetables, green beans with a side of corn and vivid orange circles of carrot. I ate it all. It reminded me of Veg-All in the school cafeteria. I'd eaten all of that, too. I fought an urge to lick the plate.

Well, there's mustard in here. I guess we could live on condiments.

I need some meat to go with it.

You could break into the neighbor's.

You could go to a store.

What an unimaginative solution. She straddled my lap. *Don't you have any more imagination than that?*

Do I lack imagination? She laughed and shook her head. Sand rained down from her stiff hair. I wasn't the only one who needed food. She was nothing but bones and scars and salt.

She shifted, I moaned. The kitchen chair creaked. *Is it Tuesday or Wednesday? Thursday.*

We have to go back.

In the morning, after we sleep. Sleep. And I was tired, so tired, I wanted to sleep, my eyes begging for oblivion, but she rocked hard with no mercy. We were burning and we didn't care.

A crack, a hard fall to the floor. I lay there for a minute, trying to feel if any splinters were driven into my backside. She was still on top of me. *Look at your face,* she giggled. *What's going on in that beautiful brain of yours?*

Just lying here wondering what will Baby Bear say.

She broke into great peals of laughter. The laughter was too large for that house, it was going to blow it down. She laughed and laughed until I picked her up and carried her through the house, threw her into the bed full of salt and sand and sin and made her quiet.

⌒

I had to go back and work on that last paper. I had to go back and apologize to Paige and Sandy, the friends who'd probably waited in their tiny living room on Saturday, waiting to help me with the defense of my thesis. They would have looked for me at Mass on Sunday. I never missed Mass, ever.

How many days ago was Sunday? What day is it?

It's not day. It's night. That's what the dark means, that it's night time.

We should leave. She rolled away from me. *Jillian. I need to get out of here.* I touched her back, beautifully ribbed and curved. I uncrossed her wrists, held them apart. The scars were taut, like strings. I thought of kneeling behind Becca, looking down at her shape. Like a cello. This was Jillian, not Becca. Not a cello, but a higher range, bowed and plucked. A viola.

She rolled over, moved on top of me. *We could go to Mexico.*

I put my hands on her hips to slow her down. *What would we do in Mexico?*

The same things we do here. But with tacos. My stomach groaned so loudly that she laughed. *We could get married in Mexico. You'd have to tell me your name if we got married.*

We have to go back.

She pulled herself off me so fast that I gasped. She curled away, holding her stomach. Her shoulders quaked. I let my hands travel down her thin arms. *Jillian. Hey now. Don't cry.* I wrapped myself around her and slid us deeper into the sheets. *We're the pages of a letter,* I whispered. *We're folded together in an envelope. Every word of us is written in salt.*

I held her close and gave myself over to exhaustion.

$\backsim$

I woke to a double-barreled shotgun.

I assessed in an instant. My opponent was older, shorter, weaker, but the length of metal connecting us put him in charge of my life. The barrel jammed hard against my throat, blocking my air. I looked around for something to hit him with, but I had lost sensation in my arms and legs.

I was going to die.

So this is what you're up to. With some little boy.

Daddy.

God sends us daughters and they ruin themselves.

Daddy, now . . .

Do you all have to ruin yourselves?

Daddy, calm down.

Cover yourself, you little whore. She got off the bed and began to dress. She moved slowly, as carefully as I'd been warned to move if I ever saw a bear in the woods. He stared down at me, shaking his head from side to side. *Is that what you boys are for? To finish the job?*

I was going to die. He moved the gun from my throat to my stomach. *If I gut-shoot you, it's a nice, long death.*

My hushed voice was the only sound in the horrible still of the room, *Hail Mary Full of Grace, the Lord is with You, blessed are You among women and blessed is the fruit . . .*

He jammed the gun back to my throat. *A northerner and a Catholic?*

Her shoes were in one hand. She lay the other on his arm. *Daddy. Daddy, listen to me, it isn't . . .*

He tossed her arm away. *Your mother out of her mind with worry, no one knowing where you were, I sent you to that school for a reason, you were supposed to be safe.* The gun moved from my throat down to what burned, Oh GOD, don't let him, GOD help me . . .

God had mercy. The gun moved back to my heart. A shot in the heart would be faster.

PLEASE Daddy . . .

Oh, you get out of here, little girl. You get in your car and you wait for me, I'm going to take care of this boy and then follow you back to college where you belong. He pressed the metal hard against my heart, the heart that thudded, boomed, drowning me with sound.

Daddy, I'll go, but Daddy, please . . .

GET OUT THERE AND WAIT FOR ME!

She broke for the front door where she'd met me wearing only her glory, I'd cried at her glory and it would cost me my life.

Sir, I do not want to die.

Shut your mouth, you dog. Before I put this gun in it.

Not in my mouth.

He looked down and smiled. *Have you heard this one before? "The wages of sin is death." Romans 6:23.*

⁓

A miracle, the right prayer rose from me, the prayer I needed.

A new litany to the father who held the power of God in his hands, a prayer to the god on earth who could take away my life.

Please don't kill me, please, please don't kill me, I never meant to hurt your daughter, I swear I'll never touch her again, never another girl at all, oh please sir don't kill me, I don't want to die, my dog will miss me, this will kill my uncle, please sir, I'll quit, I'll stop, I'll confess, please, PLEASE sir, I'm only twenty-one years old and I can't die, I can't die . . .

The words failed and the prayer was only a sob from a sinner cowering on the bed, the bed that belonged to this man with the shotgun pushed against my heart.

The barrel of the gun moved to my forehead. He was going to blow my head all the way off. Mel would have to see this when they called him, he would have to see my head blown off my body. I felt so sad that Mel would have to see this.

I whispered the words that prepared me to die. I repented all of it. I foreswore it. I despised my sin. I was ready.

The gun moved. *Open your eyes, boy.*

I opened my eyes.

The gun pressed into the bed beside me. The tired, small man leaning on it studied me with something like wonder. *How the hell am I supposed to shoot a boy with a face like that? It would be like shooting a girl.* He stared for a few more moments before he pulled the trigger.

The crack, the buck of the mattress. The thump of blood in my ears. Deaf but not dead. I was only deaf. But just for a moment. I heard a wail. A girl, not a siren.

She was out there wailing.

His footfalls moved around the bedroom, through the hall, out the door. There was shouting out there, one last plea, and the slamming of car doors. The engines started, they left in a dual roar, displaced gravel thrown like bullets against the dirt. My fingertips found the hole that could have been torn through me instead of a mattress.

The wages of sin is death.

I wound myself tight in the stiff, salty sheets.

ᔕ

I went back to school, delivered my thesis, got a shot of penicillin and shut myself down. For five years. But God, Kathryn had brought me back to life. I was alive again. And I would do the right thing this time.

Amen.

ᔕ

Mel was disappointed that I came a day late. He was disappointed that I left early. His eyes told me. I was such a sap while I was there, barely taking the time I needed to check the servers, talk about tech support with him, work on the filters, I was cursory and distracted and he knew why, he knows me, and I couldn't care, I couldn't be ashamed, I couldn't be sorry. My heart was singing in that stupid way.

I was happy.

I drove about a hundred miles an hour to get home. I needed no sleep, I needed no coffee. I plowed through mountain passes, barely registered a small blizzard near Spokane. I skated through the Columbia Gorge. I was invincible.

Happiness does that to me.

I don't know what I expected to find. Kathryn waiting for me, I guess, her sharp body in her warm bed. I kept thinking about that. I allowed myself a few other thoughts, of family, finally, please God, my own, finally. God, I would do it right this time. This was different, this was completely different. We would be a family. Gretchen would be happy. Marci would come around. And I would kick that Mumford guy off a cliff.

Nothing like that waited for me when I reached the dark and empty house. No Volvo, no Kathryn. Still, I was demented with hope. Bosco ran off to the beach and I decided to clean out my Jeep, to get the tin foil and waxed paper and balled up plastic wrap from the leftovers that Loren sent with me thrown away before Bosco came back and chewed up everything, looking for crumbs.

I knew it was a bad sign when I lifted up the trash can lid and saw Kathryn's pink robe balled up in there.

Kathryn drove up while I was studying the trash. I never believed it could be that difficult to raise my eyes from garbage. I looked at her face, her eyes, and she didn't need to say one word, but she did.

"We need to talk."

Needing to talk is never good.

〜

I sat at Kathryn's table and listened to words. Nothing she said made any sense to me. It was like she spoke in a language I didn't understand. "It didn't mean anything." She sighed. "It was wonderful. But these things happen, Gentry." She shook her head and lit a cigarette. "Age is an issue."

"I want to marry you."

"*Marry* me?" The look in her eyes. She wasn't horrified. She was amused. "I can't *marry* you."

"Why?"

"Because I don't love you."

Ah. I was beginning to understand.

She smiled, patted my hand. She refilled my coffee. I looked at her and remembered the feel, the smell, the sound of her. I wanted to say to her, I made you cry, I made you tremble.

I drank my coffee and looked out the window because it would hurt to look at her. Everything about her was sharp and beautiful and merciless as rocks in water.

"I've never seen you need a shave before." I felt her hand on my arm. Located her pale, puzzled eyes. "Gentry? Have I ruined everything?" Her face gave a little twist. "Can we still be friends?"

She wanted to be friends. To sit across the table, smile, talk about work and weather. Do the crossword. Because, no matter what it meant to me, no matter how it felt to me, what happened meant nothing to her.

The spectacular cruelty of this.

I thought about taking her in my arms, taking her back up those stairs, reminding her, persuading her. Making her kiss me. But I would never make her.

"Of course we can."

Blue words.

Gretchen

When they pulled up to the house, the Jeep was there. "He's back early!"

"Whoopee." Marci sounded grumpy.

Gretchen opened the door, jumped out and ran to the top of the stairs. There they were! She could hear her dad yelling something as she ran down the steps, but who cared what he was yelling?

Probably just good-bye.

∽

Gentry held out his arms, bracing himself. She ran as fast as she could and jumped high and hard into his arms. He spun her around five times. Bosco barked, then barked again. "Bosco wants you to put me down." As soon as her feet hit the sand, Bosco ran away to look for a stick.

Gentry had on a new coat with a hood, which he needed to put up because the rain in December was pretty bad. She adjusted the cord. "I like your new coat." He smiled, looked at his sleeve, and Gretchen could tell he liked his new coat, too.

"Did you and your sister get good stuff for Christmas?"

"Yes. Way too much, though. We opened presents until I wanted to go back to bed. Marci and I went to the mall the day after Christmas and spent all our gift cards on Mom. It was Marci's idea. Dad was so pissed. But Mom needs everything. Especially sweaters. She gets so cold in the winter." He walked along, looking at the sand and listening. "And we needed to get her a better bathrobe. She hated that bathrobe we got for her. I could tell. It was a stupid robe, anyway."

"Why was it stupid?"

"It was pink. My mother never wears anything pink. Marci said she'd hate it, but I wanted to get her something to keep her warm. My mom is always so cold."

He stopped walking and looked out at the ocean. He blinked from the rain falling in his face. To Gretchen, he was beautiful and terrible, like a storm.

"Are you okay?"

"Yes."

"We should go up. It's almost dinnertime."

"Good. I'm starving."

"Marci says you'll end up fat if you keep eating so much. She says you'll be so fat someday."

"Would you still like me fat?"

"Yes, of course, dummy."

"Then I don't care."

"Me neither." She took hold of his hand and led him in from the rain.

Marci

She just wanted to eat and get out of there, so Marci started dishing up as soon as they entered. "God, Gentry. Are you wet enough? Hello, it's Oregon. There's this thing we have called shelter. Animals and people with any intelligence seek it when it's pouring."

He finger-combed his hair off his face and ignored her.

Gretchen set a bowl in front of him and he bowed his head. Marci banged a tablespoonful of chili into her own bowl. She'd had enough of family togetherness. Eve's idea of family togetherness was shopping, and Marci hated shopping this time of year. The crowds overwhelmed her. Marci felt sure she'd be fabulous in New York. It wasn't like it was crowded there or anything.

She hated Christmas at her father's. The first night they got there, Gretchen barricaded herself in her little pink room and refused to come out for dinner. Her dad was furious. He scowled around the perfectly decorated house while Eve fussed over the food and pretended everything was fine. Eve concentrated very hard on making things look perfect, because to her if it looked perfect then it was perfect. But there was nothing Eve could do about Graham. Graham was one of those puffy mean kids. He was so mean that whenever Spencer asked for another aquarium pet, her dad and Eve traded nervous looks and changed the subject.

It was tense enough, and then Evan had dropped by. Taller and geekier than ever. Eve was all excited and hostessy. They'd sat down in the formal living room, which was a room she didn't usually go into at her dad's, seeing as how it was formal. Evan had smiled at her. She'd looked at him in parts, his wavy hair and narrow shoulders and big nose and the smooth white hands he kept brushing on his jeans. When she asked him what was new, he flinched. He was afraid. He'd always been afraid of her.

She'd known Evan her entire life. He was one of her Roxaboxen friends, the boy she could push into doing anything because he was afraid of her. He was afraid to climb that rock wall, but he did it. He was afraid to walk across that giant piece of half-burned driftwood, because it was full of rusty spikes and (he told her this at age seven) he didn't want to have to get a tetanus shot. But he did it, because otherwise she'd call him a baby. And he did have to get a tetanus shot.

When they were older, he was afraid to sneak out and night swim in the waves because of the dangerous floating logs. He was afraid to steal his mother's car and go on joyrides. He was afraid to break into empty second homes and steal the good wine. But he did all of it, because he was more afraid of Marci's scorn. And when they were sixteen, it was something new. Something that terrified them both.

She'd been daring him, teasing him, tormenting him all summer, and he'd done everything she dared him to that night. He'd walked up the beach in the dark the half-mile from their place. He'd arrived at midnight. He'd climbed the steps and thrown pebbles at her window. But when she came down and met him by the door of the little house, he stood there, too afraid to go in.

She said, *What's your problem, Evan? Why are you always so afraid?*

He stood there with his hand on the door of the little house. *It will change everything, Marci. If we go in there, everything will change.*

They opened the door and went inside.

Afterwards, when it was over and they lay there on the bare mattress under the window, the moon shone through and lit them. She looked at their new bodies, the strange, hairy, bumpiness. She remembered them as kids, when they'd run around naked on the sand, how flat and smooth and innocent they were, his little boy stick, her little girl line, but other than that basically the same. Now, they had bodies like adults. How strange. They weren't adults.

So, that's it? I mean, that's all there is to it? That's seriously all there is?

He stood up and started to cry. *I've never done it before. God. You're so mean.* He got dressed and left, and didn't speak to her for three days.

⌒

He was right. Everything had changed. But he kept calling her mom's house like she'd want to talk to him, and coming by her dad's when she was in town. He kept trying to be friends.

So they sat there in Eve's version of a formal living room like normal friends who'd never had sex, and sipped lemonade and talked about the people they both still knew like nothing was different, like they were still friends. Eventually Spencer had come in and started talking about gerbils, and then Graham had stomped in to stare at all of them with his tiny, confused eyes. Eve had also come in to get the glasses before they set them down and made rings on the tables.

Evan had finally stood up. "I guess I should go."

She'd walked him to the door and opened it. A dark-haired neighbor boy was standing on the sidewalk, staring intensely at the house. "He's so *creepy*, why doesn't he ever *knock*?" Marci had called back into the house, "Spencer, Tristan's here!" Spencer rocketed out the door, quick as a gunshot. Eve started to shout about, don't you leave, it's almost dinner, but Spencer had to make his escape before Graham could tag along.

That left Marci alone with Evan's sweet, hopeful face.

He'd smiled. "It was nice to see you."

"I have to go, Evan." She'd shut the door and gone inside to not eat dinner.

⌒

Once she emerged from her room, Gretchen had found a way to work Gentry into every conversation. She revealed an exhaustive knowledge of personal trivia. His shoe size (huge). His shampoo brand (expensive). The manufacturer of his scanner (who cares). How much his car payment is (tiny). Where he banks (his account was still in Detroit, imagine that, fascinating). What music he listens to (Marci heard it in the car, she was aware). The last twenty books he checked out from their tiny library (seven poetry collections, ten novels and three books on computer science). What day he was born (June 25), where he went to school (expensive), when he got his master's (22), how old he was (27), how tall he was (6'), how much he weighed (185, which was more than he looked), what his uncle's name was (Melvin). What was in the packages his uncle sends (homemade soap and sometimes books). She told him everything but the Big Mystery. His name. She only knew his initials and she wouldn't tell anyone what they were.

Her father had a theory. "He's probably in the witness relocation program. I'm heading down to the post office to look through the wanted posters. Want to tag along, Gretchen? Maybe he's a Colombian drug lord. Those guys are all Catholic, aren't they?" Her dad could be funny, mostly when Eve wasn't around. Gretchen never laughed, though.

Dad was worried.

⁓

So, there was the man her little sister had memorized, sitting at the table, not looking at anyone. Gentry stared at his chili like he was counting the beans. The word was "stricken." He looked like his best friend just died, but Bosco was there waiting for falling food, so Marci didn't know what was wrong, or care, really.

"How was South Dakota?"

"North Dakota."

"Whatever. You came home early."

"So did you."

"That's your fault. Gretchen talked about you so much that Dad gave up and brought her back." He brightened at this. He wouldn't be so happy if he knew her dad wanted to be more "conscientious" about their monthly weekend with him. Her dad had also called Mom to see about adding some Gretchen-only weekends.

Gretchen was having none of it.

"Well? How was it?" He frowned. "Gentry, Christmas?"

"Cold."

"How was your uncle?"

"Fine."

She waited for a minute. "And that's it? Christmas was cold and fine?"

He stared at his bowl. A drop of rain ran down his nose and he batted at it with his hand.

Mom came in and stood with her hand on Gretchen's hair. No drink tonight. She had on one of the sweaters they brought her, a black cashmere that dipped low to show her sharp clavicles and hugged her hipbones. Her mother's bones were art.

Gentry pushed away from the table so hard that his chair hit the floor with a crack. "Did you have fun at your dad's, Marci? Mike, right, his name is Mike? He has a great car. How was his wife, what did you say her name was, Eve? How are your little brothers? What are their names again?"

Her mother's mouth made a little round "o" of horror. She whirled back into the kitchen. Gentry followed.

Marci looked at Gretchen, like, do you know what this is about? And she gave Marci a look back with a shrug, like, no idea. They carefully placed their spoons by their bowls as if they were setting the table, and tried to hear the low voices in the kitchen.

Gretchen's eyes were so silvery blue they looked like mercury.

She heard the door slam, once. Her mother had never slammed a door in her life, so Marci knew who that was. Close behind it was the rumble of Garret's truck in the driveway. "You're on your own, little sister. I'm out of here." She slipped out the front door and ran around the side of the house as fast as she could.

∽

The date with Garret, if that's what you would call it, was nice, even though they just drove around, telling each other about Christmas. The truth was, Marci had never liked Garret's voice. It was a little too high. But that night, it rolled along like his truck on the highway, easy and soothing. "Dad got me ten cartons of smokes. Nice, huh?"

"Nice. Cancer for Christmas."

"You're funny."

"As funny as cancer." She stared out the window.

Marci hadn't formally met Garret's dad. Sometimes he was there staring at the television, tipping back cans of beer in a determined way when they stopped by the house. But Garret had never actually introduced Marci. Mr. Blount always ignored her, and said something to Garret like, *Remember we're out early tomorrow, kid.* Something to remind Garret who was boss.

Garret worshipped his dad.

Their house was tiny and crooked. A living room, an odd little kitchen wrapped around some stairs down to the basement, two bedrooms and a bathroom. Marci didn't know where they ate. Probably in front of the television. She'd only been in Garret's room once. It was as immaculate as his truck, but the rest of the house stank like beer and cigarettes and fish and something dark she couldn't place.

"What did you get, babe?"

"Clothes, mostly. Some gift cards. I hate gift cards. It's like, Merry Christmas. Go shop for your own present." She described her little brothers fighting over a game, how Spencer finally lost it and called Graham a "fucktard." "It was really the highlight of the whole holiday because Spencer never says bad words."

"Really?"

"Really. No one in my family ever swears." Garret drove along, trying to absorb the idea of a family where no one swore. "How was your Christmas?"

"Mom had a furlough. Dad said she could come over for Christmas dinner, so she did. She made that casserole with the green beans. Dad's favorite."

"Which casserole?"

"You know, that green bean casserole."

"No, I really don't know."

"Sure you do. It's got green beans and mushroom soup? There's onion rings on top. Those ones that come in a can."

"Barf. Don't talk about whatever that is anymore." She reached over and took his hand, and he said nothing, but his mouth tightened in a suppressed smile.

Before he'd asked her out, Marci had assumed that Garret hated her. It was the fall of their junior year. Vu was the only friend she'd had since grade school, and they sat together in every class. Their classmates ignored Marci, but they stopped by Vu's desk and talked to him about the weekend. Then they'd look over at her, embarrassed that she could hear their discussions of mud running and bowling and keggers. Like she couldn't possibly care, like she'd never want to know.

She was dying to know.

Marci was tired of sitting in class on Mondays hearing about what happened while she was at her dad's. She'd ride away in his car, leaving Gretchen alone with their mom. She'd spend her Saturdays wondering if they were all right, and her

Saturday nights wondering what everyone else in her class was doing. Probably not getting pedicures or golfing at Dad's club. Probably not going to fundraisers at the Portland Art Museum or playing tennis at the indoor courts at the MAC. Probably not shopping with Eve and all her platinum cards. She imagined this dark, rainy world of coastal partying, in which all her mundane classmates were glamorous because they drank beer and had sex with each other down at Short Sands.

She knew Garret was at every party that mattered because he had older friends and reliable drug connections. Garret was short, and so good-looking that it made her chest hurt. She sat behind him in class and couldn't keep her eyes off his arms, how ropy and hard they were. Broad shoulders and bowed legs and that dark smell. His square jaw, his full lips. His thick, brushy hair. He was always running his hands through it, so she said to Vu that he probably had head lice. His eyes were so small, so mean. She remarked to Vu that he looked like he had fetal alcohol syndrome. Sometimes he reeked, *reeked* of sweat and fish. She stood near him just to breathe it in. He was stupid, awful. How could someone that awful be that hot? He carried a *knife*.

She began her campaign. She goaded the teachers, she needled her classmates. Especially Garret. *Why don't you ask Garret?* she'd say to any teacher naïve enough to lob a question out, hoping for classroom participation. *I'm sure he knows.* Garret pretended to ignore her, but she knew he heard her.

Vu warned her. *You don't want to mess around with Garret Blount. He went out with a senior girl when he was a freshman, Marci. Now he hooks up with girls who already graduated. I think he has a kid in Warrenton. He's like a demigod to all the coastal young ladies. You'd be poaching. Every girl in this school will hate you.* They already hated her. So why not?

One day he showed up, just sitting in the driveway in his truck, idling. *Who's that?* Gretchen had peered out the window, her pointy little face knit up and suspicious. *Who's that out there in that truck?*

No one. Don't tell Mom.

Marci went out to the passenger side of his Chevy short box, put her palm against the door. She stood there, her hand against that door like she could hold it closed, push it away, shove it over the bluff because if she opened that Chevy short box and climbed inside, her life would change. She didn't know exactly how, or how much. But everything in her life would be different. If she climbed in there and sat next to that stupid, beautiful boy who wasn't afraid of anything, she would have him. But she wouldn't have something else, something she'd never, ever get to have or be or do because she made the decision to pull on that door handle. And she would never even know what it was.

She opened the door. Her chest opened, too, with a sense of something beautiful and painful being removed. Something perfect. But the deed was done. She had opened the door.

She clambered in, graceless and unsure. The entire time she was making her clumsy entrance, Garret watched, his eyes at half-mast. It took two tries to get the door to latch.

The word was "awkward."

She turned her face to the passenger window and waited for something mean to come out of her mouth. Anytime she opened it, she could find something mean to say. It was just a matter of time before she spoke, and insulted him.

He grabbed her by the back of the neck and yanked her towards him, used his hand to force her chin around. His eyes were narrow and purple, his voice barely more than a grunt. *You know what? You talk too fuckin' much.* She smelled tobacco and beer on his breath. He leaned down, menacing and stupid, and kissed her. She couldn't move, she couldn't breathe. He let her up for air, just for a second, and she gasped like a drowning girl. He smiled before he kissed her again and shoved a hand between her knees to pry them apart.

That was when everything changed.

⌢

That was a year ago. No, more than a year. She'd been with him for over a year. They were parked at her house, listening to the radio and looking at the moon. With his face and his arms lit like that, Garret looked like an Italian statue. He took a pull on his cigarette and threw the butt out onto the drive. "So clear tonight. Wish I was out on it."

"Wouldn't that be dangerous?"

"Sure." He almost smiled. Oh so dangerous, right? But after a year, Marci knew that underneath the swearing and the muscles and the drugs and what he did to her until she couldn't breathe, Garret was like any other boy. He kept his room clean and got his hair cut. He sent postcards to his mother and visited her in prison. He had a savings account and a smashed penny collection. She'd brought him flattened pennies from the zoo and the Forestry Center for Christmas, and he'd been so pleased. She'd spent less than five dollars on those pennies.

"Babe. I'm sorry I didn't get you anything."

She remembered Dad's living room, that overload of presents. "It's totally all right."

He put his arm around her. "No, I should've got you something." His arm tightened, his face in her neck, his arms too tight. She couldn't breathe.

"Would you stop? My mother might look out here."

"She never looks out here."

"Well he might."

"Who gives a shit? I'm sick of that faggot. Let's do it right here, right here, and I'll throw the rubber out the window at his Jeep."

"Oh my god. Would you get OFF me?"

He shoved her away and started the truck, put it in reverse.

"What are you doing?"

"You don't want him to see us, fine. I'll pull around the other side of the house."

"Stop." She put her hand on his arm. Her heart was pounding, pounding.

He sat for a moment, holding on to that steering wheel so hard she expected it to come away in his hands. "Listen. Don't talk, babe. Just listen."

She didn't say a word.

"I been thinking. Portland's less than a hundred miles away. Brian says there's a shit ton of colleges there."

"So?"

"Don't you get it? It would be a lot more better if you went to school there."

"A lot more better?"

"Yeah. A whole lot more better." He gripped the wheel and stared straight ahead. "Listen, Marci. I want to marry you."

"*Marry* me?" Okay, her ears weren't working. "Did you just say you want to *marry* me?"

"Sure. I always figured . . ."

". . . that we'd get *married*?" She couldn't contain the horrified, bawling laughter that came pouring out of her mouth. She couldn't stop it, even though Garret was turning to stone right in front of her, inch by inch, a boy made of stone, a boy who couldn't be hurt.

"You know what? You're a cunt." He reached across her to push open the passenger door, and shoved her out onto the gravel. The truck roared backwards up the drive, the passenger door swinging open as the truck fishtailed. She lay there for a minute unable to breathe, her head ringing, listening to him gun the engine and pull out onto the highway, tearing off. He'd called her a cunt. He'd said that once before. Except he wrote it in a note.

Your a cunt.

Gentry will find me here, she thought, and he'll pick me up like a cigarette butt and throw me away, so Bosco doesn't eat me. She stood up and shook her head, combed her fingers through her hair. She felt like she had bugs in her hair, in her brain.

"It's my fault." She said it out loud, to test the truth of it.

Yes. That was true. It was her fault.

The moon shone down on this wreck of a night, bright and unreal as what had just happened to her, like a stage set, glowing and cold and eerie in a completely artificial way, and there was music.

Music? She walked around the side of the little house. There on the edge of the world sat Gentry, leaning on his dog and drinking from a bottle of something brown and listening to his boom box.

All boys were the same.

He tipped up his head and squinted. "Hey."

The rain had stopped, and that meant it was freezing. "Gentry? What are you doing out here?"

He appeared to be thinking about it. "Getting drunk."

"Obviously. But have you ever heard of hypothermia?"

"Low heat." He tapped his temple with a fingertip. "Latin."

"Well you should go inside."

"Not yet." He tipped up a bottle.

The word for Gentry was "smashed."

"Gentry, seriously. Are you going to stay out here all night?"

He spoke with quiet dignity. "I might."

Marci shivered. She wasn't sure if it was being wet or being angry that made her shake, but she went inside to get his sleeping bag.

She sat down on the other side of Bosco and put the bag over all three of them. Gentry handed her the bottle. She took a drink, and as she handed the bottle back to him, it hit her, made her gasp and wheeze and breathe out fire. "Oh my god, Gentry, this is the worst."

He nodded. "It's the bottom left."

"The what?"

"The bottom left. The bottom left is where they put the worst. This is seven dollars and fifty cents worth of the bottom left." He took another drink.

"Do you always know what everything costs?" Gretchen said that Gentry ran a mental tally when they went to the store. He was within a dime every time at the checkout.

He stared up at the sky. "The moon throws the knives."

Okay. Fine.

The CD stopped, and he pushed the button to start it again and moved his head in time to the music. He handed over the bottle. It wasn't as foul this time. "So, why are you getting drunk? I mean, I know why I'm getting drunk, but why are you?"

He laughed a little, an involuntary eruption that sounded like a milder version of her laughter in the cab of Garret's truck. "I had a bad day."

"So you just get drunk every time you have a bad day?"

"No. No, it has to be a really, really, really, really, *really*. Bad. Day."

Nothing that happened to Gentry could be as bad as what had happened to Marci that night. "Gentry, whatever it is, it can't be worth freezing to death over."

"I won't freeze. Now. This is a down sleeping bag." His logic was starting to make sense. Marci took another drink.

He tried to lean his head back against the house, misjudged the distance, and slammed his head against the siding. He peered back over his shoulder at the little house, surprised. "Ouch. That hurt." And then he did it again, harder, and laughed.

Marci tried it. Bam. "Ouch. Yes, it really does hurt." They were both laughing. She gave him back his bottle. "Garret has this CD. It's his favorite."

He put his finger to his lips. "Sh. I like it."

"I like it too. It's rougher than what you usually listen to. I mean, some of that stuff you listen to sounds so poppy. Sappy. Like, the early Beatles, or something."

"I like the early Beatles."

"So does Mom. She saw them in concert the first time they came over to the States. A neighbor took her. Was that like, 1962 or something?"

He slammed his head really hard against the house.

They sat in silence for a while, passing the bottle back and forth in companionable silence. He sipped. She sipped. It didn't taste so nasty awful anymore, and it had a nice effect on an empty stomach. He stopped the CD, put it in a shirt pocket from which he took another. "Hey Marci? Does Garret like Jeff Buckley?"

"Garret *hates* Jeff Buckley." Marci shook her head. Great. Garret proposed and then called her the c-word, she was getting drunk with a teacher because she had no friends, and now she had to listen to Jeff Buckley. "So, Gentry? You're supposed to be so nice. But you're not, not really."

"Thank you."

She had another drink. "Seriously. Why do you make him so mad? On purpose?"

"I have no idea what you're talking about."

"Oh yes you do."

"Oh no I don't."

"You so do."

"I so don't."

"Don't lie. Lying is weak."

He took a minute to consider before he spoke. "All right. Listen. Teaching Garret is like catching a salmon. As opposed to teaching someone like your sister, which is like catching a trout."

"Since I know nothing about fishing, these metaphors make no sense. But whatever you say. Everyone is a fish."

"Okay. Listen. Again." He took a drink. "Trout are hungry. They want the bait."

"So you're saying Gretchen is like a trout because she has a hunger for learning."

He slapped his thigh with his hand. "Exactly, Marci, that's *exactly* what I'd be saying if I were not so impaired. A trout is hungry. This is as opposed to salmon, because salmon are not hungry. They just want to spawn."

"No kidding."

He ignored that. "The most you can hope for with a salmon is that he'll notice what you trail past him." He made a little motion, like he had a fishing rod in his hand. "He'll never be hungry for it, but he might snap at it out of irritation. And that way, he takes the bait. Except," and he stopped to take a sip, "I'm just snagging Garret."

"Snagging?"

"Fish talk." He lurched to his feet and walked at a slight angle around the side of the house. Bosco followed. Marci drank while they were gone. She really avoided drinking because of her mother, but she decided she should drink more, and more often.

Gentry stumbled back, buttoning his jeans. He was having a little trouble.

"What took you so long?"

"This tree back there. It . . . scared me." He sat down again and very gingerly put his head back against the house.

"Hey, Gentry." She slammed back her head as hard as she could. "I better stop before I get brain damage and end up a cheerleader."

He threw back his head to laugh again, and accidentally slammed it into the house. He reached back and rubbed his head. "I'll end up a Garret."

"You're so mean. You're hilarious, you know that?"

"Yes, Marci. I'm hilarious in more ways than you'll ever know." He stared out over the water and sighed. Oh, please, enough sighing. She wanted him to be mean again, she loved it when Gentry was mean. Except when he was mean to her mother, of course. She'd forgotten about that. He was mean to her mother.

"Why were you mean to my mother at dinner?"

"I'm not answering that." Gentry took another drink, she took another drink, and Gentry hit the forward button on the CD player. "Too sad. Too sad for me. Here's a good one."

It was a good one, much as she hated to admit it. "Gentry, can I ask you a question?"

He shrugged. "Ask me anything."

"Except why you're getting drunk and why you were mean to Mom."

"That and my name. Anything else."

She considered asking him if he actually had sex with Darlene, but she thought of something even more gross. "Okay. Have you ever, in your life, had a casserole with green beans and mushroom soup and onion rings on top?"

"Yes, and please don't talk about it."

"I could have sworn Garret was making that up."

They'd finished the bottle. Marci decided there were worse places to sleep. She tucked the sleeping bag around her and Bosco, who'd settled down on the ground for the night. Bosco smelled, but he was warm, at least. She leaned over him and so did Gentry, his eyes closed, his hands in Bosco's fur. Even though they were shoulder-to-shoulder, he'd probably forgotten she was there.

One song ended, another started. She'd thought she couldn't stand this CD, but maybe she'd never really heard it before. The guitar notes were high and full of echo. She decided the song was personal. It was the most personal, private song she'd ever heard in her life.

Gentry started to sing. Note for note, sweet, deep and strong. Marci couldn't sing, but she knew a beautiful voice when she heard one. If her mother heard this, she'd smile and her eyes would shine and she'd fall in love with Gentry. Because it was that beautiful, how he sang.

Why was it that everyone could sing besides her?

He couldn't get anywhere near the last notes. So he just listened. When it was over, his head dropped forward and he mumbled something. "What?" He mumbled again. He was passing out. She shoved his shoulder and almost knocked him over. "Gentry, what?"

He repeated himself with the exaggerated care of the very drunk. "I said, I forgot to wash my hands."

"You're drunk and sleeping in the dirt with a dog. Why do you need clean hands?" His head fell to one side. "Gentry?" Nothing. He was passed out cold. She leaned in, closer than he'd ever let her get if he were awake. His mouth smelled like her mother's. But she didn't care.

As dry and light as the wing of a sparrow, she brushed his sleeping lips with hers.

Gentry

It was morning. Gretchen was brushing my hair. She'd taken to doing this almost every day when I came over for coffee. I had a one-cup arrangement Kathryn brought me the first week, I could have had my coffee out there. But then, Gretchen wouldn't brush my hair.

I closed my eyes. The room spun. The room spun and I had to think about last night.

I thought this was as low as I could go, getting drunk with a student. I didn't think I could sink too much lower as a teacher. No, I could do worse. I could put my hands on a student in anger, or take one into my bed. But since I wouldn't ever do either of those things, getting drunk with a student would have to stand as my worst.

It was time to get a handle on things. I needed to buck up. How?

I'd buy something. Something electrical and expensive. That would cheer me up. I had an excessive amount of peripherals at that point, so I'd have to do something with the Jeep.

Marci showed her face in the kitchen, looking as sick as I felt. "How are you even alive?"

I was too sick to answer.

Earlier, at dawn, we'd woken up freezing. I could hardly stand. Marci had to help me up and into my house, where she ran me a hot bath. Bosco, misunderstanding the full bathtub, jumped in with me. He needed a bath almost as much as I did.

Had Marci guessed who had me howling at the moon? If she did, it didn't seem to matter. I appreciated her kindness, especially since she could easily have had me arrested for furnishing alcohol to a minor.

I'd never been arrested. I'd been accused, suspended pending investigation, brought before an angry panel of suspicious administrators, questioned as to my personal life in front of my colleagues, and grilled by the media about how awful it was to be grilled by the media. If I continued to draw from the deep well of my own stupidity, I'd be arrested.

Gretchen brushed vigorously to get the dog hair out of mine. She hit a snarl. Ouch. My head. I had a fuzzy memory of banging it into the siding, which accounted for the tender spot. Why was I slamming my head against the house?

"Marci, do you think I should put some gel in his hair?"

"It might clump. Use mousse." I heard the sound of Gretchen's feet on the stairs, going to get some mousse, whatever that was. God, I was so sick.

I felt a hand on mine. Marci patted me as gently as my uncle patted me.

I wondered what kind of a man Mel would think I was.

⌒

I'd been thinking about the girls in college.

I thought about how it was, back then, what made me want a girl. A sigh. Just that sound. Or another would bend, and something in the way the back of her thighs stretched would set every nerve in my body singing. Becca, I remember her hand holding back her hair at a drinking fountain. I wanted to be that hand on that riot of red hair, holding it back, letting it loose to set a young man on fire.

I didn't know what they saw, what made them want me back. It felt like it was a new girl every day. I didn't remember any damage. Did anyone feel a great loss when whatever it was we were doing was over? Had I hurt anyone?

Becca, my first girl. She was my first, and I was hers. When I remembered her, I remembered my disbelief. I couldn't believe she was actually going to let me do it. I broke into her like a grateful thief, and she wept, welcoming my trespass.

The sweet, fumbling fire.

I didn't usually let myself remember Becca. To remember Becca was to consider the depth and breadth of my own youthful stupidity. She wanted to get married. How could I tell her I was only sixteen? I couldn't get married. I ignored her, avoided her, loved her in a way that hurt me still. Dear God, You knew how sorry I was. I saw the betrayal in her face and hated myself for putting it there. But that was not the point. The point was, I was a coward.

That's why I tried not to remember Becca.

So yes, I'd caused pain. But I refused to count the students, the Tiffanys of this world. I didn't know what to do with a lovesick student. I hated the whole mess when that happened. Not that it happened all the time. Maybe twice? Three times per year? Some poor kid came to me, and I could see it in her face. Sick with love, handing me everything I'd ever need to destroy her. And, somehow, I had to do it. I had to. Because if I didn't, I'd be destroyed.

This was a time for prayer, when I saw those hopeful eyes. Prayer for kind words that didn't lead to false hope. Hope was something I couldn't allow.

When it came to Kathryn, I could allow myself no hope.

Gretchen's voice, mercifully soft. "Is he asleep?"

"I don't know. Let's leave him alone."

The scrape of Marci's chair, four bare feet padding away on the floor. The television coming on. The ocean rolling. A light step on the kitchen stairs. The click of Bosco's nails, his happy pant, the thump of his tail on the table leg. The tap and rattle of a bottle of aspirin set on the table.

Kathryn was there. I knew I couldn't hope. And I knew I could never leave her.

It was almost the New Year. A New Year, a new chance.

I staggered to my feet and dialed Lorrie's number and carried the receiver into the laundry room and shut the door. I wondered why the laundry room had a view of the ocean, but the living room didn't.

Garret's truck pulled up in the drive and sat at idle. If he blew the horn I'd have to go out there and teach him some manners, but he just sat out there in his truck, waiting in a vaguely malevolent way.

Lorrie answered on the fifth ring. "Yello" as opposed to "hello" by way of salutation.

"Um, hey. I called to apologize."

"To me?"

"Yes."

"For what?"

"For hitting you."

The kitchen door opened, the kitchen door closed. Through the window I watched Marci pick her barefoot way across the driveway to stand by the driver's side of his truck. He rolled down the window. And though I couldn't hear them, I could tell by how she stood, the rocking of her small body, how she held her chest, the careful way he wouldn't meet her eyes. They were making up.

I stopped watching.

Lorrie cleared his throat. "Well, leave it to you to make me feel like a jerk. I come over there and embarrass you, I call the old lady names, I laugh at you, and you apologize to me for hitting me, which did hurt, at least more than I thought it would coming from you, Gentry."

"I'm sorry."

"Hell. You're a pansy. It didn't hurt so much."

"What are you doing New Year's Eve?"

"Jeannie dumped me. And I don't want to drive with all those drunk assholes on the road. Do you wanna come over here and watch TV?"

No, I didn't. Not at all. "Sure. That would be great."

I would spend New Year's Eve with Lorrie.

⁓

His apartment was interesting, yes, interesting was the word. I'd been here before, but I'd never really been at leisure to study it.

He had a black leather-like couch. Several of those framed posters of girls in extremely short shorts and high heels leaning on long, powerful cars adorned the walls. His coffee table was glass, and smudgy. His lamp started behind the couch and leaned forward, terminating in an arrangement of balls that reminded me of the pawnshops I went to in Detroit, hoping to find my stolen CPUs. There were no books here, but there were magazines of a type I avoided. He didn't have a desk or a dining room table. We ate our take-out fish and chips and drank our beer sitting on the plastic couch.

God, I own no furniture. I never have. Forgive me my disgust. Amen.

Lorrie did have the largest television I'd ever seen. I told him his television was the biggest, bar none. He beamed. He liked to have the biggest.

The only object in this apartment that signified an inner quest, a spiritual path, was a large plastic wheel with all the signs of the Zodiac in gold-painted bas relief. This item hung over the television. Maybe this injection molded shield thing, in combination with the world's largest television, combined to create Lorrie's altar.

I could have been wrong. It might have been decor.

Lorrie offered me pop, calling it "Coke." To Lorrie, every type of pop was "Coke." So what he actually offered me was "an orange Coke." "All I've got in here is orange Coke. Would you like an orange Coke, little buddy?"

Was he from Georgia?

We drank beer instead. Since I hated movies, we watched a martial arts tournament tape. "A buddy of mine taped this." I was astounded, completely affected by how bad the camera work was. The camera operator put on the lens cap and forgot to take it off for seven minutes. This gave me a break from the lurching, swinging violence of the filmmaker's art.

The actual competition, I didn't mind. After my hands stopped itching for a joystick, I watched real combat. I was grateful Lorrie didn't hit me back after watching him smash up a few opponents. "Lorrie, you kick high. Ouch." This, next to the homage to the big television, was the highest compliment I could pay Lorrie.

He was off, again, on the subject of me and martial arts. "You gotta try it, Gentry. Seriously."

"I try not to hit people."

"Well, it's about more than hitting. There's all that metaphysical shit."

Lorrie was not at that advanced a level as far as martial arts. The philosophical elements seemed to elude him. I tried, but I couldn't imagine Lorrie mounting a ladder to spiritual enlightenment. "I'm too much of a pacifist."

"A pacifist? I thought you said you were a Catholic."

And, then, after this amount of time and this amount of beer, Lorrie was asking me the list of questions I'd been asked by non-Catholics, all my adult life.

"Do you believe in that Pope guy?" (Did I believe in him? He seemed real to me, not like the tooth fairy. Yes, I believed in the Pope.)

"Do you really do that confession deal? I mean, do you really tell everything? EVERYTHING?" (Yes, I did. EVERYTHING.)

"Were you an altar boy?" (Yes.)

"Do you really believe that cracker is the body?" (Yes.)

And here was a new one, new from Lorrie. "Ever run into any kinky nuns?" (Kinky nuns, this man had watched too many movies, nuns were SCARY, kinky nuns, the thought of it made my flesh crawl, NO, I have NOT, Lorrie.)

I had to hand it to Lorrie, at least he came up with a new question.

I stood up and went into his kitchen and checked the clock. Midnight. He watched me pour what was left of my beer into the sink. He didn't say a word.

Happy New Year, Sink.

I went back to the living room and sat down on the leather-like couch. "Little buddy? What happened between you and that Mumford woman?" I'd thought that was pretty clear. But he was pressing for particulars. "Is she as skinny as she looks in her clothes? Is she a natural blonde? Is she freaky? Is she a screamer? I bet she goes crazy."

I had limits.

Oh, God help me out here, okay? I'll never ask You to help me find my keys or pray for sunshine or pray that I'll make it to the gas station on fumes or pray that Bosco will stop barking at a squirrel when I'm trying to sleep. All extraneous, unnecessary and selfish prayer will cease if You just shut him up. Okay, God?

"Well? Are you still knocking boots?"

"I don't want to talk about this."

"Well, don't get all testy on me, little buddy. I just wondered, seeing as how she was 'truly wonderful' and all."

She was that. But what kind of a man would talk about it?

"Hey, Little buddy? Did you ever hear about how a blonde parts her hair?"

"No. But if you tell blonde jokes, I'll probably hit you."

He was quiet. The tournament on tape continued. I watch Lorrie decimate a man three inches taller than himself. I thought about a man that large, that strong who only hit people of his own size, according to rules. I thought about how he sat me down on this couch the day I hit him. I thought about his warning, crude and correct.

"Hey Lorrie? No. We're not."

"I'm sorry, Gentry. I'm real sorry about that."

He was no master, but he was trying.

JANUARY 1997

Marci

The big day had arrived. They were all going on the Internet.
Worried parents had been calling the house about it all week. Calling Marci's house, since Gentry didn't have a phone. She had to go fetch him, listen to him try to explain what the Internet even was to people. Tiffany's mother was terrified by a big Newsweek cover story on the Internet and pornography. Gentry's end of the conversation sounded something like this. *Hey. Hey Jeannie . . . Hey, Jeannie, um, yes? . . . Of course . . . I understand . . . That's right, the Internet, yes . . . no, no, um, no . . . I'm sorry, I mean, um, it's not like that . . . no . . . I know what it said in Newsweek, but the World Wide Web is not all, um, pornography. It's out there, but that's not what we'll be looking at. No, it, I, we, um, Jeannie? Um . . . we have special software . . . I see, um . . . JEANNIE. Would you like to come in and meet with me?*

Marci had started counting the "um's." He'd said it twenty-two times before she stopped. And now they were going to put his special software to the test.

It felt strange to walk into a classroom and have the teacher say, "I need you to listen and listen carefully. If any of you are uncomfortable with this you may be excused, but I need help testing out my porn filters." A couple of kids left, not because they objected, but because they could. And then they got to work.

"Please type in the most perverse, obscene web address you can think of. Try anything."

Vu looked over her shoulder. "That's more of a technical term, Marci. You should misspell it a few ways, and maybe search all the euphemisms."

She began to type them in, but ran out after "going down" and "giving head."

"Vu? I know we're out of your realm of experience, but can you help?"

Vu glanced over. "Hummer. Blowjob. BJ. Cocksucking."

"How does a virgin know all these euphemisms?" She typed everything in and got exactly nowhere.

Gentry was up at his computer, watching his software work. Vu said something in Vietnamese. Gentry said something back. They laughed, and she had no words for how much she hated it when they did that. Mrs. Green walked into the room, her acid wash jeans tight enough to cause circulation damage. Vu's eyebrows lifted. "Camel toe alert."

"You're *disgusting*."

Gentry blanched, leaping up to guide her past all those screens. "Let me, um, let's . . ." He nodded. "Okay, we're fine, now."

It was easy to see where Tiffany learned her flirtation skills, watching Mrs. Green. They liked to work the helplessness angle. "So, show me this Internet, Gentry. Because I just don't know anything about it. At all."

"What, um, are your interests?"

Mrs. Green batted her mascara-caked lashes. Marci wondered if Tiffany had learned her special trick of separating them with an open safety pin from her mother. "You know I just love to bake for a man. Especially pies. I love to bake pies for men."

Vu twisted and squirmed. He looked at Marci and mouthed "pies."

She mouthed back "pies for men."

"All right. Pies for men." Gentry kept his eyes on the monitor, but he sneezed so hard that his body flew backwards and his hair flew forwards like he'd taken a blow to the stomach.

Vu yelled out, "BLESS YOU!"

"Thanks." Gentry looked at the computer screen, Mrs. Green looked at the computer screen. He got out a cloth and started wiping it off. "Sorry about that." Vu was dying.

Marci wished Garret could see this.

He sneezed again. She frowned. "Are you getting a cold?"

"Um, no. It looks like crisco.com would be good site. Any particular type of pie, Mrs. Green?"

"Oh, let's see. How about lemon. Do you like lemon?"

And he sneezed.

Vu bawled out "BLESS YOU GENTRY!" Gentry gave Vu a bland, half-lidded look that somehow carried a stern warning.

They made a nice pair up there in a compare and contrast essay question kind of a way. Gentry wore clothing so old and faded out that he was camouflaged, able to melt seamlessly into the forest. He even smelled like wood. In contrast, Mrs. Green had outdone herself in a country western superstar mode. The matching jeans and jacket were set off by earrings that resembled Christmas tree toppers.

She reeked of that lemon body splash, like Pledge and rubbing alcohol. Tiffany wore the expensive unisex fragrance for heroin addicts that smelled just the same.

The word was "redolent."

Gentry kept sneezing into the crook of his arm as he performed the miracle of the download, the magic of the printer. She was just *amazed*. "I'm *amazed*. Would you *look* at this? This is just *amazing*." She probably chalked up his discomfort to her irresistible charms. She finally left, all a-flutter. Like mother, like daughter. Marci wondered how soon Tiffany would turn up with a lemon pie for old Gentry. Marci hoped it would make him sneeze.

"Okay, enough. The filters work. Everyone stop, now. Stop. Close the browsers, I'm going to reboot everything and clean out all the filth."

Vu said, "Filth." He laughed.

Marci didn't. "Filth is actually a terrific word." She watched Gentry, working away, his face so closed and calm. "There's something sweet about how he thinks he can deflect all of it. Keeping his students safe from filth. Ridiculous, but sweet."

"Don't, Marci."

"Don't what?"

Vu tapped the top of the table with a pencil, choosing his words. "Don't do this to yourself. It will wreck you forever."

"What are you *talking* about?"

"You know exactly what I'm talking about." He turned to regard Gentry through his new, fashionable glasses.

"I hate you, Vu."

"I know."

"Oh shut up." She gathered her books and went to find Garret.

Kathryn

Life's ironies had never been lost on Kathryn.

When she was nineteen, Kathryn was a full-time voice major and a part-time clerk in a vintage clothing store. She lived in a roach-infested studio in Northwest Portland, went to school, sang her heart out, and bedded boys who looked remarkably like Gentry.

Her mother didn't understand why Kathryn wanted to live on her own. She refused to convert Kathryn's bedroom to a den, as was done in those days, preserving it in case her daughter wanted to move back. Kathryn had lived through more than enough years in the parental love nest. Her parents were so intoxicated with each other, they could hardly have missed her. They were too engrossed with their own love story.

She was raised on the official version, in which two young adults from neighboring towns in the Iron Range didn't manage to meet until they both moved to Minneapolis. *I'd heard of your mother, of course, her father told her. Everyone had heard of Lynne Jordahl and her beautiful voice.*

And what about you? Hadn't she heard of you?

He would shake his head. *Me? Plain old Pieter Tingstad? No one heard of me. No one at all.* But her mother's voice was legendary in her small town for its power, range, and clear beauty. Well, at least according to her father and her nana, it was, but her mother wasn't singing in the official version, where her parents worked side-by-side at one of the many Minneapolis dinner theaters that were popular at the time. Her mother painted sets and sewed costumes. Her father had a natural gift for comedy, and played various witty sidekicks. He also wrote plays, and the official version said it all happened during rehearsals for his first professional production. In this play, the Ice Queen was drawn by love out of her fairytale into a modern setting. This was followed by spritely musical flirtation, heartbreaking duets and a choice between the rewards of mortal life with a rather mundane young man, or a return to ruling a kingdom of magic. Guess how she chose?

This must have been a welcome diversion in its day. When Kathryn read the play twenty years later, it seemed insufferably clever. But this was her father's first staged play, and he was very, very nervous on that night so long ago. He was sitting in on rehearsal, and her mother was up on a scaffolding, touching up the glitter on the Ice Queen's conveyance, suspended over the stage. During a break, the female lead slipped on an icy sidewalk and suffered a compound fracture of the ankle. There was the hubbub of the ambulance, and her father's dismay as he walked back into a production that suddenly had no star. When he walked back into rehearsal, stage snow was still floating down, scattered by her mother up in the scaffolding, sifting glitter and singing his witty score as she worked.

And that, Kit, is when I found my Ice Queen. It was fate.

That was the official version. But of course the real story was much better.

They were both married to other people when they met, her mother to a boy she'd known her entire life, her father to an older German woman. Her mother's voice actually was well known, and her father wrote the play specifically to tempt her out of the wings and onto the stage. She refused to succumb to temptation. But when the original actress fell on the ice, the show had to go on. Her mother took the stage as the Ice Queen, and she also took up with Pieter Tingstad.

Scandal ensued. So did pregnancy.

Lynne liked to tell the official version at parties, and she liked to talk about the ice. *I owe everything to ice. Ice brought us together.* And she would put some ice in a glass, and have a cocktail. They loved their parties and their cocktails. But the role of drinking wasn't included in either version of the story.

They moved out to Portland to reinvent themselves, setting up shop as young marrieds in a sweet little cottage in upper Burlingame. It was a house full of music; Pieter's piano, a record player, the big radio tuned to the opera every Sunday. Her parents were small and fair, quick with their tongues and their laughter. Pieter was a drama teacher. Lynne raised their daughter, whom they always called "Kit."

Kit inherited their eyes and hair, her voice, his laugh. She did not inherit her mother's ability to bewitch a man in the manner of the Snow Queen. Pieter was in his wife's thrall, there was no other word for it. Lynne curled onto his lap. *My Ice Queen*, he'd murmur. She would smile her teasing smile and lay her hand on his heart. He had no heart left for his daughter.

They laughed and sang and bantered, that constant Midwestern teasing. They argued over the eventual fate of their daughter's spectacular soprano. *Kit's a little ham, Lynne. Listen to her. She can do the accents.* Pieter referred to Kit's childish penchant for mimicry, the flattened tones of her Swedish grandmother, the southern drawl of a neighbor, the same mannered British mockery that she would indulge in with her own daughter generations later. Her mother saw it differently. *She can use that gift for accents with Puccini.* Lynne knew her voice had gone to waste. She was determined this wouldn't happen with Kit.

What did Kit want? She wanted to be a poet. Emily Dickinson, in particular. She didn't understand a bit of her poetry, but admired her style. She spent a lot of time dressed in white, sitting in her room writing hyphenated verse in a small notebook, occasionally lowering a basket out her first-floor window. The attic would offer more of a drop, but that was where Lynne kept her sewing machine. Kit was only welcome upstairs for fittings.

Outside her sewing room, Lynne was a playful wife, a devoted mother. Inside it, she was an artist. Oh, the clothes she sewed for her daughter. Pieter's voice, teasing. *That child isn't dressed, Lynne. She's costumed.*

Lynne indulged Kit's penchant for wearing white with pinafores and petticoats, and Lynne's own penchant for pageantry with stiff little dresses embellished with subversive detail. Other girls had candy canes and hollyhocks smocked across the bodices of their Christmas dresses. Kit had a dancing line of wild-haired trolls. A chain of red along the hem of a navy blue jumper seemed to be flowers from a distance. Up close, it was a scarlet garland of skulls and crossbones. Dolphins leapt up her arms from her wrists to her shoulders on a play coat. The hem of her favorite Christmas dress was embroidered with tiny icicles.

When Kit grew up and needed a different costume, Lynne quietly collaborated with microscopic miniskirts, plaid maxi skirts, knitted vests and caps, pieced smock tops and patched jeans. Her mother designed, modified, embellished all of it. *Kit? Butterflies are groovy, yes?* "Groovy." It sounded so ridiculous coming out of her mouth. But Kit nodded. And Lynne sewed for her an azure wool cape with swarms of butterflies embroidered along the flaring edges. Women stopped her on the street every time she wore it, begging to know where they could find one.

Her mother's rebellion was confined to the sewing room. Her parents were Republicans who believed in the war, but Kit felt they had potential for enlightenment. After all, their original story, the story that resulted in Kit, bespoke rebellion. Certainly they could understand her passion for social change, for peace? They could not.

You have no idea, Kit, her father would say. *You have no idea how much your grandparents sacrificed to get here, to have a chance at a better life. And when you show disrespect for this country, you show disrespect for your grandparents and everything they did for us.* She never bothered to hide how distasteful she found the idea of respecting her elders, or her opinions about the immorality of military involvement in Vietnam. What she couldn't understand, looking back, is how she confused the one with the other.

And so, that year, when her parents made their annual Christmas trip back to see Nana Marit in the iron range, Kit refused to go. She was trying to recover from the loss of a boy named Christian who'd been shamed by his father into honoring his obligation to defend his country. She was not interested in riding in a Buick sedan all the miles to and from Minnesota. She stayed in Portland and went to a midnight candlelight vigil for MIAs on Christmas Eve at Riverfront Park. It was very cold. She held her candle aloft and thought about Nana Marit attending the Christmas Eve service without her. Hearing Kit sing the hymns was Nana's favorite part.

She'd woken up alone the next day in her dingy little apartment. In Minnesota, they would be waking to pastries and hot cocoa. She'd be wearing whatever hat, scarf and glove combination Nana Marit had knitted over the year. Kit never wore any of them once she got home, of course, it was too temperate in Portland for that. But she wrapped them in tissue and mothballs and saved them all. That morning, Kit had risen and found a tasseled hat in a dresser drawer, pulled it down over her ears, and stared out at the grey skies.

Christmas was just another day.

It was an ice storm that killed her parents on their way home. But she rejected the reality of their death. She refused to believe that her parents had died in a car accident.

Oh, she'd seen their broken bodies. She'd accompanied the coffins back to the Iron Range, stood beside her bent little nana as the pastor officiated over a joint funeral. Both their ex-spouses attended, the plain German woman with big hips who had been her father's first wife, the stooped man who had been her mother's first husband. If Kit hadn't been so blasted apart by grief, she might have been amused by the irony of their story. In some misguided attempt at revenge, they'd married each other. *I think we did it to spite them.* The man laughed. *Of course they never cared!* Holding his wife by the hand, obviously glad at how it all came out. *My but you're a little beauty, said the woman,* eyes wide. *The image of your mother.* And this strange, aging couple told her of their happy ending, their three children, as if it were the last chapter in a story she'd been waiting all her young life to hear. They spoke with the distinct Iron Range diction of their nationalities, the "dis" and "dat" of the man whose parents came from Sweden, the harsh, wide Germanic vowels of his wife. Kit's parents had trained away their accents.

Kit nodded, maintaining her chilly silence in the face of their offensive familiarity. These people were old. Her parents had never been old. They never would be. That's why they were all standing there in that Lutheran church in rural Minnesota wearing navy blue. Kit kept an arm around her bent little nana as her parents were committed to their frozen graves. She lifted her carved jaw to the winter wind and refused to believe they were really gone.

She returned to Portland and rendered moot her parents' discussions about exactly the best path for her voice by smoking. She stopped being "Kit." "Katrin," her given name, was too much. She became "Kathryn." She switched her major to art history. Certainly her parents would have been horrified. Logically, she understood that her parents were not going to show up and demand that she stop ruining her life. But logic had nothing to do with her pain.

⁓

She met Michael soon after the accident. He was a finance student, tall, blond and intense. He was older, returning to school after several years at an agricultural commune in northern California where he'd had an economic epiphany about how easily they could convert their communal nonprofit model into a means to make an enormous amount of money supplying goods to key restaurants and businesses in the Bay Area. His fellow commune dwellers were not interested in joining Michael's conversion to capitalism. He officially declared the sixties "a steaming pile," moved to Portland and enrolled in school. If he was going to play by society's rules, he wanted to win.

They met in a required science class, Rocks for Jocks or something like that, and became friends. She was too hard, too angry, too funny for Michael to want more than that. Michael feared his father, hated his brother. His mother had died when he was seventeen, so he thought he understood loss. Kathryn rejected the idea that anyone could understand her loss. She smoked and joked, trying to hide the fact that she believed in nothing. All around her, political corruption flowered while young men like Christian were shipped away to die. Her protest singers signed lucrative recording contracts. Her fellow feminists traded empowerment for the culture of victimhood. The country was entering a period of political cynicism so intense it made everyone sound like Lenny Bruce after his arrests: furious, plaintive, accusatory.

Her generation was going down in a cloud of pot smoke.

⁓

Why was she doing this to herself? What was the point of dredging up the past, the pain of a life that she'd never appreciated until it was over?

Kathryn returned to the here and now, where she sat at the kitchen table, on the phone with the most objectionable person in her entire town, taking down a phone message. "Yes, Jeannie, I'll tell him you called. Again. I'll tell him you called, again." Kathryn hung up and added Jeannie's note to the pile.

Yes, women were calling, girls from his classes, random women who had traded conversation with Gentry at the gas station, the restaurants where he lunched with Gretchen, the libraries. They tracked down his number and called her phone. And it was her job to deliver the messages to him. Wasn't this ironic, since she'd scorned him?

She took a sip and lit another cigarette.

When Kathryn made it in to a meeting, she could listen to a coarse bartender conversing with an overprocessed convenience store clerk about Gentry, speculating on the specifics of his age, experience, his endowment. "Well, Dar*lene* says . . ." Trading their grubby, inaccurate tidbits in public. And then their reddened eyes swept over to Kathryn, speculating. No wonder she'd stopped attending meetings. What did everyone do before Gentry drove his Jeep into their little string of coastal towns? He was the stuff of legend, a mythical beast. Like the unicorn.

She stared at the stack of notes, the stack of mail. She'd had enough. She felt like an answering service. "Gretchen?" No answer. "Gretchen, will you run this out to the little house?"

No answer.

Kathryn trudged unsteadily up the kitchen steps and pushed open the door to Gretchen's empty bedroom. Where was she? It was after dark.

⁓

The curtains on the door's window were open. Gentry sat at his computer. He typed, read some words, typed again. He was "chatting" with someone. He actually laughed at what he read on that screen. She pushed open the door. Her voice was perhaps a trifle too loud. "Who are you *talking* to?"

"Paige Sanderson."

Ask a direct question, receive a direct answer. A direct answer that told her absolutely nothing. "What's Gretchen doing in here?" Yes, definitely too loud, though modulation was difficult to control in her present state. "It's getting *late*."

He looked surprised to see Gretchen sleeping next to Bosco. "I didn't know she was in here." He went to the bed and leaned down, frowned. "She doesn't smell right."

Kathryn rushed to breathe it in, the hot, sweet smell of a sick child's breath. She knew without trying that her daughter was too big to lift, too heavy to carry. She was taller than her mother. How had that happened? Gentry gathered Gretchen up in his arms while Kathryn blinked back tears.

⌣

Gretchen's room was the color of butter. Gentry lay Gretchen down atop the tangle of white sheets, duvet, a great-grandmother's disintegrating wedding quilt. He averted his eyes discreetly while Kathryn undressed her and drew a nightshirt over her head. Kathryn straightened the bedding, smoothed covers over Gretchen's long limbs. She drew the wispy sheers over the windows, guarding her Gretchen from the night with these layers of soft cotton. Bye bye, baby bunting. He lingered by the shelves full of shells and starfish and bones and rocks and feathers and nests and eggs, studying Gretchen's posters, her tidal chart, her hand-drawn maps with their careful notations, which bird, which nest, how many eggs, how long.

Yes, Gretchen was a prodigy. It was not news to her. She would not speak of it to him.

"She's fine now."

He nodded, but stopped before the framed illustrations from the book of fairytales she'd read at her grandmother's house. His eyes widened with something, fear or recognition. Perhaps he had it as a child. It was hard to imagine him sitting on someone's lap, turning those leaves, scared and thrilled by those bloody, cautionary tales.

He left for a moment, returning with a wet washcloth folded neatly in thirds. He settled it on Gretchen's hot forehead. At the cold, her eyelids flickered, opened. Through the fog of her fever, she saw him. "I think I'm sick."

He sat down and took her hand. "I'll be right here."

And across her face flowed such love, such contentment, even though her teeth chattered from a wretched fever. "Promise?"

"Promise." He would sit there all night, keeping vigil. Sick. Kathryn was sick too. Sick at what this had become, what had happened.

And she was too sick to fix it.

Marci

Her dad wanted Gretchen that weekend. Her mother told him she'd been sick. For once, Gretchen was really sick, not just pretending in order to get out of school, but Dad insisted.

Gentry wanted to go into Portland and have a CD player put in his car. When Marci mentioned this to Dad on the phone, he told her to put Gentry on the line. "Dad, he's *outside*."

"Can you go get him?"

"He's in the *driveway*."

"Well, go get him. I'll hold."

She set the receiver down on the table and walked out in the driveway. It was sunny but still cold. The Jeep was making kind of a racket. Gentry was barefoot, wearing nothing but a pair of jeans, and leaning over the engine. She stared at his bare shoulders, the ponytail snaking down to the small of his back, the muscles working at the base of his spine, the curve just above his jeans. She ignored the ache this caused, the stupid ache that made her feel like she'd been hit by a car. She wanted nothing to do with it.

"Gentry?"

He pulled his head up and turned around. He was actually brushing his teeth. The brushing slowed down as he straightened up. Marci guessed that working on his car and brushing his teeth at the same time was doable, but having a conversation tipped the balance.

He spit out a big mouthful of foam on the driveway and stuck the toothbrush in the pocket of his jeans. He wiped his mouth with the back of his hand and wiped that on his leg. She stared at the gob of toothpaste on the gravel.

"Every single thing you've just done repulses me."

"I'm, um, sorry. I couldn't decide what was worse."

"I understand your dilemma but it's still revolting." She stared at the spit so she wouldn't stare at his chest, which was as sculpted and perfect as Garret's, maybe even more so. She didn't understand why, because Gentry didn't actually do anything. "You should get some sun, you're as white as a mushroom. And my dad's on the phone. He wants to talk to you."

"To me?" He loped into the house, and they talked, and before Marci was really sure what happened, this *thing* happened. How did this *thing* happen?

This thing being Gentry driving them to their father's house.

"Why do I always have to ride on this stupid jump seat? It's like sitting on a ping pong paddle." They couldn't hear her, apparently.

Gretchen huddled next to Gentry like a hurt animal. "Do you have to drive so fast, dummy?" He drove with one hand on the wheel, an arm around her. She gave him hateful looks.

Marci didn't blame her. How could her dad be so okay with Gentry driving them in? They didn't seem like best buds. Gentry lived in a converted tool shed and her dad lived in the West Hills in a three-story house that overlooked downtown. She hoped that Graham had soccer games, birthday parties, play dates, anything to keep him away from Gretchen. But Graham never seemed to get invited anywhere. Spencer did, and he had his little best friend who ran away from Graham with him. And the worst part was that she didn't blame him. Graham was so awful.

The word was "repulsive."

And yes, she felt guilty for finding her own brother repulsive.

⁓

When she was in grade school, kids asked Marci why her mother's hair was white if she wasn't old. This made Marci angry, so she'd say something like, "At least she's not fat, like your mom." She knew her mother's looks were different, that platinum hair and straight, full mouth that often looked angry. But she knew her mother was beautiful.

When she was seven years old, she was over at the Barnards' playing Olympics, and she fell off the railing of their back porch. Kirsten told her that gymnasts always got back up on the beam. Maybe Kirsten hadn't noticed that Marci had bloody knees and she wasn't really a gymnast, either. Marci ran home and found her mother standing at the counter, her pregnant stomach straining against a print caftan, dry strands of her hair floating around her face like cotton candy. She pressed a hand against a scaly rash on her cheekbones. Marci said, "You look so ugly, Mommy. And fat." Kathryn burst into tears.

That was the first time Marci realized that children could hurt their parents.

⁓

Gentry pulled to the curb in front of her father's house. His face was a mask, but he swallowed so hard that his Adam's apple bobbed up and down. Dad came right out with Eve and the boys. "You made it!" So friendly, even.

Gentry hopped over the side of his Jeep and held Gretchen's hand while she climbed out. Marci was left to get out on her own, which was fine. Eve was all smiles, so glad to meet him, showing off her gravestone teeth. Spencer took Gretchen's backpack and Graham gave her a sideways shove that nearly knocked her over. Gentry raised his eyebrows. Graham was yelling the rules of some game at Gretchen that she HAD to play, she just HAD to, she had to play that game RIGHT NOW.

"Hey," Marci said. "She doesn't feel good. Knock it *off*, Graham."

Eve scurried off to referee.

Of course, Dad insisted on having Gentry in. Gentry squared his shoulders and walked up that flagstone walkway, up the stairs and through the massive double doors, both of which Dad had left open in welcome. Yes, welcome to the Lord's Manor, serf.

What a pissing match.

Gentry looked like a prisoner out on work release coming to trim the hedge, but he took stock of the house, the view, the furniture, the art, the rugs. He swallowed more, the muscles of his jaw clenching. His face got harder and harder. Dad smiled. There was a long pause. Standing there in his formal living room, her father said so much without words. See what I have, see who I am. Will you ever have any of this, be any of this? Go back to the shack beside the home I don't need with the woman I don't want, you insubstantial, grubby teacher. That's what her father was saying, and Gentry heard him.

Marci wished she didn't.

Eve, having restored peace, entered the room and smiled. "Would you like something, Gentry?"

Gentry frowned at her for a moment. Thinking. "Could I have an apple?"

An apple? Gentry never asked for food. He was embarrassed, Eve was baffled, and Marci was dying. Because Eve's teeth were false, and Gentry could tell, and that had to be what made him ask for an apple.

Eve brought him an apple.

He took an aggressive bite and sat down on the dining room table, he put the butt of his worn-out jeans on a twelve-foot stretch of mahogany and bit and chewed that apple. He and her father talked a little about audio equipment options. But soon, Gentry just focused in his single-minded way on the apple in his mouth. "This is one great apple, Mike. This is maybe the best apple I've ever eaten." Of all the things in the house, the apple got the compliment.

Eve smiled. "It's a Hood River."

And then Gretchen, unable to hold out, came in and wrapped herself around Gentry in a hug that made her father's face deflate. Gentry hugged her with all proper care and restraint, patting her back, quickly cupping the back of her head with his giant hand before she let go of him and took the rest of his apple. She walked away, finishing it. Eve ran after her to retrieve the core before Gretchen set it down on something expensive.

Dad swallowed. Gentry smiled. "Take good care of Gretchen, Mike. She's been sick."

Dad made a big deal out of loaning Marci his cell phone, "just in case." "I'll get it tomorrow night when I bring Gretchen back." There was no cell reception at the coast, but whatever. She took it to shut him up.

⁓

They took the curves down Vista and the city stretched out below them to the river, which was where Portland stopped existing for Marci.

The word for Portland was "beautiful."

"What did you think of Eve?"

"She has beautiful hair. But . . ." He shuddered. "He left your mother for her?"

"It was complicated. Graham's only six months younger than Gretchen. I know you tutor all the kids in calculus, so you can probably do the math on that one."

"And your mother used to live in that house?"

"No, we never lived in the Heights. Mom didn't want to. She considered it 'excessive.' It was one of the ten thousand things they fought about. We lived down the hill in Northwest."

"Will you show me?"

"I guess." It was weird that he wanted to see, but she was secretly thrilled.

⁓

"Why do new owners have to change everything?"

He stared at the house for a long time. Up the street, down the street. He took some time looking at the cars, which weren't usually anything special in this neigh-borhood, even though some of those houses cost almost as much as anything up by her dad. Finally he said something. "Lots of stairs."

"I fell down these stairs once when I was three. Mom ran all the way to Saint Vincent's with me. I had a concussion." She could see her mother, crying, running, holding her. "That's how her legs got so buff, packing everything up and down those stairs. And she used to, like, actually run."

He cleared his throat, embarrassed. Well, he had to have noticed. Her mother's official drinking costume was leggings and a T-shirt, and in leggings, it was clear that her legs were still great. But her mom had been wearing that official drinking costume a lot lately.

"That's a perfect porch."

"We had a porch swing. Mom would sit out here and watch me ride my Big Wheel up and down the sidewalk. Shut up, Gentry, I'll bet you had a Big Wheel, too."

"I didn't."

"That explains the Jeep." She stared at the front door. "I wish you could see the inside."

"We can come back another time."

"Promise?"

"I promise. What time is it? I need to get the car in."

⌒

Gentry consulted with the service writer, gave detailed instructions, left her dad's cell phone number in case of emergencies. He looked back on the Jeep one last time. "The Jeep will be fine. And think about the CD player. It's the only *way*, Gentry. Now, let's get some lunch."

This was her favorite neighborhood. She couldn't understand how her mother could ever leave it. She pointed to a metal fire escape. "My mother used to live there. She would lie out on that fire escape in a tie-dyed bikini. She grew pot out there, too."

"Your mother grew pot?"

"She says everyone grew pot back then."

"What year?"

"1970. The year you turned two, right?"

"Yes." He had a really funny expression on his face.

"Here's one of the places she used to work. It was a vintage clothing store that sold clothes to hippies." He stopped, peered in the window like he'd see her mother in a flowered dress and army boots, hair frizzed out, turquoise rings on all her fingers. "My mother was a flower child. She even has a little tattoo on her hip of a . . ." He opened his mouth, pressed it shut. Marci guessed he didn't want to hear about her mother's butterfly tattoo.

And then they were at Papa Haydn. A friend worked there, Kirsten Barnard, and she seated them. Kirsten was one of her Roxaboxen friends. Her family lived near Dad and had a house at the coast near Mom, one of those funny relationships that balanced between all Marci's worlds. But things had been a little weird between them. Kirsten had asked Marci to fix her up with someone "coastal" the summer before. She'd wanted to sample those rough boys she'd been hearing Marci mock for years. Marci fixed her up with Trent. He was tall and cute in a coastal way. He was also stupid.

They'd all gone to a kegger and sat on a log by the fire. Kirsten kept talking. She was witty, silly, sarcastic to Trent. She made fun of the music, the brand of beer they drank, what people were wearing. Trent gave Marci a look, like, thanks a whole hell of a lot. Marci shrugged. Garret sneered. *Is there a switch or something?* He looked at Marci, hard. *Could you maybe shut her up, now?* Kirsten laughed. She thought that was a joke. A coastal joke. She kept talking. Garret said something low to Trent, and they laughed. It was not a nice laugh.

When Kirsten was drunk, Trent dragged her off to his truck. Marci watched it bouncing up and down, thinking, that's my friend in there. I should do something. Kirsten was smiling when she got out of the truck, a stunned smile. She could hardly walk.

Welcome to the coast, Kirsten.

She made Garret take them back to her house.

Kirsten was upset that Trent never called her. She was even more upset when she found out she had gonorrhea. The entire episode was completely grotesque. Especially, Marci thought, her part in it.

"Marci, what are you doing here?" Kirsten spoke a little too loudly. She kept sneaking glances at Gentry. "Are you at your dad's? Can you go out tonight?"

"No, I'm just here for the day. Gretchen's up at Dad's for the weekend. I'm just showing Gentry here the old neighborhood. Gentry, this is Kirsten, Kirsten, this is Gentry."

"Gentry! I've heard SO MUCH about you."

Oh god, Dad and his big mouth. Did he tell Eve? Had Eve told the neighborhood about what was supposedly going on? And now, a sighting.

Gentry looked confused. Kirsten looked a little embarrassed. "I'm sorry. Do you want to start with coffee?"

"Yes. I'd like a short double half-caf nonfat mocha, one pump shy on the syrup, no whip, and foam the milk a little."

"Got it." She wrote that down. "And you?"

"Do you have just, um, coffee?" He smiled as he said this, and Kirsten's face lit up.

"You mean drip? Of course. Today we have hand-roasted Sumatran and fair-trade Guatemalan."

He gave Marci a direct appeal with his eyes.

"Give him the Sumatran."

"Cream?"

"No thanks." She floated away in her Danskos.

"Hey Marci?" She'd never seen that particular expression on his face. "Does that girl think I'm your mother's, um . . ." He let it sit there.

"She does. Because of what you did at Christmas."

He went a little pale.

"You know, when Dad came to pick us up? How you put your arm around Mom? Do you even remember doing that?"

"Um. Yes. I get it."

"Well, it was hilarious at the time but it gave Dad the wrong impression." He actually started to blush. "Does it embarrass you that much?"

"No. I'm thinking of her. Your mother. Being, um, embarrassed by me."

Marci looked at him. Really looked at him.

He had on a white thermal shirt with a stretched-out neck, tucked into his jeans. He wore his jeans loose and there were holes in the knees and shreds and threads around the holes. His belt was old and worn out and black, and the buckle was pulled over to the side. His ancient brown work boots had white salt rings on them from the beach, and one was coming apart a little. His plaid flannel cotton shirt, untucked and hanging open, had strings hanging off the cuffs and big frayed holes in the elbows. If the holes were any larger, the shirt would have been short-sleeved. The thermal shirt had holes, too, and his elbows showed. She wondered if his knees and elbows got cold. He'd topped this all off with a trucker cap. He had the cap on backwards, and some random hair stuck out through the gap over the adjustable strap.

That was what he wore to work every day.

All he needed was LOVE tattooed across one set of knuckles and HATE across the other, and a Camel straight, and he'd be right at home taking donations at the Goodwill drop box.

This was going to be hard.

"Gentry," she said, as sincerely as she could. "You look fine. Really. You look just fine."

"You think so?" He brightened a little. He took off his hat and ran his fingers through all that hair. Marci thought maybe he should put the hat back on.

"Yes, don't worry about it. What do you want to eat?"

Kirsten stepped back up to the table with the mocha and "just coffee," ready for their order. It was bad enough before, but when she saw him without the cap, she staggered a little at the shock of his outrageous male beauty.

Absurd.

"The usual, okay?"

"Sure." She turned to Gentry. "Do you want to hear the specials?"

"Specials? No! I mean, I'll have the first one."

"But I haven't told you what they are yet."

"That's okay. I'll just have, um, the first one you were going to tell me about. The first special."

"What, are you psychic?" She walked off, giggling.

"So, do you have a problem with specials, Gentry, or were you flirting?"

"I was not flirting."

"You were too. And everybody's going to hear about it, and everybody's going to be jealous of my mother's imaginary relationship."

He stared out the window, and took a sip of coffee. And then, the expression on his face. The word was "rapturous." "This coffee is *amazing*." Was he going to pray about it? Marci heard a little gasp from the woman at the table next to them. She was just *staring* at him.

Oh for god's sake.

In Portland, it always took longer for the coffee than the food. Kirsten set down their plates. Gentry did his little prayer, then stared at his plate. "Hey Marci? What, um, what *is* this?"

She checked it out. "Well, this is radicchio I think, and some fennel root, maybe this is jicama, and these are peppercorns . . . this looks like raspberries." He snorted in disbelief, dangerously close to the edge of outright laughter. "But what's this? Did you taste this? Is it some kind of meat, or fish maybe? It smells like fish. It looks like Spam, doesn't it. I think you call it a terrine. What's this brown stuff? Is this some kind of custard?" She poked at it. "It's firm. It's like, meat Jello or something." She gave him a brilliant smile. "I'm sure these are all members of the four basic food groups." She picked up the lemon wedge and squeezed it all over the plate. "There, does that help?" He let out a thunderous sneeze, followed by a clap of laughter. And so did she. And neither of them could stop.

Kirsten appeared. "Everything okay here? Is the special okay?"

"Special *what*?"

Gentry threw three twenties on the table and rolled to his feet and out of there, holding his stomach with laughter. Kirsten handed one of them back to Marci. "I'll take the salad back to the kitchen. Tell Gentry I'm sorry he didn't like it."

Marci wiped her eyes. "It's okay. He's okay. He's fine."

"Oh, he's fine all right. Where did your mom *find* him?"

The woman next to them smiled like, yes, tell me. Because I want one, too.

Marci thought about her dad's face at Christmas. She thought about all her mother's smug, bored friends. Talking about her mother and her divorce and how absurd it was that they lived in that shabby place at the coast, that falling-down second home full of hand-me-downs because her mother was too proud to spend her divorce settlement, how she was renting out her guest house of all things, and now she was actually *with* that scruffy young teacher. Marci could set it all straight.

She could see him through the window. Gentry waited on the corner, and the eyes of every woman in the restaurant were on him. Marci was pretty sure the eyes of every woman who walked past (and at least half the men) were on him, too. And they weren't watching him because he made them worry about whether or not they'd locked their cars.

He really was that beautiful.

"He came out here to set up the computer science program at my high school.

He's the best teacher I've ever had. He's so brilliant. He's read everything there is, and he fixes his own car. And he's wonderful with Gretchen."

"Your mom is *so* lucky."

"Yes. She is." And wasn't it true? Her mother was lucky. And she would also kill Marci if she had any idea what her daughter had just done for her.

⌒

She gave him his twenty and half of her sandwich, which he ate in two bites. It looked like she'd just made a homeless man's day. Other people were going to start handing him spare change if they didn't get out of there, so she took him by the arm and steered him into Music Millennium.

Gentry bought CDs with warning stickers on them. He even managed to buy music in an amusing way. He knew which songs he wanted, but not by title or artist. Only by the melody. He sang a little, and then the clerk joined in, and then they got a two-part harmony going, and then the clerk said, "OH! That one!" And one of them ran over, grabbed it, slapped it on the counter. It was like a game show.

That Jeff Buckley CD was on the pile. "Gentry, you already have this."

"I wanted to listen to it on the way home."

"Then what will you do with it?"

"Give it to you?"

"I do NOT want this." She put the CD back in the rack and held out her father's cell phone. "Call the place and see if your car is done." Though he'd clearly never used a cell phone before, Gentry was delighted to play with such a gadget.

⌒

He hummed as they walked, a musical preview of those new CDs. But would he sing along with the foul words? Marci wondered.

When they brought out his Jeep, all ready to go, the technician wanted to talk to him a little about the ancient wiring, some suggestions for updating it, making it safer. Listening to them, Marci was possibly the most bored she'd ever been in her life.

He paid with a debit card so there was something to sign, and he had to "um, borrow a pen, if you have one?" because the only writing instrument he ever carried was that old mechanical pencil he used for the crossword each morning.

The girl behind the counter had a head full of the tiniest brunette ringlets. She kept shaking around those curls, and a few other things. Please. She couldn't be any older than Marci. She was cute, though. When she pushed his receipt back to him, there was a little piece of paper with it, one that said, "Call Me! Angie!" The "I' was dotted with a heart. "Anytime!" Again, the heart. Her phone numbers were there, both Home! and Work!

He smiled, but when she turned away, he crumpled up her number and put it in an ashtray in the waiting area. "Gentry, she was really cute. I loved her hair."

He shook his head. "Too much punctuation."

He grumbled about Oregon's self-serve law all the time he was hunting down a station. "I don't see why they won't let you pump your own in Oregon. These kids track gas all over your vehicle. They forget to put the cap in."

"I don't know. My dad turned down a job offer in Seattle because he didn't want to have to pump his own gas."

That made him laugh out loud, his bark of a laugh, and the warmth she felt when she heard it was even more ridiculous and unwanted than the ache she felt when he walked around without a shirt on.

Ridiculous.

The attendant came up to his side quickly, but Gentry jumped out anyway. He wanted to at least take out his gas cap. He stood, hands jammed in his pockets, lips pressed together, supervising the gas pumping process. He put in his own gas cap.

A woman next to them asked the kid to check her tires.

He shrugged. "Sorry. I don't have a gauge."

Gentry slapped Marci's knees out of the way, and got a gauge out of his glove box. He met the woman over by the air pump and spent five minutes getting everything pumped up. She looked okay to Marci, even if her hair was a color never found in nature. A little old for him. The woman gave him a card.

When he got back in the Jeep, he handed over the gauge. "Would you please put that away?" Marci stowed the diagnostic instrument in the proper place next to the ice scraper, the emergency flare, the flashlight. Yes, there was a First Aid kit in there. The woman pulled away, making a little telephone pantomime through her window, like "call me."

The word was "desperate."

He politely waved. As soon as she was down the road, he threw the woman's card out the window.

"That's littering."

"She drove a Tempo."

~

On the highway home, Gentry sang along with the swear words. He loved to drive. She imagined him driving across the country, leaving a little trail of rejected women's phone numbers, like Hansel and Gretel going into the forest.

And the trail led right back to her mother's house.

FEBRUARY

Kathryn

She'd had the phone calls from her friends, now ("Kathryn, what are you *up* to?"). Her misadventures had been broadcast to a select group of women within a small radius of the present Mrs. Mumford ("Please, Kathryn, I *know* you. Quit *lying*."). Originally, the news remained geographically isolated to the West Hills, but it leaked into Northwest via 23rd Avenue, traveling up us far as Forest Park like a rare and fatal African virus ("Kirsten says he's absolutely *beautiful*."). The word on Vista Avenue was that Kathryn Mumford was seeing someone closer to Marci's age than her own. She was forty-six. He was twenty-seven. Despite her icy denial of any involvement ("Oh Kathryn, come *on*. You can tell *me*."), the amusement she currently provided was considerable.

The idea of it.

He was so *young*. Everything about him announced this. The state of his clothes. The enormity of his feet. The length of his hair. The volume of his Jeep. It was loud before, but since he'd had that CD player installed, the entire vehicle reverberated.

So young.

But Michael had been young once, as well.

⁓

One night, over a year after her parents died, Kathryn had asked Michael to drive her to the old neighborhood. He'd given up trying to get her into bed, moved on to other prospects, but if she wanted a ride somewhere, all Kathryn had to do was ask.

He let her direct him without asking questions, maneuvering that old Karmann Ghia past the houses tucked up on their small lots, the bushes trimmed, walks swept. The neighborhood was clever, like one of her father's plays. Her parents' home was still tidy. The neighbors must have been helping with it, though she'd never asked anyone to do that. She just paid the taxes. But it was that kind of neighborhood. Wood-handled hedge trimmers and push mowers were sharpened up and put to work helping out the widowed, the sick, the bereaved. The orphaned.

Michael followed her to the front door. Painted red, of course, though it was peeling a little. He kept his silence as she felt around by the mailbox, found the loose board, the key. The house smelled vacant.

She led him through the small front room with the white hearth and impeccable red sofa. The galley kitchen opened to the left, with its glass jars of staples, pine cabinetry unmarred by hardware, the nook, the indestructible table and chairs. On the red Formica of the tabletop sat a wooden bowl of wooden fruit, covered with that fine white dust particular to closed rooms. She inspected everything, suspicious and hopeful, but found no fingerprints.

She checked the sheets on the sleigh bed. Taut as a drumhead, just as she'd left them. Her mother's tiny knitted slippers sat side-by-side on a rag rug, her white-blonde hair threaded the bristles of the ivory-backed hairbrush on the dresser. A saucer beside it held a small pile of change from Pieter's pockets and their wedding rings. His wallet, that sleek bit of folded leather, had been tossed nearby. Lynne's smart little handbag hung on the closet doorknob. Every artifact remained exactly where Kathryn had put it.

In the hall, she peered at the photos. Searching. Her parents laughing, their expressions so similar that they might have been brother and sister rather than husband and wife. Kit wearing her outlandish little garments, white-haired and blue-eyed.

Michael tried to put a hand on her hair. She ducked away.

She reached for the rope in the ceiling and pulled. Michael gently moved her aside to finish the work of unfolding the attic stairs. They climbed into the realm of her mother's sketchbooks and boxes of patterns and neat shelves of unused fabric, organized by seasonal weight. The big Bernina resided in one eave. A dressmaker's form haunted the other, draped with a project that would never be finished.

Michael stooped low, waiting. He could not pretend to be interested in this room. The arts of women were invisible to men.

The last room held a twin bed with the metal frame painted white. A crib waited in a corner. She'd never let her mother put it away. She spent her childhood waiting for a sister. She was Emily, so her sister would be Lavinia. But Lavinia never arrived.

Rage pricked her eyes. How could they leave her without so much as a sister?

Michael put a hand on her shoulder and she flinched. He tipped up her chin with his hand and met her gaze with fierce eyes the color of a Chinatown jade bangle.

Listen to me, Kathy. They're not coming back.

He pressed her to his chest as she struck him. He picked her up and lay her down on the bed of her childhood, where he carefully, gently made love to her while she wept in fury and loss.

⁓

They bought their place at the coast while they were still renting. Well, Kathryn bought it. She wrote a check out of the insurance money, the first of it she'd spent. The place at the coast was all hers. She took her time, sorting, evaluating, choosing what to bring. The Nordic silverware, the old pots and pans, the wool blankets, the vivid Scandinavian rugs that probably belonged in museums. The long red sofa with its superior hardwood frame and elegant lines. The dressmaker's dummy moved to the garage. When her nana died, she stuffed the back of the Volvo with knitting supplies, sweaters, hand-carved wooden bowls, an eggbeater, that silly souvenir spoon collection. She tied the table and chairs on top and drove back to Oregon.

Certain garments were deemed worthy of storage in cedar-lined chests in her room and closet. The wooden rocker was in Gretchen's bedroom with the old iron bed. Kathryn slept in her parents' sleigh bed, something they never let her do while they were alive. There had been a box with her father's scripts, the photos, family papers, Nana's prayer book. But Kathryn was afraid she'd lost that box somewhere.

It took time to arrange it, to get it all right. Michael was patient as she evaluated every jar, every book, every dishcloth. And when she was done with the last selection, the final arrangement, he quietly disposed of whatever was left and sold the Burlingame house. They used that money to buy their grand Craftsman in Portland.

Michael was always so good at taking care of things.

Somewhere in there, they'd married in a meadow. But with all his careful planning, Michael hadn't timed things quite right. He was furious when the judge decided that both properties and all her remaining insurance money were Kathryn's assets. The judge awarded her a huge settlement, besides.

Kathryn had everything. Everything but Michael.

Michael was never coming back, either.

⤾

She was standing in her driveway smoking a cigarette and scanning the sky when he pulled in. He had to cut the engine to hear her. "You'd better watch the volume when my girls are in that thing with you." He nodded, vaulting over the side of his Jeep. The window in his door shook when he slammed it.

"I need help with the storm windows."

"You're worried about the weather?" He smiled and frowned at the same time while looking up at the sky. It was warm, beautiful. But this was Oregon.

"The weather reports say an Arctic front is on the way, and this is the month for sou'westers. That's a bad combination. If you're too busy to do it, I can hire someone."

"I'll do it right now." He peeled off his T-shirt and threw it in the Jeep. And she led him, shirtless and ready, to the airtight and carefully arranged garage.

The windows were neatly stacked inside. "They're all marked."

He studied a penciled notations on a frame. "SSUR?"

"South side upper right."

"Oh. I get it." He carried them out one by one, and set each window against the correct wall. Kathryn got busy cleaning them as he went after the ladder.

He climbed the ladder, wrested away a screen. She watched the muscles in his stomach and arms as he brought it down and leaned it against the side of the garage. He lifted a clean storm window and climbed again, straining with the effort of carrying a wood frame filled with heavy old glass up a ladder. His face went pink, and the color in his torso rose steadily.

He climbed that ladder eleven times. Two windows for each bedroom, one for each bathroom, and three more for Gretchen's windowseat. She had trouble keeping up with her rag and her Windex. If she wasn't quite done washing the window when he was ready for it, he stood beside her and panted softly, like a dog. Sweat rolled down his shoulders into the small of his back, but she didn't believe he was really exerting himself. He was too young, too strong for this to wear him out.

After he finished installing the storms on all the lower windows, he hosed off the screens and put them away in the garage. He hosed off the side of the garage. And then he hosed himself off, a trail of water, sweat and dirt running down his back.

He pulled his shirt on and stood waiting, hands on hips, his face flushed. Standing there like a Greek god, too immortal to be tired. She wanted to tear him apart. "Don't forget to coil up the hose."

He gave her a look of pure outrage.

She got in her car and left for the liquor store. How had it even happened? How had this particular humiliation happened to her? She'd been hurt and furious, raging at Michael. How dare he take her children away on Christmas. He had *other* children, he had two *boys* he could celebrate with. She only had her daughters, and he was taking them away.

Gentry had come into that kitchen and found her crying. He'd wrapped his arms around her, hushed her, held her. His intentions, she was sure, were pure. He wanted to comfort her. He'd looked so good, so pure. She'd convinced herself that he wasn't a beast, but that's what he was. A perfect, innocent, tireless beast. And so young.

And only one thing would comfort her.

It was just one night she'd asked for, not stopping to think what it might mean if he stayed. *Could I just have one night?*

The way he said this in her ear. *Whatever you want.* He carried her up the stairs, lay her down in her parents' double bed.

You'll have to be careful with me.

His voice so low, it was almost a whisper. *I'll be so, so careful with you.*

⌒

Somewhere in that one night, she'd finally fallen asleep. When she woke, he was propped on an elbow above her, looking down. Looking down, watching her, and how many years had it been since she looked into eyes that held that for her? Reverence. Desire. Gratitude. When a tear rolled down her cheek, he brushed it away.

She'd tried to explain, what it felt like to nurse Gretchen, how she thought that was the end of anyone needing her, the pain of feeling like her physical life was over while this baby used the body that no man would ever want again. She described how it felt when the milk came down, like tiny hammers behind her

nipples, and how it made her breasts hard and hot, and Gretchen's pink mouth
would clamp on and pull, and the milk would pour out so fast that she would
choke, but then she would settle in, and Kathryn would cry, feeling like a husk
even as she fed her baby.

And he fixed on her eyes and groaned, and fell on her one more time.

She was amazed. Was there no end to it?

He fell back and looked at the ceiling. *Okay.* His voice was soft. *That actually
hurt.*

She knew she was going to be unbearably sore, too.

Gentry? How long has it been since you did this? Tell the truth.

He looked up at the light fixture. *I always tell the truth.*

Well? How long?

He let out a sigh through his nose. *A long, long time.*

A long, long time. But not, she'd wager, as long as it had been for her. *Were
you actually in the monastery, Gentry? I mean, were you a monk?* She had to ask,
because of his strange emanation of purity.

He quietly studied that light fixture, which Kathryn only found remarkable for
its midcentury banality. *No. I have never been, nor will I ever be, a monk.* His eyes
sank shut in immediate, exhausted sleep.

She allowed herself the luxury of examining his face, the masculine jaw, gen-
erous brows and straight nose. She lost herself in the precipitous architecture of
his cheekbones. All of that symmetry balanced on a strong, smooth neck with a
pointed Adam's apple. As beautiful as a man could be without being feminine.
Looking at him made her shiver.

She crept out of bed to shower away her exertions and remedy her hair's inherent limpness with a blow dryer. She put on a warm robe and yes, just a bit of
makeup, all right? She went downstairs to start some coffee, and glanced out the
window.

Bosco looked back. He was in the Jeep, and he couldn't get out because the
cover was on.

That poor dog.

After she let him out, and watched him go on the tire for an obscene length
of time, she took him into the little house and filled his bowl with kibble, which
he finished in several slobbery moments. Was she supposed to give him more? He
gulped a bowl of water, then jumped up on the bed and turned around. He lay

down with an old dog groan that sounded reproachful. She patted his massive, shaggy head. She apologized.

It was a cold morning. When Gentry woke, he'd want his robe. She looked around to find it. Not difficult, since he owned perhaps ten things. She looked around, realized how immaculate the place was. He actually had all the proper cleaning solutions stored under his sink, and they'd been used. Impressive.

She put the robe on over her own and went outside to smoke another cigarette. Her eyes were open to the ocean's beauty that day. She pressed a hand to the soreness between her legs and shivered.

She was bruised by beauty.

⁓

He was singing in the shower when she came back upstairs, a low tenor swelling out clear and fine, with occasional rough-edged tones Kathryn's best voice instructor would have called "woody." But still, good enough for training. Another surprise, another hidden part of the mysterious man.

He came out of the bathroom in all his young glory. And though she wanted to resist, though she longed to hold her robe shut and make small sounds of protest, her pride kept her standing still. She didn't want him to see her skinny back, her empty breasts. She didn't want Gentry, so perfect, to see her, so old. But she let him make her naked, she allowed him to look at her body in the cold, clear light of day.

His eyes were gentle with what was left of her.

He tried one last time to kiss her, but she ducked away, knowing how foul her mouth would taste from smoking.

She let him lay her down and finally let him kiss her somewhere else.

She cried. She cried because she was tender. She cried because the truth was, she'd always hated what he was doing to her as much as she loved it. When she reached that unbearable place, balanced on the edge of orgasm, she wanted to fight him, to push him away and fight it. It was painful and precious and she never wanted to do it again. He kept his hands on her hips and gave her no choice. It rolled through her body like a wagon riding over her bones, breaking her over and over and over.

There was no end to it.

He pulled himself up to the top of the bed on his elbows. He rolled onto his back and collapsed beside her. His eyes were closed, but that smile. She lay a hand on his hammering heart. *You're so very pleased with yourself.*

I waited all night for it.

Then I guess you win. She was determined to retaliate, but when she moved down, he groaned and rose up on his elbows.

Hey Kathryn? There is a limit.

So you're saying five is your limit?

Five? It was five? Awe in his voice. *No wonder I hurt.*

She lay her head on his taut belly, studying his exhausted implement of destruction. Unbelievable. She wished she could sketch it, but sensed he might object. His big hands were gentle, patient in her hair, but under her ear, his stomach sounded like breaking timber.

Are you hungry?

No, he said softly. *I'm starving.*

⌒

Was that it, then? The circumstances of her life, which seemed so uniquely humiliating, so profoundly devastating, barely registered, really. Just one infinitesimal point on the incomprehensibly huge graph of human despair. She was supposed to put this all in perspective and get over it.

She couldn't get over it. She would not be relieved of her anger. She'd lived on it for ten long years. And a beautiful young man who could efficiently install her storm windows was not enough for what she'd gone through. His sweetness would not cure her. She would not allow that.

She knew she was beginning to verge on caricature. An angry divorcee by the sea, the woman set aside. The starter wife. Didn't she used to be more than that? She remembered being angry as a girl, angry at her parents for their closeness. Angry at her classmates for their banality. Angry at the war, and the establishment. When was she not angry?

She'd been more than her anger. She had her voice, her journal filled with poetry and sketches. That's who she was in college, the promising soprano who sketched. She'd been creative. Could she revive that? Her voice was shot, so she could take up painting. Or pottery. She could invest in a wheel and throw haphazard little vessels to present to her friends, a handcrafted place to stash their pencils.

Poetry was her other great love. Possibly she could publish some bitter little chapbooks of excruciating confessional poetry. Or sewing. Her mother had never taught her to thread a needle, but with time and some classes, she could learn to make lumpy pictorial quilts that pieced together a narrative of her healing process.

Wouldn't that be quaint.

She pulled into the parking lot, hit the concrete parking guard, killed the engine. The nausea might kill her.

Relief was in sight.

The familiarity of this door soothed her. The pneumatic resistance. The clanking chime of the small brown bell attached to the handle. The shelves and shelves of bottles. The current of air that smelled of nothing but dust and old carpeting, really, because glass and cardboard hardly had any smell at all, and what she came for was tightly sealed.

The clerk had carefully styled hair and a gin blossom nose, his legs thin, his stomach tight against a shirt with snaps, a large turquoise ring on his right index finger. "Afternoon, Mrs. Mumford. Let me help you." This was Duke. Before his collapse into his current life, Duke was probably attractive in the way of a workingman who knew his way around a woman. And he was still a knowing man. He knew exactly what she'd come for, what and where and how many. They were all creatures of habit, and Duke knew hers. It was graceful, the way he packed her order, handled her debit card, smiling all the while. His chivalry comforted her.

She left with her anger and her liquor replenished. She would need both to make it through the storms ahead.

Marci

Marci stared out the window at her mother, who was staring at Gentry. She knew her mother had this great reputation now, thanks to her imaginary affair with Gentry, but she looked like a vulture out there. Stop staring at him, Mom. Go to the liquor store already. Good, go.

She went.

The door opened. "Hey. Is there any coffee?" Thank God he'd put on his shirt.

"I think so. Help yourself." She affected a casual lean against the counter and snooped through his mail. A bank statement. A special appeal from the Society of St. Vincent De Paul. A lumpy letter from the local food bank. The food bank? Didn't they feed him enough? An ivory letterpress envelope looked personal.

He washed up, disposed of the unsanitary towel, drank three glasses of water, and sat down in his dry shirt and wet jeans at the table. His hands were shaking. "I think I gave myself a hernia."

"Will you be able to lift this?" She handed him a hot cup of coffee and his mail. That hint of a smile. "I think so. Thank you."

"Why, you're welcome, Gentry. My pleasure. Anytime. Really, it's no trouble at all to serve you." He ignored all that, he didn't rise to the teasing occasion. But, from what she understood, Gentry didn't rise to any occasion. She heard Garret laughing, his gleeful words. *"Darlene says he can't even get it up."* Marci supposed that was why her mother rejected him.

But what a waste.

He opened his mail at the table. Would it even occur to him to get his own mailbox? To keep his mail private? He frowned at his bank statement, and because he left it right where she could pick it up, Marci read it too. "This is ridiculous. Do you *ever* spend any money?"

"Gas. Library fines. Insurance. CD player. Car payment." He was still a little out of breath.

"You can afford some clothes, Gentry. Buy some clothes. What's that from the food bank? Do you need more food or something?"

"Information about volunteering." He scanned the letter. "They usually need people to drive around and pick up donations."

"You can't volunteer there. Everyone around here uses the food bank. It would embarrass your students to have you give them their free food." Especially Garret.

He shrugged. "I always volunteer somewhere."

"Why don't you shelve books at the library. None of your students ever go there."

More than a hint of a smile, this time. She'd gotten to him.

He finally came to the letter. It was clear he recognized the sender. His face lost the flush and went a bit pale, and she wondered who could have sent it. He set it on the table and let his huge hand hover over the envelope, as if he could divine the contents with his fingertips.

"It's going to kill me if you don't open that. I mean it. I will actually die, right here."

He slid a finger under the flap. A flat card with a piece of parchment over it, a folded note. He read them both.

He set it all down in the middle of the table and pressed his hands to his eyes.

She picked it up and looked at it so she wouldn't have to look at him. It was an engraved birth announcement on handmade paper so elegant and crisp, it looked edible. Someone named Ariel Rossetti Shaw had been born on January ninth. There was a short letter on similar paper in full, slanting handwriting.

Hey, Gentry.

How are you? Do you love Oregon? I always did. It has to be better than Detroit. I never understood just exactly what you were doing there. Sandy said it was probably penance, but I'm glad you're in a better place.

So all of a sudden I have a baby.

She has my red hair and Daniel's eyes, and no freckles. I intend to raise her under a parasol. She is covered with golden fuzz, and I remember, when I look at her, what you used to say about peaches. Babies are magnificent. I suppose you'll never do this "family thing."

Dan says "hey" and "send money." He asks after the "teaching thing," and asks how the "uncle thing" is going. How is Bosco? When are you coming to visit? The Sandersons aren't that far away. Well, they are, but you could manage to see us all. If you wanted to.

I miss you, Gentry.

Yours,
Becca

When she looked up, he was staring out the window and drinking his coffee, looking, well, fine. He seemed just fine. Maybe his eyes had been hurting from, oh, she didn't know, maybe the altitude up there on the ladder while he was putting up the storm windows.

"Who are these people with the weird names and expensive stationery?"

"Friends from college. This is their first baby."

"What are you going to send them?"

"I don't give presents."

"You should at least send a card. Mom will have one in the buffet. She has cards for everything in there."

She brought him a stack, some as nice as the birth announcement, but he quickly set those aside. He didn't want to use her mother's "good" cards. He looked through a group of cheap postcards sent to her mother by some charity. They all showed fine art of women and children, and Kathryn had never used one of them, but she liked them enough to keep them.

She held out a Madonna and child. "Don't you want that one?"

"Every picture of a mother and baby is a Madonna to me."

"Seriously?"

He smiled and nodded. And that thing in her sparked and hummed, that connection.

He finally selected a woman holding a red-haired baby painted by an Impressionist and carefully printed out a message on the back with his mechanical pencil. She immediately picked it up and read it.

Hey to all. Congratulations. I love the name. I wish I could smell her. Please send a picture so I can eat my heart out.

I'm teaching in Oregon. Bosco is fine and loves it here. We live right above the beach in a house the size of a dorm room. It feels roomy to me because I don't have to share it with anyone but Bosco. We watch the sun fall into the ocean every night, unless the clouds make that impossible.

My uncle is fine. I saw him over Christmas.

I guess I need to get to work on the wife thing and then maybe the family thing will follow.

> *Kiss her for me.*
> *Gentry*

"This is fine. But, I mean, Ariel Rossetti? Do you actually love that name? What kind of a name is that?"

"She was probably named after the spirit in *The Tempest*."

"Or the Disney movie."

"The what?"

He was so unaware. "*The Little Mermaid*? The redheaded mermaid in the Disney movie?"

He shook his head. "Becca loves Shakespeare."

"Okay, well, Rossetti?"

"Christina Rossetti was a poet. Her brother painted the most beautiful women I've ever seen."

"Really? What does a painting by this Rossetti person look like?"

"Like Becca." He smiled. "Becca has hair like Easter."

Easter hair? All Marci could think of was that nylon grass in the bottom of the baskets. That stuff was usually pink or green.

"Where did you go to college?" He mumbled the name. "Really? That's a good school."

"And you sound surprised."

"If I'm surprised, it's because you have a job here. Will I go off to a good school and end up back here?"

"No. You're not staying here. Colby's a fine school. You'll love it."

"I doubt it. I'm used to being the smart one."

"Hey Marci? Are you afraid of academic rigor?"

"Absolutely. I've never experienced any, and I'll be at school with kids who went to preps."

He laughed. "Don't be too worried. I went to a prep."

"Seriously? Where?" If she was shocked by the college, she was more shocked by the prep. Her mouth actually fell open. "That's a really good school." She tried to picture it. Gentry at a prep. Him at her age with short hair, wearing a navy blue blazer, crossing the quad, taking Latin, playing lacrosse and crewing, whatever it was they did at preps. "Was it like *Catcher in the Rye*?"

"Full of phonies?" He smiled and she did too, feeling that crackle of recognition. "Not so much, Marci. Things have changed. But when he goes on about everyone cutting their toenails? That part is the same."

She stared at this smooth skin, how it stretched over his cheekbones, and wondered if he'd ever had a pimple in his life. "What were you like back then?"

"Short. I was really short and I didn't talk very much. I liked math."

"Math? You liked math?"

"I liked the security of math. How . . . orderly it was. That was important to me. Then I had to take advanced chemistry, and it was all over between me and math."

"Advanced chemistry in high school? Was college boring after a school like that?"

"Boring? No. I tested out of enough classes that I was almost a junior when I started college. They put me in advanced classes. It was . . . stunning. Everything about college was stunning to me, in the sense that I walked around in a state of stupidity most of the time." He swallowed hard and stared out the window. "I made great friends."

She knew Gentry hadn't made too many friends in Oregon. Coach Gilroy, ugh, there was an intellectual peer, and her mother, but she was way too busy drowning herself lately to be much of a friend. He didn't have anyone to talk to, not really. Marci knew how that felt. But what if no one at Colby would talk to her, either?

"I wonder if Colby will be stunning. I guess if I bomb out, I can come back here."

"You won't bomb out." He reached over and took her hand in both of his. He had such big, square hands. "Marci, it will be a change, and it won't be easy, but you'll rise to the challenge. You'll still be the smart one."

"Promise?"

"Promise."

They sat there for a minute, quiet and calm. Marci wanted to sit in that kitchen forever, her hand pressed gently between the hands of a man who'd read Salinger, who understood college, who appreciated her sarcasm, who believed she'd always be the smart one.

The word was . . .

Her mother's car lurched to a stop in the driveway. Marci pulled her hand away. They watched as Kathryn almost fell down trying to jam the car door shut with her bony hip. She slammed into the kitchen carrying a bottle, looking for knives to throw, a head to tear off, or maybe just a glass. She had on black leggings and a dirty sweatshirt, and Marci wondered how long it had been since Kathryn had washed her hair. The best part was that her shoes didn't match.

"I hate that heap of a car. Carry in that box in for me, would you?"

The air in the kitchen was silent and still, like someone was going to say something important. Gentry gave Kathryn one long and furious look.

He gathered up his mail and left.

Gretchen

Gretchen hated going to her dad's. Eve was stupid, Graham was mean, Spencer was always running off with his friend. And her room was pink.

Gretchen's brothers had regular rooms in colors that were not pink, as did Marci. Gretchen wondered why she had to suffer with pink. Eve had always wanted a girl, that had something to do with it.

Her dad was always trying to get her to talk. She never talked to her dad.

She'd insisted on staying at the coast for the weekend, but Gentry had gone off somewhere that morning without her. When she came outside after he got home, he was busy putting up the storm windows. That was not interesting. She went down to the beach with Bosco, but Gentry hadn't come down to the water.

She should have just gone to her dad's. It wasn't like anyone cared that she was home.

Gretchen climbed up the steps, Bosco huffing up ahead of her. At step nineteen, she could hear her mother screaming at her sister in the kitchen, and her sister screaming back. She listened to them scream for twenty-five steps. The back door must have been standing open. She couldn't stand to look at either of them. They were so much alike.

She sat down in the driveway with her back to the laundry room wall. Bosco settled beside her, groaning a little. He stared at Gentry's door. Gretchen stared, too. She thought if she stared hard enough, that Gentry might come out. She decided to test it as a hypothesis.

He didn't. He could probably hear her mother.

She considered knocking on his door. Marci had given her another lecture about how Gentry was a man, and men had to have time to be "private." She spoke slowly, like she thought Gretchen couldn't understand what she was saying. No one thought she understood anything. Anyway, she highly doubted that he was in there being "private" with all that screaming going on.

She lay her cheek on Bosco's broad back and looked at the world sideways. It wasn't really an improvement, sideways. It was different, but not any better.

"Do you ever hate everyone?" Bosco started to snore. He probably hadn't ever hated anyone in his whole entire dog life. She wrapped her arms around his broad back. The wind started to really blow, and she blinked against the grit it kicked up. Her sister and mother had finally stopped screaming. Gentry's door was still closed.

She decided to go make soup.

❧

She was making what her mother called "garbage soup," so she looked through the fridge and got out everything that needed using up. She washed it and chopped it and sautéed it and added some frozen turkey stock from Thanksgiving. She stared at the vegetables swirling around, all the separate things trying to be one thing.

The wind was really blowing. Gretchen hoped all the boats were in, which they probably were by that time of day, so she shouldn't have worried. But she did worry. She even worried about Garret a little. If he died, he wouldn't bring over any more fish.

She wanted Marci to come downstairs and call her an incompetent dork who cooked as stupidly as she dressed. She wanted her mother to come downstairs and call her an "industrious little duckling," to tell her that garbage soup was "just the ticket" for a stormy night. The house filled with the delicious smell of onions and celery simmering in salty stock, but no one appeared to eat it.

She felt like there was no point. No point to soup at all.

❧

It was dark out and Gentry's lights were on. She watched him through the window in his door, ducking under the table to get his boots, hitting his head on the table as he stood up. A regular man would have sworn, she knew that from observing just about any male she knew. When a man hurt himself, he swore.

Gentry didn't swear. He sat down on the bed, rubbing the back of his head.

Gretchen had made Gentry buy socks in December because none of his matched. He said since he always wore boots, he thought it didn't matter. She told him that even if it didn't show, it mattered. They went to Fred Meyer and he got six pairs of gray socks so that when he started to lose them, the leftovers would match. That was her idea.

He told her she was brilliant.

She stood outside in the dark and watched through the window while he put on one sock, one boot, one sock, one boot. He tied his boots and stared down at his feet, looking so sad. His boots were pretty sad. But not that sad. He put his hands over his eyes. His shoulders rose up and he started to cry so loud that she could hear him over the ocean. It made her throat hurt to hear it.

This was the most terrible thing she'd ever heard in her life.

She opened the door. He held up his hand like "don't come in," but she had to, there was no way she could just let him cry like that. He rolled to his side and put a pillow against his face to hide it, and she sat down beside him.

Crying was probably private. What did you say to a man when he cried?

So she did what her mother did, and said what her mother said. She rubbed his back. "Go ahead and cry. It's okay. Just cry." It was the strangest thing, but when someone gave you permission, you usually didn't have to cry anymore. That's what happened to him. He lay there, very quiet and still.

Her stomach hurt so much that she wanted to curl up in a ball beside him, but she didn't. She sat there until she heard his breathing change, until he was asleep. Whatever made him cry, it wasn't about her.

Bosco jumped up on the bed and lay down next to him. Bosco would take care of him.

The wind sounded like someone crying.

Kathryn

Kathryn found it absurd that he wouldn't give up and come in. The temperature dropped thirty degrees in one hour. Gale force winds ripped away whatever they could. Those winds had teeth. The power kept browning out.

He stayed in his little house.

He was afraid to turn on his computer, so he used her phone to check in with his uncle. He took the receiver into the laundry room and sat cross-legged on top of the dryer with the door closed, but she could hear him. He talked, laughed, sometimes argued. Kathryn had no idea he kept in such close contact. Were they doing this with the computer? Gretchen said yes, they were. "Every day, Mom." What were the chances he hadn't talked about Kathryn? But after those conversations, he went back to the little house.

Still, he stayed in his house.

And then, the ice came. The power lines sang and snapped. Trees fell, tipping up in tangles of root and earth, taking down more lines, blocking the roads. The phones failed. The cars stayed in the garages. Four-wheel drive, chains, nothing works on the glaze of a silver thaw. The boats stayed lashed up at the docks.

In the main house, they had a gas hot water heater that they could light manually, fireplaces in the living room and Kathryn's bedroom, firewood, lanterns, candles, stocked shelves. They were prepared. Gentry had no power, no heat, no hot water. He had no plan.

Bosco, being a smarter animal than any human male, moved in first.

One evening, Gentry knocked. He never knocked. Kathryn opened the door to his stony, whiskery face. He was shivering. "Hey." He held his little assortment of toiletries. "Gretchen said you had hot water?"

"Yes. Do you want a shower?"

"Please." She took a lantern and led him up to the girls' bathroom, started the faucet, put out towels. "Thank you, Kathryn."

"You're welcome. You're welcome to stay at the house, too, you know. It's too cold out there."

"I just need a hot shower." The steam curled around them as he waited for her to leave.

She closed the door behind her and stood in the hall imagining him in there, peeling off his rags, moaning at the hot spray, leaning back under the showerhead, his white form behind the frosted glass, the arch of his back, the patches of dark. She gave herself one minute to indulge in visions of what she wouldn't be touching or seeing.

She went downstairs to avoid disgracing herself.

It was a long shower. Long enough for Gretchen to settle everything. When he came down, warm and shaved and relieved, Gretchen smiled and pointed to his sleeping bag on the couch. "You're staying here, dummy."

He didn't argue.

⌒

The downstairs hearth had a hook and a removable grate, and both were put to work boiling water for coffee and oatmeal in the mornings. Lunch and dinner were cooked in old black cast iron pot that had been Nana Marit's, a pioneer artifact with a spiraled metal handle and three short legs. It could hang from the fireplace hook if Kathryn wanted to heat up canned chili or soup, or sit in the coals if she wanted to bake johnnycake. The girls roasted hot dogs on long metal forks, setting buns to toast on the grate. The cuisine was a little on the summer campfire side for Kathryn's taste, but most of her caloric intake was liquid.

At night, Kathryn built a fire in her bedroom hearth and braved the icy sheets alone, while the kids set up camp in front of the living room fire. Kathryn left her door open so she could drink quietly in her room and brood upon their every word. And every word was harmless.

He instructed Gretchen in the fine art of marshmallow toasting. "Pay attention. I have a system."

"A marshmallow system."

"Yes. The secret is patience, and turning."

"I thought you couldn't cook."

"Coffee and marshmallows, that does it."

"How nutritious." Marci told Gentry she really liked those yellow sweats. "They are so magnificently ugly. I wonder where I could get some."

"I can ask Mel. They were his."

"Great. Priest sweats. That's dead sexy."

"Don't I know it."

It continued in that mode. Endless, harmless teasing. Gentry asked Marci if Garret would be giving her dead fish for Valentine's Day. She said yes, and she'd give him yellow sweatpants. He laughed low, Marci laughed loud, Gretchen laughed last, a high harmony to theirs.

They told ghost stories. Gretchen's involved animals and were never all that frightening, eventually becoming mired in evolutionary detail. Marci's always featured a comic reversal. Gentry's were the best and the worst. He was capable of beautiful turns of phrase while telling stories, which didn't surprise Kathryn. She knew he had poetry in there somewhere. But his ghost stories were absolutely terrifying. It took her a few listens to understand that he was simply telling fairytales. The strangest, most macabre of them.

They told their ghoulish yarns, heated cider and popped corn. Kernels flew out and Bosco chased them and they laughed, they all laughed. Having fun. Kids, all of them. Bosco settled by the fire. Gentry zipped into his bag. Marcialin and Gretchen on the floor below him like kids at a slumber party. "It's not fair that you get the couch."

"I'd be uncomfortable on the floor."

"Right, because old, skinny people need to sleep on something soft." Thumping and squealing like children while she stayed in her room alone. Kathryn's fires were haphazard, undependable. She could have asked ask Gentry to make a fire in her room that would last the night. She drank, alone.

She was trying to live what was left of her life as a block of ice in an ocean frigid enough to allow her suspension, floating forever in Arctic latitudes, only the glacial hardness of her frozen parts buoying her, allowing her to keep her head above the black waves that churned against her, calling her down to the tempting depths of oblivion.

But she kept popping up like a stupid cork.

⟋⟍

When she was a child, they had driven to Minnesota twice a year. The winter trip was always a near-death adventure. Her father wrestled the car through blizzards, black ice, the senseless lunges of starving deer along the highways. No one ever suggested that they might spend Christmas in their temperate home state.

When they arrived, Nana Marit transformed Kit. She braided her granddaughter's hair and wrapped the braids around her head, dressed her in garments she remade every few years, consulting Lynne over the phone as to her growth. Pieter would laugh. *She should be driving a team of reindeer in Lapland!*

Yah, you're right. Nana took that as a compliment. She insisted that only her native garments would make Kit impervious to frostbite.

Kit ran out into drifts as high as the modest houses. The neighbor kids accepted her instantly. With her skin, hair, eyes, and Nana's outlandish winter wear, she was one of them. They knocked loose icicles, waged slush ball wars, stole candles and made snow caves. They slid and slid and slid, screaming in frigid velocity. They were children of ice.

When her mother came to take Kit in, she would protest. *I'm not cold! I'm NOT cold!* Lynne was all business. She pulled off boots that were as full of snow as they were of feet. She tugged off hat and scarf and mittens, knitted in ragg wool in Nana's even chain stitch, inches thick with crusted rime. She unbuttoned the boiled wool jacket, the pants that could stand alone, retaining Kit's shape. She rolled down the long, grey socks with orange stripes that reached her daughter's thighs, left from a dead grandfather. Last were the cotton tights and turtleneck.

And then Kit was cold. Her fingers, ears, nose ached. Even her teeth hurt. Her bottom was so numb that she couldn't feel it when she sat. Nana Marit wrapped her in heated blankets, sat her in one of her creaky kitchen chairs near her combination electric and wood-burning cook stove. She set cup after cup of hot chocolate before Kit, urging her warm from the inside out.

Sometimes, she would let Kit play with her spoons. She'd never been anywhere, but she had racks of souvenir spoons on her walls. Anyone who ever went anywhere brought Nana Marit a spoon.

Kit ranked them by beauty, by ugliness, by size. She alphabetized them. All the states, most of the major cities, immortalized by flower or bird, an inaccurate engraved map, some tiny, geographic totem. A boot for Texas. A cable car for San Francisco. Nana seemed to have a spoon from every tourist destination. Virginia City, the Grand Canyon, the Trees of Mystery, the Empire State Building, the Statue of Liberty, Wall Drug, all the Washington D.C. sights.

Nana could tell Kit exactly who brought every spoon, and when. *The Swensens brought me that one when they went to Idaho in fifty-four. They went to a place where you can pan for your own gold. That right there's what a real gold nugget looks like.* Kit studied the plated lump. In her mind, it was authentic gold that the Swensens had sifted from a stream, so she handled that spoon carefully.

A penny for your thoughts, Kittycat.

Nana always gave her a real penny when she said that.

Kit swore to Nana Marit that when she was old enough to go places, she would see the world. *I know you will, that's for sure.* Nana smiled, her eyes misting. *You'll go everywhere in the world, Kittycat.*

And I'll bring you a spoon from everywhere. Kit sipped cocoa and imagined a wide world just packed full of commemorative spoons for her nana.

She never sent her one.

She never returned to the Iron Range in December. She and Michael visited once before Marci was born, and he hated it here, hated her quick little grandmother with her cold blue eyes and hunched back. But Gretchen would earn the same inclusion that Kathryn did with her white-blonde hair, her pale, unsettling eyes. Kathryn's eyes. Lynne's eyes. Nana Marit's eyes.

Gretchen had never laid those eyes upon the winter regions of her mother's secret heart.

She heard Gentry say, "Bosco's tired. Hush." They all went quiet at his command.

Kathryn lay in the cold and listened to the crack of logs in her fireplace. Outside, she heard the snap of freezing wood, tree limbs breaking away from the trunks. Burning, freezing. All the same. It was sap that made trees vulnerable.

This wouldn't last forever. The cold would lift as suddenly as it came. The weather would warm, the ice melt, the world thaw. The earth would reel under a false spring. Everything and everyone would forget it was still winter.

Almost everyone. Kathryn wouldn't forget.

She knew the winter was there.

Gretchen

The TV startled Gretchen. It had been so many days since she heard it. But there it was, blaring away about the roads, the fallen tree branches.

"The power's back." Marci sounded confused.

"Great!" Gentry rolled up his sleeping bag. "Thank you!" He went out the back door with Bosco, smiling. Gretchen stared at the floor, biting her lip.

"Thank God. If I had to listen to one more night of him snoring, I'd die."

Gretchen hated Marci. "He doesn't snore. Only a little. Sometimes. You're the one who snores."

"Oh my god. Get over it, Gretchen. Is it that awful, just having our family here?"

She ran up the front stairs and into her room.

The windowseat had always been her favorite place, but that day, it was just one more place where Gentry wasn't. She wanted the electricity to go out again. She wanted to have her birthday by the fire. Her mother wanted her to invite somebody for her birthday dinner, someone her own age. Right. Who would she invite, anyway? Gentry was her only friend, and he was back out in his house.

She hated electricity.

Hoan-Vu

I guess you could say that I've been pretty instrumental for old Gentry in getting his network set up. That's why I'm so hurt, no, I'm devastated, that's what I am, by Gentry's lack of response to my latest idea. I think Gentry needs to approach things in a more innovative way. Grades are fine. My "A" was fine. But I think Gentry should explore bonuses, you know, cash incentives. Money is a motivator, and I'm trying to explain this to him, but he's not taking me seriously. In fact, he seems to be getting angry at me. He's sort of abusing me, actually.

"Shut up, Vu. If I graded on effort, you would have an 'F.'"

Now, this hurts. He denigrates my effort. Who followed him around, carrying boxes and watching him drop things all last semester? But I take into account the general listlessness and disrepair of Gentry, and I decide to cheer him up. I offer him one of my chips.

"Get that food out of the lab RIGHT NOW or I'll make you clean every keyboard in here. I mean it."

Okay, maybe I need to think a little harder.

Gentry is trying to get us students to brainstorm, to come up with an idea for our web page. I have several ideas. I suggest that we upload the entire yearbook, thereby saving thirty-five dollars per student. Marci is not as impressed by the innovative nature of this idea as I had hoped. She suggests that we post the school paper.

"Excellent, Marci. Did you hear that, Vu? That's what an idea sounds like." Fine, fine. I have other ideas. Tiffany, for one. She's talking, oh, to Gentry as usual. She's a beat late, she's back at the yearbook idea. She's asking if we can sign the Internet, "Can we sign the Internet, Gentry?" She loves to say his name aloud almost as much as I love to say hers.

I talk to her. "Tiffany, no, we cannot sign the Internet in that sense you mean with the Magic Marker hearts and smileys, no, we cannot, though we can allow people to leave messages containing hearts and smileys in a guest book. Tiffany, if you paid attention to the information imparted in this class, you would know that. I have an idea for a web page, one that even you would figure out a way to visit, how about 'gentry.com'? Would you like that, Tiffany?"

Gentry tells me to visit "shuttup.com." I do.

Marci speaks. "I know, we can put pictures of Vu and all his little friends up there. Virgins.com. How about that, Vu?"

"You can help me out with that any time you want to, Marci. By the way, do you like my new glasses?"

Marci rolls her eyes. "How many months can they still be called 'new'?"

"I need you and Tiffany to go work on the web page, now."

"Together?" Marci looks as betrayed as if he'd shot her. Tiffany is delighted because she's always happy to work with someone smarter than her on projects. So she's always happy because every single person in this school is smarter than her, to be honest, not that this detracts from her charms.

"Work on it together. This is a group project and you'll be graded on your ability to collaborate." The look she gives him. A normal man would hide behind his desk cowering in fear if a woman looked at him that way, but Gentry is implacably serene as ever, or maybe he's medicated, who knows, I don't understand this guy.

Speaking of help, Gentry asks for some. Or rather, he doesn't ask outright for anything. He waits until the girls leave, and then he quietly announces, "I could use some help, Vu."

Then, because I'm a sucker, and because he's pathetic, I ask, "With what?" And he outlines his problem. It's his boots. I think he must buy a new pair every fifteen years whether he needs to or not. You have to understand the look of this guy. A grunge reject wearing a cap with the name of a heavy equipment manufacturer on it. Sort of spoils the look, not that I think Gentry ever goes for a look, actually. He wears his jeans loose enough to appear gang-affected. And these boots. If he offered these boots to a Burnside bum, the bum would turn him down, I swear, it's pathetic. He's pathetic. And he wants boots. But not crappy boots, no. He tells me the brand he's after, and I study those boots hard. You mean, once, those twisted ruins cost hundreds of dollars? This boggles the mind, frankly.

This will require a trip to Portland.

∽

This is how I come to find myself in the grinding, lurching vehicle that Gentry favors. I understand everything, now, rolling down 26 and then over the Markham, my balls nearly shaken off my body by this rig. I understand the hat. Gentry puts on the hat, he climbs in here, and he's driving a tractor. And he likes it. What does Tiffany see in this guy? And of course Gentry has located the alternative radio station and tuned it in. I fear that station is going to provide the soundtrack for this entire excursion, even though Portland actually has some good radio stations.

"Gentry, have you been to Portland before?"

"Once. I drove the Mumford girls in." I do like Marci, but she typifies the west side mentality of Portland, Oregon. The west side folks stay over there. They know the east side exists but see it as composed of blocks and blocks of whores and crack palaces between the Willamette and the airport. The east side is beautiful. This side of town has character, style, danger, ethnicity, and some neighborhoods that make the one Marci's dad lives in look like the neighborhood my uncle lives in.

I point out to Gentry the landmarks of the east side skyscape. "To the left, please note the Portland Rose Garden, our new arena. In architectural style, it has been favorably compared to an open diaphragm case. As a backup, please note the twin receptacle tip condoms of the Portland Convention Center." I see Gentry laughing in spite of himself. Do I have birth control on my mind? I do. No action yet, but when the day finally comes, I plan to be prepared, educated, nothing is going to stand in the way of my chances with Tiffany, no way.

"How old are you, Vu?"

"Seventeen." Gentry ponders this. He's mulling it over, he's digesting this knowledge.

"When I was your age . . ." He trails off, possibly due to an awareness of the overwhelming lameness of that phrase. How long ago was Gentry my age? What can he possibly say that will have any relevance to the situations I face? Is he planning to give me some bullshit Catholic lecture on the sin of using of birth control?

He continues. "When I was your age, I guess I was incredibly lucky." And he laughs, laughs hard. Fine, rub it in, I'd wondered if he was still a virgin at the advanced age of twenty-five or whatever the hell he is because he sits in church every Sunday with that strange, ethereal glow, that virginal air. But, no, even Gentry was luckier than me at seventeen.

I figure Gentry is hungry because as far as I can tell, Gentry is always hungry, so I take him to the Saigon Kitchen. He tells me to order for him, fine, I start to, but as soon as I say a dish, he jumps in all excited, questions the waitress in embarrassingly bad Vietnamese about the ingredients, asks for certain sauces and sides. When the food comes, he's shoveling it in, smiling, smacking. Gentry is the king of chopsticks. He's better at chopsticks than I am.

This guy knows my mother tongue, and even with how badly he speaks it, I can at least understand him and that makes me curious. "Gentry, were you a feral wolf child raised by benevolent Vietnamese foster parents or what? Who taught you to mangle Vietnamese?" But he's too busy eating to answer. I don't mind if he talks with his mouth full, I have terrible table manners according to Mrs. Mumford, our coastal etiquette expert.

Finally, he says, "Neighbors."

"Neighbors?" He nods, chewing and chewing. He eats until all the food is gone, he pays the check, and when we leave, he carefully notes the location of the restaurant.

The parking lot of Lloyd Center is crowded, lots of people, the prospect of which seems to have Gentry cowering with fear. How did he survive in Detroit? He explains it's not the people, it's all the "stuff." I'm going to earn my lunch, I can tell you this right now. I remind him that he desperately needs boots, the irresistible allure of a new pair of boots gets Gentry into the mall.

Gentry doesn't even know what size shoe he wears, that's how helpless he is. No holes in his socks, though. That's a relief to me at this point. I marvel at the fact that a man can survive with the lack of basic knowledge that Gentry displays. He tries on three pairs, and I remind him to choose carefully as it will be twenty years before he gets another. I tell the clerk it is too bad they don't make Velcro boots for people like Gentry, and the clerk actually goes and finds a pair. Gentry is not amused. He won't even try them on. Boot choosing is a decision of enormous, life-confirming magnitude for Gentry, so I shut up.

He buys a black pair. He wears the new boots, and as he pays, I see that he has quite a bit of green in that runaway wallet of his, the one he keeps chained up. Over Gentry's protests, I instruct the clerk to toss, no, to burn the old pair. The clerk smiles as if nothing will make him happier. I think about the green in Gentry's wallet, and I am struck with inspiration.

I'm fucking brilliant.

Gentry has a dashing personal style that seems to involve rolling out of bed, groping around for whichever of his disintegrating garments are closest to hand, and dressing in the dark. He always has strings hanging from his cuffs and elbows and knees. His shirts are often incorrectly buttoned. He does manage to keep his fly closed, however. I'm surprised that he accomplishes this, because I think he chooses his clothing for its ventilation capacities, based on the amount of holes his apparel seems to have.

The problem is getting Gentry to go into Nordstrom. I push him, that works. My cousin Vinh is working, and I explain the situation. It doesn't take so much explanation, actually, a glance at Gentry says it all.

"This guy is a teacher? He looks like a fucking bum." Vinh thinks talking in Vietnamese is safe and before I can tell him otherwise Gentry growls, "I'm leaving." But we apologize, we calm him down. My cousin has some ideas.

We consider the Dockers option. He runs his fingers across the tiny front pleats with an expression of loathing. I see. A pleats phobia. I show him the flat front Dockers, but no, Dockers are now the Devil's work. We find some store brand flat front khakis, they cost twenty dollars more per pair because they're a Nordstrom store brand, but that's fine with Gentry as long as we have no Dockers. Fine, whatever. He insists on getting them two inches bigger than he needs. Frankly, I'm finding this difficult to understand. "Gentry, is this some kind of contingency plan in case you get really fat someday?"

He frowns at the pants. "They're not, um, finished at the bottom."

"That's because you have to put them on, and then the tailor hems them."

"Really?"

"Really."

"So I can get them as long as I want?"

I can see where this is headed.

We take the pants back to get them marked and I suffer the additional humiliation of seeing that under those rags he wears, Gentry is ripped. I mean, cut. I mean, hewn out of fucking Carerra marble. He stands there telling the tailor no, longer, longer. But at least they don't sag too badly, he has lost that aging white homeboy look, and I decide not to push it.

We fail to reach a compromise on jeans, but he is adamant. At least the new jeans have no holes.

We shop for shirts. I discover that there is an entire color family that inspires a physical rush of distaste in Gentry. Gold, mustard, orange, burnt sienna, these colors get a response stronger than the Dockers reaction. Gentry stares at a plaid involving these particular colors, and he looks like he might spew any moment. I remember the lunch, all that Saigon shrimp, and even though on this fabric it wouldn't show much, I decide to act. "It's okay, Gentry, here, let's look at the denim shirts, see? And here's some flannel. These are safe colors. Colors of nature. Colors of the rainforest."

Three denim. One of each dull color in the flannel.

All right, this is working.

I'm thinking turtleneck sweaters because maybe he can work that ponytail with a turtleneck and look artistic or maybe just gay, but that would calm the girls down a little. He shakes his head. "No turtlenecks. I hate that choked feeling." Well, then, a crewneck sweater. He frowns. "Reminds me of my school uniform." Well what about a V-neck? He frowns, suspicious. "I've never worn a V-neck."

Okay, sweaters are either violent, emotional or just too foreign. No sweaters for Gentry.

I do get him to buy a new belt, and anyone who has seen Gentry's belt, which might have belonged to a dominatrix in a former life, a busy dominatrix, would thank me. He picks a black one, and I suggest that while he's at it, he could get a brown one. He gives me that unbalanced look, and I see that Gentry has a brown belt phobia, too.

Whatever, let's just wrap this up, shall we?

My cousin brings out the hemmed khakis and mutters, "Where did you find this fucking loser?" He's getting a fucking commission, he can fucking shut up, he should be fucking thankful for this fucking loser. Gentry pays and my cousin thanks him. They should both thank me. And they could both give me some cash while they're at it.

On our way out, Gentry stops at one of the jewelry counters. He seems to be shopping for jewelry, which does not coordinate with the look I have so carefully wrought here today. The salesgirl is smiling way more than her puny commission would warrant because we're not at a fine jewelry counter, just a nice jewelry counter. They are head to head, talking over the bracelets.

Now Gentry's wrapping his fingers around her wrist.

When my esteemed educator encircles the bones of the salesclerk's slender wrist with his baseball mitt of a hand, their eyes lock. Something passes between them. Something, you know, special, something magical. Something I've never actually experienced while standing that close to a member of the fairer sex. I am basically not allowed to stand that close to any girl I know, but for some reason, Gentry can. I understand at that moment, that his innocence is a front, that this purity he radiates, those absurd clothes, that girl hair, it's all some kind of camouflage.

Gentry is a sex god.

It's a good thing they aren't on the same side of the counter. If they were, based on the amount of electricity in the air at this moment, the teacher I spend most of my day mocking for his ineptitude could move her hand behind her back, turn her away from him and gently bend her over the top of that glass display case. He could lift the back of her skirt, pull aside whatever expensive scrap of lingerie he found under it and push himself into whatever it had minimally covered. And he could do this without any objection from the salesclerk, or security, or other customers because it would be an act of such primal prowess that we would all stand there in awe and envy. And then we'd clap. Well, I'd also be taking notes, because this is a move that I myself have mentally practiced many times over on Tiffany and/or Marci, and I need all the pointers I can get to avoid a slap in the face for even touching a girl in the first place. No woman would ever slap Gentry.

He lets go of her wrist, and leaves her blushing like a startled virgin. He's buying a bracelet, she's boxing it up, smiling, handing him a little box to go in one of his large shopping bags, and get this, she gives him her card.

He puts the card in his shirt pocket.

⌒

We drive for a while, and it's getting dark. Gentry is quiet. I am frankly exhausted by the physical and emotional effort of steering this man around.

I'm turning something over in my mind as we head west, back to the land of empty crab pots stacked on tarry decks and exhausted women who work at motels who are obsessed with inculcating their children with the desire for an education and bars full of unemployed men who have failed to act as positive role models for their sons. I'm thinking that when it comes to Gentry, he could help himself to any woman in town.

I'm aware this privilege extends into the senior student territory I have (so far unsuccessfully) marked out for myself. Tiffany's modest intellectual attributes might not be all that appealing to a man whose most-visited Internet sites include the Walt Whitman Project, the complete works of some dead Arkansas poet, an extensive critical database for "The Wasteland," as well as www.ILoveJeeps.com. No, Tiffany is not his type. But Marci is twice as attractive as Tiffany, and she's scary smart. I could take some comfort in the fact that she appears to hate Gentry, but I remember how she despised Garret right up until the day she began spending her lunch hours making out with him in his truck.

He sighs. "Thanks Vu." That's all. That's all he says, but it is all he needs to say. In his own pathetic way, Gentry is a great guy. I am happy to help. I try to ask him about something I need a little help with, myself.

"Gentry, is there anything special you do, you know, I mean, specifically, to get . . ." I can't figure out how to ask this. I'm not talking about sex. I'm talking about getting a girl to notice that you're alive, and male, and that those two facts might add up and make a difference to her in any way. This guy, who I am sure has never done one thing in his entire life to get the attention or approval of a female, and if he has, he's probably done it wrong, has women falling all over him.

"Hey Vu? The woman thing is a mystery to me." He takes the card out of his pocket, flicks it out one of his unzipping windows. He doesn't know why he can get women, not any more than a lion knows why it can take down a gazelle. It just can.

"Gentry?"

"Hm?"

"You know those neighbors you had? Did they happen to be named Nguyen?"

He stares straight ahead out the flat windshield. "Yes."

"Great. Maybe they were cousins of mine."

And he laughs.

That's what I like about Gentry. He gets jokes like that.

Gentry

I never give presents. Ever.

I saw that silver bracelet with the shells and knew she would like it. I should have waited to give it to her. I should have known that Mike Mumford would take Gretchen on her birthday. He came *here*. He gave her another bike. He forgot that he gave her one last year. He *forgot*.

God, I'm failing the brotherly love lesson. Failing badly.

I wanted to take her out to breakfast and then to the kite shop. I wanted us to fly a kite. And then I wanted to take her to Broadway. I go down to Broadway all the time. I go to the arcade and play games and get bothered by students who can't believe I'm down there, but I like it there. Gretchen likes it too.

I know this, and Mike Mumford doesn't. He doesn't know anything about Gretchen. Even so, I knew that he'd take her there, not because he'd figured it out himself, and not because Gretchen would tell him, but because Marci told him on the phone where to take her. Mike Mumford had no idea, NONE, where Gretchen would like to go, what she'd like to do, or what she'd like to have.

I offer the second bike as proof of all those things. Amen.

⌒

Well, they didn't go to the kite shop. That was a relief. I didn't exactly follow them. I just went where I usually went, and they happened to be there.

The arcade was dirty, loud, dark. Mike peered around, disgusted.

Yes, this is it, Mike, this is what local kids do for fun. What do you expect? Your older daughter dates one of these kids. Have you ever even met Garret, Mike? Pick out a son-in-law, Mike.

Gretchen ran over and threw herself at me and I picked her up in a hug. He followed. "Hi, Gentry." He wasn't smiling. "You come down here often?"

"Hey, Mike. As a matter of fact, I do."

"I almost didn't notice you. You fit right in, don't you?"

Ah, not nice, Mike. True, but not nice. I do fit right in. You look like the idiot, for a change, instead of me, in your suit. A suit on a Saturday.

Mike probably had fifty suits, each of which cost more than my monthly salary. So, I did the math, I figured out that he had more money hanging in his closet than I'd made so far in my lifetime.

God, I'm failing, I am.

Gretchen had me by the hand and she wouldn't let go. Kids kept coming up to us, curious about the jerk in the suit at the arcade, saying "Hey, Gentry." Some kid said, "Hey, Gentry," again.

"I'm going to get some caramel corn."

"We are, too." Surprises, surprises. How did I know that Gretchen would want her favorite snack on her birthday?

We walked over to Leonard's Saltwater Taffy Parlor, home of the world's finest caramel corn. That's what Gretchen said, and she was the smartest person I knew. The man behind the counter said, "Hey, Gentry."

"Hey. Three, please. Thank you." I didn't even have to tell him three of what. He knew, because we were regulars there.

No, put your wallet away, Mike, I can probably afford it.

We left.

"Was that Leonard?"

Gretchen was embarrassed. "Dad, everyone knows that's Joe. *Everyone* knows that."

Yeah, Mike, you idiot. In your suit.

Okay, God, I know. I'd seen her, she was fine and I should have left. But she was insisting that I go with them to the Tilt-a-Whirl, and she had hold of my hand, not his.

Gretchen and I had a counterweight body-flinging system that made a tilt-a-whirl car do a lot of tilting and whirling. I hoped Mike appreciated the partnership involved. We always rode twice, and the operators, usually students of mine, knew this. They said "Hey Gentry" and sent us around another time and we did our system. And she loved it, she laughed like bells.

I hoped Mike enjoyed the free second ride as much as we did.

He was turning an interesting color. But Mike wouldn't quit, no, he hadn't had enough. He said of course we could do the bumper cars, it was Gretchen's birthday, she decided what we did on her birthday. So we did the bumper cars.

I always took a blue car. Gretchen always took a red car. Mike and his stupid suit got into a yellow car. "No one takes the yellow cars, Dad. *Everyone* knows that."

Everyone knows the yellow cars get hit the hardest.

Gretchen and I had a system for the bumper cars, too. We kicked backside in the bumper cars, we reigned supreme in the bumper car arena. Those signs up about "No Ramming"? Those signs were not for us. We were above those signs, we were fearless, ruthless, we showed no mercy, not even to Mike Mumford.

Especially not to Mike Mumford.

Dear God, I didn't mean to break him.

I had to help him out, and the owner probably wanted to ban me from the place for ramming, yes, it was me, I did it, but I looked so repentant that the owner forgave me. I couldn't forgive myself. I expected Mike to flip out his lawyer's card, but there were signs up every six inches about "Ride at Your Own Risk." Right next to the "No Ramming" signs.

Her fine face was sharp with worry. "Dad, are you okay?"

He wasn't okay.

I drove his car back to the house. I wanted to take him to the hospital, but he said, "I'd like to retain my ability to walk, so I'll seek medical care in Portland. Just get me some Tylenol and an ice bag."

I had to go in to get them from Kathryn. I had to tell her what happened, and she gasped, said something about his herniated discs, and oh no, and what was he *thinking*?

Mike hobbled in. "Kathy, something's wrong with my car charger. Can I make a call?" Mike was in Kathryn's house taking Kathryn's Tylenol and using Kathryn's phone to call Eve. Not good.

And I am so sorry.

I sat in his car feeling ashamed of myself.

Marci came out to the driveway, arms crossed. She leaned in the window of her father's car. "How could you let my dad do something so *stupid*?" And I didn't defend myself, because I deserved it.

Sorry. So very, very sorry.

Marci followed me in her mother's Volvo all the way to Portland. I drove Mike Mumford's Saab. He reclined in the leather passenger seat, flinching, and I felt so bad, God, I'll back off, I'll get some perspective, I'll remember whose child she is, I swear, God.

God, I am sorry.

And Mike? This car is awfully nice. I'm impressed with the drive, the handling, everything. Impressed. Gosh, these windows roll up and down electronically. My windows just zip. These nice heated seats sure keep your backside warm. Your sound system is much better than mine, everything here is so much better than mine.

God, I am sorry.

He was nice, he would actually speak to me. I told him my sub-woofer was shorting out, and he wanted to know all about the sub-woofer situation.

Well, Mike, when I go over rough terrain, say at the driving beach, or on logging roads, ("You take that thing on logging roads?") the sub-woofer crackles.

And Mike was concerned, he recommended Northwest Cartunes to me, and it took his mind off his sore back to talk to me about the sub-woofer, to advise me, and I listened to his advice.

God, I am sorry.

And you know, Mike, what is it that you actually do? Because I'm not sure. Oh, you manage pension funds? Hm. I have a pension, I think. I'll wager there's a connection, and you can tell me about it, at length and in detail. As much as you'd like to talk about it, I'd like to listen.

Finally it was over, that drive with Mike, and I delivered him to a grim-faced Eve.

Eve, if you gave me something sweet to drink, I'd drink it and gag all the way home, that's how sorry I am about your husband.

I'm sorry, God.

"Mike? I'm sorry."

"It's not your fault."

I believe it is. I always will.

∽

Marci let me drive. She must have still trusted me a little. Or maybe she didn't want to drive over the pass in the dark.

We drove in silence. The pass was icy, but Consumer Reports was right, that wagon did fine, just fine. Marci stared ahead, partly because she hated me and partly because she was nervous about the ice. We passed the summit and began to drop, and the ice went away.

Oh God, I know, I'm a jealous idiot, more jealous over this eleven-year-old girl than I was when my friend married my girlfriend. God, I'll figure out a way, I'll devise a penance, I'll pay. I'm sorry. Amen.

I pulled in at a place called Oney's just to sit for a minute. I needed to go in and find the bathroom, because relief did that to me, but I was afraid that if I got out of the wagon, she'd drive off and leave me there. "I'm sorry, Marci."

When she spoke, she sounded far away. "When I was little, Dad used to take me down to Broadway and I'd beg to ride those bumper cars. He never would, ever. He always said if he got into one, he might not be able to walk afterwards. So I stopped asking." She sounded sad. "You keep apologizing, but it isn't your fault. He should never have gotten into one of those things. It's not your fault, Gentry."

She didn't know. It was my fault.

I need to make this right. Amen.

MARCH

Marci

Marci had always thought chemistry was science, but when she asked Gretchen about it, her blue eyes lit up with excitement. "It's math and science *together*. I have a couple books you could borrow." Her big brain ticking away, eager for the day when she could finally take chemistry.

The word was "brilliant."

Marci decided never to take chemistry, because math was the place where she'd finally discovered that she was stupid.

Garret wasn't stupid about math, even though he was stupid about everything else. He did math in his head related to the catch, and he was always poring over navigational manuals. He dreamed of learning how to use a sextant. That was all math. But Marci wasn't speaking to Garret that week, so she was in the dining room trying to do calculus by herself. It was going badly enough that she was actually considering asking Gentry for help.

As if he knew she was thinking about him, he appeared in a side window. He was dragging fallen tree branches around, clearing the paved part of the driveway that no one ever used. She heard him rolling open the garage door.

She went to the front door and opened it. Gentry had rolled out Gretchen's bikes. One was a little bigger, blue, the new one. He got out the red one from the year before, too.

Gretchen stood there with her arms crossed. "No."

"Just watch." He got on the red bike, which was way too small, and rode around in tight circles. "See? Easy." He looked absurd. But he earned a smile. Just a small smile on that serious little face.

He rode down to the end of the driveway where it turned into gravel.

Marci called out to him. "You can use my bike, Gentry, it's in the garage, it's bigger!"

"Thanks, but your bike isn't red!"

"Oh, right, Gentry, I understand. Not red, what was I thinking?"

She ran up the stairs to her room, past her mother's closed door. Her mother was "resting." Her mother needed quite a bit of "rest" lately. Marci came back down with her camera and took some pictures of him on that ridiculous little bike. He smiled, popped a wheelie. Would he smile so big if he knew she was going to put it in the yearbook? "You look like a clown!"

"Thank you!"

Gretchen stared at her, arms crossed, frowning. "Why are you even *out* here?" Oh god, Gretchen was starting to cry.

He put his face right down next to hers. "What's wrong? You can tell me. What's wrong?"

She spit it out. "I'm afraid to fall."

"I won't let you fall, Gretchen. I promise. I will not let you fall." But Gretchen stood there crying, so skinny and awkward and upset.

"Don't make her do this. It's too late to teach her. No one learns to ride a bike at eleven."

He smiled. "I learned when I was eleven." He pumped up the tires on the other bike, tightened the chains, checked the brakes.

"She's too uncoordinated. Have you ever seen her try to run?" Where was their mother? She could make him stop, because this was too painful. He needed to give it up, like Marci had last year. "Gretchen is just a brain on a stick. You shouldn't try to get her to do anything physical."

Gretchen wasn't crying anymore. Her eyes were like their mother's, so pale they took on the color of the sky, which was gray that day, low and cold. "Would you just go *away*?"

"No problem." Marci's stomach hurt a little as she sat back down at the dining room table. She kept her eyes on the textbook, willing herself not to cry.

She absolutely refused to cry.

When she let herself check again, Gretchen was on the new blue bike and he was on foot. They went up and down the driveway, her wobbling, him running alongside.

"Tell me when!"

"NOT YET!"

Like he was ever going to be able to let go.

Marci went into the kitchen and dialed Vu's number.

"Nguyen residence, may I help you."

"You need to come over here and help me with my calculus. Also, there's some kind of spectacle going on outside involving Gentry and a small red bike. I think you'll want to see it."

He cleared his throat. "I'd love to, but I have too much to do at home." She could hear his mother yelling, so he must have been in trouble for something.

"What could possibly be more important than helping me with my homework and watching Gentry be an idiot?"

"I'm on the shit list over here. I think need to stay home and use my tears to do the laundry."

"Please don't tell me what you're using to wax the car. I understand that you're on lockdown, but can you help me over the phone?"

"Sure."

She took the receiver into the dining room, that stupid yellow cord stretching across two rooms, and Vu talked her through it.

His mother's voice rose again in the background. "Listen, Marci, can I call you back in just a moment? I need to go defuse a potentially explosive situation, here."

"Like, a bomb?"

"No, just my mother."

"Sure, okay. Call me back, okay?" She took the phone back to the kitchen and opened the back door. They were riding down the driveway together, him on the smaller bike, her on the larger. Whenever she wobbled, he'd reach over and steady her. Gretchen grinned, the happiest grin in the world.

"The trick," Gentry called out to her, "is to speed up!"

"Speed up?"

"Yes. The faster you go, the easier it is!"

And Gretchen did it, she sped up and she was really riding that bike, riding a bike like a regular kid.

The phone rang again. She knew it would be Vu. "Mumford residence. Marcialin Lavinia Mumford speaking." Vu always laughed when she answered like that.

"The fuck?"

She sighed. "What do you want?"

"I called, like, ten times and it's always busy. Who's on the phone?"

"Me."

"Who were you talkin' to?"

"Vu."

"The fuck are you talkin' to *him* for?"

She hung up. Ten seconds later, the phone rang. It rang and it rang and it rang.

She watched Gretchen ride past, laughing and enjoying herself, her hair flying around in the sun. She didn't look hopeless and uncoordinated. She didn't look awkward. She looked perfect. "I guess you'll be all right," Marci whispered as her sister rode away.

She wondered if Gretchen would even miss her.

Kathryn

It began when Marci went under Kathryn's bathroom sink to borrow a tampon. "Wow. Can I take a whole box? Or three?" Kathryn hadn't had a reason to keep track of her cycle for so many years, she'd forgotten about it. But she bought a box of what she used, a box of what Marci used, two boxes a month. Gretchen did the same if she went to the store with Gentry.

There was a stockpile under her bathroom sink.

Kathryn called her doctor in a panic, demanded an appointment, threw on some clean clothing and drove to Portland. What kind of a middle-aged idiot, a front line soldier in the sexual revolution, a woman with thirty years of sex under her belt, no accidents, not one unplanned pregnancy, ever, what was wrong with her, what was she thinking, she felt so stupid, so unbearably stupid.

Her doctor scanned her chart. "Happy birthday."

"What?"

She frowned a little. "It's your birthday today." And then she smiled, kindly, placating, a perfect smile to extend to an insane woman. "Kathryn, I know you're worried, but this is what happens to women your age."

"We get PREGNANT?"

"Pregnant? You think you're pregnant?" She gave her middle-aged patient a fixed stare of disbelief and pity. "I don't mean to dismiss you. We'll make sure." And after the familiar, humiliating exam, it was clear that there was probably no reason at all for Kathryn to be afraid of pregnancy. "We'll draw some blood, check your hormone levels."

She waved away that idea. "Don't bother."

"Aren't you in a relationship? Menopause progresses in fits and starts. You could ovulate again in a year. We need to make sure there's absolutely no chance that you could *get* pregnant."

"There's nothing to worry about."

"If you're sexually active, there certainly is."

Kathryn stared at the doctor's capable, invasive hands and burst into tears. The doctor patted Kathryn's back and suggested hormones. Kathryn was perfectly ready to dry up, grow whiskers, blow away. Did she need to torment herself with the secret, humiliating hope she felt at the thought of a baby? Gentry's baby? She was forty-seven years old, twenty years older than the man she knew would be her last lover.

She would drive herself home to the museum of dead family possessions in which she lived out her toxic half-life, one bottle at a time. But she needed some cigarettes for the road, her monthly check was overdue and she had no cash. She drove up the hill to Strohecker's, where she could still charge to Michael's account. "A carton, please." She smiled at the clerk, who knew her brand. Without being asked, he started to write up the charge record.

"Kathy?" Only one person in the world called her that. He was behind her with a cart, which held three six-packs of beer. His eyes widened in surprise. "Kathy. That's so strange, I was just thinking about you."

What a ridiculous thing to say. Why would Michael be thinking of her? She was painfully aware of her straggly hair, the sagging knees of her cotton leggings, the fact that in her haste, she hadn't bothered with lipstick. "I just stopped in for some cigarettes."

"Well, I'm glad I ran into you. We need to talk." Which meant, of course, that he needed to talk. She would just stand there waiting for her cigarettes, invisible, while he delivered his state of the dis-union message. "Listen, I'm concerned about Gretchen. She's too attached to Gentry. I wonder if this is healthy, how attached she is."

The tone in his voice was unmistakable. "Michael. You're *jealous*."

"Well, sure, maybe. I'm her father."

"Yes you're her father, Michael. It's nice of you to finally *acknowledge* that." That was harsh enough to make the clerk's eyebrows jump.

"Jesus, Kathy. You're so bitter," Michael sputtered. "You've always been so goddamned bitter."

Her voice was a lethal hiss. "Do you really want to have a scene at *Strohecker's*?" She scribbled her name and thrust the pen and slip at the clerk.

"Did you just put those on *my* account?"

"Of course."

He threw back his head and let out one of the hearty laughs that had so endeared him to her in college. "Well, then. They're on me." He wiped at the corner of his eye. "Happy birthday. That's why I was thinking about you. Because it's your birthday. So happy birthday, Kathy."

She left the store before she started to cry.

Gentry

A child was alone, outside. A boy. The boy, dressed in nothing but a dirty white shirt.

The cold made his hands and feet blue, his teeth chatter. He shivered, he was cold and tired of being cold and he knew he had to look for a place, any place, to get warm.

He had to look in windows.

But she was there. She was there with an open door, naked, her skin like chalk, her eyes almost purple in the gloom.

Please make me warm.

Her hands pulled him inside to her bed, she was cold but that was warm and he stood before her as she rubbed his hands, blowing her breath inside. She blew and he grew and he was a man, older, no longer a child and he wanted that warm bed.

She smiled and pulled off his shirt. Her eyes went wide. He looked down.

Someone had written words all over him in a language he couldn't read, blue words all over his chest, his arms, his stomach, his thighs.

She traced the blue words with her fingers, with her tongue. "This is what makes you so cold." She took him into her mouth, her soft, urgent mouth. Please, come here, use your mouth to make me warm, I think I'm warm, I am finally warm, oh, oh.

Here I am.

He finished his thrashing, his kicking. She was over him, looking down on him, her mouth full of him. She spat it out all over the blue words. He was hopeful, happy, would this wash off the rolling, round blue script?

He looked down. Where she spat, all over, there were more. More cold blue words on him. Even more.

He froze.

❦

It was Saturday morning. I woke up, curled around the ferocious aftermath of a forgotten dream that demanded a quick release. "Bosco, get down." I nudged my dog with an elbow. "Get off the bed, Bosco. Now."

A little laugh rang like a bell.

That wasn't Bosco against my back.

"Gretchen?" Oh God, please, why was this girl in my bed? "You need to get out of my bed." She laughed again. "Gretchen, get out NOW. GET OUT."

She gasped, the smallest, sharpest sound of pain. The bed barely rocked as she left it. The door slammed. Hard. The window in the door was probably broken. A broken window and no lock, why did I even have a door?

God, if I were a good man, I would go after her. But I was only a man, and I wanted to do this first. It wouldn't take long.

I rolled over on my stomach and let out a groan at the contact.

The door *banged* open. "Knock, knock," she said, and "Oh, were you sleeping?"

No, why would I be sleeping? I didn't sleep, not there, not in my *bed* of all places.

I rolled over and sat up. "Marci, has it ever occurred to you that this isn't just a room of your house? That this is actually its own separate house? *My* house?"

She made one of her exaggerated faces. "God, bite my head off."

I pushed my hair off my face and counted to ten. "Sorry. What do you want?"

"Gretchen told me what she did. I'm really sorry. I'll have Mom talk to her."

The thought of this. This talking to her. "No, um, I'll talk to her. Or, actually, um, maybe both of us should. Your mother and I should both talk to her. But . . . can you give me five minutes?"

Why did I need five minutes? It was all the way gone, now. Probably permanently. I'd been awake for maybe four minutes. Four minutes, and the day looked like this.

Where could it go from there?

❦

That was how I came to be sitting at the kitchen table with Kathryn and Gretchen, hearing words like "appropriate" and "respect" and "privacy" leaving the lips of the woman I was ready to marry three months before. Gretchen hung her head and Marci smirked over the sink, enjoying this.

She did pour me some coffee. She was redeemed. Sort of.

Kathryn was using the word "boundaries." I disliked the word "boundaries," and I didn't think it made sense to Gretchen. I sipped my coffee. Silence. I looked up and Kathryn was staring at me. Oh. It was my turn to talk.

God, I would pray to You for words but Your silence is deafening.

I cleared my throat and swallowed. When I spoke, my voice sounded like I'd just woken up. Which I had. "Gretchen, you know I think you're pretty special, right?" She sniffed. She couldn't even meet my eyes. I had to clear my throat again. "And I like it when you come out and see me. It's the best part of living here. I'm always happy to see you. Always." She was really sniffing, then. "But I'm a man, and you're" (careful, think fast, get it right) "almost a young woman. So no matter how close we are, Gretchen, we have to have some lines. And getting into bed with me, it crosses a line."

She shattered right in front of me.

Between great shuddering sobs, she explained that she got in bed with her mom sometimes. And Marci. And when she was younger, she even got into bed with her dad and Eve when she was scared at night. "I like to sleep with people. It's just something I do," said Gretchen, hardly able to speak for her tears. "I'm sorry. I know you're not my dad. But you feel more like my dad than my dad does."

I opened my arms, my heart, my life. "Come here." She did.

I took her on my lap and rocked her while she sobbed, put my face in her hair and hushed her. I held her like Mel held that starved and hurting child with his thumb in his mouth. Oh, Gretchen, my Gretchen, forget the lines, I hate the lines, there are no lines.

Because I want you for my own.

⌢

It was quiet in that kitchen.

I felt a hand on my shoulder and looked up into Marci's concerned face. "Gentry? Do you maybe want some more coffee? Or something?" I shook my head.

Kathryn stared at me. "Are you all right?"

I wiped my eyes with the back of my hand. I felt like I'd been someplace else. "I'm fine, just fine."

I smoothed her hair and patted her back and carefully returned Gretchen to her mother. Just as carefully, I rinsed my coffee cup. I went home and back to bed, because I wanted the day to start over.

⌒

I slept until Mike Mumford slammed in my door and shouted, "HI!"

I flattened myself against the wall behind my bed in panic. He stared in amazement at how strange I was. "Sorry, didn't mean to wake you. Marci said you were up. I just wanted to say hi." I removed myself from the wall and sat down on the bed while he strode forcefully around the room, magnifying how small it was with how tall he was.

Why are you in here, Mike? We're not buddies. Your back is fine, I'm off the hook, God knows how sorry I am. I've done my time, I've confessed many, *many* venial sins, and we're even. But I guess you have a need to come in here and see what I have. This is it, this and the Jeep. Anything else I want in the world you're either carrying off to Portland for the weekend or you don't want anyway. Check out my books! Is poetry the secret language of your soul? Touch my computer why don't you? Ask me to explain why I have two printers, I'm sure you're fascinated with my scanner, yes, fascinated. I know, let's talk software and then I can ask you about investments and false teeth and Saabs and all the other things you have in your life in which I'm not interested.

"Hey, Mike."

He left.

"Bosco, you know you could bark at some of these people."

I heard his tail thump from where he lay in front of the refrigerator.

I got up and ate some cornflakes.

⌒

An hour later, I sat in my bed reading a library book, not attempting to abuse myself for once, and in popped Marci with her verbal knock. "Knock, knock." Was I "okay," of course I was "okay," she thought I was "so sweet" this morning. "You were so sweet to my weird little sister." Great. I was so tired of being sweet, especially to her. Who accused me of preying on her mother and then said sorry, like that made it all better.

"I hope Gretchen has a nice weekend at Dad's."

She kept telling me she wouldn't be home that night. Did I care? I knew where she'd be, of course I knew about that, I wasn't deaf at the school, and she thought I was so gullible that I believed she was staying with Tiffany? Maybe she was telling me I had a clear field in case I wanted to go up to her house later for some condescending rejection.

"Have a great time, Marci."

I ate more cornflakes.

⌒

Another hour. Another bowl of cornflakes. And in swept Kathryn, the smell of poison on her so strong that I craved a drink. She stared at me, her arms crossed. "I won't be *cooking* tonight."

What a grave announcement. "Okay."

She could barely stand, but she could sweep out, Kathryn in all her inebriated, unsteady, beautiful glory.

Excuse me, all I did was share the one night that you asked for, yes, you were the one who asked, and then I made the idiotic mistake of caring about you. Forgive me, I've left you alone, I've been polite, mostly, I have, and I put up your stupid storm windows, Kathryn you never thanked me for that, and on those nights in February when I slept on the couch, right below that bed where you, on that couch where you, Kathryn you drove the thought of any other woman out of my head, but you wouldn't even kiss me and I wish I hadn't done it, any of it, your bed and your windows, it's all stupid, stupid, stupid, and besides I'm *not hungry*.

Because *I have cornflakes.*

I was getting locks. Seven locks. And I'd sit in there alone and die of onanism and no one would be able to stop me.

Or maybe I'd just have some more cornflakes.

⌒

Finally, in came Lorrie.

"Saddle up, little buddy. Time to eat something besides cornflakes."

Lorrie Gilroy

Fishing sucked this afternoon. We didn't catch a thing, he couldn't even haul anything in, but that wasn't the point. The point was to get him out of that box of Bibles he calls home.

He out and out refused to go to the bar to eat. Which is good, I think. I've checked around his place, he doesn't have any booze stashed or anything, just milk in his fridge, cereal in his cupboard. I ask him is that all he eats, cornflakes, and he says, Sometimes.

Sonofabitching cornflakes.

So, no bar. We're sitting in the cafe. Nan's talking shit. "Why aren't you mighty fishermen home cooking up the catch?" Nan's kind of cute, for a skinny little tuna wench. Freckles and big teeth, smart, too, she gets the crossword done in about five minutes. Skinny and smart, what a goddamn nightmare in a woman. Gentry likes that Mumford bitch, so he likes nightmares. Maybe I can get Nan and Gentry fixed up.

Hell, it's worth a try. "Whatcha got, Nan?"

"Clams."

"Who the hell went out and dug those, Nancy? It was a five AM minus three or something like that."

"Gus was out there. With lanterns."

"Crazy sonofabitch. Well, he dug'em, so let's eat'em." She walks away. Gentry didn't even notice her.

Our clams come. I take a big whiff. "Hey, little buddy, what did God say after Eve went swimming in the ocean?"

"What."

"God says, Great, how am I gonna get the smell out of all the fish."

I crack up. Gentry doesn't. He's staring down at his plate, which I might add has twice the amount of food that mine does. "Look at that," I say. "A little custom sizing, there."

He does his little prayer, crosses himself, looks at his food. Usually, he chows right down on whatever I get for him. Gentry's poking at them, not so hot on clams tonight. I dig in, I love clams. These are big ones, though, a little too chewy.

He puts one in his mouth, chews and chews and chews like he's got a rubber band in there. Must be a tough one.

"Don't chew it all day. It's not like gum, you can swallow it." He tries, he kind of gags, and he chews on it some more. "You can spit it out, I don't care." The look on his face is making me sick, I swear. "Look, little buddy, it's either a spit or a swallow and it looks like that one's a spit." He spits it in his napkin. I flag down the tuna wench. "Nan, get these slingshots out of here and bring us some cheeseburgers to go."

It's good to see him smile.

~

At my house, I open the fridge and get us beers, but he shakes his head. He's on the wagon. Well, good. I turn on a movie. "Lorrie, I hate television."

"It's just a movie."

"I hate movies."

"Shut up and watch it." It's the stupidest movie I ever saw, the screwing isn't even any fun to watch because the woman's too damn skinny, but Gentry's scared to death.

"Do you need me to hold your hand, buddy? Cover your eyes? Do you want to sit on my lap? How about I pull this couch away from the wall so you can hide behind it?" He has to stand up and jump around a little during one part. It's a car chase. He doesn't blink once but he's as white as chalk. A big block Chevy ends up in the river, and he stuffs his hand in his mouth so he doesn't yell over it. It's a sonofabitching car chase. By the time it's over, as shook up as he is, I ask him if he wants to sleep on my couch, but no, he's ready to go back to the box.

"Whatever you want, little buddy."

On the way there, we talk about the morning. I want to make sure he'll be up because the Chinook are running and I want to get up the Kilchis River before every asshole and his brother gets there. I've got a feeling about the Kilchis, this year, a real good feeling. "So, I'll pick you up at Oh-dark thirty, little buddy."

"What?"

"Tomorrow morning?" He isn't even listening to me.

"Lorrie, have you ever been married?"

"What? Where the hell did that come from?"

He looks out the window. "Forget I asked."

Oh, hell, what the hell, I never talk about this, but he asked, so I will. "I was married for about ten minutes when I was twenty."

"What happened?"

"Well, I wish somebody would tell me, because I really don't have a goddamn clue. I got married thinking I was pulling up a chair to the biggest pussy banquet of all time. But let me tell you something. I figured out that the quickest way to kill a woman's sex drive is to marry her. Marriage for a woman is like Depo-whatever the hell you call it for a man." He doesn't laugh. Good, because it wasn't funny, at least when I was twenty. It tore me up.

"Do you have any kids?"

"None that I know of, Gentry, none that I know of." He looks at me like he knew I was going to say that and how the hell did he know I was going to say that? Is he a goddamned psychic?

I'm pulling up to his house, and Her Royal Highness' Volvo wagon is there. Maybe she's curled up in her coffin, afraid of the dark instead of the light. Gentry looks at her door and it's all over his face, everything's always all over his face. Bosco's there on the back steps and he's standing up, sitting down, making some dog noise. Opera, I hear that stupid opera. Loud music and a nervous dog. "Little buddy? There's a broken window up there." He jumps out, he's in there so fast, and back out just as fast, white-faced and tight-lipped. "Should I call Emmett?"

"No. Where's Short Sands?"

"Short Sands?"

"Just tell me where it is."

"I'll take you, it's not that easy." He doesn't know where the hell that is, how the hell would he find his way down the trail, hell, I better drive him.

Goddamn that crazy bitch.

Marci

Marci recognized his walk when he was half a mile away. Garret saw him too. "Look who's here. Faggot."

"Quit it." She'd have shoved him, but he'd have shoved her back. "Hey! What are *you* doing here?"

Gentry stopped just outside the ring of light made by the fire, shoved his hands in his pockets and rocked back on his heels. "Hey Marci? Can I talk to you?"

"I'm having *fun* here, Gentry." Garret threw him a beer. He caught it without looking and pitched it right back, which Garret wasn't expecting, so he dropped it, which made Marci laugh because she was high. Garret popped the tab and it sprayed everywhere, which made her laugh again. He held out the foaming can. "Hey Teach, this is a kegger. And keggers have rules. Have a fucking beer or get the fuck outta here. That's rule number one."

Gentry met her eyes.

"Marci. Come here."

$\backsim$

Coach Gilroy drove fast, dropped them at the back door and got out of there without coming in. Which was good, because it was bad. Her mother was splayed out on the kitchen floor like she'd been thrown down and broken. "Don't touch her." Glass all over the floor. Vomit and blood and glass. Opera shrieked out of the stereo. Turandot, of course, a roiling tide of angry soprano surging in from the living room. "I'll do this, just go away. Go *away*."

"But there's blood."

"Don't *touch* her." He stepped through the mess and picked up her mother from the floor, and carried her easily up the back steps. Marci ducked into the living room and turned off the stereo, knowing with every step that he'd seen her mother that way, he'd smelled her and touched her when she was like that, so everything was contaminated.

Even him.

$\backsim$

He had turned on the shower, full force and too cold. He stood, holding her mother under her arms in under the icy spray. He watched Kathryn's face for signs of life. Kathryn opened her eyes, blinking and lost. She opened her mouth and vomited all over herself, all over him, gagging and spitting ropes of her filthy poisonous liquor. "Just let it out," he said, angling her so it went down the drain. "Don't fight it, that's okay."

But her mother was awake, and she started to fight.

"Stop," he said, trying to restrain her fury. He grabbed her fists. She began yelling. Accusing. Cursing. Marci wanted to vomit herself when she realized her mother was talking about *him*. This hatred was for *him* and what they'd *done*. How he was. She kept yelling at him about, oh god, Mom, don't *say* it.

"Kathryn," he said, his voice hoarse with shame. "Stop."

But her mother never stopped when she was like this. She went on saying those grotesque and unforgivable things until he clapped his hand over her mouth and she bit him, hard. He cried out and yanked his hand away while her mother screamed, filling the acoustic chamber of the bathroom with soprano anger. He clapped his hand back over her mouth and pinched her nose closed.

"Enough of that. Enough, Kathryn. No more."

Was he smothering her? Was he putting her out of her misery, finally, wouldn't someone just put her mother out of her misery? But no, he moved his hands, letting her mother pull in a long, jagged breath. She caved in on herself. Surrendering. He'd gone from restraining her to cradling her under the water, speaking in that calm, familiar voice. "I haven't forgotten. I could never forget. I wanted to marry you. Remember? I wanted to marry you." She gagged and sputtered and sobbed, apologizing and pawing at him while he stroked her wet hair.

The war was over.

"Please let go of her."

Gentry looked up, blinking. He left the shower and tracked down the stairs, leaving a trail of icy water, leaving her mother alone in the shower. Cold, confused, shaking. Her mother was disgusting, snot pouring out of her nose and a trail of vomit down her nightgown. But Marci still loved her this way. She still loved her mother.

And so did Gentry.

She made the water warm and peeled off her mother's gown. She rinsed that familiar body, like a ghost image of Marci's, shaped the same but smaller, fainter. The beloved body she'd come from.

The body that had been with Gentry.

Kathryn was still crying. She tried to choke something out, but it all came out sideways. "Don't talk, Mom. It's okay." She turned off the water, and her mother stood there shivering, so much more naked than she was supposed to be because her skin was so pale, her hair so blonde, her nipples so faint that you couldn't really tell where they began. The only color on her body was the tattoo on her hip.

Gentry knew all these things about her mother's body.

Marci dried her with a soft towel and slid one of the fine cotton nightgowns Kathryn ordered from Europe over her head, over her sharp hipbones. "Hold out your hand." The cure for this was so simple; tweezers, hydrogen peroxide, some gauze, and tape. Like pulling bloody little teeth from the palm of her hand. "There. All better."

She remembered Gentry's hand covering her mother's mouth, pinching her nose closed. She'd thought he was going to kill her. She wished he had.

Marci held onto the bathroom counter for just a moment, just to breathe.

⟡

Kathryn lay on her side, staring at something that wasn't there. She barely dented the duvet. Marci pulled the thick wool blanket over her mother's lined neck to her fine, chiseled jaw. Her mother's hair under her palm was fine as a baby's. Her papery eyelids closed, so thin that Marci could see the movement of her eyes behind them.

She was still beautiful when she slept.

⟡

Marci concentrated on the aftermath. Rinsing the blood out of the washcloth, mopping up the watery boot prints in the bathroom and hall, taking down the bloody shower curtain, piling the towels on top of it, wrapping it all into a bundle in the tub. She'd come back for it after she swept up.

She got another wool blanket from the hall closet and carried it downstairs.

⟡

Gentry was on his hands and knees in the kitchen, going over every last inch of the floor with damp paper towels. He was probably thinking of slivers and shards poking into bare feet, days after all this seemed to be over. When he lifted the trash bag to carry it outside, she heard the shards tumbling with that sharp and shattered sound.

He came back and stood in the doorway, making sure the kitchen passed inspection. All signs of her mother's rage were erased, everything but a square of cardboard he'd taped over the window. Every inch of him was soaked with water and blood.

"You look like you've been in a knife fight."

He glanced down and shuddered.

It was quiet in the middle of the night. Quiet enough to hear the washing machine filling, the sound of the coffeemaker, hot water being forced through coffee grounds. Under it, the soft, steady churn of the ocean. All water.

She poured out two cups of coffee and sat down.

He came out of the laundry room wrapped in the blanket. The little chair creaked when he sat, and she wondered how much he weighed. Those pounds of bone and muscle and hair. What he measured in total.

He reached out a hand for the cup, closed it to hide the ugly purple rose that bloomed in his palm. He used his left hand to pick up the cup.

"You've done this before. I can tell. Was it the priest? Did he drink?"

A negative shake of his head that so small, it almost wasn't. It had never occurred to Marci that Gentry had parents. But of course he did. And one of them drank.

"Your mother?" Another shake of the head. "What was she like?"

"I don't really remember." He took the smallest sip of his coffee. "I don't remember much. I took care of myself."

"Hey Gentry? It kind of sucks, doesn't it."

Tears sprang to his eyes and he choked, not on the coffee, but on a sob. Her mother's drunken words, what she'd said, the horrible way she'd she said it, that hadn't made Gentry cry. But this did. His face was too open to bear.

The word was "vulnerable."

She ducked away, busying herself, pouring more coffee, bringing him a napkin to wipe his face, anything so she didn't have to witness this loss of dignity. He scrubbed at his eyes, blew his nose. "She'll go to meetings again. She always does after it gets like this. Things will be better for a while. But never for that long, Gentry. And I'm leaving Gretchen here. Alone."

"I'll be here."

She shook her head. "That's not enough."

"What more can I do?"

She stared at him, and his eyes widened as he understood the sacrifice she would need him to make. "I can't do that."

"You have to."

"I *can't*."

"You have to promise, Gentry. I can't leave here and go to college unless you promise."

He started to cry again, but she made him promise to do the hardest thing she could imagine for him. She made him swear it to God. He swore it.

If it got bad next year, he would take Gretchen to her father.

APRIL

Gentry

School was done for the day and I wanted to be quiet, I wanted to pray. I wanted to pray about leaving. I have always been able to leave, God. As hard as leaving can be. I have lived my life with my eyes on the exits at all times. I don't want to leave this place, but I want to be able to.

⁓

I left Detroit after a morning of stops.

I started at church, of course. Any light was welcome in Saint Bartholomew's, where the stained glass windows were boarded over to preserve the few panes that hadn't been shot out. Back in the pew, I spent some time on my knees considering, then rejecting a plea to Saint Christopher for safe travel. The saints offered me opportunities for intercession. I pictured them arrayed like tools on a pegboard, the right one for the job always handy. But I prayed only to God.

Church, even with boarded-up windows, felt silent and safe.

I approached Father Harold (some called him Father Hank, but that was too folksy for me), who had heard my somewhat monastic confessions for the last five years. *We'll miss you*, he said, shaking my hand. *Your presence here has been remarkable.* As a solitary white man with long hair who brought his dog to church, not just on the day he blessed the animals, but every Sunday, I was not sure what the priest meant by "remarkable."

He patted Bosco. *What you read at Hoan-Vu's funeral? It was beautiful, Gentry.*

I pressed my hands to my eyes. I pressed them hard, holding myself in.

When I took my hands away, Bosco and I were alone.

⁓

A stop at the corner store to say good-bye to the couple who had scolded me about my short shopping list (milk, cereal, bananas, dog food) for five years. They scolded me a little more about my dietary habits and hair. I told them the money I saved on haircuts helped me afford their ridiculous prices. We all spoke Vietnamese. Well, they spoke it. I mangled it, as was my way.

They wished me well.

A stop at the bank to figure out what to do with my account (nothing yet, I could leave it alone and do everything with my debit card). I told them where to send the statements, delivered a brief but impassioned lecture about the possibilities of Internet banking (it was 1996, what was the holdup, when were they going to see that this was the future, and so on). I withdrew a hefty amount of cash, put a few hundreds in my shirt pocket and stashed the rest in my wallet.

The banker patted Bosco. *I'll miss you, Bosco.* He shook my hand. *I'll miss you, too, Gentry.*

My money will still be here.

He burst out laughing, which was a relief.

We made a stop at the post office to file a change of address. That, at least, didn't seem overwhelmingly sad. It just seemed like the post office.

⌒

We waited at the stop until a bus wheezed to the curb and swung open the doors. *Afternoon, Gentry. You too, Bosco.* Outside the window, the static tableau of furtive human activity (drug dealers) and deliberate human inactivity (homeless people) passed us by. I'd grown up in a different city, where everyone rushed around. In Detroit, no one seemed to have anywhere to be. Was life supposed to be this hopeless and repetitive?

I put my hand on Bosco's back to calm that thought.

Our life was repetitive. Every day, I'd gone to work and Bosco had slept. We had recreational time at night, when we walked these same streets for miles to get to a park that had some grass in it. The streets were so much more alive at night.

Bosco couldn't play with the pit bull mixes favored by the homeless people, or the strays with bad fleas and worse worms. Inner city dogs live too close to their pack to play with strangers. But people who looked like they wanted to kill me would stop to pet Bosco. Bums would ask me for change, and then pull out some Dumpster delicacy for Bosco. Prostitutes would talk baby talk to him and offer me a discount. They still liked Bosco after I declined.

These people wouldn't even know I had left.

It had all been repetitive. God, tell me it hadn't all been hopeless.

I stroked Bosco's fur. It always calmed me to touch him, it steadied me.

Our life is going to change, Bosco.

He greeted this news with canine complacency. He was more interested when I pulled the cord. His ears lifted. He sniffed the air, and stood in the seat. His tail began to beat the air with strong, possibly dangerous strokes. *Settle down.* He couldn't. He was too excited. He wove a path around me, a dance of dog joy as I checked in at the booth and settled my bill and surrendered my key card. When he heard the jingle of keys in my hand, Bosco danced even more.

I held his collar so he didn't bound up ahead of me. We walked up a filthy, spiraling concrete ramp, periodically moving over to the side when a car came winding down on the way out. Six floors up, the highest space I could rent.

There it was, safe and sound. My 1968 CJ5, all original.

This garage had cost me a monthly fortune, but that was my vehicle. It was worth it. Even though the windows zipped, I had never even lost the radio. In comparison, I had seven locks on my apartment door, and had lost three computers in five years.

I should have kept my computer in the Jeep.

Let's go, Bosco. But he was already in the co-pilot's seat, panting deeply with excitement. *Your breath.* He smiled and panted more. He thought we were going to go see Mel in North Dakota. Usually that's where we were going when we got in the Jeep, but we'd spent the summer with Mel. We wouldn't be able to stop on the way if I wanted to get to Oregon by Thursday night.

How do you explain things like this to a dog?

I started it up and cranked it out of the space and wound my way down the ramp a little faster than was probably safe. It drove like a tractor, the gears grinding, rattling. Just the way I liked it. Thanks to the lack of road maintenance and the Jeep's stiff suspension, we bounced high out into the streets of Detroit.

All I needed was a job, a dog, and a Jeep. I had all three.

We drove through the unremitting grey that had become my daily landscape over the last five years. When I drove out of town every summer, the first shock was the color. The second was the smell of fresh air. When I'd first arrived, I thought the city smelled like despair. Since one of my undergraduate degrees was in English, I was occasionally guilty of thinking like that. The truth is, the city smelled like auto exhaust and rotting garbage and cigarette smoke.

Or maybe just despair.

Bosco was a little confused when we went back to the apartment. *It's okay, Boy.*
We just have to get our stuff. I maneuvered into a tight space relatively near my front
door and waited. Waiting for some color. The color of the day.

Three young men approached the Jeep in casual synchronicity. What they
wore signified exactly what they would die for. They froze into a triptych of casual
male postures. A furious heat came off young men like this, a roil of bravado and
vigilance. They hypnotized and repelled me. They illustrated perfectly my failure
as a teacher.

I nodded. They nodded back. Bosco wagged his tail. One of the young men
almost cracked a smile, then recovered. Bosco gave an urgent little woof, such a
small sound from such a big dog. The young man gave in and held out his hand.

How you doing, Bosco?

Grudging conversation followed. I didn't ask what they were doing, because I
knew what they were doing. They didn't ask me what I was doing, because they
weren't supposed to care. So we discussed my Jeep, and the recent graduation of
a younger sister. But not their history in my classroom. School was a remote and
forgotten territory for these young men.

Why you down here with your Jeep and all? This time of day?

I'm moving.

Moving?

I nodded, swallowed, cleared my throat. *I could use some help.*

A glance from eye to eye, as subtle and fast as the flicking tail of a snake.

Two positioned themselves by the Jeep, elbows out. Bosco refused to get out
of the Jeep, he wasn't going to miss a chance for a road trip, so he remained with
them. The third young man followed me upstairs to help me carry down my computer and peripherals, three boxes of books, one box of detritus and spare parts,
Bosco's bowls and bag of food, and a duffel bag full of clothes.

It took two trips and ten minutes.

I made one last trip up by myself, because I didn't want to have to use a rest stop
until I was far from the city. In the bathroom, there were some paper cups on the
windowsill. Under the sink, there was a toilet brush and some cleaning products.
An empty cereal box sat under there, too. It held spent razors, some swept-up hair,
nail clippings. DNA. I put everything in a garbage bag and tied it shut.

I walked out into the other room and stood there, holding my bag of trash and considering what I was leaving behind. One dirty window that looked out on flashing signs. A futon on the floor. A hotplate sitting on top of a dorm fridge, a plastic bowl and a spoon sitting on top of the hotplate. I'd never actually turned on that hotplate. A broom and dustpan leaned in the same corner where they'd been leaning when I moved in. The only marks on the walls were a nail, where I'd hung the cross over my bed, and a phone number written in pencil. I decided to leave it. A mark to prove I'd been there.

I thundered down the stairs dragging the rolled-up futon and knocked on a first-floor door. It was opened by my landlady, a woman who smelled like red wine and sweat. She scowled at me through her glasses. *What do you want.*

I held out the keychain she'd given me five years earlier. *I'm moving out.*

Don't I get any notice?

I paid my last month in advance five years ago.

Well, I still need notice.

I paid the rent early this month? So, um, it's paid through October.

Fine. She shook her head, grabbed the keys and slammed the door in my face.

I knocked. She didn't open it. I knocked again, and waited. I called through the door. *Hey Mrs. Melloy? I gave you a thousand-dollar pet deposit.* I heard her feet as she walked away from the door to a chair. *That was supposed to be refundable.* The volume of her television rose in reply.

Bosco hadn't done any damage, but she'd never admit that.

⌒

I hauled the futon to the curb. Bosco and the young men waited by the Jeep. *Well, that's it. Thank you.* I held out a hundred for each of them. These young men were proud to wave away my money, but would have been insulted if it hadn't been offered.

You really doing this. You really taking off.

I am. I received three congratulatory fist bumps in reply.

⌒

I took Bosco into the school, which was technically forbidden. Technically and explicitly and repeatedly forbidden since I'd started doing it at the beginning of the school year. But the way I saw it, not bringing my dog with me to work was part of my employment contract. I was working without a contract. I'd left him in the apartment to listen to the warring neighbors for five years and he never complained, but for these weeks, I'd brought him to work.

When I first started at this school, six ornate wooden doors spanned the front of the building. Those doors were fit for an Italian cathedral. Now it was crudely bricked off, a pair of reinforced metal doors positioned in the middle. Like a Cyclops with his eye closed.

We climbed the concrete steps, pushed our way into the security foyer. Primus was there. *Hey, Primus.* I presented my pass and surrendered my backpack for searching.

Good morning, Gentry. A little late this morning? Rose won't be happy.

Rose is never happy.

He smiled. *That, young man, is God's honest truth.*

I stepped through the metal detector and raised my arms for the secondary sweep of the handheld unit. I submitted to the morning pat-down. So did Bosco. I think he actually liked the pat-down. I didn't, but I was used to it, the price for reclaiming my pass and backpack. Normally I'd have headed to the cafeteria for breakfast, but I needed to resign more than I needed to eat.

On the way to the office, I remembered the old spelling helper I'd learned in grade school. The principal is your pal. This had rarely been the case with Rose Brewer, whose name reminded me of tea. She pretended not to see Bosco and received my resignation, effective immediately, with a familiar combination of stoicism and head-shaking. *This is what I always expected of a white boy from a private college. You lasted longer than I thought you would. But I always knew you'd turn tail and run.*

I did the math. Five years, a thousand students, twenty-two funerals, three teaching awards and one humiliating suspension that involved a restraining order and media attention.

Hey Rose? I think it's time for something new.

Something new. Well, that's nice for you, I guess. Her tone was mildly challenging. *I wonder what will happen with the lab. I suppose we'll just . . . close it.*

I expected this when I walked in. I knew she would talk about closing the lab I'd built and maintained over five years, five years of going before a school board composed of people who'd never touched a computer to talk about hardware, software, results, success, and the need for more money. Five years of begging for a bigger budget. Five years of keeping my students in the classroom while they struggled with poverty, drugs, pregnancies, sick babies, hunger, parents who disappeared and grandparents who died, little brothers and sisters they had to raise, the deaths of their classmates, the disinterest and dislike of their teachers. Most of all, I fought to keep my kids succeeding in spite of the general apathy of a country that was more than willing to let them rot in this infested, hopeless world, hoping they'd never leak out.

This was how she would punish me.

I swallowed and made myself speak. *Why not just replace me?*

With who?

Times have changed. It's 1996. There are other technology teachers out there.

Maybe. But they won't want to come here and teach. And without a teacher . . .

I stared at her. She stared at me. Her eyes were so dark that I couldn't distinguish her pupils from their surrounding irises, which were ringed with strange, milky circles. I wondered what those rings were.

Oh Rose, thou art sick.

She permitted herself a bent little smile. *I suppose you'll want to stay through lunch.*

My appetite for cafeteria food was legendary. I smiled back.

She rose with her usual heavy weariness and extended a hand. *I guess I can't blame you, really. So good luck.*

I shook her hand. I took my leave.

⁓

The news of my resignation preceded me out of her office, thanks to the open heat registers. School secretaries had been making a fuss over me since I started kindergarten, and the two women who sat outside the principal's office had carried on the tradition. *You're LEAVING? Oh, Gentry, we're going to miss you.* I nodded, answering their questions, accepting their apologies for what had happened last year, their condolences for a loss we all shared. *I miss Hoan-Vu. This place isn't the same without him.*

I nodded.

What will they do in that lab without you?

I wished them both well.

Bosco and I walked down the central hall. It was as wide as a street, floored with ancient linoleum that had only taken a week to lose the glassy sheen of the summer's buffing. Not that it would have shown much. The lights were off to save money, and the high windows over the entry doors were masked with wired Plexiglas to minimize the danger of incoming bullets. All the doors had been taken off the lockers. They stood, empty and dented, like broken teeth. Sirens, as always, wailed away outside. The edifice was like a decaying Gothic ruin, boarded up and systematically looted of anything noteworthy. Everything beautiful had been declared a fire hazard or a security risk.

But the students were still beautiful, I reminded myself. They would remain.

One last lunch in the cafeteria.

I went through the line, nodded at the hairnet ladies with their plastic gloves, answered their polite inquiries after my uncle. I sat down at one of the two tables in the corner of the room designated for faculty. No one really sat at this table, it was there as a buffer between us and the students. But since my reinstatement the year before, I'd chosen to sit at it alone. I began to methodically empty my tray.

There was a period in my life when I probably ate like a normal person, three times a day at a table, eating off a plate until I was excused. This was before I turned five. Between the ages of five and twelve, I ate breakfast and lunch at school. At age twelve, I entered boarding school. The meal system was, you walked in, sat down, and someone (another student, we took turns) set a plate in front of you. You prayed, and then ate as much as you possibly could in the shortest amount of time possible so you could be served seconds. When the food was good, you enjoyed it. When the food was bad, you ate it anyway. But you had to eat carefully, politely, making sure not to get it on your tie. Otherwise, the Jesuit brothers would excoriate you with shame for eating in a savage and unmannerly fashion. For someone like me, this was both a form of torture and a necessary reintroduction to the world of table manners.

College was easier, but my manners were better. And then I was back in school as a teacher. Breakfast and lunch on weekdays were there for the taking. Dinner and weekends presented a problem. But that was why cereal existed.

I sat in the cafeteria on that last day in Detroit, eating my lunch. One table over, my fellow faculty members ate, argued, gave me looks that were guilty or suspicious or, in the case of Pam Gerrity, overtly hostile. They had to have heard, but no one said anything.

Finally, Mike Orr walked over. *I hear you're leaving. Where are you going, again?*

A direct question. I usually tried to answer those. He leaned in, staring with his abnormally bugged eyes. *I wonder what they'll do with the lab once you're gone.*

I wiped a dinner roll around the edges of a compartment to get the last gravy and wondered if Mike had a thyroid condition. Graves disease, which I had only heard of because Christina Rossetti had it. I chewed my roll.

Well, good luck, Gentry. He went back to the other table.

I drank my second carton of milk and did the math. Two cafeteria meals a day through six years of grade school. Three meals a day in high school, college, graduate school. Then teaching, so two meals, five days, forty weeks for five years.

I decided the only people in the world who had eaten more institutional meals than me were probably incarcerated for life.

I opened the door to the lab and just stood there, having a moment. My kids were working away without me. The radio played softly, they talked and joked. Everything felt quiet and productive and calm. Perfect.

It was time to ruin it.

They started looking up, and I could tell they'd already heard. But I did them the courtesy of personally delivering the news.

Bad news, I'd noted, broke my classes into thirds. Some kids reacted immediately and loudly, with denouncements and shouts (*Oh screw that! No way!*). Other kids were encouraging and positive (*You don't need these pendejos, Gentry, you're gonna be all right*). And the last third retreated behind a wall of silence, glancing out from behind it with accusing eyes that said, *Fine. You're leaving, too. I don't care.*

I told them exactly where I would be, and wrote my new address on the board in case any of them wanted to write. I added my personal email address. Heads bowed, furtive lines were scrawled. I hope some of them carried through and wrote to me.

The questions all ended with "out there." Was I taking my dog out there. Where would I live out there. Did I have some family out there. How long did it take to drive out there. Would I make more money out there. Would I finally get a girlfriend out there.

None of them had to ask why I was leaving.

Some of the kids didn't know exactly where Oregon was, but they immediately went online and found it. *Man. This is on the other side of Idaho, Gentry. I wouldn't be going through Idaho.*

Idaho is supposed to be beautiful.

Oanh was one of my best students, and she sang in my church at the earliest Sunday Mass. Her voice rose like a bird in the computer lab. *That's okay, Gentry. I'm glad you're getting out of here.* She switched to Vietnamese. *After the way those assholes screwed you over last year, who blames you?* I didn't allow swearing in my lab, but I had never been sure if the words I condemned in English were all that bad in Vietnamese.

Hey everyone? I think you should all try to get some work done.

Latrell, who in general said very little, spoke up. *Once you go, no one's here to grade it.*

Grade it yourselves until the new teacher shows up. You know what good work is. You'll probably be harder on each other than I am.

He rolled his eyes. *No new teachers be showing up here, Gentry.*

The students would forgive me for leaving. I wondered more about my ability to forgive myself. The school would close, I knew that. And the church, too, maybe even sooner than the school. A neighborhood without churches and schools was a body without organs. I knew what happened, I'd seen it all over Detroit.

God, forgive me my part, however small, in what was going to happen to that neighborhood. Amen.

I finished cleaning my personal files off the server as the students left the room. It hurt too much to look at them. I stood in the empty lab for one last look around. The cool light of the monitors, the chairs every which way, the blackboard full of my rules, which no one had bothered to erase. *This is it, Bosco. This is over.* He looked around with appropriate solemnity.

I had my little moment.

I closed the door, but didn't lock it. I had always trusted my students in there. Only one had ever let me down. She broke my trust and ruined my reputation and nearly ended my career. But she didn't steal any equipment.

⌒

I didn't know how they got the word, or why security let them do it, but they were waiting, and they were all there. The central hall was lined with hundreds of students. All those students. All those brown eyes on me, some shining with tears. They clapped together, like syncopated thunderclaps. The cheer squad started to chant my name. They took my name and threw it around. They spelled it out and mocked it, they shouted it and praised it, they gave my name a life of its own. With their hands and feet and voices, they made my name into something else, something not of me, something like music. This was a call-out, a ritual I heard every year at commencement. This was something they did for each other.

The floor reverberated. The ceilings shook. The empty lockers sang like a church organ. Bosco walked beside me, his head high, his tail wagging. I kept my head up, too. I passed through a wall of syllables and celebration on my way to the security foyer, where I surrendered my pass and shouldered my backpack and walked through the metal detectors and the metal doors and down the concrete steps for the last time, carried by a thunderous cacophony of farewell.

I was graduating.

Bosco and I got in that Jeep, and we flew.

∽

We flew to Oregon.

I stood at the window in my Oregon classroom, thinking about lines. Drawn with a stick, a pencil, pixels, words. What were lines were made of? I was taught early on that lines were made of points, and points are separate. Lines were not barriers, they were not walls. Lines were agreed upon. Lines didn't exist without agreement, without some rudimentary code of honor.

I made a line in my dorm room in high school to protest a roommate's chaos. I ran a strip of duct tape from the windowsill to the doorway. I didn't say a word, but the message was clear. Here was one side of the line. Here was the other. He honored it, he kept his filth over there.

I didn't make a graceful transition into being a man. I was completely out of line. I sinned as joyfully and as much as I could, and I nearly died for it. But whatever I'd done as a man, it stayed on one side of a line. Students were always on the other.

I needed my lines back. Or I would have to leave.

But I couldn't leave, could I?

God, how could I ever leave Gretchen?

Amen.

∽

"Gentry? What're you doing?" Tiffany stood in the door, tentative as always, her face as white as the breast of a seagull. "Can I talk to you?"

"Sure." I sat down at one of the tables, and Tiffany sat beside me. I waited.

"I'm late."

"Late? Late for what?"

She looked up through sparse little eyelashes. "I'm *late* late, and I don't know who to talk to about it."

That seemed easy enough. "The attendance office. Or do you want me to write you a pass or something?"

She gave me a look of pain and betrayal. "Not *that* kind of late, Gentry." She burst into tears. She was late for something and crying, and I was confused.

"Tiffany, what are you *late* for?"

She took a deep breath. "My period. It's late? And I took one of those tests? And I guess I'm pregnant?"

I said nothing, because I was so stupid. Breathtakingly stupid. I just took her hand. I shouldn't have taken her hand, that crossed a line. But I was too stupid for words, so I took her hand, and I held it while she cried.

She cried for a long time.

⁓

In defense of my stupidity, I would like to point out that I was enrolled in Catholic boarding school at age twelve. Pregnancy was not an issue there, as we were all boys. I started college at age sixteen in a state of astonishing naïveté. Through a great stroke of luck, I left with Biblical knowledge of an embarrassing number of young women. Through an even greater stroke of luck, none of them ever got pregnant by me.

Pregnancy was not real until I went to Detroit.

I taught girls who were mothers before I met them in their freshman year. They showed me pictures, told me their names. Sometimes the girls had to pause, thinking, to get those names right. Lasharaya Davonne. Jantoine Jamalika. Swantelle. One girl named her son Malario. I was polite but confused. For me, names will never be neutral. I couldn't understand what these girls were doing to their children with these names.

I talked about it with Hoan, a boy from a culture that seemed to use the same four or five names for everyone, like a Gabriel Garcia Marquez novel. Hoan who told me the African American names had Swahili and Bantu meanings, like "Shining Son of the Morning Erection" or "Dutiful Daughter of the Dunes I Laid Her Mother Down In." "Bastard of the Blood-Drinking Nomad Who Passed Through Nine Months Ago."

At Hoan's funeral, I met his mother, and I met his baby son.

He'd named him Hoan-Vu.

～

Tiffany was finished crying.

She wiped her nose on the sleeve of her cheerleader's sweater. That was just wrong. I wanted to offer her my sleeve, instead, but that would have been wrong, too. I let go of her hand and reached up and stroked the back of her head, her soft little ponytail. I rested my hand on her shoulder and gave it a squeeze.

Crossing every line.

She closed her eyes and sighed. "My mom is going to kill me." Something about crying had made Tiffany stop speaking in questions. "I was going to coach at a camp for elite squads in Tualatin this summer. I was supposed to stay with my aunt in Tigard."

Dear God, what could I say? "Have you talked to . . . the dad?" What a stupid choice of words, calling Alex a dad, but I couldn't think of what else to call him.

She nodded. The tears rolled down her face. "I talked to him yesterday."

"Okay. Will he help you?"

"He says if I was stupid enough to get myself pregnant, I can figure it out myself."

If she got *herself* pregnant? Even I knew that girls didn't get *themselves* pregnant. I thought about Alex, and well, that kid was weird enough, maybe he didn't know.

"Do you want me to talk to . . . Alex?" And say what? I couldn't stand to look at that kid, how was I supposed to talk to him?

She shook her head, her eyes on the tabletop. "It's not Alex. It's Garret."

Blood in my eyes, blood in my mouth. Please, God, take that away, clear away the lust for violence and give me something real and good, something that helps, that's all I ask right now, the right words to help this pregnant girl. I clear my mind of all blood, all anger. I make myself Your vessel. Amen.

"Tiffany, you should go talk to Mrs. Newhouse."

Thank You, God. I prayed for the right thing to say, and You sent a referral to the counseling office. But You know, that worked. I knew my limits, I couldn't help this girl.

Even God agreed.

～

She walked like a broken thing down the hall, my arm around her shoulders. We walked as slowly as she needed. Mimi Newhouse received her. Mimi was smart and kind and she knew what to do about teenage pregnancies. I only understood computers.

After I handed her off, I wanted a phone. I needed to talk to Mel, but Mel was in Italy at a place called Castelmonte, at a retreat. I couldn't figure out how someone who lived in a monastery needed to go on a retreat, but there it was, Mel was in retreat and even with a phone I couldn't find him, couldn't lay this at his feet and beg him to help me understand why God let stuff like this happen to children. And it hit me so hard and so foul that I had to stop walking and let it settle, shuddering with the ugliness of it as the blood rose in my gut, my mouth, my eyes.

It was Garret.

～

I heard him before I saw him.

"Did you HEAR me? GO. I don't CARE. I'm tired a you and your FUCKIN' SHIT." I could finally understand him, and everything he said was ugly. He started to punctuate his words by slamming his fist into the locker next to hers. "I don't CARE. I've HAD it."

"Good, because so have I. I'm DONE, Garret."

"Go on and LEAVE, then."

"Fine." She started to walk away.

"Where do you think you're GOING?" He pulled her back, her books slipping from her arms, falling to the ground. He pushed her against the lockers. "What, aren't you LEAVING?"

He raised his hand.

The metal wall of lockers rang like a bell with the impact of his body.

He dared to try to twist away.

My hands, wound in his jacket, longed to close his throat. My breath felt like fire pulling in and out of me, gorgeous, furious blood sang in my ears, urging me to do it, roaring at me to take him apart, to tear him to bits and kick the pieces down the hall on my way out the door.

I leaned into his face. "Don't fight me. Don't you *ever* fight me."

I stepped back and pressed my hands to my aching eyes. He slipped away.

That voice. I knew that voice.

Her voice pierced through, high and nervous as a bird call.

"Gentry?" I'd forgotten she was there.

"Gentry? Can I have a ride home? Please?"

I took my hands away from my eyes. I had to leave. She gathered up her books as I walked out through the rain, rain in my eyes, I needed to get *out* of there.

"Would you WAIT for me?" I stopped and she slammed into me and dropped everything all over again. She scrambled to gather it back up as I walked on through the rain to my Jeep. She slid in beside me, put a hand on my arm and I pulled it away. My ears ached from the ringing. God, make it stop. I don't remember. God, please. "It's just a stupid fight. He's mad because I'm leaving, so we keep fighting. It's not all his fault."

I started the Jeep, gunned the engine, and we were out of there in a spray of mud and gravel. She bounced beside me, a little toy on a rough ride, a dog being kicked around a room while someone raged and swore and tore him apart. There was a movie playing on the back of my brain, and I hated movies. That's all it was, a movie.

God, please.

"Don't tell my mother."

I slowed down, pulled over for a minute, just a minute, that's all I wanted was a minute to make that movie go away.

I knew I had to leave.

Gretchen

Garret hadn't been around at all that week. Marci had to ride in to school with Gretchen and Gentry. Gretchen just ignored her, which was easy because she rode in the back on one of the little seats, and she was quiet, weirdly quiet.

That morning on the way to school, Gentry was quiet, too. The two of them didn't look at each other or speak to each other, and even though it bothered Gretchen when they joked about school stuff, the silence was too heavy. Gretchen was a little tired of it. "What are you giving up for Lent?"

His eyebrows went up in surprise. "Hey Gretchen? How do you know about Lent?"

"I read about it in a book. One of those Catholic books I got out of the library. So, what are you giving up? It's supposed to be something you like, right? It's supposed to be a sacrifice." Gretchen thought for a bit. "You could give up coffee."

"Never."

"Bacon?"

"I don't think I can live without bacon."

"Okay, how about fishing?"

"Not a lot of fishing right now, Gretchen."

"Well, what else is there?" Her mom could give up smoking or drinking, but she never would. Her mom should eat for Lent. Gretchen could give up TV or caramel corn. Marci could give up being mean.

Gentry didn't have anything to spare.

⁓

She'd had to catch the bus home, because he was working late. So she'd gotten on with everyone she hated and ridden home pretending to be deaf, dumb and blind. It was the only way she could stand to ride the bus. When it stopped at the top of her drive, she'd already been standing, ready to burst out the door and into a dead run. The driver had yelled something after her, but she didn't hear. The deafness part, that lingered.

She slowed when she saw Garret's ugly truck in the driveway. He usually didn't say anything to her, but he opened the door, letting out cigarette smoke and the smell of fresh fish. "Hey. C'mere. I got something to show you."

She felt something like panic, a surge of disgust like she felt for that old man on the beach. But Garret was holding the most beautiful fish that Gretchen had ever seen. The skin shone like a rainbow. The only dead part of it was the eyes.

"Can I cook it?"

He shook his head. "It's for your sister."

So she brought him in. Marci, who'd ridden home on the high school bus, was working on homework at the kitchen table. Garret set the fish on the counter. Marci took one look at that fish and her eyes shone. Garret sat down watched her while she got out the boning knife and cut it in half.

"You know what would be good? Chunk it, and fry it in the Frydaddy."

"Frying will ruin it."

"I like fried salmon. Nobody else does, but I do."

"I'm not frying this beautiful fish. And this other half is mine, too, so don't get any ideas." Marci wrapped one half in tinfoil and put it in the freezer. "Why don't you make some potatoes. And salad. But don't use all the fresh parsley."

"Parsley has no taste, why would you put it on the fish?"

"Because I *want* to."

So Gretchen made new potatoes with butter and parsley, but not all the parsley, while Marci steamed half the fish with herbs. They worked together on the salad, bumping and teasing. The kitchen smelled so good, so salty and fishy, that Bosco smelled it and scratched to come in. Garret sat at the table, and Marci didn't say a word to him. She didn't even look at him. But everything she did was for him, and he watched it all through his weird little purple eyes.

Gentry came in looking pale and tired, and washed his hands up to the elbows. He didn't look at Garret, either.

For some reason, Garret was invisible.

When the fish was done, Marci arranged it on the big white platter, with some fresh rosemary next to it from Mom's herb pots and little wedges of lemon and lime. She set it down in the middle of the dining room table. They all stood there staring at it.

Gretchen wasn't sure about the lime.

"That's a masterpiece," her mom said, and she lifted the fish to see the skin on the underside. "Look at the color."

Marci smiled. "You should have seen it before it was cooked."

"I wish you'd called me down. Well, let's eat."

Everyone dished up. Gentry put some potatoes on his plate, and some salad. He did his praying and crossing. Everyone started to eat but Gentry.

Gretchen's first bite convinced her that the lime was actually an excellent idea. Marci said, "Oh my God. I know I cooked it, but this is *amazing*."

Her mom made a little "mm" and closed her eyes. "This is the best fish I've ever eaten. Think how good this would taste if I stopped smoking. Beyond description. Garret, this is magnificent. You've outdone yourself." Garret's squinty little eyes almost closed because he was smiling so much.

Her mother looked at Gentry's plate and frowned. "Gentry, what are you waiting for? You've *got* to have some of this." She slapped a big slab onto his plate. His lip curled. She stared at him, frowning. "Well? What's wrong?"

He stood up and carried his plate into the kitchen. They could hear it clatter in the sink, they could hear the back door slam. Garret's face went white, then red. Definitely the fight or flight response.

Her mom crossed her arms. "What was *that* all about? Lent?"

"Maybe he just didn't want the fish." Marci's voice was quiet. She didn't sound mean at all. Just tired.

"He could have *said* that. And he *always* eats fish."

Marci pushed back her chair. "I'll go talk to him."

"Talk to him about eating fish?" Gretchen decided that was even more stupid than some of the things that she'd tried to talk to him about.

She and her mother traded looks. Then they looked at their fish. Gretchen couldn't help it, she took another bite. It was like putting the entire ocean in her mouth, all the brine and seaweed, all the plankton and sand and foam and fish, all in one flavor. It was the best fish she'd tasted in her whole entire life.

And it was ruined when Marci came back into the house, crying so loud that they could hear her in the kitchen. Garret sprang up and ran into the kitchen, asking "What did that *faggot* say to you?" Her mother's hand went up to her throat like there was something stuck there. The door slammed and the kitchen was quiet.

Her mother's voice, cold and commanding, broke the silence. "Gretchen, finish your dinner." The two of them sat there, eating the fish. It still tasted like the sea.

But the sea was full of mysteries and dead things, and it was very, very cold.

The little house was dark. Gentry never sat in the dark. Because of the moon, she could see him through the window of his door. He sat on his bed with his back against the wall, petting Bosco. She went in and switched on the bedside light. "Hi."

He reached over and turned it back off.

She didn't sit on the bed anymore if he was in it, so she sat on the chair. "What are you doing out here?"

He didn't say anything.

"Are you really giving up fish for Lent? Because Marci froze half of it. We can have it after Lent is over."

He still didn't say anything.

Gretchen knew he loved his church, but what she'd read about it gave her nightmares. Especially the saints. If you wanted to be a saint, you had to let people burn you alive or rip out your eyes or shoot you full of arrows. Then, after they tore you into little pieces, they felt really bad and called you a saint and fought over the bits of you so they could put them in a church. Churches in Italy were full of these things, these relics. Mummified feet and fingers.

"Do you *like* being Catholic?"

He finally looked up, but she couldn't see his eyes. They were shaded, as dark and heavy as if they'd been taken out, only sockets left behind.

"Gretchen, I need you to leave me alone tonight."

It felt like someone had pulled her stomach out through her throat, that empty and awful. She wished she could just disappear. Just not exist anymore. She wished she had never been born.

Gentry spoke again. "Will you please take Bosco with you, too? I need to be alone. Because I need to pray on something."

And she understood that he didn't hate her. He didn't want her to go away forever.

He just needed to be alone.

Kathryn

Marci was off with that brutal boy, and Gretchen was upstairs with Bosco. Kathryn had let her take the dog up to bed with her, another example of her superior parenting skills.

Both her daughters off with dogs, and it was Gentry she worried about.

❧

A fresh fire, a good book, a warm throw and a stiff drink. This was her formula for peace, but she felt unsettled. Life seemed to be spinning out of her control, like those moments before a car wreck, agonizing camera clicks of time in which the impact is on its way and there's nothing surer than collision. She had been in three wrecks in her life, and though she believed in no gods, she remembered praying to live, having no idea whether or not it might be kinder to die.

Did her parents pray to live? She doubted it. They were each other's gods. In those eternally long moments before it all hit, she assumed that they took each other's hands, grateful to end their lives as they'd lived. Together.

She lifted her head to listen. Through the sound of the rain and the wind, she heard her least favorite sound in the world, that foul engine gunning up in the driveway. Brakes, gravel.

A girl crying. A man shouting. An unfamiliar man's voice, full of threats and profanity. That was not Garret's voice, and it certainly wasn't Gentry's.

What man was in her driveway, raging like thunder?

Bosco lumbered down the steps to the back door, barking like a mad dog, scratching, whining, almost mad. What was happening out there?

Marci's cries cut the night.

Kathryn's hands worked. The door opened, and wheels spun, and gravel sprayed, kicking up rocks at the furious dog that flew up the drive after the truck, snarling, teeth bared, chasing it away. Kathryn was whipped by the wind and lashed by the sound of her beautiful daughter weeping. Gentry stood beside her, arms at his sides, and Marci clung to him, pulling at him, howling her pain and disbelief, hands scrabbling over him like a wall.

He turned his face to Kathryn. His eyes, oh Gentry, those were not his gentle eyes.

She moved towards him and he lifted his hands, palms out, a gesture of warding to get her away from him, to get Marci away from him, to just get them away but it was too late. She didn't know how, she hadn't meant to. But she'd done it, she and her daughters.

They had torn Gentry to pieces.

Lorrie Gilroy

My classroom has a view of the teacher's parking lot, and I see him pull in. He sits in his Jeep for a minute, finishes listening to whatever song, just sits there. And when he gets out, he moves like an old man. Slow-like, and so sonofa-bitching sad.

It breaks your heart. He's what, twenty-seven?

I don't know how he keeps his classes going, but he does. The shit they do in that advanced class amazes me, he doesn't miss a beat in the classroom. And every time I walk down the hall I see him in somebody else's classroom. You know, I'll take a class for somebody during my office hours if they've got a dentist appointment, I will, I'm a good guy and what goes around comes around but I just sit at the desk and maintain order. When Gentry's in there, he's right in there, believe you me. He teaches the crap. Biology, Math, English, whatever, he does it, he likes it. He's happy at the school. But out of it he's one sorry son of a bitch these days.

And, I'm wondering what the hell it is. I'm wondering is it the Mumford woman? Because I'll take the bitch out and be happy to do it.

⁓

A little later, I put my head in the lab. "Hey, little buddy."

"Hey." He has something all tore down on one of the tables, and he's just staring at it.

"What're you doing there?"

He sighs and scratches the side of his face. "I don't know."

"Looks like you're doing something."

"I took this apart, and I can't remember why."

"Where were you last night? Teacher's union meeting. You need to go to those. I told you about it three times."

"I forgot." He starts to put the machine together, sets down the electric screwdriver, stands up and walks out of the room.

Okay, something's up.

It isn't Darlene, he looks through that little skank like she isn't there, and she loads his tray without a word. He won't talk about the Mumford bitch, I ask him but he won't say anything at all. I'd like to beat her skinny ass, I would, I've never hit a woman in my life but she's what I call an ankle, because she's three feet lower than a cunt, get it? She's part of it.

That's not all of it, though. It's some kind of deep shit.

I think it's that religion of his, because that shit'll screw you over if you take it seriously, it will. I watch him like this for a week, and I think, I need a game plan.

Well, I take him fishing a lot. On weekdays I come to get him at five o'clock in the morning and he's sitting there at his table reading. He looks up at me like he doesn't know who I am. Then he stands up, changes his shirt, gets his jacket. I can tell he hasn't even been to bed, but I don't say anything.

This morning, a Saturday, I brought a little brandy for the coffee and he just shook his head. That's okay, see, because he can't hold liquor anyway. He's a good fishing partner, because he's quiet. Fishing's the only time I like the quiet, and Gentry's as quiet as death these days.

We're out at the jetty. I can't get shit, but occasionally he gets a nice steelhead but he doesn't hardly notice. Mostly it's greenling, rock cod, sea bass, stuff I don't usually bother with. He baits his line and they all make a run for it, they fight to get caught by Gentry. He won't throw anything back, he'd keep the sonofabitching sculpin if I didn't point out to him that they are not edible.

He loses all his bait to the sculpin but that's okay, I brought a ton of bait. Usually, he makes fun of how much I bring, but not lately. He runs out of bait pretty quick so he walks over and gets a handful of herring.

A gull circles, hoping for guts. He stares up at it and gets distracted by that high, crying sound, and puts the whole mess of herring in his pocket. Then he looks down like he can't figure out what the hell's going on. He looks so goddamn lost. I'd laugh, but I can't laugh at the guy standing there pulling fish chunks out of his jeans. He'll stink like fish all day but so does every other fisherman's son this time of year.

He's holding out the end of his line, and I tie a hook on there for him, bait it. He walks off, fishes. After awhile, he walks back over and throws a sea bass in the bucket. He comes over and stands by me which is fine because maybe he'll bring me a little luck, like in Vegas. He stands beside me with those dead eyes.

And all of Vu's goddamn uncles come pushing in with their goddamn light sinkers and their goddamn Kmart bamboo poles, and I'm not in the mood to have my line fouled this morning. A person gets sick of the whole sonofabitching outfit and a person can't say a goddamn word about it to Gentry or he'll get pissed off. I reel it in and we go over to where Bosco is, by the fire. He hunkers down, puts his arm around the mutt, so sad, so goddamn sad. Bosco gets after his pocket.

"Do you want some coffee?"

"Yes."

"Do you want it in your cup, or should I just pour it in your pocket?"

He doesn't even laugh. Just holds out his cup, the one I keep for him. And after I fill it up, he whispers, "Thank you." Like the whole goddamned world would fall apart if he didn't remember to say thank you one time in his life.

You know, I've never seen such a miserable man. I know I'm not a deep thinker, I know this, hell, I don't want to be a deep thinker, but I think a little. And I think I've got this one figured out. "Gentry, I think you're letting this religion get to you."

"My religion?"

"Yeah. Your religion." I expect him to jump on me, because he's done that a time or two when I rib him about it. I tell him how nice and holy he looks in the cafeteria praying over the tray like that and he shuts me up pretty fast. But this morning I'm not joking, so he doesn't get his back up.

"What do you mean?" He's going to listen. I better not screw this up.

"Every Saturday night and Sunday morning you go to church, right?" He nods. "And you're a good guy. I mean it, you're one good guy." He looks like he'll cry, oh please you little pussy, no crying. "Well, what I mean is . . . what I want to say is . . ." I can't think, and I can't talk, either. "Gentry, you're the most miserable sonofabitch I've ever seen in my sonofabitching life. So what's the goddamn point? What's the point of sitting in that church asking to be forgiven for whatever piddly-ass sin you convince yourself you're guilty of, jacking your dick or telling somebody they look nice when they look like shit or whatever the hell you think you do that's so goddamn terrible, what's the point when it doesn't even make you feel any better?"

I'm halfway expecting him to hit me. He doesn't.

"Well?" He doesn't answer. "Well, does God forgive you or not?" He won't answer. "If God forgives you, Gentry, then you better forgive yourself."

I hate to hug a man, there's always that point when your balls bump up together, but I hug Gentry because if anybody ever needed somebody to hug them then he does. I don't even care if he cries.

And he cries a little, and I don't care, because he looks a little bit better after that. He looks a little bit better.

⌒

I had coffee with Jeannie a couple of days ago. Oh, we're not going to try again, I made her miserable enough and don't need to do it again. But she's upset because her daughter went and got herself pregnant. Leave it to Tiffany to do that to her mom.

It's that little asshole Garret Blount knocked her up and he won't even talk to her about it. I'd like to kill that kid.

I know I'm an asshole but I sat across from her and watched her cry and Jesus have a heart attack Christ how I hate it when women cry, but I'm kind of getting used to crying what with being around my little buddy all the time. Then Jeannie got herself calmed down, and she started talking about Tiffany's options. That's what she called them, options, like Tiffany's life is one big all-you-can-eat buffet of options and all of them wonderful. Jeannie sounded excited. And I told her I didn't see a whole hell of a lot of options for a junior in high school, did she? And she told me, "Maybe she could keep it. I could help. It's an option."

And probably this was harsh as hell but I know how hard this woman works so things can be a little better for her daughter, she's driving that bus and cutting hair and giving those perms and picking up a night shift or two every week at the cannery during the season, all that and she scrimps and saves for the lessons and the camps, and I sat there and listened to Jeannie talk about how she could help her daughter if she went ahead and had a baby.

I had to say it.

"Jeannie, honey, no offense here but do you want her life to turn out *exactly* like yours?"

And she cried some more.

Well shit, I'm no good at this stuff, but we talked and she agreed with me after about an hour of my talking to her about it, and I'm awful glad of that because the last thing this town needs is one more girl having a baby at seventeen while whoever the dad is turns his back and gets out of this town like he should and she spends the rest of her life on food stamps and hooking up with assholes like me until that baby grows up and has a baby of her own, and so on and so on and so on like that old shampoo commercial, except with stupid little coast rat baby girls who don't know any better than to grow up and get themselves pregnant.

I made her let me give her the money for it.

⸱⸱⸱

So I guess that's what I have to do these days, keep people together.

We pack it in and I want to take him to eat but he says he's not hungry, so I take him over to my house. We clean the fish and put them in the freezer, except for that nice bass, which I cook up for us. He doesn't say a word, just eats his fish. I turn on a game. I watch it while he falls asleep on the couch.

He sleeps until it's dark and then he wakes up crying. Crying bad. He starts to settle down and then he falls to pieces. I sit in my recliner with my eyes closed, pretending to be asleep. Bad enough a man has to make that noise, but having another man hear it is a whole other ordeal. He cries until he's all cried out, then he gets up and does the dishes.

All I can say is, there's something seriously wrong with the guy.

⸱⸱⸱

I'm driving him home. It's getting late. I'm a little spooked driving up to the house but it all seems okay. He gets out of the truck and walks to his house. I back up and turn around, start up the drive again, and I get to the top and about piss myself because a big head raises up out of the cab behind me like Frankenstein or something. It's the dog. I guess he forgot to get out because he was asleep in the truck bed on an old tarp.

I cut the engine. My hands are shaking. "Come on, boy." I decide to walk him back and make sure he gets in okay. He makes some noise, a little growl. "Keep it down, the bitches are asleep." He swallows it up, what a good dog. We go up the drive and when I get nearer, I see someone going toward the Mumford house, quiet-like. It's Gentry. He's stepping light in those big boots, head up, shoulders squared, stepping as careful as one of the Indian guides you rent out by the day up the coast. He goes around the north side, walking so slow.

He's tracking.

I put my hand on the dog's collar, because his tail's gone into a point. I set that dog down on his little front step and hold up one finger to tell him stay. And he will, because that's one good dog. I walk around the house to see what the hell my little buddy's up to. I stop by the corner of the house. He's back a bit, just a dark shadow against a stand of trees. Nobody on this planet can be as quiet as Gentry.

There's a little piece of blue light coming out a window, so somebody must be in the big house with the television on. That light catches Gentry's face. If I didn't know it was him, I wouldn't recognize him. Because I've been charged by a bull moose, cornered a badger, seen a grizzly rear up ready to fight. I've seen a good dog gone mad, a dog I had to shoot if I wanted to live myself. I never knew a human being could look this angry.

He's watching whoever that is at the window.

It's all so perfect, see, the night and the silence and something big's going to happen, like watching a mountain lion take down a deer, but then of course my boot catches a stick and the guy at the window hears it and he turns and breaks and runs over me like a cold wind. I know who it is, I know who it is, Jesus in Heaven Christ I would give my left nut not to know who it is.

Only one person in town runs that fast. Only one.

Gentry takes off after him and I want to say, don't bother, don't waste your breath. You won't catch that sonofabitch. Nobody can catch that sonofabitch. Goddamnit all to hell.

What kind of a team can I field without him next year?

Kathryn

Kathryn was on the phone, attempting to reassure Michael.

"Kathy? What the hell? Marci says some boy was taken away from the house in a police car?"

"It was nothing, Michael." She saw Gentry at the living room window, his arms spread wide as an eagle's as he lifted a storm window out of the frame. Gentry's

Lenten depression had lifted. The act of chasing down a spying boy had miraculously restored him, and he poured his excess of physical energy into pruning the roses, cutting the winter's growth of grass, raking the gravel. And the storm windows, of course. "It was a misunderstanding."

"Marci said he was in handcuffs. And where the hell was Gentry? He wasn't home? And where was this kid parked?"

Parked? Why were men always concerned with where someone was parked? "Up on the highway, just past the turnoff. He'd walked down the drive."

"The dog didn't bark?"

"The dog knows this boy."

Michael sighed, a gusting huff of male frustration. "And Marci knows him."

"Not very well, but she knows him."

"What, did he claim he was up there to see her?"

"No. He isn't her friend." Alex Fournier was not the objectionable local boy who came to see Marci, but she wouldn't say that out loud. "He said he wanted to talk to Gentry, and that he was just trying to find him, that's why he went up to the house. He was checking to see if anyone was home. He said he ran because he was afraid."

"Afraid of what?"

"Just afraid. The boy panicked and ran down to the beach. Apparently Gentry spooked him."

"I'll bet he spooked him." Michael's voice carried a pang of envy. "But he chased him down?"

"Yes."

"And you'd already called the cops?"

"Yes. I overreacted." The sheriff had come almost immediately, Emmett with his lights flashing, hurtling down the drive. Kathryn had been so afraid he'd hit poor old Bosco. "They took him in, but didn't charge him. He said he was there for a valid reason."

"But he ran away, Kathy. Only guilty men run away."

Her head was starting to hurt and she needed a drink. But she would not have a drink. "This boy is the track star, Michael, the quarterback. That's what he does. He runs."

"Quarterback. And Gentry chased him down?" Michael's voice carried so much emotion, so much admiration and frustration and grief over his own aging. "I can't believe Gentry caught him."

"I can." He'd never seen Gentry naked. He had no idea what was underneath those baggy clothes. But Kathryn knew.

She really wanted a drink.

"And where's this kid now?"

"He went to stay with his aunt in Bend."

"And you're sure that's all it was? You're sure things are under control?"

"Yes, Michael. Things are under control."

All the row of it, the shouting and sirens, that hunting down and taking away. She'd finally gotten the girls calmed down, sending them to sleep in her bed. She sat at her table and drank coffee with Gentry until the sun rose, convincing him in whispers that Gretchen was best protected by not knowing. Gentry pleading that the boy needed help, asking her, *Kathryn, what if he does this somewhere else? What if he does something worse?*

Kathryn didn't care what that boy did, so long as he stayed away.

She put a hand on her stomach, lit a cigarette to calm it. The physical sickness would pass, she had to remember that. The nausea and sweats would leave her alone soon. All that would be left was the great mounting ache of addiction, the panic at facing life without it, the fear of never having another drink, the anger that other people could drink and she couldn't. But the sickness would pass.

"Kathy? Are you sure you're okay?"

She said the only honest words she could find. "I'll be fine. Don't worry, because Gentry's here. That boy is lucky Gentry didn't kill him."

"Why would Gentry kill someone?" That was Marci's piercing voice. She'd caught the tail end of the conversation.

"I have to go." Kathryn hung up the phone gently.

Marci frowned. "Why is everyone acting so weird? So Alex was up at our house. So what's the big deal about that? He came up here to talk to Gentry about something, right? So why would Gentry kill him?"

Gentry came in as if on cue, dirty and sweating. "Is there any coffee?"

Marci let out a dramatic, huffy sigh. "I'll make some." He washed his hands, took the towel to the laundry room, sat at the table and waited while she rinsed, filled, ground. "Do you know why Alex left town? Tiffany's been absent for three days. What's going on?"

"What's going on is that I was hoping for some coffee." Marci set a cup in front of him, and he blew, sipped, sighed. "Thank you. You make great coffee, Marci."

"You're welcome." Her face took on a narrow-eyed, devilish mask of amusement. "I wonder if Miss Lazarre makes great coffee."

He shrugged, studying his cup.

"Miss Lazarre? The new PE teacher?" Something settled along Kathryn's limb, a sort of numbness, not quite shock. Something more akin to disbelief.

"Yes." Marci batted her eyes. "I bet she makes *fantastic* coffee. Or maybe it's *amazing*. I had no idea you were into Amazons, Gentry. She probably outweighs you by forty pounds. Forty awesomely distributed pounds, but still."

He stared at the cup in his hand. Kathryn tried to absorb it. Was this the source of his good mood? This new PE teacher?

Gretchen wandered in, opened the fridge. The other three people in the room watched as she found herself some cheese. It was happening, Kathryn could see it in the long, graceful sweep of her back, the fall of that white-blonde mane. Gretchen was starting that shift from an awkward child to beautiful young woman. She turned around, saw the eyes on her.

"Hey Gretchen? I need to go to the hardware store. Do you want to come with?"

She shook her head and left the room.

Gentry sat for a moment, absorbing the blow. He rose up and carried his coffee cup out the back door. Such dignity in the face of rejection. Certainly Gretchen would have to forgive him for being male. Eventually.

Marci poured herself some coffee and joined her little sister on the couch in front of the TV. Their voices drifted in. "That cheese gives you horrible breath."

"That coffee makes yours worse."

Kathryn poured a cup and worked the crossword.

Victoria Lazarre.

She'd met Miss Lazarre at a meeting to plan the senior all-night party. Kathryn was trying to accomplish her own return from the dead, she was trying to participate. Her inattention had resulted in that strange boy prowling around her house. She was determined to be present and involved in the lives of her children. And this Miss Lazarre was on the party committee. Oh, she was calm. Dead calm. She reminded Kathryn of the bathtub in the little house; huge, smooth, and white. She was gorgeous.

When Kathryn introduced herself, Miss Lazarre took her hand and said, "Pleased to meet you." Her voice was almost as low as his, and she looked at Kathryn and somehow she knew. Maybe Gentry had told her. Kathryn thought of them together, his long, strong body, hers even longer, even stronger. Her body could take him. Nothing on Vicki Lazarre would be sharp, or poke, or hurt. He'd taken such care of Kathryn, but when he left her bed, a row of little bruises marked the front of his hips. Her pelvic bones had bruised him. He left her bed carrying her mark. She'd spent that night memorizing the contours of his face, the particulars of his body, the way his thighs joined his torso, the dips and curve of his stomach, where his hair grew. She'd seen his face in ecstasy and in sleep, and he had seen hers.

She hung her head and heard the call of a drink. If only she could tie herself to the mast.

She had thirty days. Thirty days of sitting in meetings with men who reminded her of Garret Blount, grown up. Thirty days without her only coping device. Thirty days to survey her failure, stretching as far as her mind's eye could see.

She'd never had thirty days.

"Mom?" Gretchen's ice blue eyes, her long hands. "Mom, if that Alex guy was just trying to find Gentry, then why did you call the police?"

Kathryn pulled a kitchen chair next to her and patted the seat. Gretchen sat her narrow little behind down and twined her legs around the chair legs like ivy. "Because I was scared, honey. Coach Gilroy told me someone was prowling around the house, so I overreacted and called the police." Kathryn stroked Gretchen's shining white hair.

"Okay. But you could have told them it was fine and to go away, and you didn't. You let them put Alex in the car."

Gretchen had seen all that. Lorrie and Gentry walking their prisoner up to the house where Emmett waited, that boy looking as sick and pale and sad as a corpse that had washed up on the beach. Lorrie had him by the scruff of the neck, moving slow and solemn like it was a last walk to the electric chamber. Gentry moved with the same implacable intent, glowing in the mercury light, delivering this boy to justice.

"You're right, they took him in and questioned him. But it was all a mistake. When they questioned him, they realized it was all a misunderstanding."

Gretchen's eyes flashed with anger. "I'm not an idiot. Please don't talk to me like I'm an idiot, all right?"

"You're not an idiot, Gretchen. You're my baby girl."

"I'm not a *baby*. When will all of you realize that I'm *not* a *baby*." She stood up and began to pace. "I was asleep on the couch and he was looking in the window at me. Right? I figured that out. He was doing something. And it was gross, whatever it was. He was doing something *gross*." Her eyes were glacial with accusation. Kathryn opened her mouth to reply, but Gretchen cut her off. "I know, Mom, I *know*. I know there's that part of men, Mom, I know that. They have that, that . . . *side*."

"Men aren't all like that."

"Yes they are. All of them. Dad is like that. Graham is already like that. Spencer's going to grow up and be like that." Her body was rigid, her teeth clenched. "Mom, even *Gentry* is like that." She threw herself into her mother's arms. Grieving. Kathryn smoothed her hair back, rocked the baby girl who was taller than her.

She did not drink.

Gretchen

Before this all happened, he'd been so sad. For weeks, he wouldn't talk to anybody around but her. Normally she'd have liked that, but when a person was that sad and you were the *only* one he'd talk to, it was weird.

He went to church a lot. He'd stay up all night and read. Then, at about five o'clock, she'd hear Coach Gilroy come to take him fishing. She'd go back to sleep until seven, and come downstairs to a big pile of gutted fish in the sink. Gentry would be at the stove, frying those fish up for breakfast.

That was an interesting way to start the day.

She'd sit at the table and wait. Marci would come down the stairs with her hand pressed over her mouth like she was going to barf from the smell, but she didn't say anything. She sat down with a plate and waited, too. He'd fill up their plates and get one for himself, and they'd all sit and eat together, picking little bones out of their teeth. Their mom stayed in her room with the window open while the rest of them ate bony little fish for breakfast. Sometimes for dinner, too, depending how much he'd caught that day. He always cooked it, and he did it right, that was the funny thing. Every fish he cooked was perfect.

That went on for three weeks.

Marci said he kept falling asleep in class. She said nobody wanted to wake him up, because he was so startled. She wanted Gretchen to find out what was wrong. She could have asked if she was so worried. But things changed after that night. Gentry got better. He was happy again. Maybe lying to her put him in a better mood, who knew, but he was lying to Gretchen just as much as anyone else in her family, and she was tired of it.

Garret didn't come over anymore. The only part she missed about Garret was the fish.

∽

She knocked.

His face looked surprised when he opened the door. "Hey."

"How was the hardware store?"

"It was . . . the hardware store."

"Oh." Bosco shoved himself up from the warm spot in front of the refrigerator and came over to get petted. "Can I take Bosco for a walk?"

"Of course."

"Do you want to come with?"

Gentry smiled. "Sure."

∽

They walked down the steps without talking. Bosco first, then Gretchen, then Gentry. She liked hearing his boots on the steps behind her. When they reached the sand, Bosco took off running. She reached over and took Gentry's hand, and he let her.

She liked Gentry's hands. He had a calipers and he showed her how to use it, and then he let her measure his fingers from joint to joint. She used her mother's measuring tape to measure digital circumference. Measuring tapes were not at all precise, but she did the best she could and recorded it all in a notebook. The best part was that he didn't ask her why she wanted to do it. He probably knew about the Golden Mean.

Bosco barked at a gull that kept gliding down to bother him.

"I think he wishes he could fly."

"I think we all wish that."

"I think you're right."

It was windy, but she had on a very old, thick sweater. It might have had some reindeer on the front. She said might, because they looked like guinea pigs with antlers, not reindeer. It was from one of her mother's boxes in the garage. She pulled the sleeve over both their hands to keep them warm. "Where did you catch Alex?"

Gentry frowned. "Over there."

She couldn't see anything special about that place. No clue, no sign of what happened. "Marci says he moved away. Marci says Coach Gilroy will probably make everyone on the football team wear a black armband."

"He's gone to live with his aunt in Bend." Gentry didn't laugh. "Lorrie is upset about the team."

"Why did he have to leave? What did he do wrong?"

Gentry's hand tightened around hers.

Looking in windows was wrong, but she did it all the time. They *were* made of glass. If Alex had just been looking in a window, Gentry would have said, "Hey Alex? Can I help you?"

"I'm not stupid, Gentry. I know that Alex Fournier was looking at me." Gretchen was worried about how she was sleeping, what he saw. Was her underwear showing? She was eleven years old. There was nothing about her to be looking at.

They walked.

⌒

Her mom had never said anything to her about sex. But she knew about it. Marci and Gretchen were watching a special on lions and two of them were doing it and Gretchen said, "Is that what people do?" Marci frowned at the screen and said, "Well, sort of."

Gretchen had sat in Health on the days when the boys went to another room and they all watched those insulting videos that treated sexual development like a disgusting idea they couldn't handle unless the teachers made it seem like a Disney movie. But Gretchen did pay attention. She was interested in the human markers for being ready to reproduce. Boys got shoulders, hair, and bigger parts. Girls got hips and breasts and hair and periods. Those were the markers, and she didn't have any of them.

There were girls in her class who wore bras, who complained about their periods so everyone would know they had them. Gretchen was taller than anyone in her class, but she didn't wear a bra because she didn't need one. No breasts, no hair, and that was fine. She had no markers, none at all. There was no reason for anyone to want to look in a window at her or show her his penis on the beach.

She didn't understand.

She'd yelled at her mother about it. She'd never yelled at her mother before. Her mom asked if she wanted to "see someone," which meant go to a therapist. Gretchen wanted to figure it out herself. It was biology, so if she studied it, she could probably understand it. But how to study it? You had to observe the species in its natural habitat. And that was the trouble with men. How could you see them in their natural habitat?

It was like wolves. If she wanted to know about wolves, she'd have to penetrate the habitat and habituate them to her so they'd let her observe. The wolves would have to trust her and what if they didn't? Wolves were scared of people.

And people kept secrets.

They were almost to the tide pools. "Gentry? You've had girlfriends, right?"

He smiled and frowned at the same time. "Yes, Gretchen, I have."

"More than one?"

He reached up and scratched at his jaw with his free hand. "Hey Gretchen? Why are you asking?"

"I wonder why you don't you have a girlfriend."

"For a lot of reasons. None of which I want to talk about." She dropped his hand and pulled hers up into the sleeves of that old sweater. He sighed and put his hands in his pockets. He cleared his throat. "I have a friend named Sandy Sanderson."

"Is that a boy or a girl?"

"A man." They walked for a minute, but she knew he'd start again.

"When we were in college, Sandy had an old two-stroke Kawasaki motorcycle. He loved that bike. He used to say, 'You should try it, Grasshopper. It's so fun, you can't believe it's legal.' And then he married our friend Paige, and Paige was having a baby, so Sandy sold the bike. And he missed it. He really, really missed that bike."

He got quiet again, but Gretchen knew he'd have a point.

"I talk to Sandy all the time. Almost every day on the computer. Sometimes on the phone. Every so often, he says, 'Grasshopper, do you have another woman?' I say I don't. I ask him if he has another two-stroke 1974 Kawasaki H2C 750 Triple." He kept his eyes on the sand, his hands in his pockets. It took him a minute to talk. And when he did, his voice sounded choked. "He says, 'No, Grasshopper. A motorcycle will be the death of me.'"

The death of him. Gentry was afraid. She'd never thought about a grown-up being afraid of all of it. She'd never thought of that at all.

She didn't have to ask him why he was afraid, since she was, too.

"Why does he call you Grasshopper?"

"I have no idea."

"You should ask him, dummy." She put her arm around his hip. She liked the way Gentry felt, how she could feel the muscle groups he used when he walked. He puts his arm around her shoulder and just for a second, he leaned down and put his face in her hair. All mammals did that with their newborns, they imprinted the scent of their young on their neurosystems. Even human mothers did that. Gretchen thought he'd find that interesting. But she kept quiet.

Gentry was a sand-watcher, because he didn't want to step in anything dead. Gretchen usually watched the sand because she wanted to stop and study anything dead. But that day, she watched the water. The whales were migrating, moving through that water, only breaking now and then to send up a spout or slap a tail. Biologists tried to observe the life of whales with divers and cameras and microchips. The pods migrated thousands and thousands of miles and most of the time, and they swam at crushing depths.

On TV, she watched some orcas swim up around a grey whale cow and calf. They surrounded and harried them until the calf was so exhausted that it fell away from its mother. Orcas, the most beautiful whales, ripped its jaw away. The calf died, and the orcas didn't even eat it. They were just killing for sport.

Those orcas were all males.

The last thing she watched was the whale calf sinking to the ocean floor with its jawbone torn away, looking like a little mailbox with the door hanging open. Its mother swam away, vocalizing. After that, she decided whales were exactly like humans. Men killed things they didn't have to, and mothers cried over it. But why?

You had to study something to understand it. How could you study humans? People were animals, but never thought of themselves that way. Humans lived so far away from how they were designed to that studying their behavior was useless. Studying humans would be like studying wolves that lived in zoos, or whales that performed at aquatic parks. You'd understand some of it, you'd see echoes of how they'd evolved. But not enough to make any real sense.

The way men acted made no sense to Gretchen. She didn't understand how Gentry and Garret acted, how they never said anything but were always fighting. It was the same with her dad and Gentry. Even though they seemed polite, they weren't. Her dad was telling Gentry he didn't have anything, and Gentry was telling Dad he didn't know anything.

The stupid thing is, they were both right.

She didn't understand what went on at school, and she'd stopped paying attention to most of it because she hated every single boy there was. She didn't understand fistfights or bullies or shoving matches or swearing or spitting or why her brothers thought throwing boogers at each other was hilarious. She didn't understand why her Dad was married to Eve instead of her mother, who was so much prettier and smarter and better, even though she did drink. She didn't understand why Alex Fournier looked in the window. She didn't understand that old man on the beach with his running shorts and his penis. She didn't understand any of that on the couch.

She didn't understand Gentry.

Gentry was a man. He was probably her best chance for understanding one. She'd studied him, she'd tried to understand. But he took that whole entire side of himself and turned it away from her. He was a wolf and a whale. Part of him was too wild to trust her, and the other part was too deep for her to follow.

MAY

Gentry

For years, the oldest brother at the monastery was Brother Harland. Before he gave himself over to God, he was a criminal. Loren called him "Felonius Monk."

This was a jazz joke, and I hate jazz.

Brother Harland could pick locks, crack safes, empty pockets and forge signatures. Harland relieved me of my wallet countless times, even after I chained it up. He liked to tell me about these lost skills he'd worked hard to master before he gave them up to dedicate himself to Christ. He spoke to me with the earnestness of a man seeking an heir to his expertise. *You have crime in your blood, Gentry. You're a natural.* How to wash a check. The quick and dirty flashlight process for projection, used in forgery. How to turn a five into a twenty while talking to a store clerk, a combination of conversation and expectation. I tried it once with Sandy and it worked. I found it all, as Gretchen would say, interesting.

The last summer he was alive, I was there. I must have had a day with no work, which was rare, but when I had one I put myself at the disposal of the brothers. We were pacing off a field on the grounds. Brother Harland could have done this himself, walked a field, reckoned its size. Maybe he just wanted the company.

I walked beside him as he poked and muttered, checking the existing vegetation, grumbling about moisture content, weeds. *How the hell*, he said, and *Maybe when hell freezes over*, and *When pigs fly out my ass*. He wasn't the only brother who swore.

And then he whistled. *Son of a bitch. Would you look at that.* He knelt, clearing long blades of prairie grass from something black and metal. I crouched down beside him as he used both hands to sweep dirt from the gold filigree painted along the corner. It was a safe. An old black office safe, sunk part of the way in the middle of a field on the grounds of a monastery. *Looks like an old Herring-Hall-Marvin.* We were on church property. Whatever this was, however it got there, it belonged to God. I knew it, Brother Harland knew it. God knew it, too. *Gentry, go get me a shovel and the vet kit, would you?*

I ran back to the biggest pole barn, my mouth dry, my heart beating. I found the old leather medical case, a shovel, a cracked pair of gloves to wear because he'd make me do the digging and it would tear up my hands. I ran back before he changed his mind.

He said we needed to level it. That took a good part of the morning, digging a space big enough for both of us in front of the door, and then gently digging under one side. The summer sun had no pity at noon. I didn't have a hat and felt heat sick. We knelt in the square pit that I'd dug as carefully and precisely as a grave, the prairie at eye level around us. I put a hand on the cold black metal to steady myself.

Good enough for government work. Give me the scope.

I found the stethoscope in the flaking black leather suitcase and handed it over. He put it on, moving it around the door as he manipulated the dial with movements soft as whispers. He sighed in criminal bliss. *You should see the mechanism in a door like this. It's amazing what you can't see. But it's all in there.* He traced a path with the bell of the stethoscope. *Gentry? Put this on and pay attention.*

I tried to do as I was told, but when I felt those earpieces in my ears, the world around me fell back to a heart beating, beating away. Not my own heart. A man's heart and a woman's voice, *Big men have big hearts.* Big hearts, pumping a wide slick of blood.

My head spun and the funereal smell of deep earth overpowered me.

I felt a hand on my shoulder, a touch so light it almost wasn't there. *Hey, you, this isn't nap time.* I opened my eyes, saw the rich brown of the earth, the eerie threads of prairie grass worked through it. White witch hair in the dirt.

I shrugged away his pickpocket's hand, shivering.

Now pay attention. Listen while you turn the knob. It's your ears and your hands. What you feel and what you hear. And your blood.

What am I listening for?

You'll know it when you hear it. And you'll feel it more than you'll hear it. Trust your hands and your blood. I tell you, you're a natural. You've got crime in your blood.

I knew he had faith in my inherent criminality, but these were not precise directives. But I listened where he told me, turned as he instructed me. Slow, incremental. He was right. I could feel it in my hands, when to stop, to reverse. And the way it turned over, the way it fell into place. That gentle thump and tumble, that almost silent settling that let my listening hands know I'd found the combination that would open up all the mysteries, all the secrets.

It's like a woman, I whispered.

He threw back his bald head and laughed.

⌒

Some things are in the blood.

I knew he was back there because I smelled him. I smelled someone who didn't belong and tracked that smell, crept the edges, found where he was. When I saw him standing outside the window, that unmistakable rhythm of his arm, I felt that same thump and tumble, that same locking in. And it was me that cracked open. What came out was an animal.

Chase.

He panicked and took the steps to the beach. Forty-four steps. I knew every riser, board and landing, every loose handrail and rusting nailhead between the top of the bluff and the beach. I could have taken him down on those steps, but to where? We'd both have fallen.

I would take him on the beach.

Thought fell back and the body came forward to do what the body does. He must have known when I launched myself to bring him down, because he was flinching before I ever touched him. The moment my body connected with his was one of the most satisfying of my life. Now I understand why Lorrie loves football.

It might have been different if he fought me, but he didn't. He cowered on the ground. I stared down at his terrified face, the blankness at his center that repelled me and always had. I felt nothing. Nothing, like what was inside that old safe when Brother Harland slid the nickel crossbar over and opened the door. I was empty.

I sat on him until Lorrie came. I stood, and he pulled the boy to his feet looked him over. "Good, you didn't mess him up. I thought you might mess him up. Adrenaline, you know. I'm glad you kept your head." Then he clamped his huge ham hands on Alex's shoulder and shook him until his jaw rattled. "DAMMIT! DID YOU EVER THINK WHAT THIS WOULD DO TO THE TEAM, YOU SONOFABITCH!"

"Lorrie, don't shake him. Don't."

He stopped himself.

By the time we reached the top of the steps, lights flashed in the driveway.

Kathryn stood there, arms crossed, face hard. Was Gretchen still asleep on the sofa? I hoped she would sleep innocent through all of this and never, ever know. But no, innocence never lasts. She came out in her white nightgown and bare feet, frowning and rubbing her eyes. Then Marci came, stumbling and grumpy, demanding to know what the "deal" was. "What's the deal?"

Kathryn's eyes flashed a command to enter into collusion with her. To protect them another way, to save them from information. I watched demand turn to supplication in her eyes as the lights flashed, red and white, red and white, on the trees and the big house and my house, on Alex's blank, staring face, on Lorrie's face as he stood there, more blasted apart than anyone else.

Marci's eyes widened as she watched Emmett handcuff Alex. She called across the driveway to me. "Gentry, what's going ON?"

I shook my head. "Ask your mother." Because I had no clean words to explain what I'd seen. Emmett said he'd be back to take my statement in the morning.

Kathryn was adamant that night. She's adamant now. This was something that had never happened. Except it did. I told Emmet what I saw, but Kathryn wanted no charges filed, no information released. They let Alex go.

Kathryn demanded that I stay silent.

⌒

Gretchen didn't trust me for a while. She knew I was lying, a lie of omission.

But she let me drive her to and from school, she watched me from the corners of her eyes. I knew it would pass, that she would trust me again. I knew what it was not to trust. I remembered Mel, his quiet presence during the year I could hardly speak out loud.

Marci was oddly tolerant of my presence, which I didn't understand because she wasn't supposed to know what happened. And of everyone, it was Marci who had no trouble with the official version. She handled the fact that I drove her to and from school, monitored her whereabouts. This would pass. Marci would go back to disliking me.

Kathryn was furious and grateful. I'd usurped her somehow, stepping in where only a parent belonged. She couldn't forgive this. I had to defer to her, obey her, let her decide how this would be handled even though I knew she was wrong. But this would pass. I worried more about me. I was still locked in and ready to give chase.

God, tell me that this vigil will lessen. Tell me I'll relax. My heart, my breath, my vision, it will unlock. I'll be a man again, not an animal. I wasn't made to take children down like prey. I was made to teach them.

God, tell me this will pass.

Amen.

⌒

Big men have big hearts. Someone said that to me once. I don't know who or where or when I was told that, but I looked at Lorrie and knew it was true. His big heart was broken.

He went through his days defeated. He wouldn't rant. He barely swore. He wouldn't even tell me any terrible jokes. He'd lost his best player, his only hope. I needed a remedy for him, God, I had to find a way to make a repair.

I thought I'd figured it out. Our girl's PE teacher had left to have a baby. For the remainder of the year, the girls would go through their paces under the relentless direction of a substitute, Miss Victoria Lazarre.

Ah, to describe Miss Lazarre. She was an abundance of riches. Her face was calm enough to suggest paralysis, but her eyes danced with intelligence. Her voice was low enough to make the hairs on my arms stand up. She was taller than me, and substantial. When she sat down next to me on a lunch table bench, I flew up in the air a little. She had deadly steel biceps, strong thighs, a backside so high and hard that I could set up my computer on there. She had magnificent breasts. Those were Your handiwork, God.

But I wasn't thinking of myself, for once.

⌒

When Lorrie and I had coffee in the teacher's lounge, he drank out of his mug that said "Football Forever, Work Whenever." I drank out of the mug he bought for me, which said "Byte me." He shook his big buffalo head. "Did you see the size of her feet, Gentry?"

"Her feet?" I was too busy looking at all the other parts.

"Yeah, her feet. Jesus, little buddy, look at those feet. Those feet are enormous. I've never seen feet like that on a woman. Where the hell does she get her shoes, that's what I want to know." Who *cared* where she got her shoes? Lorrie was a fool, and blind to his destiny. This was Betty Page made young, a woman who could knock Lorrie across a room without trying. Couldn't he see?

I saw. I saw the future. I saw Lorrie Gilroy and Vicki Lazarre, I saw an uber race of children, children who will lead us across that bridge into the new millennium. I saw many, many children, an entire football team, offense and defense. Foul-mouthed children, swearing children, children who habitually took the Lord's name in vain, fishing children, hunting children, children who competed in martial arts tournaments, children who knocked people around, children with enormous feet.

And enormous hearts, as well.

Marci

"Wha do you two talk about? I didn't know she could talk, actually. Does she actually talk?"

Gentry just smiled.

He seemed better to Marci. He didn't stare at his hands all the time, and he stayed awake in class. He was even noticing what he ate again. She'd made lasagna, and he did the little smile and chew after the prayer. She hadn't realized how much she'd missed that little smile.

"This is excellent lasagna, Marci."

"It certainly is." Vu was there for dinner. "So, Gentry, as you probably know, I'm the token nonwhite in the junior/senior prom court. I'm nominated for king, along with our fair Tiffany. Who finds herself in need of an escort, so . . ."

Marci used her fork to pull apart her noodles and scrape out the cheese. Poor Creepy Alex. He'd probably come over to talk to Gentry about Tiffany being pregnant. He had no father, he lived with his grandmother, who else would he talk to besides Gentry? The coach? And he ended up being shoved in a cop car. Tiffany was completely devastated. Marci would have felt sorry for her if she weren't so pathetic and annoying.

"At any rate, I need you to consider something." Vu was gearing up, switching into his persuasive student-government mode. "I'm supposed to ask if you'll do the student body the honor of acting as a chaperone at the prom."

Gentry looked skeptical. "What exactly *is* a prom?"

This was so typical. "You don't know what a prom is? Where were you raised, Mars?"

Kathryn gave her daughter a look, and Gentry an explanation. "It's a big formal dance."

"A *dance*?" Gentry set down his fork and stared at his plate, moving his head from side to side as if wondering what outlandish idea the Mumfords would come up with next.

Vu continued his pitch. "Come on, it will be an interesting life experience for you. Maybe you can take Miss Lazarre."

Please. Miss Lazarre belonged on that late night gladiator show. Black, shiny hair, big, sharp horse teeth as white as Eve's, and boy, could she ever blow on a whistle. She believed in stamina, in cross training, in endurance. She was killing Marci in PE, which unfortunately she'd delayed until her senior year. "Yes, you should take her. After your pursuit and capture of Alex, you can probably handle anything, even the Anabolic Amazon Queen."

Gentry ignored that. "Is Lorrie going?"

"What, you'll only go if your *friend* will be there? Do men ever grow up?"

Vu smiled. "Yes, Coach Gilroy will be honoring us with his presence. He's bringing the nurse who helped remove that lovely mole from his neck."

"Lorrie had a mole?"

"Yes, it looked like a big hairy cockroach."

Gretchen leaned forward. "Did he have it *biopsied*?"

"Gretchen, please," murmured her mother.

Gentry picked up his fork, started to eat again, but he was thinking, something going on in that head, something to do with Miss Lazarre, Marci would bet on it. "Do I have to dance?" He shook his head. "Because I can't dance unless I'm drunk."

Marci cracked up, as did Vu, but her mother was irritated. "Honestly, Gentry."

"I think it's very honest, Mom."

Thankfully, the phone rang. Her mother went to the kitchen to answer, and Marci could tell by the defeated curve of her neck that it was her father. She'd been going to meetings, but talking to her father might do it.

Vu was offering to teach Gentry to dance. "Seriously, Gentry, you just have to listen to the inner rhythms of your sexuality. The beast, as it were."

"Whatever, Vu, your inner sexual beast is a gerbil."

Gretchen giggled, and Gentry laughed in spite of himself.

"You're all so pleasant here, while Marci razors up my fragile adolescent male ego."

Her mother started to talk louder. "It isn't me, Michael. It's her. Gretchen refuses to come." There was the pause while her dad talked at her mother. "She says she doesn't want to come to your house and get beaten up by that son of yours anymore." Vu snickered, but Gretchen shrank into herself, so horribly embarrassed. "I'm talking about the older one, the one who yells all the time. He shoves her around and he picks his nose and wipes it on her bedding. No, I'm serious. She told me." Marci hadn't heard her mother talk to him like this for ten years. "I'm sure that Gretchen isn't making this up. Gretchen does not lie. And frankly, whatever's wrong with that boy, if you don't deal with it, I'm not sending her to your house. I'll see a lawyer. She has enough trouble at school. She shouldn't have it at your house, too."

Gretchen stared at her plate. Her mother brought the receiver to her, that dirty mustard yellow cord stretching across the room. "Your father wishes to speak with you." Gretchen crossed her arms, and she looked just like her mother when she did that. Kathryn finally held the receiver up to Gretchen's ear. She listened for a minute. Apparently her dad had been talking the whole time.

She said one sentence. "I'll only go if Gentry drives me."

Her mother pulled the receiver back from Gretchen's delicate white ear to guard it from her father's yelling, and his words spilled out through the line and over the table.

". . . *one more goddamn block in that heap!*"

Kathryn put the receiver up to her own ear. "Watch your language, Michael. Now, Gretchen will come if you deal with your son, and if Gentry drives her. And that's that. I'm going to go finish my dinner." She trotted back into the kitchen and hung up on him.

She sat down in her chair and tucked into her lasagna with an unfamiliar delight.

Vu finally broke the admiring silence. "You preside over an interesting dinner table, Mrs. Mumford."

"Thank you, Vu. Please don't talk with your mouth full." Her mother frowned at Marci. "Are you going to prom?"

"Of course."

"Really? In Portland? With Evan?"

"No, Mom, I'm not going to prom in Portland." Evan had called out of nowhere and asked Marci to his prom. Her mother couldn't contain her enthusiasm for the whole idea. "I'm going to the prom here. At my school. Where I go."

Kathryn arched a white eyebrow. "With whom?"

And then it was her turn to look down. "Well, that's the funny part." Marci studied her plate the way Gentry did when he didn't know what to say. "I'm going with Garret. We're not, you know, back together, but we're going to prom. We're on court."

Her mother's sigh said it all.

Gentry's expression was somewhere between furious and sick. Vu was, of course, utterly fascinated. The phone rang again.

Gentry stood up. "I'll get it." He took the call in the kitchen, but Marci could hear just fine. "Hey, Mike. How's your, um, neck? I'm so glad to hear it, I'm so . . . No, no, I haven't done anything about the sub-woofer thing yet, no, I haven't . . . oh, you did? What did they say? . . . This weekend? I guess I'll drive in and have that done, then . . . a favor? . . . Sure, no problem . . . No, that's no problem at all. I would be happy to. I'll just fire up the heap, I mean, the Jeep, and bring her over. Yes? . . . okay . . . okay. See you then. Hey to Eve. I, um, have to go. Bye."

Well, wasn't that chummy.

Gentry came back to the table. They were all staring at him. He shrugged. "What? I need to have that speaker rewired. And Gretchen said she would go if I drove her."

Gretchen started to cry. Gentry was confused. Marci spoke softly to him while her mother tried to calm Gretchen and Vu watched the floor show. "Can I come along to Portland? You promised you would take me back to . . ." She stopped. No sense getting her mother upset. But she wanted to go to Portland with Gentry more than anything, she didn't know why.

He answered softly. "Yes, of course you can come along. But Marci? You're going to go to this prom thing with Garret?"

"Yes."

He blinked once, and raised his voice.

"Okay, Vu, I'll do it. I can chaperone. But I need some help."

Vu rolled his eyes, shook his head. "Gentry, I'm never taking you shopping again. That trip still haunts my nightmares. You're on your own, unless . . ." Vu stopped. "Never mind, I know what size you wear, I'll take care of it."

"Do you need money?"

"Nope. I'll go to the Vietnamese Nordstrom."

And they both cracked up.

Gentry

When we arrived, they all came out to greet us. Mike Mumford seemed fine, he was recovered, Thank You, God. Mike clapped me on the back hard and hearty. Ouch, Mike. Maybe Mike was hoping to cause some reciprocal damage to my spinal column.

"Just want to say thanks," he said. "I mean it." And again with the mauling, the whacks. I felt his pounding in my kidneys. I'd had about fifty cups of coffee this morning.

"Could I, um, wash up?"

The bad son, Graham, was my guide through the paterfamilian mansion that Mike Mumford called home. He took me through the kitchen with its industrial-sized stove and mortuary-sized refrigerator, through a short door and down some narrow steps that didn't have a grown person listed on their capacity permit. I banged my head on a beam halfway down. Stars, ouch. Quite a bit of wine down there, and many spiders. As I pulled the webs from my hair, I kept my eyes open for nitre, piles of bricks and mortar. Not that I was paranoid or anything.

Basements. Not good. I wondered if the place has an elevator. Probably.

Graham showed me to a rotting, filthy little bathroom. The door didn't shut right. Mid-stream, I noticed a piggy little eye glinting through the crack. Fortunately, I didn't have a shy bladder. Boarding school and dorm life would cure you of that.

I was concerned with this spying. The whole world couldn't be a threat to Gretchen, could it?

I washed my hands, but there was no towel, towels were upstairs on heated racks in the bathrooms with functioning doors, heated marble flooring, panoramic views, steam showers and whirlpool tubs. I used my wet hands to smooth back my hair.

I opened the useless door. "Hey Graham? Spying is rude."

He had a puffy face and teeth that seemed to have been ground off into stumps. He sneered. "You look like someone I know."

"Is that right." No one ever said that to me. "Who?"

"Someone I hate." He bared his horrible, stumpy teeth. "Your willy's bigger than my dad's." My willy? It was a CJ5, everyone always thought it was a Wrangler. "Your willy's way bigger than mine or Dad's." Ah, that. He sounded dejected.

"Are you mean to girls?" He glared at me, shocked. "If you're mean to girls, your willy shrinks and shrinks. I don't know why, but it happens that way. So don't ever be mean to girls."

He headed off into a corner of the basement to torture insects, and I found my own way back upstairs, bumping my head, asking God's pardon, because there was some truth to this, isn't there? If you were nice to girls, your willy did grow in a way, yes?

I stopped in the kitchen to admire the appliances. I stood in awe of the range. In the summer I ate in farm kitchens where harried women fed starving combine crews. I wondered about the meals a farm wife could make on something like this.

I didn't think Eve fed very many combine crews.

The refrigerator was even more impressive than the range, with visible dials and gauges, tempered glass doors to display the contents. A regiment of bottled water and fruit juice filled the top shelf, an artful still life of wrapped cheese sat on another. I imagined my solitary quart of whole milk on display in this gargantuan vault.

Back at the Jeep, Marci waited in the front seat, exchanging some heated words with her dad. Hm. I decided to chat with Eve. She smiled at me and I shuddered. "Gretchen said you like iced tea." She handed me a glass.

"Thank you." I took a swig to be polite. Oh, please, sugar, this was not the south, no one sugared the tea in Oregon, no one but Eve, no wonder she lost her teeth. I spat it all back in the glass. Eve wasn't impressed with the precision of my spitting, she just seemed puzzled when I handed her the glass. I didn't know what else to do with it.

I scratched my head and cleared my throat. "Your son, um, Graham, he spied on me in the bathroom, Eve. The one in the basement. I thought you should know."

The horror in her face. "He took you to the *basement*?" She seemed more embarrassed by the basement than her son. Thanks to the pension funds, there

seemed to be plenty of money around there. If I were Eve, I'd have traded that kid
in on a better model.

Eve rushed away to scold her son and Mike left his angry daughter and came
over to thump me a little more. I forced myself to stop gagging from the tea because I needed to talk to Mike and if I gagged in front of him, he'd pick me up in
a huge, manly Heimlich maneuver and crush my ribs. "Hey Mike? Can I tell you
something?" This question got me more reassuring back claps. I'd earned this, I
submitted, God, this was penance. Part of my penance.

"What can I do for you, Gentry?"

You could stop shaking me by the shoulder, Mike.

"Um," I hated myself when I "ummed," "Hey Mike?"

God, do You know how hard this is for me to say?

"Mike, there's something I want to, um, tell you about Gretchen."

Go ahead and spit it out, I hate this more than sweet tea.

He seemed concerned. "What is it?"

"She, um, has, um . . ." Maybe he could hit me again, maybe it would knock
this loose. I gagged a little more, and that made me stop umming. I hated myself.

Okay, enough.

"Look, Mike. I taught Gretchen how to ride her bike. And she's practiced quite
a bit on her own. She's good enough to go down to the cove with it. So I just
thought, um, well, I mean, um . . ." Oh, get a grip. "If you have a bike and you
brought it along, you could take her down there. Or maybe you could ride Marci's,
or rent one, but you could go to the sidewalk on the cove? To ride bikes together.
I think she'd like it."

"The promenade. Sure. Great idea!" He was pummeling me, get your stupid
hands off me, Mike, I don't like you, I just owe you. Never ruffle my hair, please
Dear God, this hair ruffling must stop.

I left before he hugged me because I had limits and if he hugged me I'd hit him
and I'd have to start all over again with penance.

∽

Marci didn't say a word as we drove down the beautiful hill into the beautiful
city. I took the opportunity to let out some quiet gagging. I didn't know if it was
the sugared tea or the effort of penance that made me gag more.

"My dad is such a prick." No, I think your dad is a willy, Marci. "He expects me to stay there tonight, and when I said wouldn't, he accused Mom of turning me against him. Like I can't figure out what a prick he is all on my own."

I'd never heard Kathryn mention him to either girl. She pretended Mike doesn't exist. "Maybe he's worried about you."

"Dad's only worried about Gretchen."

⌒

We dropped off the Jeep. The service writer was contrite to a level of absurdity. "We are so sorry about this." "We want to offer our deepest apologies, Mr. Gentry." "I can't tell you how badly we feel." No one died, a wire just came loose.

I needed air. "Hey Marci? Let's walk up to your old house." She brightened. It was a nice day, a nice walk. When we got there, Marci gave me a quick visual appraisal before we climbed the steps. I passed muster. I'm trying Marci, I am trying. I left the John Deere cap at home, and that's my favorite cap.

We climbed the stairs to the entry. The front door stood open. Classical music, Pachelbel's Canon. Thank you, Music History 201. It sounded nice coming out of that big white house. "Knock, knock," Marci called.

Hey Marci? Come on, no verbal knocking. I rang the bell. A woman about my age came to the door. Her face was bright and cute and reminded me of a ferret, and I meant that in the most complimentary way possible. She looked at our hands, no weapons, no religious literature, no soap samples. I felt stupid. Incredibly stupid.

"Can I help you kids?"

"I used to live here. I'm Marcialin Mumford."

"Mumford? I recognize that name. You lived here for years, didn't you?"

"Yes." We all stood there, quiet for about two of the longest seconds of my life. "Did you want to come in?"

I didn't think Marci had ever wanted anything so badly in her life. I was relieved for her. "Yes, I know it's weird, but I really want to show the house to . . ." She waved a hand over at me. "To Gentry."

The woman gave us the sweetest little grin, and her eyes flashed with sympathy, understanding. "It's not weird at all. I understand."

Once inside, Marci took over as tour guide. She showed me the beveled and leaded glass, the inglenook, the mullions, the wainscoting. The rectory had all these features, but I never knew what to call them, other than "old house stuff."

This was a Craftsman bungalow, and did I know it was built from a Sears catalog kit in 1921? No, Marci, I didn't know that, and neither did the woman who owned the house. She was delighted.

We entered the kitchen. Marci stopped, shocked. "You changed it."

"Yes, we opened it up, it was so dark, and the utility porch was useless, so we took it and the half bath out . . ."

Marci recovered, praised the room, which was full of sunshine. Marci sounded relieved when she said, "At least you still have the butler's pantry." I saw no butler in there, just a bunch of shelves, glasses.

Well, there we were. This woman was so nice to us, it was embarrassing. She smiled the most endearing smile, but I could tell she was wondering "what next?"

God, send a sign to end this awkwardness.

We heard a funny little noise from a speaker on the counter. "Would you like to go upstairs?" Of course Marci wanted to go upstairs. The tour continued. Marci pointed to a door on the landing and said "attic." Ah, the attic. We continued up into a hall, and the woman opened a door.

Oh.

A baby, pulling up on his crib bars. He had blond hair and blue eyes and the froggiest little face. He didn't have very many teeth, but those he had were much nicer than Graham's. The baby looked right at me and smiled. He held out his arms. There was a feeling in my heart, a tightness.

Dear God, the beautiful pain of it.

I knew this feeling from a trip to Oklahoma to see the Sandersons and their kids, Lucy Rose and Byron Branwell. Those kids made my heart hurt like this. I felt chosen. I took that soaked boy into my arms, and he made a wet little "crrr," and pulled my hair.

Oh God, someday? Please?

The kid had a good grip. "What's your name?" I asked him. He didn't tell me.

"How old is he?" Marci asked.

"Seven months. Today. And his name is Max." Hey, Max, Happy Birthday. Only seven months old, and what, five teeth? You're an amazing young man, Max. Standing up in your crib, pulling out my hair, you have all kinds of tricks, don't you?

"Can I hold him?" Marci, I suppose so. Though, I would like to point out, he asked me, I didn't do the asking. He picked me. But I suppose it's only fair. If you have to. I guess.

His mother wanted to change him first, and my shirtsleeves attested to the wisdom of this plan. She dealt with the diaper thing while Marci poked around Max's room, which she told me was Gretchen's. Marci showed me the laundry chute. It fell two stories into the basement, and Max's mother sent a diaper down by way of demonstration. The landing thud was wet.

Marci smiled. "I used to drop all kinds of things down there."

I was glad she never tried to drop Gretchen down there.

Marci stopped in front of a shelf full of stuffed animals, staring at a doll that didn't seem to merit much attention. The doll was about three feet tall, and it was all yellow, the yarn hair, the dress, even the face. It was a strange doll, to tell the truth, not that I was a doll expert. "Oh my God," the woman blurted, awe in her voice. Something about this doll . . . was there a hidden message, a resemblance I didn't see? "Was it yours?"

"No." Marci sounded far away. "My sister's."

The woman pulled the doll from the shelf. "The *box*. I have to give you the *box*." The woman handed the doll to Marci, and Max to me. I definitely got the better end of the deal in *that* one.

Hey, Max.

And we went back down some of the stairs to the landing and entered the attic by way of more stairs. The attic that was some sort of home entertainment center that still smelled strongly of attic. The woman opened a closet door and pulled out a dusty box. "We found this and the doll when we finished the walls up here. I always meant to track you folks down. Your mom has an unusual name, yes?"

"Yes." Marci recited in a wooden voice. "Katrin Marit Tingstad."

Katrin Marit Tingstad? Who was that?

The woman smiled. "Yes. Oh, I meant to find you all, I'm so sorry, there's so much important family stuff in here, your mom must have been heartbroken to leave it behind . . ."

Marci's voice sounded young. "No, she was burning everything. I hid that box from my mother so she wouldn't burn it." She kept on in that sad little voice. "I tried to get everything important in there, but I know I missed some. I tried to save what I could, but I was only seven."

We all stopped. Even Max. The woman took Max from me, wait, we were fine, me and Max, but she gave me an urgent look, then glanced at Marci.

Oh. All right.

It was like hugging a pillar at first. She was a stone girl, stone except for the tears tracking her cheeks. And then something inside her gave way, and the woman carried Max away downstairs so he wouldn't see it, and I sat down on this couch sort of a thing and pulled her into my arms. Her entire body shook, and her arms went around my neck, she held on and sobbed. I thought of Gretchen, Marci was just a girl like Gretchen, a girl who could break and cry. It was easy, then, it was safe to let her cry into my shirt, to hold her and pat her, because she was seven years old right then.

It seemed like a long time, but she finally settled down. "I'm okay."

"Are you?"

"Yes. Okay? I'm okay."

"Okay. If you're okay. Then everything is okay."

That made her smile through her tears. "I'm sorry."

"It's all right to cry." And beneath my own words, I heard Mel's, reassuring. *It is all right to cry, my boy. Hush now. Don't be afraid to cry.*

I pulled her close, kept her safe. Some things are safe to remember.

Max's mother had come back upstairs. She was beaming down on us with a goofy fondness based on a fundamental misunderstanding of what she saw. But I would let it stand, because all of a sudden, I loved this woman. "By the way, my name's Jenny." Jenny. What a fine, average name. "Would you two like some lunch?"

And that got Marci up, straightening her sweater, wiping her face with her hand. "No, I'm sorry to do this, to fall apart in your attic." She gave an embarrassed smile. "We have lunch plans. Oh, Gentry, your shirt."

My shirt? I wore one of these new shirts, was there something wrong with this shirt? I glanced down. It was soaked, big dark patches of wet all over the shoulders and chest. It looked like I'd been hit with a hose.

"I can put it in the dryer!" volunteered the splendid Jenny, no trouble at all, and nothing would do but that I remove it and hand it to her, no, it was no trouble, she took my shirt and I crossed my arms over my bare chest and we all made our way downstairs.

I could hear Max, where was Max? I thought he was calling me. I found him in the kitchen in one of those baby prisons with the webbed sides. "Gentry? Could you handle Max?"

I believed that I could.

Marci and the terrific Jenny took themselves down more stairs to the basement, and I liberated Max. "Hey, Max." Max went for the ring of hair around the nipple, "Whoa, wait a minute, Max. Let's check out some of these toys." Max had more toys than Mike Mumford.

Peerless Jenny called up the stairs to me, "Could you give Max his lunch? It's all set up."

Lunch? Baby lunch. I didn't have a lot of practice here, but I saw some bowls on the counter by the microwave and yes, a highchair. Hey Max, let's get all the proper safety restraints fastened, and let me wash my hands. Well, Max, I see we have some orange stuff, and some green stuff, and hey, if it works for you, Max, then I guess this is lunch.

I spooned in the orange stuff, ooh, it wasn't so great, huh? We just scraped it back into this yellow plastic spoon and retried. And the second time, some of it seemed to be going down the hatch, we were getting it, yes we are Max. We're on a roll now, let's try the green stuff, Max. Hey, I'm sorry, what is it that Jenny feeds you? I sniffed it but I had no idea what that green stuff was before it went through the puree process, and it made Max shudder, poor little guy.

Hey Max? Would you maybe like some juice? Here's some apple juice in a cup. This is clever, this cup doesn't tip over. I would like one of these cups. Hey, you like that stuff, I never have, but that's purely a matter of personal taste.

Max's eyes moved to a point over my shoulder. He smiled, held out a little orange-smeared hand. I turned. There was a surprised man there in the kitchen. I had an instinctive understanding that this was Max's dad. He seemed confused and I didn't blame him. He'd come home to have lunch with his family, and a shirtless stranger was feeding his son.

There was a long moment.

I was trying to decide how best to explain the situation when the superb Jenny came up the basement stairs. With a remarkable economy of words, she made the arrangement understood to her husband. Marci came up, which added to the veracity of Jenny's explanation, and all of it seemed to satisfy the other genetic contributor to Max.

What pride he must have felt at the besmeared and multicolored young man I got to finish feeding. Max and I came up with a system. We worked in a sort of a scraping and spitting partnership. We got a respectable amount ingested.

Well, what time was it getting to be, lunch plans, etc.

My shirt, still damp but warm, was returned to me. I buttoned, I even tucked in, the box and doll would be waiting on the porch for us, thanks so much, sorry about the attic, not a problem, and it was time to shake hands once again.

We bade farewell to that fine family.

Marci

Marci ordered a frittata for him. "You'll like it. It's like an omelet with potatoes." He hadn't eaten at the house that morning. She knew he had to be starving.

Kirsten wasn't working, but her mom and Evan's mother, Sally, were sitting over by the window with dessert and lattes. They saw Gentry and licked their lips. If her mother had any idea . . . Marci stopped herself. This was fine. He had on decent clothing. His hair was combed. His boots were new. He looked fine.

And of course, it helped that he was beautiful. He didn't *mean* to be so beautiful, he didn't *know* the effect he had.

She picked at her usual sandwich and watched him eat. He'd never given a repeat performance of how he ate his dinner that first night. Marci remembered that night, how embarrassed she felt every time she looked at him, how furious she was that she'd no longer be able to meet Garret in the little house. All those nights on her parents' old bed. She'd had to help her mother drag it out there when she was how old? Seven?

Had Gentry been in that bed with her mother?

She couldn't stand to think about it.

Her mother's friends stopped on their way out. Sally was an inch shorter than her mom, but she drew herself up and beamed. "You must be Gentry." He rose to his feet, so tall and gorgeous, just awkward enough to be forgiven for being perfect. He nodded and smiled while they told him who they were, obviously expecting that he'd heard their names. Marci was so glad he'd worn his new clothes. It was different now that she knew what she knew about, well. What she knew. Which she refused to think about.

They left. He sat back down and glanced at her plate. "Aren't you hungry?"

"Not really." But she took a bite.

He sipped his coffee and his eyes got soft. "That Max. Wasn't he something? His poor dad. What did he *think* when he walked in the kitchen?"

"That you were a strange shirtless burglar who broke into people's homes and fed their babies lunch." They burst out laughing. She gave him the other half of her sandwich and he ate it in three bites. "Speaking of babies . . ."

"What about them?" He brushed at his smile with a napkin.

She couldn't say it.

He had to have heard that Tiffany was pregnant, but just in case he hadn't, she thought she'd tell him. He thought Tiffany was so great. But he was happy, smiling, thinking about that little boy, and she didn't want to ruin it. "Speaking of babies, let's go pick up yours. The Jeep. It should be ready, right?"

⁓

There was the emotional reunion of man and vehicle. Gentry personally inspected the soldering of the wire, and Marci realized that he could have fixed this himself. They drove back to the house on Northrup for the box and the yellow doll, and those people who lived in her house came out to wave good-bye from her front porch.

She wondered if her parents had ever been that happy.

She kept the doll on her lap. Her dad had brought it home the day after Gretchen was born. Marci was stuck at home with a babysitter. He walked in and Marci saw its happy gingham face and reached for it. "No, honey, this doll's for your new baby sister."

He brought it to the hospital when they finally went to bring her mother home. Kathryn was tired and weak and sad. She didn't smile when she saw Marci, but she held out her arms for a hug. Her arms were loose. She couldn't hold on to anything, not the baby, not Marci. Not her father. But her mother held the doll on the way home. She went up to her bedroom and took that doll with her. Her dad had to take care of the baby.

Gretchen, a strange, pale baby, kept crying.

After her mother put that doll in the nursery, Marci snuck in there and took it. She hid it in a secret place in the attic, and occasionally she played with it in the dark. Her dad could never find it. Her mom never tried.

And six months later, when they had their last awful fight, when Marci heard him say he was going to leave, and her mother said, *good, get the hell out, you left so long ago but you just forgot to walk out the door*, and the door slammed and her mother was yelling and breaking things and burning her wedding pictures in the fireplace, Marci went into the hall closet and found that box. It was already half full, but she stuffed in her baby book, her first-grade report cards, whatever else she could fit before she dragged that box up to the attic and pushed it under the eaves by the yellow doll. She didn't know she would never be able to get it back.

Until that day.

She'd started to cry again when she was down in the basement. She'd looked around and remembered riding her bike down there when it was raining. She'd remembered her father's wine in the room next to the laundry, all those bottles her mother had come down and smashed until the floor was covered with sticky glass, and that huge furnace her mother had painted to look like a monster. None of that made Marci cry.

What made her cry was putting Gentry's shirt in the dryer, remembering Gentry taking off his shirt. He'd shrugged it off and stood there half naked. Marci had wondered how many times her mother had watched him take off his shirt.

She had to stop thinking about her mother and Gentry.

But she'd started to cry with the horrible hopelessness of what she felt, and that Jenny woman had patted her. *It sounds like it's been rough for you with your mom.* Marci, embarrassed and miserable, kept bawling. That woman had put her arm around her shoulder. *Listen to me. Life always offers us the chance to do it differently. Some day, you and your Gentry will have your own babies. Look at him with Max. He's a natural. The two of you will be such good parents.*

Her and her Gentry.

⁓

They drove down 25th and passed the Surgicenter. It was only blocks from her old house. Open on Saturdays, now, she saw. There was a yellow line painted on the sidewalk, and on one side of it stood a group of protesters, shouting, waving signs with pictures of bloody fetuses on them. An old man yelled at a girl walking in. "Don't slip on the baby blood when you go in there! Don't slip on the baby blood!"

That same psycho old man had yelled at her.

Gentry slowed the Jeep, stared. "What *is* this?"

"An abortion clinic. They're saving babies. Look, one of them is a priest." A priest waved a sign with scripture on it at the girls who'd come to save their own lives. A right-to-life carnival. "Tiffany had an abortion here. She wanted to have things taken care of before prom, since she's up for queen."

"This is taking *care* of it?"

Oh, please. What gave him the right to be so angry? What did any of this have to do with him? He was right there on the street side of the yellow line with the lunatics, she could tell. She wanted to tell him to just go over there himself, join the fun, wave a sign, scare some girl, save a baby. "What else was she going to do? She's so *stupid*. Anyone who has to cross that yellow line is so *incredibly* stupid."

He said nothing.

Gentry slammed it into gear, hard enough to hurt. "Tiffany tries. You have no *idea* how hard she tries. And she could use a friend."

"She has you."

He actually scoffed. "I'm no help in a situation like this."

"There were kids who thought it was you, you know. Who got her pregnant."

He looked outraged. "Why would anyone think that?"

"Because she wouldn't tell anyone who it was. People assumed she was protecting someone. Your name came up. She's in love with you, if you hadn't noticed."

He made a sound as tortured as his transmission.

"I should quit. I should just . . . give up teaching."

"What? Don't be a drama queen, Gentry. Nobody thinks it was you anymore. I mean, it was hard to believe anyone had sex with Creepy Alex, but then he left town. The timing was pretty obvious."

He didn't say anything, just kept grinding the Jeep up the hill, furiously slamming it through the gears. She was so busy being disgusted by him that she didn't notice where they were going until they were parked at her father's house. "Gentry? Why are we here?"

"I think you should stay here tonight."

"What the . . . I don't want to stay *here*." She hated Gentry. She never wanted to speak to him again as long as she lived. He was a prude and a religious weirdo and a hypocrite who had some secret, weird relationship going with her mother. And Marci hated him.

Gentry's face looked like someone had cast it in plaster. A death mask. That hard and white. "You'll be safe up here."

"Fine. I'll stay. And then you can go back to my *mother*."

"Don't."

She was still sitting there, and so was he, and there were miles between then, not feet. They were so far apart. But they weren't. Didn't he see that? They were not that far apart. He had to feel it, that warm crackle and hum when they connected over books, laughed at other people, liked the same songs. They were not that far apart.

"Gentry, could you just explain it to me? Explain why? Could you help me understand?" She put her hand on his arm. When he wouldn't look at her, she let herself touch his face, her palm against his sharp jawbone, the tips of her fingers grazing the faintest hint of whiskers.

She pulled her hand away and got out of that ridiculous Jeep, walked up the flagstones with the doll under one arm and her hand burning like she held a coal. She climbed the stone steps and pushed in the huge door to her father's house, expecting her hand to leave a char mark on the wood. She bumped into Gretchen, all arms and elbows and white, flying hair. "Watch it, you little albino." Her sister ignored her and ran outside to throw herself under the wheels because she'd rather die than be left behind by Gentry.

Marci guessed they were made up.

Her dad was in the front room, watching out the window while his new favorite girl threw herself at the man she loved more than anyone or anything, more than baby seals or dolphins or penguin chicks or her mother or her father or her sister. Her father turned to face her, and Marci had to look away from the piercing pain in his eyes. "Looks like you and Gentry were having quite the heart-to-heart out there."

She shrugged. "It was nothing." She crossed her arms over the yellow doll to muffle the thump of her guilty heartbeat.

"It looked pretty serious." He put a firm hand on her shoulder. "What were you talking about, honey?"

She rolled her eyes and thought of a million funny things to say, a million lies to tell. She'd sat out there longing to tell Gentry about Evan. The need filled her to bursting, to tell him and see if he would forgive her. She'd never told anyone but her father.

And her father put a hand under her chin and angled up so she had to look at him. Her father's face was so strong and manly, tanned from the golf course, silver in his eyebrows, lines around his deep green eyes. Eyes full of worry. "Marci? You can talk to me."

She could. When she'd told him she was pregnant, he was completely calm about it. He said she had two choices. She could deal with it that week, or deal with it every day for the rest of her life. So she could tell him the truth now, she could tell him about this pain lodged under her breastbone like a knife, and why she felt it. Her father would know what to do. He'd take her to see someone, someone good, one of those gentle neighborhood therapists in black pants and Birkenstocks and a colorful ethnic jacket, and she'd sit in that woman's office and talk about bad patterns and destructive urges and how to stop what she was feeling.

But she didn't want to stop feeling it.

She was trying not to cry, so everything she said came out like a question. "We passed the *clinic*? On the way *up* here? And there were *protestors*?" She sounded like Tiffany, like stupid, stupid Tiffany, and that was enough to start the tears. "He's so *Catholic*, Dad."

"Ah, honey." He pulled her into his arms and held her too tight, that yellow doll crushed between them. "You know you did the right thing. Don't you?" She did know that.

But when she closed her eyes, she felt Gentry's face in her burning palm, the bones of his jaw, the scratch of his whiskers, the beat of his pulse as he pulled away from her touch.

Gentry

Dear God, tomorrow You rise.

I should be at reconciliation right now, but I've missed the five o'clock.

Is it true that You forgive all? Everything? Sometimes, when I confess, I wonder at Your ability to stand it. I feel like the fairytale. I open my lips only to let out toads and snakes and lumps of filth. Where does it all go? Do You have an infinite ability to absorb poison? I have to let it out, and I used to believe You took away all of it, but so much is still inside of me.

Why will Tiffany carry this one alone? Why will she carry the judgment, is that fair, oh I don't question You, I just pray for understanding and if You won't grant me that then could You at least help me not to kill Garret? Because I thought we'd worked something out, here? I'm a teacher, God. I can't have that in me.

Am I ever going to have a child of my own? Or am I ruined for parenthood? I can't blame You, if that's what You decide. I pray for this, God, I pray for a chance.

Amen.

⸰⸱⸰

It was dinnertime when I got home. The Volvo was here. So was Bosco, waiting by the door of the little house. Hey, Bosco, were you a good dog while I was gone? I'll pet you in a second, let me put this box in my closet. Bosco, let's go let Kathryn know that Marci is at her dad's. And maybe there will be dinner for me, would you maybe like some dinner?

I know I would. I'm starving.

I went to the door. I felt like I should knock. I walked in that door every day, many times a day, there I stood like an idiot, not sure if I should knock because the girls weren't there.

Bosco. Let's go in.

The kitchen smelled like something good. Very good. There was a note on the table.

> *Gentry,*
>
> *A friend gave me a ride to a meeting.*
>
> *Marci called. How brave of you to insist that she stay at her father's. I'm sure she will eventually forgive you. I made some lentil soup with that venison sausage Vicki Lazarre sent home with you. Please help yourself and do your own dishes.*
>
> *PLEASE Do Not Let Bosco eat out of my bowls.*
>
> *Kathryn*

What was she talking about? I always did the dishes. What friend?

I got down two bowls. Bosco and I ate in the kitchen, because it would have seemed strange to eat in the dining room without the women of the house. It was too quiet. Kathryn played music, sang. I'd lived there for almost eight months and had never been in the house without Kathryn. Not once.

Are you enjoying your soup, Bosco? Would you like seconds? I would.

I found some bread, so we had bread. So quiet in there.

Bosco, I have an idea. Let's put on Kathryn's Patsy Cline CD and do the dishes. Let's sing along. Yes, you can sing too.

I was drying a bowl when I heard a car, Kathryn calling "Goodnight!"

That was Rob Renton's car.

I quickly put away the two bowls. She came in. "Oh, hello, Gentry." She said it like a song. She was beautiful, God, she'd always been beautiful, but even more so since she stopped drinking. I poured myself some coffee and sat at the kitchen table. She sang along with the CD while she got herself a bowl of soup. She sat down across from me. "It's good?"

"Hm. The best." I watched the spoon rise to her mouth. I watched her lips as she blew on it. She tipped the soup onto her pink tongue, and I watched her throat as she swallowed. I wondered if she was eating out of the bowl that Bosco ate from. I hoped so.

Seven-thirty. I could make seven-thirty Mass.

JUNE

Gentry

When you give something a name, you make it into something, but you also set it apart from everything else. You erect a barrier of classification.

I needed to explain this to Lorrie.

"Are you going to hog all that for yourself?"

"Yes." I needed all of it in order to tell the story the right way. I was trying to tell Lorrie one of my favorite stories. Lorrie was not listening. I wished he would. Listening is the first step in learning, but of course Lorrie knew nothing of that. Lorrie was too busy to listen. He had something more important than listening to do.

It was after the prom. Did I mention that the prom was over?

How did the evening degenerate to this point? Where did all my plans for the evening go? I had such fine plans, I did. Now all I had was a bottle of poison.

I wanted to tell Lorrie about a story about Eve. Not Eve Mumford, this wasn't a scary story. This was a great story, a story I loved in college. It was the best story I knew.

What was it again?

Oh, the Eve story. Okay.

In it, Eve, the original Eve, removed all the names that God gave things, removed the barrier of classification from her relationships with the animals, the wind, the trees. Wasn't that a wonderful idea? I'd have liked to tell Lorrie this, but we'd been out there for some time and my powers of speech were affected. I couldn't talk. But I could still think.

I always started out by saying, "I'm not that drunk, I can still . . ."

Still what? First it was talk, then walk, and then it was focus my eyes, then think. I couldn't *say* anything right. I certainly couldn't walk. My eyes hadn't focused for some time, now. But I could still think. And I thought that Lorrie, like Adam, had named this thing. We had the barrier of classification, now.

I rejected this barrier of classification. I rejected it.

◡

The evening started out okay. I looked fine, thanks to Vu. I smelled like moth-balls and I had to staple the cuffs of the shirt, but I looked fine, just fine. And Vicki, well Vicki was resplendent in white. She was a tall, virginal column of a woman, healthy and vigorous. I believe we're the same height, but she had on high heels. Vicki in white, me in black, like a wedding cake top where the groom figure got pushed into the icing about an inch. But I don't mind looking stupid in the name of a good cause, I look stupid most of the time anyway and why not look stupid for love. Not my own love, of course, my unwanted, too-young, too-poor love. No, this is true love. Between Titans.

We got to the prom, and Lorrie was there. There was crushed velvet, and a plaid thing around his gut. He told me that the tux he had on was just like the one he rented for his senior prom. How was I supposed to get these two together if Lorrie insisted on dressing like half of a bad magic act? And his date, the nurse, did he learn nothing from I Dream Of Jeannie, or did he just want someone to complete the ridiculous picture? What was Lorrie thinking?

He and Jeannie were busy ignoring each other. She'd come with someone I didn't know. I couldn't let my eyes rest for long on what she was wearing. But Lorrie looked, he stared for a moment, eyes wide. He shook his head, and firmly turned his eyes back to his date.

Idiot, I wanted to shout, look over *here*. At *Vicki*.

There's always that moment when a slow song starts when you take a girl in your arms and you start to dance. I wouldn't know, I have never been to a dance before, I've only danced in dorm rooms while sober or bars while drunk, so I'm going on Jungian memory, here. Anyway, I found that this moment was nothing to fear because Vicki was a well-oiled and relentless dancing machine, and she did all the leading. How lucky can you get?

I wanted Lorrie to look at her, to appreciate her precision, her strength. This woman is your destiny, I wanted to shout at the idiot. But would he hear me? No. Time for other measures.

I switched partners with Lorrie, I insisted, and then I had to lead. The Lorrie Gilroy date shrieked in my ear. "I can't believe you are a teacher! YOU look so YOUNG!" I smiled, nodded. "How OLD are you, ANYWAY?"

"I'm fifty-four." She laughed right in my ear. Ouch. Lorrie, don't say I never did anything for you. We were even for the fishing trips.

I tried to get a view of Lorrie, to see if his hand had moved into the channel between the twin columns of muscle that rose from this Valkyrie's waist. His hand was up on her shoulder blade. Idiot. I focused instead on Vicki's backside in that white dress. That was Your handiwork, God, and I gave You thanks. And then the dance was over.

Vicki smiled at me. We danced again. She was such a handsome woman. My hand moved from the side of her waist to the small of her back. Things were stirring, I admit it, but no, this woman was for Lorrie.

I moved away, declared myself danced out. Then, as I feared, there were other suitors. Vicki danced with the biology teacher, Bill Bongers, who always smelled of formaldehyde. He was single. After a few turns around the room, Vicki looked a little faint so maybe we were safe. Tom Seidenberg from the math department asked her next, and he had on a nice suit. I had no idea what he smelled like, though.

Lorrie, you idiot, you are going to lose out.

In my single-minded scrutiny of the field for Lorrie's competition, I didn't see Marci by my side. But I could never ignore Marci for long. She looked unfamiliar, her hair up, her mouth darkened. Reflected light played across her arms and shoulders and the smooth blue of her dress.

"Hey. You look nice."

She rolled her eyes. "You have no idea how hard it was to find a dress like this, and everyone here hates it. Oanh asked me why I just wore my slip."

"It's perfect. It's the same color as . . . as Gretchen's eyes."

"I never thought of that." She looked down, frowning. "You have to dance with me."

"Why?"

"Because Garret won't and no one else will ask."

"Not even Vu?"

"Vu's busy."

"Where's Garret?"

"Outside throwing up. He's nervous, I think."

Girls stumbled past in long, stiff dresses, some of them inexplicably wearing gloves, their hair swooping and lacquered, their makeup so heavy they looked ten years older. The young men all looked overheated, their formal wear undone, twisted, ties hanging, cuffs open. These kids had their own wrongheaded beauty, uncultivated, running headlong and half drunk into their futures.

In this room, in this town, Marci stood alone. She kept looking around, her arms crossed over the dress that was the same glacial blue as her mother and sister's eyes. "It's okay. You don't have to dance with me." Her shoulders rounded in defeat.

A slow song began. I counted it out. Okay. I could do this one.

I held out my arms and she stepped into them, wrapped her arms around my waist and lay her head on my shoulder. Her dress was unbearably soft to the touch, as were her breasts where they pressed against me. "Hey Marci?" I gently moved her back. "You have to give me some room. Or I'll step on you."

She bit her lip, nodded. We moved around the floor, where Vu adeptly moved a stiff little Tiffany across the floor. Some of the girls steered their dates around like cars. Other couples grappled, shifting from foot to foot until Lorrie blustered up and made them move apart.

"Who taught you to dance?"

"A girl named Becca." I closed my eyes, remembered dancing her around a fountain one night, counting all the way.

"You're smiling."

I opened my eyes. "I am?"

"Yes." Her eyes narrowed. "You most definitely are. And you reek like moth-balls."

"Thank you."

She laughed. Her teeth flashed, her hair shone like marigolds and honey. She smelled so strongly of hairspray that I sneezed.

The song ended.

Garret was there, pale-faced and malevolent. He jerked his head at the stage. "We gotta go up there. On that stinkin' stage."

He couldn't hurt her on a stage, could he?

Vu had filled me in on this part of the evening so I could understand the gravity of his quest to be king. Three couples mounted the stairs and turned to face the crowd while Mrs. Newhouse and Rob Renton walked behind them, holding the royal headwear and prolonging the suspense. Trent was so drunk his long body kept swaying almost to the point of collapse, then snapping up straight when Oanh poked him in the ribs. Marci and Garret were hand-in-hand. Marci looked bored, Garret looked fearful. Vu and Tiffany stood tall, their young bodies and tense smiles betraying just how much they wanted to win.

The crowns came down on Vu and Tiffany. Vu flashed a V for victorious. Jeannie made a sound that set my teeth on edge, then started to cry.

Thank You. Amen.

⌒

Lorrie came to find me. He explained that first part of the night was over, and the part that involved drinking was soon to start. That's where the chaperones came in. It was our job to confiscate their alcohol.

"So you take it away *after* the dance?"

"Well sure. You gotta let 'em have a little fun, Gentry."

While Vicki checked purses, Lorrie showed me how to frisk the kids. He chose Garret as the subject of my instruction. He frisked him down, removing most of a pint of beautiful Scotch from his suit jacket, which he turned over to me. I would have expected Garret to drink from the bottom left. "Okay, now you do it."

I didn't want to put my hands on this kid. "But you already..."

"Just do it." I patted Garret down again thoroughly, and then I had Lorrie do it to double check my work. We relieved the students of whatever they'd smuggled in. We filled up a laundry basket, then carried it around the side of the gym.

He handed me a bottle of Bailey's Irish Cream. "Pour this shit out first. I hate this pussy booze. But don't you dare pour that out. Or this. Or... this." He turned back to the parking lot. "What the hell is it now." I looked over and saw Marci yelling at Garret, him yelling back. Lorrie shook his head. "Does Garret Blount have to be an asshole every minute of the goddamned day? Can't he take one night off from being an asshole?"

Garret moved his angry face only inches from hers and whatever he said made her pull back, battered and falling like a wounded bird.

What did he say to her?

Lorrie held me back. "Whoa there, little buddy. You stay right here. Seidenberg is on it." And he was, the math teacher had taken the fisherman's son aside. He was handling it. Tom Seidenberg was a deserving mate for Vicki Lazarre. I watched Marci get in a limo with Vu and Tiffany. He was still wearing his crown. V as in Victor, U as in unvanquished. Vu is regent, long live Vu Rex.

Garret saw me and flipped me off, his face twisting. "FAGGOT!"

My night was complete. I opened his bottle and raised a little toast to him before I began to drink it.

Hello, Poison.

Which explained the next part of the evening.

⌒

"Hey Lorrie? How much do fishermen make a year?" I had another long pull of this outstanding Scotch. God, are you responsible for this tasting so good? It tasted so fine, I thought Mike Mumford would even drink it.

Lorrie shrugged. "Not very much anymore. The runs are mighty skimpy these days. Mostly those guys are running drugs. I tell you what, I'm pretty sure Garret is."

"So drugs paid for this Scotch."

"Nah. He probably broke into an empty house and stole it."

Well. This was great information to have.

He took a deep swig of something I wouldn't touch because it was sweet, and let out a thunderous belch. "I'm thinking about the team next year, little buddy. I'm thinking that with your speed, and that tackle I saw you make, that you need to come out for the team. Hell, you get mistaken for a sonofabitching student every day. You could be a ringer. I think it's a helluva game plan." He smiled. I thought, he just forgave me.

I was both drunk and glad.

"Well, little buddy, what do you think of my date?"

"It was like dancing with a coat rack."

He brayed, slapped his leg. "You should talk, you little asshole. That Mumford woman is about the size of a starved pullet. Jesus, at least my date has tits." Did she? I was usually uncomfortably aware of those when dancing with a woman, a woman like, oh, say, Vicki Lazarre. I wanted Lorrie to notice Vicki, and I wanted Vicki to notice Lorrie's finer qualities. But what exactly were Lorrie's finer qualities, anyway? Vicki Lazarre was a goddess. Lorrie Gilroy would never have knowledge of her finer qualities. And he would never have this Scotch. He could have that schnapps, though.

This Scotch was smooth. What did he say about Kathryn?

"Hey Lorrie? Kathryn has breasts."

Oh, God, shut me up, please? She would kill me, please?

"Really? She does?"

"Yes, she does."

"He daughter does, that's for sure." Yes, he was right, I was uncomfortably aware of those. "Are you going to drink that whole bottle?"

"Lorrie, my friend, I need it all. I've decided to decimate my mobility with spirits." Lorrie frowned at me like I was insane. Dear God, I missed my college friends. Nobody got drunk with more verbal embellishment than an English major. I translated. "I'm going to drink until I can't walk."

"Pass it over."

"You have plenty over there."

"Gentry, I have schnapps and vodka over here. Jesus at the Hoedown Christ, I'm not making punch, okay? That's the only good bottle we got off those kids and I want some."

"I'm showing respect for age by drinking it all myself."

"Age. God, I'm so old, Gentry. I am so sonofabitching old." Lorrie sounded sad. If I were that old, I might have been sad too, I guess. "Look at these kids. They don't know it, but they won't ever have it better than they do right now."

"You can't be serious."

"Dead right I'm serious. Best years of my life. All I ever did in high school was play football and chase pussy."

I remembered high school, the pressure, the dorms, the brothers, not wanting to let Mel down, yellow cards, detentions, how angry I was not to be first in my class, hazing, secret Catholic societies, beating up anyone who looked at me sideways or too long or called me by my first name until everyone left me alone, nuns in the infirmary, trying to speak Latin with a stammer, oh, the terror of it. I was scared out of my mind.

"Wouldn't you like to go back, little buddy?"

"Not in a million years."

"I think you would. I think you would, for one reason." He stared at me, and I tried to stare back with a matching degree of gravity, but the focusing thing, not working, no. I decided that Lorrie was far too serious. He needed to drink more. "You better watch this Mumford deal, little buddy. That shit will get you fired."

"Fired?" I didn't understand. I was drunk, so drunk, it had been five months since I'd had a drink, what did he mean, fired? "Evicted, maybe, I can see how I could get evicted, Lorrie. But how will it get me fired?"

He shook his buffalo head. "Messing with the student body?"

I was drunk but my eyes would still focus. Sort of. What was he *talking* about?

"Oh come on. Don't get all shocked. I know what I'm seeing. You have to leave Marci alone. She's worse than the mother. I'm sure she'd do it, too, and that's what I'm so goddamned worried about."

"Lorrie, you are . . . full of it."

"No, I'm not, you goddamn clueless pussy, you're so full of it you're about to bust out all over your shoes. Listen to me, Gentry, stick to balling the old lady, screw the stupid little cheerleader, at least she wouldn't tell anyone. But stay the HELL away from Marci. She's trouble."

Those were Lorrie's words.

I reject this barrier of classification. I reject it.

Lorrie Gilroy

I'll be goddamned if I let the little son of a bitch hit me another time, so I block his swing and set him against the wall. I'm trying to be easy, I am, but he's a little out of control. "Forget it, little buddy. Don't even think about it."

This poor, drunk, stupid, sorry sonofabitch. That babyface of his shows every goddamn thought he has. When he was dancing with the girl tonight I about started to cry myself, looking at him. He looked so goddamn happy. I'll tell you, I know these girls are soft and fresh but they are YOUNG, and so is he, so is he. I know who he was crying over this spring, see, I figured it out and it wasn't that old dried up nasty alcoholic bitch.

I hold him against the wall for a minute. I've got about eighty pounds on him, but it still isn't easy to shut him down. He has long arms. He doesn't say one goddamned word, and if I let him he would tear my goddamned head off. I just hope the kids don't see this, I just hope that.

After a minute, the crazy goes out of his face. "Let me go."

"Tell me you won't even think about it."

"I won't even think about it."

"Swear to God?"

"Swear to God." And I believe he means that, I do. I let him go. And he doesn't pop me, and I'm glad, because I would have to pop him back. And I really don't want to do that to my little buddy.

I would tell him a joke, but I don't think he ever gets my jokes.

He goes back to that bottle of Scotch. I let him work on it, let the night go on, dark and quiet-like. We sit there for quite a while.

He's hurting and too goddamn stupid to see over what.

～

You can't fall off the floor, that's for sure. Let's go, little buddy, heave 'em on up here. Hey Vicki, here's your date. You want to carry him yourself?

Jesus at the State Fair Christ.

Gretchen

Gretchen thought it was time for Gentry to wake up.

He'd promised they could wash cars today. He'd *promised*. She'd been sitting in a chair next to the bed for a half hour while he lay on his back in his Jesus pose, snoring. He still had on that smelly black tuxedo. His mouth was hanging open and he was snoring. His breath smelled like something Bosco would enjoy rolling in.

His eyes opened. Well, one did. He peered at her with one open eye. "What?" His voice was raspy and whispery.

"I'm inspecting your dental work. I'd say you suffered from early dental neglect."

"Bingo." He closed his eye and started snoring again.

This was not interesting.

She understood all the lectures about him being a man. She didn't get in the bed, she didn't even sit on the bed anymore. But she thought she could jump on the bed. She'd always loved to jump on that bed. And she was jumping pretty high. His head bounced up and down and he made a groaning noise but his eyes stayed shut.

"WAKE UP!"

Finally he sat up. He put his finger in front of his mouth. "Shh."

He jumped out of bed and slammed into the bathroom.

That sounded *terrible*.

～

Her mother was at the kitchen table. "Mom, he's sick."

"Sick how?"

"Sick in the bathroom. Barfing." Her mother didn't say anything, but she started a new pot of coffee. "He promised we could wash cars after church."

Her mother shook her head. "He won't be going to church this morning."

Strange. Gentry never missed church.

Gentry

It was the motion, the jarring of my head, her voice . . . Oh God, Oh God, I know I deserve this, my penance, Dear God.

I can't say Amen. I can't even pretend that was a prayer.

Give me some help, God. Or kill me. Your choice, God, and right now, either one is fine with me. Amen.

◡

I was just going to lie there, very still. Very still. It was so hard to remember that feeling like I did last night would make me feel like this the next day. It was so hard to remember that.

After that winter, I never thought I'd curse the sun. I sat through one long, gray Saturday and spent every minute of it praying for sun. But that morning, I cursed the sun. The sun was like knives, trying to slice under my eyelids.

God, send some clouds.

My stomach.

A shower. A long shower, but the water was so loud. And who thought it was a good idea to live by the ocean, didn't anyone realize how loud the ocean was? Too loud, too loud, turn it down.

What did I do? Did I get into that schnapps? What happened to me?

Dear God, did any of the kids see me like that? Did You let that happen, did I talk to anyone but Lorrie in that state?

I checked myself for tattoos, all right, at least I didn't get a tattoo. Still only one hole in the earlobe. Nothing anywhere else. And I was sure if I'd experienced the charms of Vicki Lazarre, I would remember that. I would, wouldn't I?

An old, old man with terrible balance had moved into my body, an old man who could barely dress the shaky frame he'd taken over.

"Knock, knock." Marci opened the door. It might be nice to have a lock on that door, since I just got my shorts pulled up and buttoned, but never mind. Because I had to throw up again.

Oh, God, please. Please kill me. Please?

⌒

I can't even talk about what happened in that bathroom. But when I emerged, she was waiting. "You're supposed to do your barfing on prom night, remember?" She handed me a pair of dark glasses. I always lost my sunglasses, how did Marci know I'd lost another pair? Oh. Those were mine. "You'll need these if you're going to wash the cars. It's sunny out here, and hot."

Marci, your kindness, your consideration. I was deeply moved, enough to go throw up again. After which I would lie down and stay very, very still. And pray for death.

⌒

Oh, inhuman thumping on the side of my house that echoed in my head, down the vibrating steel rod that connected my head to my neck, as I sat here on the bed with my head in my hands, oh who would be so cruel.

Kathryn, with coffee. I ran to the bathroom but she waited.

She seemed concerned when I came out. "Are you going to live?" I would live if I didn't have to talk. She held out the cup. I shook my head, oh, ouch. "It's your only hope." I sipped a little. My stomach cramped, then held. She sat there with me while I finished the cup of coffee, the ocean howling like a hurricane outside the open door. "Gentry, you know . . . you don't seem to react well to drinking."

I hung my head. Kathryn, please, please, please extend to me the same consideration I've extended to you. I've never said a word about it. Please, I know. Please don't give this a name.

She left, thanks be to You.

⌒

All three made their way out to participate in the morning's festivities, they all heard me throw up, took a good look at my pasty face, my yellow eyes. I could serve as a cautionary example for all of them. They could sing my praises in three-part, horrified harmony. And then, they could come out there with hammers and spikes and nail the door shut and every blow would shake my teeth with pain. But before they closed the lid, before the nails were driven, there was something I had to do.

I had to wash cars with Gretchen.

Because I'd promised.

⁓

It was a rare day of fierce, blinding perfection. This was the single warmest day I'd experienced since moving there. Warm air traveled into my sinuses and intensified my headache. And the sun. Even with the shades, the ocean reflected the rays of the sun with a clarity that burned into my eyes and scarred my retinas irrevocably.

Please, God, kill me now.

Oh, but it was all worth it, this pain in my head and down my neck as I washed my Jeep and Gretchen washed the Volvo, all worth it if I'd brought amusement and pleasure to the Mumford women. That's what I was there for, correct? So that Marci could sit in a chaise lounge and laugh as I lurched, and winced, and stumbled, and accidentally tripped over the straining phone cord that stretched out the back door, and yelled at Bosco for barking and then cringed at my own voice. Yes, it was all worth it, I guess, to hear Marci laugh

"Gentry, I was a little worried. The last I saw of you, Miss Lazarre had you slung over her shoulder like a sack of rice. Were you hit over the head, or what?"

Kids saw me, oh no, all I needed was a big whiff of peanut butter and I'd die. That would be best, to die.

"How long has it been since you washed your Jeep?" This was Gretchen. Her voice was not as painful as Marci's.

"Jeeps are supposed to be dirty."

"Gentry? Did you have fun last night?"

"I had a little too much fun."

"As much as you had at your own prom?"

"We didn't have proms."

"Why not?"

"Because we didn't have any girls at our high school. Just nuns." I shivered, I couldn't help it, even though the day was warm. Nuns did that to me.

"No girls? So, it was an all-boy school?"

No, Gretchen, I went to an all-wallaby school. What was so hard to understand about this concept? Gretchen was a bright girl, she shouldn't have had this much trouble. "Yes. An all-boy school."

Marci handed the phone to Gretchen, who ran in to hang it up. Marci smiled. "You boys could have taken each other to the dances, I suppose."

"The Jesuits sort of discouraged that." Oh, why did I make her laugh? When it just meant a wave of pain in my ears?

"Gentry, do you remember a conversation we had about a line?" A line, what line? I didn't remember any conversation about any line. "A line that people cross over, and then . . ."

Grotesque.

I dropped my sponge in the bucket and headed for the water.

⁓

Ah, this was better, I could lie there and let the wind blow salt into my pores. Dry me out, wind. The morning beach walkers passed me with hardly a glance, just one more dead thing on the sand, one more washed-up carcass. Pretty soon Bosco would come over and roll on me. Except he'd found a pair of big yellow dogs to play with, they dodged in and out of the waves. He was ignoring me.

Thank you, Bosco.

And I heard a little sound. Gretchen had followed me. She was singing. I could take it if it was soft. It sounded like the theme to that show she liked. She sang and sang. And to think that six months ago, I had not heard of this show, let alone heard the theme song. Not a big deal in the inner city, this show. It was one annoying melody.

"Gretchen. Hush. Now."

She stopped. Thank You for silence, at least beyond the roar of the ocean. I don't expect You to stop that. Though if You did, I would appreciate it, Amen.

"Gentry?" I took it back. Unthank You.

"Yes?"

"I'm sorry I made you mad."

"I'm not mad."

"You are too."

"I'm not fit company." I was trying to die, sort of. But she was there to bring me back to life. I stood up and brushed sand from my shorts and she took my hand while we walked.

"Gentry, what's your name?"

"My name is a secret." I would take it to the grave. I wouldn't even have it put on my tombstone. Maybe cremation, scattered ashes, to avoid posthumous discovery.

"Is it embarrassing?" It was so bad that it was even embarrassing to me, the king of humiliation, the Grand Prize Winner in the Idiot of All Time sweepstakes. "If you told me, I wouldn't laugh."

"Oh, you would."

"No, really, I wouldn't." I'd had this conversation before. Friends in college. Good friends. And all those girls. If I ever did get married, I'd have to tell my wife, but no one who knew my name would ever marry me.

She pulled on my hand. "How bad could it be?"

"Bad." I heard his voice rolling up from my twisting stomach, thick with disgust. That stupid name. *What did she expect, naming you that.*

Please, God, take it away. I sat down hard on the sand.

She knelt in front of me to bargain. "Gentry? You said it's a secret. If you tell me your name, I'll tell you a terrible secret about myself. And then, if I ever tell anyone your name, you can tell everyone my secret. Deal?"

My stomach was in knots, and it was not the hangover. It was the idea that Gretchen had a terrible secret, what could it be, who would hurt her? Who did I need to kill?

I nodded. "Deal. You tell your secret first."

"You won't tell my mom?"

God, forgive me this lie. "Whatever it is, I won't tell your mom." I was thinking of Alex Fournier, or that brother of hers, I even wondered about Mike for a moment, but I got hold of my suspicions. If anyone, anywhere, ever hurt this girl, he was dead.

"Okay." She waited for a moment. "Everyone at school hates me. Everyone."

This was the secret? "If everyone hates you, then everyone already knows that. That's not a secret. No secret, no deal."

She turned away. "I have one other secret, but it isn't mine. It's someone else's."

The murderer in me gave way to the mandated reporter. "Is it a secret someone told you?"

"No. It's something I saw. I didn't mean to." She wouldn't look at me.

"You saw it by accident? And you were the only child involved?"

She nodded.

"Is it something that hurt anyone?"

She frowned. "I don't think so. I don't think anyone was hurt by it. It was just something private that I saw by accident."

"Do you need to talk about it?"

She shook her head. She still wouldn't meet my eyes.

"Then you should keep that secret. Unless you need to talk about it." We got up and walked, and she took hold of my hand again.

"Gentry?"

"Hm?"

"Do you have any secrets besides your name? I mean, bad secrets?"

"I have secrets so bad that I don't know them anymore."

She nodded as if she understood, but how could she understand, God?

"Are all your secrets bad?"

"No. Some are just private. Hey Gretchen? You don't have any bad secrets of your own?" She shook her head. "Nothing it would kill you to have someone know?" She shook her head again. "Keep it that way, okay?" She nodded.

I wished I could follow my own advice.

Marci

Oh, he was sick. He was so sick. It disgusted Marci, and it reminded her of her mother.

Still, he was miserable.

She went out to make sure he was alive, and he was just lying there staring up at a spot on his ceiling. He looked like a corpse in a pair of baggy cargo shorts. Which of course had a bunch of threads hanging off the hems.

"When does the funeral start?"

"Not soon enough."

"Oh, come on. It's just a hangover." She sat down by him and when the bed creaked, he winced. "Do you want some aspirin or anything? Some water?"

"No." He rolled away from her. She was trying to be nice. She was no good at nice.

She lay down beside his bare and miserable back, and stared up at the spot on the ceiling. "What's that? Gentry? Up there on the ceiling? What is it?"

He rolled over and stared up. "I don't know. It's always been there."

"And you've never checked?" She stood up to see it better. "It's a painted-over spider. A big one. The word for this is grotesque."

"I'm grotesque."

And she looked down and felt that pang of guilt she always felt when her worst words came back to haunt her. "You're not grotesque."

"I am, I crossed that line."

"No you *didn't*. I was just joking. You're not grotesque, you're *sweet*. I mean . . ." She had to think how to say it. "Look at how nice you've been to Tiffany."

He sighed. "Is Tiffany okay?"

Her neck went stiff with self-loathing, remembering Tiffany's shattered face in the limo, what she'd said to her.

"Tiffany's fine. Stupid people are always fine, haven't you noticed that? Besides, there's nothing in this world that being prom queen can't fix for Tiffany." She stood there on his bed and did a little Tiffany imitation, the kind that would make Gentry laugh in spite of himself. "You *guys*? I'm only a junior, but, you *guys*? I was elected *prom queen*. Can you guys believe it?"

He laughed and winced. "Don't make me laugh."

"It's good to laugh. Laughing beats crying. When given a choice, I say we laugh." She bounced the bed a little. "Come on and jump on the bed. Come on up, Gentry. That will cheer you up. It always cheers up Gretchen." She bounced more, almost a jump. "Did you know before you moved in here, Gretchen used to jump on this bed all the time? She loved it." Her weird little sister, jumping around, her blonde hair flying out. Her innocent little sister, who had never once complained about what she could no longer do on this bed because it was Gentry's.

Marci jumped for her.

"Marci, my head." He was so pale, except for his nose, which had a little sunburn. His perfect nose. "Please just go away." She jumped some more, higher and harder. No wonder Gretchen did this, it was fun. "*Stop* that!" He grabbed her ankles, and scrambled to pull her down. Oh, fine. She'd make him laugh another way.

She went for his ribs.

He grabbed her hands, his eyes miserable and angry and disgusted. "*Stop.*"

She couldn't breathe, she didn't know why, but she couldn't. She wanted to touch him. And he wouldn't let her.

"Tiffany's in love with you, you know." He moaned and let go. "You must have this happen all the time, right? Students falling in love with you?" He wouldn't answer, wouldn't look at her, so embarrassed, poor Gentry, always so embarrassed. Because everyone loved him. "All the kids are in love with you, you know. Vu's in love with you! The two Oanhs are in love with you! Garret's in love with you! I think I'll fall in love with you Gentry, I will, because I just *love* grotesque men!"

She went for his ribs again, and he pinned her hands over her head. He wasn't laughing. He was furious, his blood was surging and he had her pinned she only had to wait for the moment of trespass when he would be hers.

The anger went out of his face, which slid and softened and he moaned. His body was heavy on hers but his lips were light and dry, barely brushing her jaw, her eyes, her mouth with kisses as dry, as gentle as moth wings. She was crushed by his lightness, ignited by it. She parted her lips for more, but his were gone, moved to her neck, her collarbone, her ear, where he whispered the most unforgivable words anyone would ever say to her in her life.

He released her wrists and pulled away.

No. She wrapped her legs around him. He pulled back, pushing at her thighs to get free, but she could *feel* him, she *knew* he wanted her. All this yearning and hoping, months of it, watching and waiting with that pain in her chest, and it would *not* end with him getting control, it would *not* end with him turning her away.

A noise. He turned his head.

The door slammed behind Gretchen, the door with no lock.

⌒

She wasn't fast enough.

Gretchen was in her mother's arms. Neither one said a word.

Marci's throat was dry, her heart thumping. She got a glass, ran the tap, drank it all down. Trying to figure out what to say. The hair on the back of her neck rose as she turned to face four blue eyes, eyes that hated her. Both of them. They would never forgive her. Never.

But she had to try, for him.

"Mom it was nothing . . ."

"Nothing? NOTHING?" Marci had never known how much hatred her mother could hold in her eyes. "You were in his *bed*? With *him*?"

"Nothing happened."

"No, *something* happened."

"Nothing, Mom. Nothing."

Kathryn stared at one daughter, then the other. "Are you saying Gretchen is *lying*?"

"I'm not saying she's lying. I'm saying she made a mistake."

"Then let's find out." She banged out the door just in time to see the Jeep tearing up the driveway. She marched into his house, Marci didn't know why, maybe to gather evidence.

Gretchen cowered over by the table, a long white bone of a girl, ugly and awkward and stupid. "You're so *stupid*." Marci still had a glass in her hand, and she threw it. Gretchen jumped as it shattered by her feet. Marci hoped that Gretchen would step in it. "Do you have *any idea* what's going to happen to him? Do you have *any idea* what you just did to him? You're so *stupid*."

Her mother slammed back in and picked up the phone. Marci didn't know who she was planning to call, maybe her dad, maybe her sponsor, who also happened to be the principal of her school. Marci knew what would happen if she got on the phone with either one so she reached over and hung it up. She'd always been embarrassed by that old yellow wall phone, but if they'd had a cordless, her mother would be upstairs by now and this would all be over.

This would never be over.

They stood there, her mother with the receiver in her hand, Marci with her hand on the button that hung it up. Her mother's face was stone. "Do you remember that morning when Gretchen got in his bed?"

Was this a test or a trap? Marci nodded.

"Did he leave that day?" It was a trap. "No. He came right in here and dealt with it. So if nothing happened, then why did he just *leave*, Marci? Why did he *run away*?" Marci opened her mouth to make up some other lie, but Kathryn turned to Gretchen. "Well? Were you mistaken about what you saw out there?"

Gretchen stood there, a stone angel among the shards. She spoke very slowly to the shattered glass around her feet. "I made a mistake. I didn't see what I thought I saw."

Kathryn spat her words. "You're *lying* to me. *Both* of you. Liars. You're *both* just like . . ." She clamped her lips shut.

Marci waited.

Kathryn banged the receiver back into the cradle on top of her daughter's hand. "Fine. You win. Do you *hear* me? The two of you *win*. I won't get him fired. But he can't live here anymore. He has to move. And neither of you will *ever* speak to him again, do you *hear* me?"

"I have a class to finish, Mother."

"YOU WILL NOT SPEAK TO HIM." And she turned and stomped up the kitchen steps. Gretchen slipped out the kitchen door. Marci was left alone with the slivers of glass all over the floor. Gentry wasn't there to clean it up.

Because Gentry was gone.

Kathryn

Kathryn drove her daughters to school each day. She could have let Marci take the wagon, as Kathryn really didn't have anywhere to be. But she drove them because she was the mother.

Gretchen sat in the backseat saying nothing. She walked into school, isolated despite the press of children around her. Then it was just Kathryn and her beautiful daughter. They rode along without speaking. Kathryn listened to the radio, trying to imagine what to say to her. She couldn't find any words.

"Do you have to sing?" Marci asked, a note of restrained hysteria in her voice. "Do you *always* have to sing along?"

Kathryn hadn't realized she was singing. She pulled into the school's drive, let Marci out and watched her walk away. She realized that her daughter had probably always hated her.

She'd probably always had good reason.

From the school to Astoria, where she sat in the basement of a church. Trying to get better. And everyone knew this, of course. Every careworn clerk at every store, every yellow-toothed man at every gas pump, they recognized her from meetings. Everyone who saw her in the post office or the store smiled and thought, oh, Kathryn Mumford is trying to dry up, isn't she? Look at her, back from the dead, living out her toxic half-life one day at a time. They smiled in a knowing way, and encouraged the woman with the privileges they had never had in their lives. They could do it. They might get stuck at the fourth step or fall off the wagon after the agony of the ninth step but they'd at least worked that first step.

She was the only person in AA who'd never managed to work the first step. She tried. She failed. She always tried again.

They were always happy to have her back. All her flawed compatriots in the daily battle to simply not drink. And she survived their support and encouragement. It was a form of humiliation both exquisite and thorough. What Michael did to her was child's play in comparison.

She wondered if she'd survive this.

⌒

On the way home, she visited a gallery in Cannon Beach that sold the most exquisite blown glass. Kathryn liked glass. She'd inherited a nice collection of Swedish glass, but left it in boxes in the Portland house. Michael had probably sold it.

The mat sounded a soft bell of warning and welcome when she stepped in the door. The sales clerk, a curvaceous blonde, smiled in greeting. She watched Kathryn move around the store, made hopeful by a customer's unerring attention to what was most expensive. "Do you collect blown glass?"

"Not really. I prefer cut." The answer puzzled her. No one liked cut glass anymore, but Kathryn admired its lead and edges, the heaviness of it, the sharpness, the way it reflected and refracted and withstood.

The clerk smiled again before walking away to the back of the shop. Kathryn was transfixed by the sight of her from behind. Her bottom was soft and round and she had on a little knit skirt that revealed every shift and jiggle. The fabric of her shirt fell down the middle of her back in a revealing cowl. There were blue-birds tattooed on each of her shoulder blades, a ribbon running beak to beak, with some words Kathryn couldn't bring herself to read. She was appalled by every dimpled, inked inch.

She turned her attention to what she held in her hand. A vase of incredible depth and delicacy, blown through with tiny falling fuchsias and grainy marks of gold. Glass like that was miraculous. Whoever blew it added substances to a molten lump, and fixed that warm mass on a tube, and blew life into it, and somehow those frozen bleeding hearts came from the heat and the breath and the minerals. It was a miracle. But what she held in her hand was too fragile. It almost deserved to be broken.

And then, it was.

"I'll pay for it." Kathryn produced a card from her handbag. "Sorry about the mess."

The clerk's eyes were round behind her intentionally clunky glasses. "We have insurance. I won't charge you for this."

"Please charge me for it."

She did so without another word, and without meeting Kathryn's eyes.

⁓

She realized something, driving home in her ancient Volvo. That was her emergency card. It drew against the account that held the divorce money. She'd cracked the settlement.

She'd finally accepted her payoff.

⁓

Cigarettes and coffee at the kitchen table, that day. She stared out at her view. It was blinding her, the taken-for-granted beauty of it.

If she called him, Rob Renton would leave his office and sit there with her, earnest and steady with his patient chuckles and caring face, helping her work this step. He'd tried so many times before, and he never gave up hope. She'd asked him if she could lay her addiction down to the highest power she knew, which turned out to be addiction.

He shook his head, slow, calm. "It has to be greater than addiction, Kathryn."

What was greater than addiction? She knew no higher power. Her lonely childhood, her forgotten church, her dead parents, her lost voice, her dear nana, her ruined marriage. The years and miles and things she'd put away, cut off, said good-bye to and fled. None of it was anywhere as strong as her desire to drink. She sat in her kitchen full of castoffs from the people who came before her, the people her girls had never known. She looked out the window, she looked in her heart. Her girls. This was too simple, but it was all she had.

She would lay her drinking down to love.

It would have to be enough.

Marci

H is uncle called. Her mother talked to him and smoked. "I have no idea where Gentry is . . . how would I know? . . . Excuse me, Father, but he's just gone . . . Yes, the dog's with him, wherever he is . . . I'm sorry, but that's all I know." There was a long pause, while someone dared to question her mother, to risk her anger. And then, her voice tamped down like a fire that could still flare up, she talked back. "How should I know? Am I *supposed* to keep tabs on him? He comes and goes as he *pleases*. Gentry is the *tenant*."

She hung up.

⁓

Her mother went to a meeting every morning and every night with all those local people she felt superior to. Gretchen sat in her windowseat, watching for a return that wouldn't happen. Marci did the dishes, did her homework, got out her mother's address book and filled out envelopes for her graduation announcements. She put on her cap and gown and stared at herself in the mirror. She counted the days.

No one spoke, no one watched TV, no one sang.

It was so quiet.

It wasn't quiet at school. At school, everyone kept asking Marci where he was. He was sick, she told them. He'd never been sick, so people were freaking out. Vu wanted to come out and see him. He kept questioning her about what he called Gentry's "generalized state of disrepair." *Do you take care of him?* Vu wanted to know.

Nobody ever took care of him, she wanted to shout.

Garret didn't speak to her but that was actually fine with her, if he never spoke to her again. He gave Tiffany rides to and from school. They were a perfect couple. Two short morons.

It was June, she kept telling herself. Only a few more weeks, and then she was out of there for good. She would finally make her exit.

Good-bye, good-bye.

⌒

She was at the sink doing dishes when the phone rang. "Hello."

"I'm just calling you to say thanks for what you said to Tiffany in the limo. This was the biggest thing that will ever happen to Tiffany in her whole life, and you had to ruin it for her."

"Vu, I'm sorry. I was going to call and . . ."

"Don't bother. Christ, Marci, you have everything. Everything. Don't you know Tiffany would give *anything* to be you? Don't you *get* that?" He hung up.

Well, she'd officially ruined everything. Everyone hated her. She looked down at the phone receiver, trying to remember where to put it.

⌒

She went up to her room, but it was too early to start trying and failing to fall asleep. The sun wasn't even down, and as Gretchen would say, those cumulonimbus clouds would make the sunset so pretty. But she didn't appreciate the sunset and she didn't appreciate the beach. All she'd ever thought about this place was how to leave it.

Her sister loved the beach.

Marci went to her door. "Knock, knock." Gretchen was in her windowseat, staring out the window as the sun fell into the water. Why did she appreciate it? "Your room stinks like garbage." Gretchen stared at the ocean. "So, I guess you're never talking to me again. Listen, egghead. You can't stay mad at me forever. If not for me, you'd be named Gudrun."

She sat in that window like something made of light. And it occurred to Marci that Gretchen wouldn't always be awkward, wouldn't remain a pariah. Because she was strange, and she was awkward, but she was going to be beautiful. More beautiful than their mother, more beautiful than anyone. "You're tall like Dad. You're going to be a model, Gretchen."

That actually got a look. A disbelieving look from a girl who thought it was mockery, because she was used to hearing how weird and ugly she was.

But Gretchen had always been beautiful. "You were always like a little fairy, not a baby. People used to stop the stroller so much that Dad would put a blanket over you just so we could get there in less than fifteen minutes. Dad used to strap you to his back when he ran. He called you his little papoose. He said you were so light, it didn't slow him down a bit."

She didn't move a muscle.

"Do you know why I call you egghead? It's because Dad used to hold your head in the palm of his hand like it was an egg."

And there was a movement. Just a little one. But it was there.

"When Mom was nursing you, he'd lie down next to her and put his hand over the back of your little bald head. And I was so jealous."

Just a glance, but Marci was grateful that someone would look at her.

"I was so jealous, Gretchen. I'd hang out on the edge of the bed and watch Mom nurse you. He'd hold your head and say, 'I can feel this one thinking.' And he'd smile. I thought you looked as ugly as a condor chick. Dad didn't think you were ugly at all. He loved the shape of your little space-alien head."

She'd heard so many things in the big house that she wasn't supposed to. Her parents' fighting in the kitchen, making up in the bedroom. Once she woke up in the middle of the night because she heard her father crying. She snuck down those wide stairs and he was sitting on the far bench of the inglenook, crying into the phone. *I know, Evie, I know. You don't understand.* He was sobbing. *I can't let her grow up without me. She needs me.* Marci had felt the sweet satisfaction of knowing her father was crying over her. He shook his head. *Marci will be okay, but Gretchen's just a baby. I can't leave her. If I go now, she won't even know me.*

And she didn't. Marci and her mother had let Gretchen think she didn't matter, because the loss was easier to share out between three. But the truth was, Gretchen was the only one who made him want to stay.

"Gretchen, he'll come back."

A high sound came out of Gretchen, a whistling moan like wind being forced through a crack. Her mouth stretched wide across her face and she stared into the space between them, blind to everything but his absence. She filled the room with her anguish, her white hair bursting into flames, her strange, alien sister sending out rays of light.

But it wasn't Gretchen. It was the setting sun through her window, and Marci's tears.

No.

It was Gretchen.

⌒

When he was teaching her to drive, her father told her how to lie. He said she might be pulled over one day, and it was important to know how to lie her way out of it. He said, pick a lie and keep it simple. So she picked a lie, which was this: it meant nothing.

What a terrible lie.

It happened to her body, not her mind. It was the warmth that spread through her chest when she made him laugh. The dull ache when she saw him without a shirt on, when she saw how his chest and stomach and hips fit together like plates of armor. She couldn't breathe when he frowned. When he told her anything about himself, she wanted to hold it inside like something tiny and living she had to guard.

Of course she hadn't recognized it. She hadn't felt it before, how could she know what was happening? And if she had known, what was she supposed to do about it? Could you weed your feelings like a garden, pulling up the invasive nuisances, feeding only the emotions that were supposed to grow there? Is that how it worked?

She didn't know, she had no idea.

You didn't die of it, you just lived with it, and forgot about it, or maybe you sealed it up inside, covered it with mental cement. No one ever died of it, she was sure.

That's what she told herself.

That it wasn't going to kill her to feel like this.

⌒

Friday night. Her mother sat in the dark, alone. The end of her cigarette glowed. Marci stood behind her, wanting to put a hand out to touch her sharp shoulder. Marci never touched her mother. "Mom? When are you going to talk to me again?" And she didn't say, but Marci knew the answer. She'd start talking to her when Marci stopped lying to her.

She sat down on the couch.

"It wasn't his fault. Okay? It was like we were playing." Marci felt shame trickle like hot water down her face, her hands. "We were . . . fooling around. Not fooling around like that, like . . ." How would her mother say it? ". . . rough-housing. It was me. Remember how sick he was? I was bothering him, I was trying to tickle him." Because she wanted to touch him, her hands wanted to feel the bare skin of his chest. "He was getting mad. Pushing me away. He was sick and miserable and the only reason he touched me was to push me away." Even that was true. Really, everything she'd said was true.

Pick a lie. Keep it simple. "So I kissed him."

That wasn't so hard, was it? It was the only lie, and it was an easy one. And now, she could go back to what was true. "It was just for a second. He pulled back and he was upset, Mom. Gretchen saw his face. She could tell you how upset he was."

The little orange coal flared as Kathryn dragged on the cigarette. She breathed it in. She breathed it out. Marci watched as she silently stubbed it out in the ashtray beside her.

"You can't blame him, Mom. I did it. Hate me forever if you want to, but this wasn't his fault." Certainly that was enough. Marci had erased the only moment she would ever have, the only moment when he'd wanted her. And that wasn't enough.

Her mother was going to make her say it out loud.

"It's not me he wants. It's you, Mom. He's still in love with you."

She heard the strike, the hiss. The lit match illuminated her mother's lined face, her pale eyes, her filament hair. The cigarette glowed in her cupped hands. Her mother didn't participate in religion. But in the darkness, Marci could have mistaken her for a woman praying.

Lorrie Gilroy

Well, hey little buddy, I didn't think you'd be up and at'em and Jesus Have a Heart Christ what happened now. Goddamn Gentry, I think that bitch just has you locked up in that box on purpose so she can mess with your head, I do. Goddamnit all to hell. Now sit down and tell me what the hell, oh, the dog, you have the dog, the dog's here, this is some serious shit.

Christ on the cross, you look like somebody just reached up your asshole and yanked out your heart. You better talk to me. Right now. This is serious-like. Yes, you can stay here, you can, Bosco too, anything you need, of course. It's okay. It's okay, look here, do you want a beer? Oh I see, you brought your own. You brought two six-packs of Budweiser. And five bottles. Five bottles?

You brought over five bottles of this lousy shit?

⁓

Monday. He wouldn't come to school this morning. If I can figure out what this is, maybe I can help, maybe I can get him off the couch. He won't say a word, not a goddamn word.

All he does is drink.

I'm just sitting there in the can at school, thinking about it. I need a game plan, and there are worse places for thinking than the can. And some kids come in talking too goddamned loud. "You're so, you know, excited about her, that's all. And she's a whore." That's Garret.

"Tiffany's no whore." That's Vu. "Shut the hell up, Garret."

"I'm just tellin' you. She'll do it with anybody. She even does it with teachers. Everybody thinks it was Riddle, but it was that faggot Gentry knocked her up, you know."

I come flying out of the bathroom stall like a goddamn bronc out of the gate at the Round-Up. I've got that asshole by the neck and against the wall so fast his balls are still sitting across the room. He won't look at me. "Tell me what bullshit you're spreading around." He's scared, he's about to wet himself, this kid plays so tough but he's a pussy underneath. I make him look at me. "Who knocked her up? You tell me." I give him a shake. "WHO? Say it."

He squeaks. "Me."

I give him a slam, then. "Say it louder."

"It was me, okay? It was me."

"Dickhead. You dirty little coast rat dickhead. Who else would it be?" I think about Jeannie and I want to slam his head on this tile until I crush it. I don't, see, but I want to.

Vu's edging toward the door but I tell him to hold his ass still because I'm not finished. I tell these boys about the dangers of gossip and that I've got big ears, big elephant ears, like satellite dishes, really, my ears, and if I so much as hear Gentry's name in a sentence with Tiffany's name again I'll personally kick their asses from here to Astoria and back again and I don't think they should worry about legal consequences because corpses don't talk.

I step out of the john and right on time, here's Rob with his big Charlie Brown head falling into step with me. "Say, Lorrie, I was wondering if I could talk with you. About Gentry." And that's a whole different level of damage control but it turns out it's the same stuff, rumors he's heard but here's the deal with Rob, you have to tell him the truth because he's one of those decent types you can't lie to. So I tell him, no, yeah, nothing to do with Tiffany and he can trust me on that one because I know her mom and I know exactly who knocked her up. Gentry never went near her. But I say, see, my little buddy might have a little bit of a bent elbow problem.

Rob lights up like a Christmas tree. He puts a hand on my shoulder and says with his voice all pastor-like, "You tell him he is not alone."

Oh Jesus Emcees a Telethon Christ. That's the thing about these twelve-steppers. One second he's ready to believe Gentry's messing with the student body, but let him get wind that Gentry's a drunk and all of a sudden my little buddy's got the special disease and Rob defends him like a hero.

These drunks.

∽

I go home and stare at Gentry, passed out on the couch. I'm not sure what's going on here. I still don't know what's wrong with him, but I'm getting a better idea, and I don't like this, not at all.

Not at all.

∽

It's just a couple of weeks until the end of the school year, and I've got to keep this guy together. He won't say a sonofabitching word, he just sits there like a zombie. Deep shit. I think about calling that uncle of his, that Mel guy, the friar or whatever. But how do you look up a monk in a phone book? Do these guys even have last names?

I'm wondering what the hell is wrong. He won't say. He doesn't hardly even move. He showed up at my house in a pair of shorts and a flannel shirt and sat down on my couch and I don't think he's moved since, except to pour himself a drink every now and then. It's like he's figured it out by hours and ounces. He's not drinking to get drunk, see. He's drinking to *stay* drunk.

What kind of a man drinks like this? A man goes out to drink, I want to tell him, drinking is for having a good time, don't you know anything about drinking? I need to teach this guy about drinking. And then I watch him ration out that horse piss glass by glass, and I'm afraid my little buddy already knows every single thing there is to know about drinking.

At school, we take over his classes. You just don't know how many classes Gentry took for other teachers until he needs somebody to cover his puny little schedule. I think Gentry took every sonofabitching class over at one time including PE and I'm not exaggerating.

So we all file in there for a week and follow his lesson plan, and the guy has it all so laid out that we could have gone on for the rest of the year, I could not believe how he plans everything out. I've been in there when he's teaching, it seems like he makes it up as he goes along but he doesn't, that guy knows exactly what he's doing.

But I'm thinking, it's been a week, maybe if I make Gentry think his classes are falling apart, he'll come out of it? I go home and stare at him. He lays there on the couch all day and all night. Sometimes he's asleep and sometimes he's awake and it's goddamn hard to tell the difference. "Boy, are your classes a mess," I tell him. "Those kids are forgetting everything you ever taught them." I stare at him. Nothing. "Little buddy? Are you in there?"

He peers up at me from under some deep, deep water. And then he has another drink and closes his eyes.

Once in awhile, he wakes up. He stands up, stumbles into the can, takes a leak. He goes and gets one of those cheap beers and chugs it down, and then he goes back in the can and throws it up. And then he sits down and drinks the whiskey. That, he keeps down.

If I turn on the TV, he looks at it, but I don't think he notices anything. I bring him a sandwich now and then, and he stares at it a while, then takes off the bread and eats the meat and cheese. The other night he ate through a whole package of beef jerky. If I bring him anything that's not meat, he stares at it like I'm offering him shit. The dog eats it. Sometimes he does pet the dog. But I have to let the poor old mutt out, which thank god he's a big dog with a big bladder or my carpet would be swamped. How can you not let your dog out?

He doesn't talk. I ask him, "Hey little buddy? You think you might want to take a shower?" It's like I'm not there. It's just him and his five bottles, rationed out glass by glass in some little system he has to keep himself shut down.

I thought he was bad in March. At least he wasn't drinking in March.

I gave him all that booze after prom.

~

So, it's late Friday night, I can't sleep and I'm watching TV, trying to ignore him. Not hard to do. He's as exciting as a Chia pet. Earlier tonight, I cooked him a steak and he sat up and ate it. I was kinda afraid he might take off a finger with the steak knife, but no, he cut through the meat, chewed it, gave the gristle and fat and all the fries to the dog. I thought, okay, maybe what he needed was a steak, you know, to wake him up. Some red meat.

Then he lay back down.

I need a game plan. If I could take him out in my boat, that would make him laugh, he was always laughing up his sleeve at my boat. I got the old Alumaweld off a guide and it probably had a million hours on it, and if I could get Gentry out on it, I can guarantee you that something would go wrong enough to make him laugh. Maybe I'll accidentally forget to put the plug in. It gives an idea how desperate I'm getting, thinking about swamping my own sonofabitching boat. He needs to go fishing, he needs to wrestle a sturgeon, that's what he needs, he needs to pull up one of those big ugly fish, those are some ugly fish, and then throw it back.

But I'd have to carry him to the truck to get him to go fishing, and, to tell you the truth, I don't want to touch the guy because he stinks. I tell you, he's as entertaining as a cat box.

That last bottle was getting empty when I left for work this morning. He probably planned it out to last through the day but he must have messed up his rationing at some point and now he's hurting. I do know he's out of beer.

"You want to go get some coffee?" Nothing.

Then I think, I'll take him over to Uptown Annie's and prop him up, pour a shot down his throat, pay for a lap dance, see if that might rev his engine, some little skank waving it in his face for twenty bucks. The thought of that. Probably do the poor bastard in.

I've got to get a game plan.

The phone rings. I let it. I have one of those old answering machines where you can hear the person talk when they leave a message. And guess who it is? She sounds nice and crisp, like the gal at the dentist office who calls to remind you to have your teeth cleaned. "This is a message for Gentry," she says.

You know, I hunt. And once in awhile, I come across a rabbit. Just frozen there, too scared to move. I poke it, clap, anything, trying to get the stupid animal to move. Hell, I won't shoot a sonofabitching rabbit. But the goddamn thing won't move. That's what he looks like when he hears her voice.

"He needs to call his uncle. He's reachable at the . . . technical support desk tonight." And she hangs up.

He lays there for a minute, quiet. And then in a rusty voice that doesn't even sound like his, he says, "Hey Lorrie?" He swallows real big. "Will you do me a favor?"

"If you want me to go to the liquor store for you, the answer is no."

He stands up, he can barely stand, and he gets in his pocket and finds his keys. I'm up just like that. I take the keys out of his hand. "No way." And that dog shame is on him so hard that he can't look at me. But he starts to walk around, he's starting to crawl out of his skin. "Just settle down. You need a shower."

"I want to go home and take one. Will you take me home?"

"That I'll do. Just settle down. It's okay." He won't get in my truck, he wants to be in his Jeep. Okay, whatever he wants. We take Bosco, that's a good dog, to just sit there for a week, a good dog, like he knew what to do.

My god but this rig is a ballshaker.

And we head north on the highway and he asks me in that raspy voice that's not his, "Hey Lorrie? Did I get fired this week?"

Well now. I wonder what my little buddy's been up to over at the Mumford house that might have gotten him fired, what kind of a stupid situation might lead to that kind of a deal, even though he's aware of those proper lines and all. Gives a person a little more of an idea just what the hell might be wrong enough to send a man to the bottle. But I don't think it could have been too bad, or that little old witch would have had him arrested, wouldn't she? Except I believe Marci Mumford is over eighteen. And he wasn't worried about being arrested. He was worried about being fired.

"Nope," I say, "in fact everything's just fine over at the school."

Out of the corner of my eye, I see him cross himself.

When we pull up to the Mumford place, I think we're both scared as shit. But nobody comes out. The dog jumps out and lifts his leg, tail wagging.

"Want me to check your place out first?" He nods, so I go in. It seems okay.

Gentry walks into his door with that old man walk, relieved. "I was starting to think I made it up."

Well, this is one weird deal to say.

"How about that shower?" I say. "You smell like a portable toilet, little buddy."

He scratches at his patchy little beard. I didn't even know he had whiskers. "Could you just . . ." He's scared, again.

"Could I what?"

"Would you . . . I mean . . ."

"What? Wash your back?"

"There's no lock. Could you just make sure nobody comes in here?"

"Sure, sure. Hit the showers, kid."

He goes into the bathroom and I make some coffee, for sure he can use some coffee. When I run the cold water in the kitchen sink I hear him holler. I bet the water in there turned nice and hot for a second, which is fine because he needed some hot water. So I do it again, except this time I run the hot water.

Yup. He's awake.

No TV, so I scout around for something to read. Jesus Macaroni Salad Christ, no wonder Gentry's so screwed up, look at this shit he reads. Nobody needs to read shit like this, ever, these guys are all dead and they deserve to stay that way. And he has all these little notes in here, he takes this shit serious, oh why does he take everything so serious.

And then his door opens. It's Madame Mumford. She's a little surprised to see me, I can tell. Thought she would come sink her fangs in, huh? "He's taking a shower." That's what I say. "He's getting some stuff, and then we'll be going."

"I just . . . his uncle has been calling, and I . . ."

"He got the message. He can call his uncle from my house."

And you know what she looks? She looks sorry. She actually looks like maybe she's done some thinking instead of drinking and maybe she's figured out that whatever it is that's messed so hard with Gentry, and let me tell you I don't know if it's the past or the present or that religion of his or drinking or what, but something has messed with this kid but good, not just this week but his whole sonofa-bitching life, and she's figured out that at least part of it is her fault.

The water goes off. I can hear him brushing his teeth. She stands there watching the door to the bathroom. He's in no goddamn shape to look at her. I get up and I move toward the door because it's time for a little offensive blocking. I back her up and out the door and I shut it behind us. She's scared. Good. "Would you just tell him that . . ." Her blue eyes dart around. Just you and me out here, honey, nobody else. She opens her yap again. "Would you just tell him that it's all right, he can come back?"

Aw, look, she's gonna cry.

"I'll tell him no such thing, Kathy." Her little wrinkled face is folding up like a bad hand of cards. "I think you had about enough fun with this one." Boy, she looks like I hit her. And I'd like to, but I don't do that. "So, Kathy, how about you take your ass up to your own goddamn house and stay the hell away from him because Gentry is the tenant of record and right now you're trespassing." And she does, she does, she hightails her round little fanny over to the house and she moves fast.

I go back inside, and he's coming out, he has on his sweats and his robe, he shaved off his scraggly little beard and my god he's a kid. But at least he's clean. "Was that . . . ?"

"Yes, but it's okay, she said it's okay." He's relieved. Goddamnit, don't be relieved, don't stay here.

"I need to check my email."

"Well then you just sit down there and do that, then." And he sits and starts reading shit at the computer, and he seems to have a lot to read.

"Mel's back."

"That's great, kid."

"He's been trying to call me." He types back at the guy, maybe three words. Sends it.

"That's old news. Keep reading, kid."

"Sandy's finally going to get that Ph.D."

"Good for her."

"Him."

"Him, then. Good for him." I've got nothing to do, so let him read, let him talk, let him type, I can wait. I just wish he had a TV or a magazine or something.

"Hey Lorrie?" He can't be going to cry, I'm sorry, but I hate this crying shit. "Lorrie, there are messages from the kids." And I go over, and I'll be goddamned, there are. I think I'll be here all night so he can read this, but you know, that's okay by me, I'll stay here all night if it helps. But I'm kinda hungry, and now that Sleeping Beauty over here woke up, I'll bet he could use a cheeseburger. I just don't know about leaving my little buddy to go get some.

Nah, it'll be okay. That bitch wouldn't dare.

⁓

I drive that Jeep up to the bar and I see the little prick's short box with the stupid lift kit that makes it look like a Tonka Toy. I look around inside. He's sitting with Darlene, those two are pretty damn cozy over there. Here comes Faye, with her wet bar rag and that enormous ass of hers. "Where you been, Lorrie?"

"Did you miss me, Faye? I bet you missed me."

"No, I just wondered how much I'd have to pay you to go back there."

Some things never change. "Well, I'm back again. I'm back, and I'm ready."

"I see that." Faye sets me up with a draft. "Lorrie, you leave, but you never really go away. You're just like herpes."

Herpes. That's a helluva thought. "Can you give me a couple of burgers to go? Load 'em up, would you?" She takes her big ass back to the grill. "And wash your hands, first."

"Hey, Coach, how's it hangin'?" That Darlene won't even look at me sideways most of the time, but she wants me to see who she's with, I guess. That's a senior in high school, lady. Hands in his lap. She's hammered, too.

"Long, strong, and free. How about you, Darlene?"

"I never been better." She rubs on the jerk a little, giggles. Hanging all over him. Christ, why don't they just get a room. "So, Lorrie? Where's your pretty boyfriend? You have him hid out somewhere?" Little bitch. Garret doesn't look at me and that's good because I'd like to hit somebody about now and I don't hit women or students. The little asshole's scared, but he's also drinking.

I nod at him. "Garret."

He nods. "Coach."

"What the hell are you doing in here? You better be careful what you pick up in a bar. You might pick up something nasty."

He smiles. "Yeah, Coach. Something nasty. Like herpes."

Well, that sets the two of them off.

"I wouldn't know about that, Garret. I don't know shit about anything like that. Why don't you ask Darlene. She's the barstool expert on all those social diseases."

She waits for Prince Charming to defend her honor.

Oh, he's going to try. "Kiss my ass, Coach."

"Kiss your ass?" I smile. "You'll have to mark that off, Garret, because you're all ass to me." I can't believe they risk their license serving the little shithead. I'm sure he carries fake ID, but Faye has to know how old that kid is. "You better get on home, Garret. Before I have to call Emmett over at the sheriff's office about whether your truck needs towing because you're too drunk to drive it."

"Shit." He gets up, walks out mad, like he has a four-by-four drove square up his ass, but he walks.

"Sorry to scare your victim away, Darlene. You'll have to go haunt yourself up another one."

"Fuck you, Lorrie Gilroy. Not that I ever would."

"Well, Darlene, the line starts behind Faye."

Faye comes back with a sack. "The line for what?"

"The line for people who won't fuck me."

Faye smiles, and she winks. "Why don't you hang around a little while till Bud gets here to close up, and we'll see about that."

I can't believe it. "You serious?"

She looks serious. "I'm serious. This is it, Lorrie. This is your big chance." I look at her, I look at Darlene, I look at the sonofabitching bag in my hand.

No way. No damn way. No damn way in Hell.

I pay for the burgers and clear out of there.

⁓

I'm thinking that I just blew the sonofabitching lay of a lifetime. Years I been waiting for that woman, years, and I just walked out of the bar and left her there. I'm thinking I'm the stupidest asshole that ever walked the planet.

Sonofabitch.

I'm thinking I should have told Garret to maybe check out Darlene's clean card before he did the deed. Christ, clean cards, I'm thinking it's a fine time to be alive when you got to carry sonofabitching clean card right alongside your NRA membership and your proof of insurance. I'm thinking about what it's like to go down there to the county to get poked and pricked and stuck with needles, and there's a bunch of your students seeing you in a place like that. I'm thinking my little buddy maybe has the right idea, after all, staying out of the whole mess like he does, I mean, look at it, what a life it is anymore.

I'm thinking Faye would have to pee on a slide before I ever slipped her the bone, I guess.

I'm tired of thinking.

I'm thinking I should have maybe got a burger for the dog.

⌒

When I get back there the dog's waiting for me and Gentry's asleep on his bed. Sound asleep. I whisper to him. "Little buddy? Do you want a burger?" He just snores a little. I put the sleeping bag over him. Christ, kid, are you on a permanent camping trip, or what? You got the sheets, but what's wrong with blankets? Are you a bedwetter?

How the hell does he live somewhere this small? My bed would fill up this whole house. I check his fridge, no beer, but there's some milk, it smells okay, tastes fine. He drank some coffee, that's good, he needed some coffee. There's a bowl in the sink, Gentry ate some cornflakes. Well, good. I eat my burger and I give the dog the other, and he eats it in two bites. Then I fill up his bowl and that dog is so damn happy to have some dog food.

I'm just sitting there licking my fingers, finishing up the milk because it would probably go bad anyway, wondering if I should stay or leave. Gentry sleeps like he's nailed to a cross. Gives me the creeps a little. Like that thing over his bed. Creepy. The ocean sure is loud in this little house. Sounds like something, in the wind, something, I don't know exactly what, but it sounds spooky.

"Don't make me."

Holy shit. He's sleep talking. I about jumped out of my skin. "Little buddy?"

"No. I won't turn around." He starts to move a little, his eyes are rolling around under the lids, his mouth kind of twitches. "I don't want to turn around."

I start to talk, real soft, like. "Hey, kid, it's okay. You don't have to. Nobody's gonna make you turn around. I won't let'em." He groans, but he settles down. The dog jumps up on the bed. Gentry rolls over in his sleep, puts his arms around that big old mutt. That's one good dog.

I could swear that dog's telling me that it's okay, I can hit the road. I don't have the truck, but I could drive the Jeep back. I could leave him alone, he had a shower, something to eat. He's okay. I could leave.

Hell, I'm not going anywhere.

I pour myself a cup of coffee and sit down at his computer, and go up on that Internet to have a look at Betty Page. I'm not leaving him alone with that vampire less than a hundred feet away. That cross over his bed won't keep her away.

But you can bet your ass I will.

Gentry

The shoes, the girl stuck to the loaf, sinking down, down into the swamp, while the toads and the snakes and the wide-mouthed fish looked at her, brushed past her, because of those shoes, the shoes she was so proud of. Dance till you die. And the iron shoes of the witch, the iron shoes heated in the fire, she danced till she died in the red hot iron shoes. Cut open the belly of the wolf, slice into it to get Grandma out, get the pigs out, get the seven little kids out of the belly of the wolf, he has flour on his paw, this wolf. Take them out, deep into the forest, and leave them, make sure they will never find their way back, because they use crumbs, you see. Is he fat enough to eat (he is in a cage), feel his finger (it is just a bone), test the oven (push her in, let her burn), don't be hungry. Bluebeard's wives, all the blood, hanging on hooks, that is what you find when you look, you will find blood. The thorns ripped out his eyes, the thorns blinded him, only her tears brought back his sight.

The boy read those stories after she was gone. She was gone, her brown eyes and her cool lips on my forehead, and the stories, I remember. He was so little and so hungry, so hungry, and he stood on the counter, climbed the shelves, looking for something, anything, finding that old jar of peanut butter under the sink for the mice, and eating it with his hands until he was sick, so sick, oh help me God I was so sick. And he threw up, and the man put the boy's face in it. Don't fight me, look at you fight me. Clean it up.

Dog.

I woke up because Bosco was licking my face. Hey, Bosco. I'm okay.

I rolled over and looked at the ceiling. Mel used to say to me, *We regret experiences only if we fail to learn from them.*

I am a teacher who can't learn.

⁓

I lived with Mel for one year and six weeks before I left for school. We ate meals at the rectory, and that was where he gave me my lessons. Officially, home was a one-bedroom apartment in the basement of an old house that belonged to a parishioner named Mrs. Prescott.

Mrs. Prescott taught piano overhead, and often cried in frustration after her students left. I didn't enjoy the sound of that, or the sound of the students hitting the keys. I would never have gone upstairs if she hadn't had an iguana. She'd found him in a city park one summer. *The poor thing was lost, of course. Ambling through the grass. All alone in the world.*

I stood outside his cage, watching. He didn't move, I didn't move. He was armored, beautiful and still. I would stare at him and he would stare at me, and Mrs. Prescott would talk enough for all three of us. *Would you like a brownie?* I never ate anything sweet. *Have you ever played a piano?* I had never touched a piano. *Are you interested in the piano?* I was, but not in playing it. I wanted to see how it worked.

I stared at her lizard.

You can stroke him. He's nice to the touch. I didn't want to touch him. I wanted to study his colors and scales, his slow-motion movements, the lack of intelligence in his strange eyes. Sometimes she would gently touch the back of my head, so softly that I barely felt it. *Sweet, sad boy. If you'll ask me out loud, you can have anything in this house.*

I wouldn't speak to Mrs. Prescott. I wouldn't speak to anyone.

Mrs. Prescott kept her home very warm for the sake of that iguana. Heat poured down into the basement apartment, and the warmth seemed to me an unbearable kindness, too much kindness, like offers of brownies and piano lessons and touching my head so gently and the opportunity to study a lizard. She only wanted me to talk to her. I was not talking to anyone but Mel, and I hardly ever said anything to him.

Mel was patient. He was learning about parenting, I think. He took me to whatever he thought a boy my age might like. Some of his attempts were less than successful. I didn't like movies because I had to sit in the dark. We made it five minutes into one, ten minutes into another before we left. We gave up on movies.

He took me to a magic show, a sweaty man in a tuxedo talking too much while a woman with frightening makeup handed him things. I didn't believe in magic and was insulted that anyone would expect me to. I knew I could figure out how everything was done if I could just examine the cards, the hoops, the cups and balls of these small shams. We gave up on magic.

There was a local puppet theater company. We went four times. The shows were fairytales that couldn't scare me because I knew them by heart. The puppets themselves were fascinating and graceful, but I knew someone was back there making the voices. I understood every single thing about the puppet show, so I liked it.

We went to the circus once. I liked the aerial acts, the tensile strength in the arms and legs of the men and women flying through the air. They would never fall, but the net was there to catch them if they did. The horses and ponies seemed fine, running and trotting, beautiful girls standing on their backs. I was quietly intrigued by those girls, their fearlessness and their bodies. I was less sure about the big cats. A bored tiger going through his paces, a lion just wanting a nap. The trainers seemed more bored than the lions. When the elephants walked out, trunk to tail, I found myself outraged. I took my thumb out of my mouth and tried to explain to Mel that the elephants were different than all the other animals, that they didn't belong in a show. He nodded, trying to understand through my stammer. Frustrated, I gave up.

Of course I hated the clowns. Even when what they were doing was funny, and often it was, they caused me anxiety. I had a sense of doom looking at a clown, a premonition of spectacular impending misfortune. I laughed in spite of myself at the little car that kept disgorging more and more clowns, but when they scattered into the audience to aggressively cavort, we had to get up and leave.

On the bus home, I remember his face in profile, watching the street through the window of the bus. He kept his eyes off my face while he spoke, knowing I couldn't stand to talk if anyone was looking at me. *The clowns are just people in makeup and costume, my boy.*

I knew that. I knew there was someone real under that ugly makeup. I couldn't explain what made me angry back then. What I hated about magic tricks, character voices, clowns.

People who pretended made me angry.

⌢

Other activities were more successful. Every sporting event was a hit. Whatever he took me to, I liked it, figuring out the rules, referring to the programs, watching the excitement or disappointment of the people around me. Hockey games made me laugh out loud. There was something about how the players would start to wrestle in a strange, padded waltz. And then they all got sent to the box for time-outs. A game where all the violence was padded and punished made me laugh.

Of all the things he tried, the very best was camping.

The first time we went, I'd only been living with him for two weeks. I hadn't spoken one word. He borrowed gear from a parishioner and packed it in the rectory's ancient Rambler station wagon. South for a while, leaving behind the city. North to the other shore. A city child, I sucked my thumb and stared out the car window at grass, trees, small towns and empty spaces. What *was* this world? *This is the world when it's clean*, he told me. *I want you to see a world that's clean.*

We got there late enough that we had to use flashlights to set up a tent that was big enough to hold us both. I wasn't sure about that. Back at the apartment, I had a bedroom. He slept on a sofa bed out in the living room. I could hear through the wall that he snored a lot. In that tent, he lay beside me in his sleeping bag and snored like a bear. I lay there feeling trapped. I thought I would never sleep.

I woke up the next morning while he was still snoring.

I slipped out of the tent and stood alone, staring at the lake in the gradually lightening darkness, the watery hush broken by birdsong, whistles, cascading trills, some jarring screeches, the low coo of a rare bird that greeted the morning with sadness.

His hand on my shoulder. *This is God's country, my boy. God's country.*

I ducked away.

He showed me how to make campfire coffee that morning. We drank it together. And then he took me out in the little boat. I clutched the sides, my heart in my mouth, but not in fear. In happiness. He showed me how to fish, which was wonderful, and how to kill and gut fish, which was not. But it was part of it. I fought back panic at the blood and slime, and learned.

The lake was calm. Mel was calm, too. He kept silent while we fished. I was always silent, so this suited me. But when he cooked our catch, Mel would sing. Occasionally I joined in. Mel didn't look at me when I sang, because if I felt eyes on me, I couldn't make a sound.

He would serve us up with the miracle of food I had helped provide, those twelve-inch trout. We'd pause over our tin plates. *Say Grace, Gentry. Just say the Grace, my boy.* I would bow my head and whisper.

Bless us, oh Lord. These thy gifts. Amen.

He taught me to swim, one hand under my stomach as I struggled and thrashed and finally understood that I had to relax. He taught me to fry trout and make coffee and toast marshmallows. He taught me how to pitch a tent, make a fire, scrub a pan with sand and avoid poison oak. I had never felt so smart, clean or tired in all my life.

Still, I kept my distance.

One night he patted the ground beside him. *Sit here. You can see the lights. The city is right across the lake.* I moved to sit beside him, staring over the fire and across the water. It didn't seem possible that the city was still there, that it could exist in the same world as camping. But he was right. I could see the lights of that vertical, dangerous, dirty world.

I shivered. He put his arm around me. I did not duck away. I let his arm stay where it was. He gave my shoulder a little pat, and we stared across the lake.

I'd thought that priests were male but not men, in the way I still fear that nuns are female but not women. It had something to do with their relationship with God and something to do with what they wore. But I'd lived with Mel for weeks. I'd seen him eat, heard him burp. I'd heard him groaning in the bathroom after a bad glass of milk, seen the hair sprouting at the neck of his pajama top. On the drive to our campsite, we'd stood together by the side of the highway making water, his hand modestly shielding his parts. I had added it all up, factored in God and done the math. Even though Mel was a priest, he was a regular man.

And he was *safe*.

We sat like that, watching the lights for a long, long, time.

⌢

After college, I moved to one of the most dangerous places in the United States. No one at school understood my determination to teach in the most difficult place that Teach For America could find for me, or how I made a life there. It was easy. My life was work, church, and walks with Bosco. When I was lonely I got on the IRC and talked to the Sandersons or Mel.

And I had the kids. Lost cases, like I was, which meant they could find their way. I considered all the factors, all the variables. The kids who made it had intelligence, support, some luck, and someone, somewhere, outside the community who cared. All of them had managed to meaningfully connect with the world of ideas through reading books. And every single one of them had determination.

Dominique Weatheroy determined. She worked harder than I ever saw a student work. She was determined to maintain a perfect GPA. Dominique had a natural ability for math and a passion for classification. I assumed she'd go into engineering. Her grandmother, who'd raised five children and four grandchildren, had saved for college since Dominique was four years old. Mrs. Weatheroy listened carefully to whatever I said when I called her. I tracked down scholarships and grants and her grandmother helped Dominique with the paperwork.

Teachers are not made of stone. I student taught at a high school in Georgia, where I learned early not to look too long at beautiful girls, because I was human and they were troubling to me. When I studied beauty, I wanted to unlock it. So I never studied Dominique's face, a miracle of angles and planes. But I couldn't avoid hearing her voice.

I would sit with my face turned away from her, listening to her soft questions and her mannered vocabulary, her coos of *Yes sir*, and *Perhaps we could talk about* . . . blowing up and over my shoulder and into my ear like a Georgia breeze. It was music dropped in from another time, another place. Formal and deferent and halting.

We sat in my lab while sirens wailed around the school, working on whatever she needed. Sometimes she couldn't concentrate. Her mind wandered and she went blank because she was starving. Her hunger made me remember a childhood ache that spread from stomach to bones, weekends of starvation that sent me to school on Mondays shaking and faint, praying for lunch. But Dominique starved herself on purpose.

I never ate in the lab, my rules. My life was all rules. But I usually had something to eat on my desk because students brought me food, most of it too sweet, but I could leave it on the desk and share it, then carry it out and find a homeless person to give it to on my way home. I would offer what I had to her. *Eat one. Please.* She stared past whatever I held out. I could never believe what I saw in her face when she turned away from what she needed to stay alive. Pride. She was so proud to refuse food.

God, I have been so proud.

And then, finally, there was the day she got too close. Her ravenous breath in my face, every sculpted bone in her beautiful young face standing out in relief. She put her hands on my hand. *All you do is go to church and teach and walk your dog. Everyone here knows it.*

She kept herself covered neck to ankle to wrist, no matter how hot it was, but her hands were bare and set before me like something desiccated from a tomb, emaciated fingers with bitten nails. I thought, these hands are wasted. I pulled mine away.

She started softly shaking her head, a desperate, hopeless shaking. *Don't you see? We have control, we're strong. We're so much better than all of them. Because they're weak and we're not. Look.* She pulled up a sleeve, showed me an arm that could be snapped into kindling. *What you're doing is beautiful, too. We understand each other.*

I turned to study the perfect geometry of her face, the lines and angles revealed by her constant self-subtraction. What could I say? I didn't think my solitude was a form of power or strength. I thought it was a penance, born from fear, carried out in pain. But if she was right, if like her, I denied myself because I believed it was beautiful, then we were both monsters.

I told her my private life was not up for discussion. No one's business.

She smiled. *It's my business because I love you, Gentry.*

I said the only thing I could. I was her teacher. She was my student. And that was it.

She stood up and walked out of that room, her shoulders high and narrow. She kept her dignity that day, but lost it the next day in a letter. She left it in the faculty mailbox next to mine, "Geritty," not "Gentry." It happened all the time. I got Pam Gerrity's mail and she got mine, and we each put it in the right slot. Because she never checked, Pam had usually opened my mail before she noticed it was for me.

This is what happened with Dominique's letter.

The principal's name was Rose Brewer. Her name reminded me of tea. She was one of the most exhausted people I had ever met, going through her days with an air of fundamental hopelessness. Rose called me in, sat me down, and had me read it.

Dear Gentry,

I'm going to write my college entry essay on betrayal. Because I know what it feels like, now, I can write about it. I'll write about the person who betrayed me worst in my whole life, and that's you.

I did everything because you believed in me. I thought I was special to you, that I was the one you chose. I could never have done all of it if I hadn't believed you loved me. I wouldn't have had the strength. My love for you gave me the strength to do it.

All those afternoons. You and me and all those afternoons.

I always believed you loved me.

                                                        Dominique

Rose Brewer looked at me. *I'd like an explanation.*

I told what had happened, that she'd come to me and said she loved me.

The principal shook her head. *You should have come to me. You come to me when a student expresses something like this to you.* And I asked, was I supposed to come to her every single time I thought a student had a crush on me? She shook her head. *I guess you'd be in here every day, wouldn't you.*

I sat there feeling hopeless.

What about this "never could have done all of it," then? "All those afternoons"? What does that mean?

She means tutoring, getting ready for the SATs, researching scholarships.

Why did she think you loved her?

I don't know. You have to ask her, Rose.

Oh, I'll be asking her. Have no doubt about that, Gentry.

She sent me out to wait in a chair in the hall. I sat in that hall in Detroit and felt twelve years old. I remembered waiting on a bench outside the headmaster's office at my school, sent there for fighting. Knowing the headmaster was going to say, *We've made so many allowances for you, but there's a limit and you have to stop this, and stop it now.* Knowing he was right, knowing I was going to be sent home to face Mel's disappointment.

I prayed when I was twelve. I prayed, again.

Dominique walked by with Pam Geritty. She kept her face turned away from me. I watched her go in with relief. I thought, she'll tell Rose the truth and this thing will be over.

After she talked to Rose, no one believed me.

༄

The school police took me back into my lab during a class, in front of my kids. Officer Primus Taft, a man who had me over to dinner every few weeks, he did the talking. *Get your things around, Gentry.*

No.

He sighed, shook his head. *You might as well take it. They'll have a restraining order in place by tomorrow.*

Hoan kept saying, *This is fucked. This is FUCKED.*

I silently agreed.

I walked away from my lab with empty hands because I refused to believe I wouldn't be back. Primus escorted me to the edge of the school grounds and walked off the distance specified by the restraining order with me so I would understand. He spoke to me so gently. *No closer than this to the school. And don't come anywhere near her, do you hear? Leave the girl completely alone.* If I came within a thousand feet of her or the school, I would be arrested.

༄

The papers picked it up immediately.

Everyone had warned me. All those earnest conversations. Other teachers, the principal, the counselors, Primus Taft. *You're very young, Gentry. It will confuse the kids.* And, *Watch your back. Don't be alone with the students, ever.* Primus telling me, *You need to protect yourself. From a few things, you need to protect yourself from a few things.* Even Hoan had warned me. *You're a good guy, so you don't know what this place is really like. Don't be foolish about anything.*

Bosco loved it that I was home listening to the screaming neighbors with him. Hoan called me every day. He offered to bring me my stuff, but I told him not to bother, I'd be back soon. I went to the hearings and I told the truth. Angry teachers, angry school board members, and one glib attorney for me, appointed by the union.

I had to answer questions, the personal questions they can ask you when it isn't court, when it's just a hearing. Had I ever been married? Engaged? Was I involved with anyone? Did I even date? *Well, what kind of man are you, Mr. Gentry?*

What kind of man?

I was a teacher and I was innocent and I told the truth. I thought that was enough. I grew up terrified of the truth until Mel made me start telling it. Basic things, like what hurt or what I'd done wrong or what I needed or wanted, and when he asked me what was wrong I had to be truthful. And then I thought of truth as something that stood, like God, with a strength and a power and a majesty of its own. I never understood the limitations of truth.

I came to understand.

∾

Everything has a limit. Everything and everyone. I was reaching mine.

Mel came. We walked my dog, went to Mass, went to hearings. There were people behind me after all, some parents, quite a few students including Hoan, who circulated a magnificently wordy and useless petition. Many, many people from my church. But not the people I worked with.

I worked with them, ate my breakfast with them, ate my lunch with them. We talked shop. I taught their classes when they had doctor's appointments and migraines and nervous breakdowns. I accepted their social invitations. No, I never reciprocated, because what was I going to say? *Would you like to come with when I visit my Jeep in the parking garage? How about Mass? I'm going extra this week.* Or I could have made this offer. *Come on over to my apartment, we can eat some Total. After, we can sit and listen to the crack of breaking bones next door.* Maybe after I rinsed out the bowl (I only had one, we'd have had to share), I could have taken them on a walking tour of some of Detroit's more colorful neighborhoods in search of a green place for my dog to lift his leg.

No, I never had anyone over. But I offered what I could, spare change for the coffee fund, use of the lab's color printer. I never offered personal advice, but I offered software advice. I did the best I could. And this was what I received in return.

Elaine Rathenkamp. *He's a Jesus Freak.*

John Rasmussen. *He never takes notes at training.*

Mike Orr. *He seems overly attached to his dog.*

Pam Geritty. *There's just something strange about him. Something weird.* The fact that she was the woman I left sitting in a restaurant when she asked me to order for her, that never came up.

Officer Taft. *He's a good man. But he seems . . . too alone.*

None of them accused me outright. It was a barely audible testimony of small doubts, uneasy feelings, faint praise. I "kept to myself." I was a "loner." I was "unusually devoted" to teaching. I "marched to a different drummer." It was a "known fact" that I spent a "considerable amount of time alone" with "certain students." I did that on a "daily basis." All these meaningless phrases. I waited for one person to say, *Gentry would never do anything like that.*

No one said that.

I contemplated my ruin.

At the hearings, Mel sat next to me. At night, he went out and found food for us because my apartment was bare of anything he could use for cooking. And he listened to me worry. *If she doesn't tell the truth, they might arrest me. What if they arrest me? What if I have to go to jail? Mel, you can't let them put me anywhere.*

Mel shook his head. *They will not arrest you. You will never even be formally charged. Trust me, Gentry, I am unfortunately familiar with how this all works. If they had anything on you, you'd already be in jail. They have nothing on you.* Next door, there was a thump, the familiar sound of bodily impact on a thin wall, the wail of fury that followed, the inevitable revenge. A smack, the yelling, and then the other part began. Hitting a mattress instead of a wall, another type of bodily collision.

Mel looked ill. *My boy, you need to move.*

I hardly hear it anymore. *I'm failing, Mel.*

Fight this battle, and then see how you feel.

I can't do this anymore.

Don't retreat.

Mel, I could still teach, it would be private school, but . . .

My boy, your vocation is teaching. If you had been called to the priesthood, nothing would make me more proud. But you weren't. And this desire to retreat is not a call. Wait, Gentry. Face this down. Ride it out.

I rode it out.

～

Mel was correct. She kept changing her story, changing her mind. Her medical history and psychiatric evaluation worked against her. There would be no charges filed. But she wouldn't recant. She had to recant so I could go back to work.

They decided to give me a chance, conditionally. The administration met, secretly, they decided, privately, that I could clear my name, finally, because they believed in me, deeply. *We believe in you, Gentry.*

Oh, they believed in me. So long as I gave them proof.

Rose Brewer came to my apartment, sat me down on the floor because there was nowhere else for us to sit, and told me this. *We need proof, Gentry. These people are sue-happy.*

These people?

You know what I mean. Don't look at me like that, I'm black. I hate it when white people look at me like I'm saying something wrong about black people, I really do.

I'm sorry.

Rose shook her tired head. *You were in grade schools guest-teaching, you were all over the city. Don't forget that. We have every whiplash lawyer in the state calling the district offices, ready to claim that you got after kids and we didn't do anything about it. Nobody has a client yet, but they will. It's just a matter of time until someone gets greedy and starts lying. We need to shut this down, Gentry. We need proof, or the district will be in court for the next ten years over this, and we just don't have the money for it. We need proof.*

I stood up, helped her to her feet. She put one hand on each of my shoulders to steady herself, and then left them there. *You're one of the best teachers I've ever had. I want you back in your classroom. But I need proof.*

It was the only way they would let me come back.

～

So they lifted the restraining order. I came back for one day. No classes, I was just there as bait. All day long, kids came in and said things like, *Glad to see you back, Gentry, I knew that was some crazy bullshit. Straight-up bullshit. Dominique, she batshit. That bitch is crazy.* I didn't allow talk like that in my lab, but that day I said nothing. There were officers in my storage closet and I was wearing a wire. All of it was "for your protection," they said, but they were ready to arrest me if I said the wrong thing, did the wrong thing, I knew that. They were waiting to see who was guilty.

I kept sweating. I was afraid I would be electrocuted, so I tried not to sweat. You can't control your sweat. Why couldn't they put it on my desk somewhere?

Finally, the lab was quiet except for the sirens wailing around the block, wailing and wailing. And she came. As sick as she had ever been, thinner than I knew a living person could be, trembling with the effort to stand. She sat down in a desk and I went over to her. I had to be near her to pick up the conversation.

Tears tracked her carved cheeks. *I'm sorry.*

Was that enough, that she said she was sorry? I knew it was not as much as they'd need.

Why, Dominique? Why are you sorry? I sounded so wrong and strange, why wasn't she alarmed?

She spoke with her careful, quiet dignity. *Because I love you and you don't want it. So then my love is a burden to you, and not a gift.*

It was a sad and beautiful thing to say.

I stood over her. She sat, examining her hands. *You're so correct. That's what my grandma called you after she met you. A correct man.* She tilted her head, searching for something in my face. *You keep yourself up there so high. There was never a way to touch you, and no way you would ever reach down and touch me.*

I choked it out. *I never did touch you, did I?*

She frowned. *No, you didn't. But you should have.*

I had it, then. That was probably enough for them.

But it was not enough for me.

Why did you lie? Why did you do this to me?

She sat there, so small and curled up and brittle, a husk outgrown and cast off by a living thing. Her pretty mouth opened, stretched, showing her brown teeth, rotting away from her own bile. *Because I love you, so I want to hurt you.*

I backed up, backed away. Reeling from her smile.

They came out of the big storage closet. A woman officer put her hands on Dominique, kept her in the desk. Two men grabbed me and I started to fight and they backed off. One of the officers held up his hands and spoke to me in the careful tone of voice you use with crazy people. *Steady, now. Calm down. We just need the wire, Mr. Gentry. We just want to get the wire off you. Remember? The wire?*

I'd forgotten the wire.

Dominique watched while I took off my shirt and raised my arms. An officer took off the box, ripping away my skin with the tape that bound it to me. She watched as they stashed it all in large plastic bags, sealed them, wrote the date and my name and case number on them.

They took her away.

I sat down at my desk in my lab and wondered what I was supposed to do next.

I put my hands over my eyes and listened to the sirens.

∽

She recanted. Mel went home to the monastery. The school said I had to do a press conference before I could teach again. I read a prepared statement about wanting to get back to my work and my students. After, all the reporters who had written lies about me for weeks had a chance to ask me about how awful it had been to have lies written about me for weeks. The media that crucified me expressed collective surprise that I didn't want to talk to the media about how awful it was to be crucified by the media.

I kept saying that I had nothing to say. And I thought, how strange, that all I have to say is that I have nothing to say.

It was nearing the end of the school year when I finally had my first day back. Hoan gave me a party with food cooked by his mother, carried in and served by his cousins. Hoan had a lot of cousins. A party in the computer lab, all that wonderful food all over the place, a clear violation of rule number one and I couldn't say a word about it. All I could do was smile and eat and speak my laughable version of his mother tongue and let them laugh at me. We celebrated.

I thought, well, maybe we can all make it through this.

∽

A few weeks later on a Monday morning, I walked in the lab. It was never quiet in there. It was quiet that day, though. No one was milling around, no one was talking, no one was swearing. Everyone was seated and waiting and silent and not one student would meet my eyes.

And I thought, she's recanted her recanting or something. I'm going to have to go through this all over again and I can't take it, I won't, I'm going into the monastery because I can't take it out here.

I remembered to breathe. I sat down and started to take roll. *Where's Hoan?*

He was never absent, never. He was my TA for three terms running and never missed a class. He even came in on the day his son was born, just to tell me all about it and show me pictures. He had called me every day I was out during the investigation, he'd made me laugh when no one else could.

Hey, does anyone know where Hoan is?

I looked from student to student, and they all looked away. Some of the girls were crying.

This feeling started to rise up in me, a calm, overarching knowledge. Not fear, not panic. A cold white prescience. And this is what I knew. Whatever I'd been through with Dominique, however it hurt me, whatever it cost me, it was nothing at all compared to what I'd feel when someone finally told me where Hoan was.

∽

I woke up in the lab, crying. I wiped my face on my shirt.

It was too dark in there, the only light my screen saver. I was working on . . . résumés. The final junior project. Résumés, and Tiffany's was the most impressive. Please God, I prayed, let Tiffany learn enough to get out of there.

It was my last day. Some movement in the hall, the janitor. I needed to get out of there and let the man do his job.

"Knock, knock." She sat down at a table. "So, I have this final paper due. It's an analysis of three poems. Will you help me?"

This was the beautiful dream, that she would say the words that could take us back to when I was her teacher, and she was my student, and all was safe between us.

I shook my head. "You need to leave."

"Please, Gentry. I need help."

I looked around. We were in a classroom. I was a teacher. She was a student. She needed my help. Maybe those were the words. "Read them out loud. No poem makes any sense unless you read it out loud."

She read to me by the dim light of a computer screen.

> *The Soul selects her own Society -*
> *Then - Shuts the door -*
> *To her divine Majority -*
> *Present no more -*

Unmoved - she notes the Chariots - pausing -
At her low Gate -
Unmoved - an Emperor be kneeling
Upon her Mat -

I've known her - from an ample nation -
Choose One -
Then - close the Valves of her attention -
Like Stone -

"I think I get this one. It's the soul as an oyster or a clam, right? An extended metaphor. She chose, and she only holds one. She closes around the one she chooses. She's not empty."

That was a matter of opinion, Marci.

"Right. Read the next one."

She read.

I cannot live with You -
It would be life -
And Life is over there -
Behind the Shelf

The Sexton keeps the Key to -
Putting up
Our life - His Porcelain -
Like a Cup -

Discarded of the Housewife -
Quaint - or Broke -
A newer Sevres please -
Old Ones crack -

"I don't understand this one. A sexton, a pastor, right? He has the key, so he has their lives locked up, right? That's probably religion. Religion is in the way."

"Yes."

"But what's this cup? Why's this cup in there?"

"It's something everyday. Something domestic."

"Things you don't notice, things you look past? It's cracked, so it means nothing? It means nothing to the sexton?"

"To anyone, I think. It's set aside."

"So their small little life is stuck away in a cupboard by religion?"

"Read the rest of it."

She sighed, and went on.

> *I could not die - with You -*
> *For One must wait*
> *To shut the Other's Gaze down -*
> *You - could not -*
>
> *And I - Could I stand by*
> *And see You - freeze -*
> *Without my Right of Frost -*
> *Death's privilege?*

"I don't get this. At all. What is 'shut the other's gaze down'?"

"One of them has to die first."

"And neither of them could stand to do it? Do you think she's talking about them killing themselves?"

"Maybe. You could possibly support that."

"So she's saying that she can't die with him, because one of them has to die first, and she couldn't watch him die without dying too?"

"Yes." She went on, Marci who needed help with a poem.

> *Nor could I rise - with You -*
> *Because your face*
> *Would put out Jesus' -*
> *That New Grace*
>
> *Glow plain - and foreign*
> *On my homesick Eye -*

Except that You than He
Shone closer by -

"Okay, so this is more religion. They can't rise up together, because her love for him is so strong that it hides God's face, right? Is that what she's saying? And you need God to rise up, right?"

"You do."

They'd judge Us - How -
For You - served heaven - You know,
or sought to -
I could not -

Because you had saturated Sight -
And I had no more Eyes
For sordid excellence
As Paradise.

And were you lost, I would be -
Though my name
Rang loudest
On the Heavenly fame -

And were You - saved -
And I - condemned to be
Where you were not -
That self - were Hell to Me -

"Here, tell me if I'm right, Gentry, because I want to know if I'm right. She says that they'll be judged because he has faith, and she doesn't." Her voice broke. "Maybe she did at one time, but her love for him drove it out of her. And she doesn't need any faith, because he's so strong to her that being apart would feel like Hell, even if she were in Heaven. Right? Is that the right meaning?"

"There's no right meaning, no wrong meaning. Only what you can support."

But she had the right meaning.

So, We must meet apart -
you there - I - here -
With just the Door ajar
That Oceans are - and Prayer -
and that White Sustenance -
Despair.

"It's not so big a distance, is it, Gentry? Oceans. Not so big. And they can pray, right? That's sustenance, what she's supposed to be sustained by, and despair. Is that what she's supposed to live on? Despair?"

I pressed my hands against my eyes.

And she was there, Oh God, I couldn't stand it, I could smell her, I could feel the air around her, how it hurt and burned. And she put her hands on my shoulders, like rope knotted up, and she started to beg. "I'm so sorry, Gentry, I'm so sorry, talk to Mom, she'll be okay, I know she'll get over it. Gretchen misses you so much, she's just disappearing right in front of me, she misses you, I miss you," but I shook my head, I would never go in their house again, never look at what I couldn't have. And her tearful face was in my neck and her hands moved down my shirt, her mouth at my ear. "I love you."

Oh, Dear God.

I rose up and slammed her against the board, I held her wrists and she didn't fight me, the tears fell down her cheeks, to taste one, the tip of my tongue, she had to stop, I had to let go of her, I had to let go. I let go. She ran away. I fell on my knees and bowed my head and begged for an answer. Oh Dear God, why didn't You make me better than this?

I thought You heard me, I thought You listened to me, I thought You loved me.

I remembered tracing my hands over Kathryn, her hipbones, that faint butterfly, her fragile spine. Tasting the silvery scar on her stomach where she gave birth to her daughters.

I remembered how it felt to hold her daughter down and look into her pleading eyes, to feel her move beneath me, against me. The taste of Marci's mouth, sweet and open, burying my face in the electric scent of her hair, searching for the scent of Kathryn.

They sounded the same when they cried.

The name for me is despair. I'll live on it. It will be enough. I'll live on this, but only for one day.

One more day.

Lorrie Gilroy

Well, Goddamnit, here he is again, can't he see I've got company? And I'm kind of embarrassed about who it is, believe you me.

Vicki was supposed to be out with him that night at the prom, but I don't know, there was something about the way she scooped him up. I was walking behind her and Gentry was hanging over her shoulder like a goddamn sack of potatoes and his hair fell down her back, see, and I looked at that magnificent ass of hers and she drove my truck up there, I drove his Jeep, and then we kind of tucked the little guy in. I looked at her, she looked at me, and I knew.

Vicki's the one.

I mean, would you look at the way she keeps her Bronco, an original, the first year, and she keeps it tip-top. My God, that rig is cherry. She even likes to fish. Vicki would make one helluva man, and I mean that in the nicest possible way.

But I didn't call her until Gentry was okay, until he was back in class, and here he is, all shaky and pale, and if he gets mad over Vicki then what the hell am I going to do? But he's talking, at least. He looks at me like a ghost's after him, and says, "Please, take me fishing Lorrie. Please, right now." Like that.

Well, what the hell. I take him fishing. I take him up to Foley Creek, and I think, what the hell am I going to say to Fish and Wildlife if they catch us up here, that I had to do some sonofabitching emergency fishing? But I take him, see, I take him.

And he calms down, he puts his line in and he doesn't talk, he just starts breathing regular. He's cold, where the hell's his coat? I give him my coat, and he stops shaking. "Will you live?" He nods. And I'll be goddamned if he doesn't get a bite. He pulls up a little brook trout. Gentry could catch fish in a toilet, I swear.

I'll miss him.

"You want to try for another?"

"No."

Packing it in.

I take him back to my house, and Vicki cooks him up the fish, and he looks at Vicki, and he looks at me, and he's all of a sudden smiling, he's the happiest son of a bitch in the world. Maybe it's the nice way Vicki has with a fish.

I told you, big women can cook.

I look at him leaning over that plate, his hair all over his lap. Eating a fish, just eating a fish, forgetting all about what's wrong with his life because his stomach's getting full. Don't do this, I want to tell him, don't live like a dog, from plate to plate and place to place. Don't forget about it. Stop packing it in. Make a stand.

He's found something he wants here. Hell if I know why, it isn't anything I'd want, but he can do it, he can sort it out and make it right. But this is the way it's going to be with him, I see that. No matter what happens to the guy, whatever crazy shit happens, stuff that's his fault, stuff that isn't, he's not going to dig in and fight it out. He's going to pack it in and move on.

And that's a real shame.

Gentry

COMMENCEMENT

SPEAKER: Hoan-Vu Nguyen

VALEDICTORIAN: Marcialin Lavinia Mumford

Marcialin Lavinia?

Why did parents do these things to their children? Give me a Max, or a Nick. I also like Zack. Those were good names. Girls should have names like Abby or Molly or Hannah.

Or Gretchen.

I felt her blue eyes on me. She was there with her dad. This was as close to her as I'd been since, oh, I wasn't going to do it. I wasn't going to think about it anymore.

I wanted to watch my kids graduate.

⌒

I don't like to look at my own face. I never have. I have one picture of myself, aside from ID mug shots. It was taken on the night of my high school commencement. I was days short of sixteen years old and I graduated second in my class. I had to wear a get-up that horrified me, there was no getting around it, I had to wear the full regalia. I wore it with pride. That night, the pride rolled off me in waves. I looked out in the auditorium. I didn't want to admit that after ten years, I was still looking for that face in the crowd.

My own.

I felt, then, not proud. I felt alone and afraid and too young. But I saw Mel standing out there next to Loren. His eyes shone. He took out a handkerchief and blew his nose. I thought, it doesn't matter as long as I have him. Nothing matters as long as I have Mel. I was proud again.

Afterward, Loren took our picture. When I look at it, I'm proud all over again.

So, forgive me my pride, God, in these kids, because it's partly made of pride in myself for my part in getting them here, and pride is a sin. Forgive me and forgive every other adult who cared enough to come here and sit on these uncomfortable bleachers and listen to Vu go on about rampant capitalism and youthful disenfranchisement and inherent alienation and the distinct moral dilemmas faced by his generation, because we're not only proud of them, the kids. We're proud of ourselves. We're proud that we helped make them what they are. Forgive me this moment of pride, forgive me the tears in my eyes, my heart is full.

I know, God, that I carry it with me. I know that the gangs and drugs and pregnant girls, the students I love and the students I lose, I was wrong to try to escape them, because You return them to me. They belong to me. Wherever I go, there will be a boy who hates me and a girl who loves me, there will be a child I can help and a child I can't.

I have prayed to You for my own children. I understand that this is how You will answer my prayer. This is to give thanks to You.

Amen.

～

A roar went up, and so did the hats. I covered my head to avoid the falling mortarboards and tried to leave. But there were kids, hugging kids, happy kids, all saying good-bye, some crying, holding on, introducing their grandparents and older sisters, I needed to go, nice to meet you, me too, yes I will, yes, this was, this was, and I was out. I was finally out, I was done.

I needed to say good-bye.

～

She was just outside the exit, having a cigarette. My throat was closed and I couldn't say a word. I came to say good-bye and my mouth would not say it.

There was no way to say good-bye to Kathryn.

"A penny for your thoughts, Gentry." She breathed in her cigarette, that sound I heard over the phone so long ago. "I keep thinking of that bird Gretchen talks about. You know the one. She nests in the grass and when a predator comes near, she pretends to have a broken wing and pulls herself in circles. She makes herself an irresistible target for predators. She does it to protect her young. But of course, Gentry, you're no predator." She dropped her smoke and delicately ground it out with a twist of her foot.

I was that cigarette.

She stared at me, appraising. I stared back at the ice of her eyes. "Gentry, Marci explained. She said it was a . . . game." She shudders. "Some game, and it got out of hand. I don't know what to make of that. But I know you. I know you would never do anything like that."

But I did.

She turned her face to me. I wanted to run my fingertips along its harsh planes, to trace the architecture of her beauty. Her face was always so still, always so beautiful. I watched as something in it gave way, a crack running through her perfection.

"Gentry, was it ever me you wanted? Was it her, always?"

Kathryn. Come here.

I took both her tiny hands. I pulled her to me, but gently, because her hands were so small. She pulled back and I let go. But her hands came back, so softly, to my hair. She stroked it back, then touched my face, my mouth, my eyes, with her cold little fingertips. She traced my neck, put her hands on my shoulders, rested them there. I wanted her to kiss me. But Kathryn never kissed me. Never. Not once.

She ran her hands down my chest, put her hand on my heart. I knew her hand would stay on my heart forever. She moved her hands to my stomach. And I thought I would die, then, as she moved her hands to the parts of me that still wanted her, I still wanted her, I would always want her. Oh, Kathryn, it was you I wanted. Always.

That was the ruin of it.

I took her hands in my own, turned them up and open, ready to receive. I brought them to my mouth. I kissed them the way I always wanted to kiss her, the way she would never let me, every other place I kissed her, but never her mouth. I covered her small, white, beautiful, ice cold hands with every gentle kiss she turned away.

I left her standing with her face in her hands.

⌒

I got in my Jeep.

Okay, God. Help.

"Gentry!" He loomed up beside me, Gretchen behind him. She peered at me like a bird through bars. "Kathy says you're taking off. She looks pretty torn up." He frowned. "Trouble in Paradise?" Mike waved his key chain at the Saab, and it chirped. He handed the keys to his daughter. "Honey, I need to talk to Gentry alone for a minute."

She took the keys and walked away, her shoulders square, her white-blonde hair shining behind her, her arms crossed over her chest, holding herself, humming. She turned back before she got in, smiled at me, waved a little wave. I waved back. She got into his car.

This was the last time I would ever see her.

"Gentry, can I talk to you for a second? It won't take long. I just have a couple of things I want to say." I sat there. Waited for his fist in my face. I almost wanted it. "First, I need to say I'm sorry."

Please, don't be sorry, don't be human. I want to despise you, Mike.

He waited for my response, but my throat was full of ghosts. It would choke me to speak.

"Oh, I don't expect you to accept it, I guess. And I don't even know why it bothered me so much. You know, Kathy getting a life. Anyway, I know I've been a jerk, and you don't deserve it."

No one had told Mike, or he'd know what I deserved.

"You just made me feel so insignificant, somehow." He studied my face. "With Gretchen. Those damn bumper cars."

I forced it out. "Mike, don't do this."

"No, let me talk. She talks about . . . she knows everything about you, Gentry. All she does is talk about you, what you do together, what you teach her. The neighbors brought home a new computer, and she went over there and had it set up and was showing them how to play Ruin in minutes. Because you showed her how."

That was one smart girl, that Gretchen.

"She doesn't know where I work. She doesn't care." Oh, she cares, Mike. Every child cares about where a dad works, what a dad does. Even I cared as a boy.

I made myself say it. "You are her dad."

"Well. Thank you. I'm trying. You know, Kathy left when Gretchen was six months old. She didn't speak to me except through attorneys for over a year. It took fourteen months and a court order before I got to see the girls again." He expected me to understand this alien world in which mothers kept children and fathers fought to get them back. I had never lived in that world. "Gretchen was twenty months old. She had no idea who I was. None. I came to get the girls and took them to Portland and she cried steady for over a day. Curled up on Marci's lap in this room Eve made for them, this little pink room with twin beds. Eve was so excited." He shook his head. "Marci just sitting there on one of the beds holding this little white-haired stranger who couldn't stop crying. Finally Marci looked at me and said, 'Daddy, will you just take us back to Mom?' I can still see her pointed face and those big green eyes. She was almost nine."

A child. Kathryn's child. This man's daughter. My student.

Someone should kill me.

"Hey Mike? I, um, have to go."

"All right, but listen." He took hold of my arm. I hated men touching me, but he held tight to my arm and I let him. "Find yourself another woman, a young one. Put her in a house by the water, and fill up that house with children, and never look away. Don't ever take your eyes off what you have. You'll make a fine father, Gentry. You were meant to be a father."

I was undone.

God Damn you to Hell, Mike Mumford.

I stared at my steering wheel until they left.

⌒

I drove too fast, played my music too loud. I thought about how good it would feel to go somewhere new, somewhere new, Bosco as my copilot, we'd fly. We'd visit Mel for a while, and then a change. We needed a change.

I hated change.

To put her in my Jeep and take her with me. How about that idea, God? The worst idea I'd ever had in my life. But she'd go, wouldn't she? Her white hair blowing around beside me, her voice so pure, her laugh like bells. We would laugh all the way to the next place.

And there was this thing, some thing that grew in me, some unavoidable, terrible, beautiful thing. It swelled and hurt and filled me until I couldn't breathe.

This was either love or grief.

I'd never been able to tell the difference.

∽

There wasn't much to pack up because I only owned what I used. I didn't use much. Bosco and I loaded it up together. The computer and the peripherals took up most of the room, the boom box, and the duffel bag and the sleeping bag and a box of books and CDs. That was it.

I put my classroom key in an envelope with a note for Lorrie, an address where he could send the box, some twenties for postage. The money would make him mad, but I didn't care. Good-bye, thank you for taking me fishing. I would put this in his mailbox on the way out of town. Lorrie deserved better, but he'd understand.

I almost forgot the crucifix, my sole graven image. I put God in my pocket.

Bosco, is this really everything? Is this all there is? Let's rinse out your bowl, let's check under the bed, let's check the closet. That tuxedo could stay in Oregon. But that box. How did I forget about that box?

Everyone had a box like this, even me, a box with pictures, certificates and report cards, whatever pieces of paper someone deemed important enough to save. Mel had one for me. But this was Kathryn's box. If I opened it, I might have understood why Kathryn loved Mike, why Mike didn't love Kathryn, I might have understood why she would rather grieve than give me a chance. I might have found a picture of Gretchen that I could take with me. I might have found a photo of Marci before this place made her what she was. But I wouldn't open it. Because that was not my box.

I slid the picture of me and Mel into the box and decided to put it in Gretchen's room. No one would be there. Gretchen was with her father, Marci was at the senior party and so was Kathryn. I wouldn't have to see anyone. I would go over there and drop off the box and stand in the kitchen and have my moment, the private little moment I earned by loving them each in my imperfect and harmful way.

I was so bad at loving them. But I tried.

Bosco, stay. No, you're not coming with. Stay.

⤸

I'll be right back.

Lorrie

Of course I don't mind driving to Portland to pick up the priest, of course not, I just guess I was expecting to see a priest, not some big farmer in overalls. Because that's what this guy looks like, an old farmer, he's as tall as me and twice as big around and he's wearing overalls and work boots. But he walks up and says, "Lorrie? Let's go." And we do, I swear this guy would have gotten out and ran the ninety-two miles if it would have gotten him there any faster.

He doesn't say much, just keeps watching the speedometer to make sure I'm going over the maximum goddamn limit and did I mention that he got in at one fifteen AM so I couldn't see what the hell his hurry was, anyway. But this Mel, he's all hot to go, and so we get to the hospital at about three AM.

I keep telling him, they won't let anyone in until morning. But since he's the next of kin (that phrase gives me the goddamn chills) he gets us in there.

And I'm trying to tell him what to expect. But Mel won't listen, and he comes in the room and sees Gentry, the light's on and the old guy takes one look and he turns to me and he draws himself up and he hollers "GREAT GOD IN HEAVEN, HOW DID YOU LET THIS HAPPEN TO HIM??"

I'm thinking Jesus Holy Hell Christ, I didn't do it, and then I realize that the guy's talking to the actual God, see, not to me. But Gentry's eyelids lift up, he sees this priest and he looks like I haven't seen him look in the twenty-four hours I've been here sleeping in the room, waiting and watching and hoping to see this.

He looks like he's going to make it.

⤸

And the old guy sits down next to Gentry on the bed, and when he takes hold of Gentry's hands, Gentry's just swallow his up. Little hands. He says "Happy Birthday, my boy." And Gentry would smile if he could, I know it, but his face is a little screwed up for smiling.

They keep Gentry pretty doped at night. Until they can set the jaw, they have to do something so he can sleep. But even with all the drugs, my little buddy looks at this guy like he's God or something. I'm thinking, what the hell's so great about this fat guy with the big glasses, but when the kid looks at him, I see he must be pretty damn special, somehow, some way.

He whispers something to the priest. His voice box is bruised and when he tries to talk, he about cries. That's another part of it. Gentry's the cryingest man I know, and he hasn't. Not once. And I remember from that week he spent on my couch, it's when Gentry doesn't cry that you have to worry.

I decide maybe I should go out and get some sleep on my favorite plastic couch and let these two talk. Except the kid won't talk, I know that. So I just sit back and watch until Gentry goes to sleep again.

⌒

It was Vicki that called me. Her little friend Rose was on duty when they brought him in, and Rose called Vicki up at the party, and Vicki called me. I admire that Vicki, believe you me. Vicki is one fine woman, let me tell you. She could make a believer of a man, that Vicki. Sort of makes you think about your whole view of women, Vicki does. Anyway, she called me and I came to the hospital. After we got him settled in, she went back up to the party to find Kathy. All I wanted was the number of the priest. I figured I could take care of the rest of it on my own. I know about the insurance and shit like that and I sure as hell have watched over a banged-up kid in my day. But Her Royal Highness showed up here, she wanted to see him, but I told her no way in hell. She gave me the phone number though. I was relieved to know they have phones at monasteries. I wasn't sure. It took a long time to get him on the phone, they weren't going to go get him until I said it was about Gentry. And then they made double time.

Gentry couldn't call, he doesn't talk, he won't say a word. He keeps reaching over to touch that creepy thing on his night stand, closing his eyes and holding on to that cross for dear life. I want to say, that thing almost took your nads off, kid, I wouldn't touch it for love or money. That sonofabitching thing was drove right near the artery that feeds the groin, one inch in the other direction and he could have died. But it's just a gash, he's gonna make it, the whole package is fine, they say.

So it was a boot party. He has four cracked ribs and the larynx, that could have killed him, too, but it didn't, I knew a guy in college suffocated when his larynx was cracked in a fight, but Gentry's isn't cracked, just bruised, goddamn lucky deal, and then he has a concussion from being hit in the back of the head, and the one tooth is knocked loose, but they can fix that up when they fix his jaw. It's a clean break, snapped, but it's dislocated, too, and they need to get in there and set it and set the break.

He won't like this jaw business, I'll tell you that. I've seen this shit before on my players. It's bad. I tell Mel this, but he's so busy staring at Gentry, who is asleep, that I don't think he hears me but I tell him anyway, I think, because telling somebody that the kid's all right helps me think he could be and he looks so bad that I really need to think he'll be okay, he will. And I guess I peter out, because there's something about the way he looks. The kid's so messed up. "Could you get Bosco?"

"Here in the hospital?" I think about it. Vicki has friends here, and Gentry's doctor's a good guy, he seems to give a shit about my little buddy. The doctor has a jaw surgeon coming from OHSU, he fixed it up so Gentry didn't have to go to Portland. "Sure. I'll get the dog. Anything else?"

"Just bring his dog."

I think I can go up there without killing anyone.

⌒

Vicki and me, we go up there at seven the next morning together. The Jeep's sitting there, the keys are in the ignition, the top on, every damn thing he has in it. I keep thinking, why didn't he just get in it? Why didn't he get in it and get the hell out of Dodge?

I see the house and wish I had some gas and matches. Vicki, she just puts her hand on mine and gets out and knocks on the door. Let her talk to the witches, if I try to I'll just kill somebody. And she comes out and she gets in the Jeep and starts it up and wrestles it into gear, my God that woman is strong, and she drives it around and parks it out of my sight.

I hope she's putting it in the garage. I sure hope so, because every goddamn thing he owns is in there and it's all up for grabs, sitting in the driveway like that. It makes you hurt just to think about it.

She comes back, and the door from the kitchen opens and here's the mutt, he comes over and pees on the tire and hops in the cab and sits down in the middle, just like he knew we were coming to get him, like he knew what to do. That's one good dog.

Well, Vicki says she's a little tired, so I drop her at my house and go back to the hospital, and they're getting ready to take him in for surgery. Gentry wouldn't do it until Mel got here but that was okay because they like to check you out pretty good before they do any cutting around here. He's ready to go. Man, is he happy to see his dog. Bosco licks all over his face, but gentle-like, like he could fix it with his tongue.

"So Bosco and I will wait out here with Lorrie, my boy. All right? All of us waiting for you. And you're going to be fine."

I can't watch this part, this wheeling him down the hall part.

Right now, I'm so damn glad that the priest is here. So damn glad. Three nights in the hospital and I want to sleep, but I can't, not until I know he's okay. It's just me and Mel and Bosco, waiting to see if he's okay.

The priest and the dog fall asleep like that. Two big shaggy ones, leaning on each other and snoring. Well, it's kinda sweet, I admit it.

Emmett comes by, looking official in that uniform of his. I have no idea why he wears it, most of the sheriffs I've known in my life wouldn't wear a uniform, but he wears it. I point to the priest and the dog. "Keep your voice down." He nods. "Whatcha got?"

"Exactly nothing."

"You talked to him?"

"He can't talk."

"He writes shit down, though."

Emmett sits down, scratches the back of his neck. "He wrote down that he doesn't remember anything."

"Well that happens with a bad concussion. But you've got clues. There's glass all over that driveway. Tire marks on the paved part. A girl to talk to."

Emmett nods. "I talked to the Mumford girl," he says. "She says her boyfriend drove her home and she found him like that in the driveway."

"Bullshit. Go talk to Garret Blount."

"I have."

"And?"

"Said he didn't know anything about it. Said he dropped her off and then went home to bed with a bad stomachache. Woke up the next morning and his truck was stolen."

"Alibi?"

"Well, his dad. And the girl. Their stories line up."

"That truck is at the bottom of the ocean by now. Along with whatever he used to do it, a bat or something."

He nods. "It still leaves me with zero."

I want to pick up one of the plastic couches and put it through a window. "Why the *hell* would she protect that kid?"

"Maybe," Emmett says, "maybe it's not that kid she's protecting." We sit for a minute. Thinking, looking at the big priest and the big dog.

I finally let my eyes close for a minute.

⌒

I guess I slept for a nice little piece of time, because he's done with surgery.

They come and talk to Mel, the surgeon and the doctor, they have this nice talk about condyles and fractures and ligaments and tendons, about appliances and braces and band lacing and sutures, enough to make you lose your lunch if you'd eaten one. And the doc says something about remarkable bone strength, all the healed fractures that show up on his x-rays. "Riddled with healed hairlines," is the exact way he puts it.

Mel starts to cry, and the doc puts a hand on the old guy's shoulder and says something about stronger at the broken places, which is a nice way of saying how great it is that kids bounce back after some asshole parent works them over.

But the whole point of it is, in six weeks he'll be good as new.

And Goddamnit, I cry. I cry like a baby. And I'm telling the priest, I tried, I did my best, I told him what I know, but I don't know shit, I don't know shit. I tried to help, I took him fishing, at least I took him fishing.

And he asks me, what happened to him. Nobody ever told him how this happened, who did it, what happened to Gentry?

You tell me, Mel. You tell me.

⌒

I go over to Emmett's office and he lets me listen to the tapes. I listened to that tape eight times. That Mumford girl calling in, panicked, crying, her voice going up at the end of everything she says like a little girl's. *He's really hurt? You need to hurry?*

Peggy's calm, telling her not to move him. Peggy over at Dispatch is nice, she says, *okay, we're about seven minutes out, do you want me to wait on the line with you until they get there?*

No, Marci says, quiet-like. *No, I'd better go.*

She's not crying, then. She's calm. She's figured out she only has seven minutes to clean up whatever she has to clean up to save her goddamned fish-stink boyfriend.

Give me seven minutes alone in a room with Marci Mumford. I'd have the truth out of her. Real quick.

⁓

So, five days, five damn days and he still won't eat.

I tell him he better get some food down his gullet or they won't let him leave, not that he says a word back to me because his mouth is a scrap heap. When he tries to talk he sounds like one of those cancer guys talking through an electronic voice box in a commercial to scare you off smoking.

I came in here and Mel was going over him with some words and oil and I listened for a minute and I thought, is this it? I went out in the hall and got busy panicking, find me a doctor, what the hell was it, was he DYING? The nurse told me to quiet down, it was something called Extreme Unction. Well that sounds BAD I said, REAL BAD, but Mel came out and explained that it isn't bad, he asked for it, it's supposed to make him better.

Well what the hell kind of crazy shit is this, I thought just Pentecostal churches did that laying on of hands bullshit, but apparently the Catholic Church does it too. But only the Catholics would have you excused from your sins caused by walking. What the hell are your walking sins? No wonder Gentry is so messed up, between sins caused by walking and "carnal delectation." Jesus on a Rubber Cross Christ.

Anyway, they can't take out the IV because he can't eat. Mel sits there beside him, praying over him and begging, mostly, that old priest is begging him to eat. "You're meant to be getting better, not worse. They're talking about a stomach tube, Gentry. My boy, I know you. You would hate it. Try, my boy. Or I'm going to have to let them put in that tube."

The food nurse keeps bringing him these Orange Julius type drinks, but I could have told these people that he can't drink anything like that, and these pussy juice drinks get Gentry to gagging all delicate-like, and Mel starts hollering. "THIS IS ALL SWEET!" His little hands fly around like quail, I watch those hands and I swear I want a good retriever and a gun. "HE DOES NOT DRINK SWEET LIQUIDS! HE CAN'T!"

He goes out in the hall to argue with them about what they bring in, I bet the staff here is getting real fond of the hallway in front of this room, and I go over and put a hand on Gentry's shoulder. "You have to eat, little buddy. They won't let you go until your gut's working again." He closes his eyes.

He's starving himself.

Mel's out in the hall, now, hollering some more in his priest way. "There has to be another way to feed him, to have him get what he needs. Besides that TUBE." Vickie comes in with Bosco, she was out walking the dog, doing something useful like usual, because she's real quiet, real helpful. She's first class, I tell you that much. We packed up Gentry's stuff at the lab today, and I was having a little trouble figuring out what went and what stayed but she just looked at this list he gave us and taped up the boxes and stacked them like it was nothing.

So we're just sitting there staring at him when the nutritionist brings in one last drink and puts the glass on his table. "I promise, it isn't sweet." She touches his hair, aw, all the girls touch my buddy's hair, and she leaves. She's smart to leave, because I never saw such a sorry bunch of rejected women as the nurses who keep coming in here trying to get Gentry to eat. They come in all sassy and walk out looking like Darlene at closing time when she fails to close the deal before the lights come up. Disappointed.

"Little buddy, you have to try. Come on. Let's try."

He looks at me, he looks at the glass, and he makes up his mind. He's going to try.

He picks up the glass, his hand's shaking, and he draws off that drink like a drunk throws down a shot. And I think about buying him those shots and I want to cry, see, I did that and this is all part of it, him laying there in that bed with the snot beat out of him, it's all part of the same thing, and he's gulping down that drink like it's the hard stuff, like he knows it's going to kill him and he can't wait to die.

Then he stops.

His eyes get big and he gags, his hand goes to his throat, he drops the glass and his hands are pulling on his throat, his mouth, he's panicked, oh Jesus Goddamn Christ don't you panic, Gentry, but he's throwing up and his mouth is wired shut, it's pouring out his nose, he'll choke on it, he'll die . . . HE WILL NOT because Vicki takes the scissors on his night table and she opens up his mouth and cuts the bands, and this dreck flows out of him and he's spitting and gagging and choking and Goddamnit, he's breathing, he's drawing breath and he's alive.

Mel runs in yelling. "WHAT WAS IN THAT DRINK?" he asks me, Gentry, Bosco, Vicki, the nurse, the food nurse, all of us in here, now, all of us who might have a hand in this.

The food nurse squeaks when she talks, she's so scared. "It wasn't sweet, I swear."

"WHAT WAS IN IT?"

And now she's got big tears in her eyes. "It was just yogurt and peanut butter."

"PEANUT BUTTER? PEANUT BUTTER?" Mel sounds like Moses on the mount, about to break the tablets. "SWEET MARY MOTHER OF JESUS, GENTRY DOES NOT EAT PEANUT BUTTER!"

No one can say a word.

Then, there's a noise.

I look over at my little buddy who almost barfed himself to death, laying in the hospital bed over there all covered with milkshake and rubber bands and puke and tears because of course he's crying. But not because he's sad.

Gentry is laughing.

He is laughing until he cries.

Until he cries.

EXODUS

I sent Mel back to the monastery, disappointed. I would always disappoint Mel, that was my destiny. And he would always love me anyway, that was his destiny.

We all have a destiny. I know that. Mine is to disappoint.

I couldn't think about that. I thought about my farewell to Lorrie Gilroy, that philosopher, that savior, that foul-mouthed fisher of men.

∽

I left my gear in his truck and almost forgot it, but Lorrie didn't.

Lorrie picked me up at the hospital at "Oh-dark-thirty." Well, not quite that. I had to sign papers and get drug instructions and other things, so it was a little later than dawn. He brought the coffee. He brought me to the place he's been telling me about all year. Every man has a place that he loves so much, he almost can't share it. He brought me to the Miami River.

First, we knocked on the door of a farmhouse and paid two dollars each to the owner of this place, Old MacDonald, to protect this spot from "the goddamn Willamette Valley sports fishermen." Lorrie insisted on paying. The farmer gave us each a note, handwritten slips that said we had "permission this day to fish." I folded it up and put it in my wallet.

Next, we came down to the river. It was already light, but the sun was low in the east. We stood about twenty feet apart. I had on enormous waders that Lorrie gave to me, because he had newer and even more enormous waders. "I don't need those, you can keep'em." I never had any waders. I always got wet when I didn't stay on the bank. I never minded getting wet. But Lorrie said I could have those.

The water was clear. As the sun rose higher, every rock in the riverbed, every speck of gravel showed through. There were shrews by the bank. Bosco kept busy with those and stayed dry. Lorrie gave me a pair of polarized glasses he no longer needed, just a cheap pair he thought he had lost. "You can have those." I was fascinated with being able to see below the surface of the water. I thought I could see before, but I was blind.

The fish went for my line, but I threw them back when I could and gave them to Lorrie when I couldn't. He tried to give me his Loomis. "I want a new one. If I gave you this one, it gives me a reason to go buy one."

I shook my head.

We were quiet. We caught fish as the sun came up and made everything new.

⌐

After, he drove me and Bosco up to the house. He insisted. The Jeep was safe in the garage, everything ready to go. Lorrie loaded in my bag, the box from school, my fishing gear. I still couldn't lift anything. I stood there on broken glass. A dark spot on the driveway might have been oil. Or it might have been blood.

I didn't remember it. Any of it. I couldn't remember.

"You all set, little buddy?" It hurt to nod. "Well, see, I was going to tell you a joke." He shook his buffalo head. "I was going to, but I figured I wouldn't. That's your going-away present."

It hurt to laugh.

We stood there for a while watching Bosco lift his leg on the tires of the Jeep, Lorrie's truck, good old Bosco. I sounded so strange, whistling through the junk in my mouth. "Hey Lorrie, did you ever figure it out?"

"Figure what out, little buddy?"

"Did you ever figure out what guys like me are for?"

He studied my face, serious and steady. "Guys like you are to make guys like me look bad. You're one helluva man, Gentry. And you're one helluva teacher."

"I'm a teacher who never learns."

"You will, little buddy. Maybe the only thing I've learned in my whole block-headed life is how to recognize another blockhead. And you're no blockhead. You'll learn." And then he hugged me, it hurt me but some pain is worth it. "I'm gonna miss you, that's for sure."

"I'll miss you too, Lorrie."

He turned his head away. "You won't miss me. I'm an asshole."

"You're my favorite asshole."

His head swung back, eyes wide in astonishment. "You swore! You actually swore!"

"That's your going-away present."

And we hugged again. My ribs sang with pain. We didn't say good-bye, we said until the next time. He dropped me like a dog told to let something go, and left without looking at me again.

Please, God. Let there be a next time. Amen.

My keys were in the Jeep. We were packed and ready to go, Bosco, but there was one more place I had to go, one last thing I had to do. To get there, we had to walk past all those windows. People who hated me might have looked out. I didn't care. I wasn't looking in.

I went in, looked around. It was just how it was when I came.

Perfect.

I lay down on the bed and began to apologize.

～

God, I've prayed to You for so many stupid things in my life. One stupidity after another. I turned twenty-eight a few days ago, and I have a few prayers to apologize for.

All the times I prayed for my keys to turn up. I'm sorry for that. The same for the sunglasses. Parking tickets and speed traps. Sorry. I'm sorry for every time I prayed my computer wouldn't crash, especially when my incessant tweaking caused it. I'm sorry for the times I prayed the paper tray was full, instead of just checking it. I can't believe I prayed about the paper tray. Forgive me.

How many times did I pray to You that someone would be quiet, God? With my mouth wired shut, I'll never pray for another tongue to be still. I prayed not to cry. You wanted me to cry, I understand that. Forgive me. But the prayers You answered, when You sent me strength, or patience, or forgiveness, or even just sleep. Thank You for answering those.

I know now that You listen, I know now that You hear, and I know that You love me.

And now, God, You must know that there's one thing I have to ask You for, one thing. I will never again pray for You to kill me, but if this prayer is not heard, it might kill me. It just might. Please.

The door creaked.

This is to give thanks. Amen.

～

She slid up next to me on the bed and everywhere she touched me felt warm. She fit herself to my side, as close as she needed to, and she fit differently. It had only been a month and she'd grown. But she'd been growing all the time I'd been here.

"Are you leaving now?"

I nodded.

"But I forgive you and so does Mom. So why do you have to leave, Gentry?"

"Because of everything." She heard me speak and sat up with a gasp.

"What's *in* there?" She had to put her fingers in my mouth, she wanted to see the wires and bands, all the garbage in there. I showed her the scissors I had to carry in case I threw up or panicked, so I could free myself from the interlaced rubber. "How will you *eat?*"

Oh, Gretchen, that was the question. I tried to explain through the clenched teeth and the taste of metal and rubber and the saliva that my tongue could hardly move down my throat, that I'd rather not eat at this point.

"You need protein. Gentry, listen. When you're on the road, stop at a grocery store, and get a little carton of milk and some ricotta cheese, like we put in lasagna, you remember? And you need vegetables. You can get baby food. And then in the car, shake it all up and drink it through a straw. It will be disgusting, but it won't be sweet, and it will keep you alive."

It would keep me alive.

"Who did it?"

"I can't remember."

"Like amnesia?"

"Yes."

"That can happen with a blow to the head." She studied the bruises on my face. "You're kind of the school colors, you know." Yes, I hadn't thought about the old red white and blue, but that described my appearance. Even as I left, I carried the school spirit with me.

"Sit up." She unbuttoned my shirt and looked at the bruises, probing, waiting for my flinches. She had to feel where I hurt, to find every point of damages. "Where does it hurt the most?" I took her hand and put it where I ached the most. My greatest pain. "Your heart?" She looked at our hands. "It will get better."

"I hope so." I let go of her hand and buttoned my shirt. And then, it was the last time to have my arms around her, to smell her hair, to hold this little girl, and she started to cry. So did I.

"Gentry, I love you."

"I love you back." I leaned to her ear and whispered through clenched teeth. She didn't laugh. She repeated it, said it out loud. I have never been able to stand hearing my name said out loud. But like everything else, Gretchen made it beautiful.

Good-bye, Gretchen.

And I'm driving down this road, a long, long way to the new place. I need a change, as much as I hate a change, even I have to admit that I need a change. I'm following Man Directions, following them south.

I'm flying.

Man Directions are clear, concise, no puzzles. But I like puzzles. I used to think that poems were the most beautiful puzzles of all, but now I know that's not true. Women are the most beautiful puzzles of all, and I've never solved one. I'll keep trying, God, until I do.

It's as beautiful on the day I leave this place as it was on the day I arrived. I'm almost happy. Almost.

I miss my copilot.

Bosco is fourteen years old, now, the age I was when he came to me. I needed Bosco then. I need Bosco now. But he doesn't need to go anywhere else. He deserves to live at the beach. He's earned this little time in dog heaven after all the years I kept him in dog purgatory.

Bosco is staying with Gretchen.

Oh, I know he doesn't have much time left, I know. I probably didn't take such good care of him. Too much people food, I forgot about his shots some years. His teeth are terrible. But he might live a while longer. He might. Some dogs live to be eighteen or nineteen years old. Bosco might. Or he might not. I explained this to Gretchen.

She doesn't care. She wants him for the time he has left.

Marci will go off to college and forget about Bosco. Kathryn will be irritated that she has to take care of Bosco while Gretchen is at her dad's. But he's a good dog. He doesn't ask for all that much. Just someone to love.

I can write to Gretchen and keep track of him. When Gretchen waits for the bus in the morning, he'll be there, waiting with her. When she gets off the bus in the afternoon, he'll be there, waiting for her. So will my letters.

Bosco likes dead things, and so does Gretchen. He will always listen to her stories. He will always watch cartoons with her. He will never ask her to be quiet. When they play games, and he loves games, he'll let her win all of the time, instead of just some of the time. Bosco is a great loser.

He'll sleep in her room. If she wants him to, he can sleep in her bed, as close as she needs. He'll always stay as close as she needs. He'll watch over her all night, every night.

Bosco begs at the dinner table. He scratches at the door. He barks at squirrels. He patrols the beach. He plays. Those are his jobs. He can look out for Gretchen. That will be another job for Bosco.

When she gets older, when the boys come, and they will, because Gretchen is beautiful, Bosco will be an old, old dog. He won't walk very well, or see very well. But he'll still be able to sniff out danger. He'll warn Gretchen, and she'll listen to him. He will keep her safe. Maybe, just maybe, Bosco will live to see Gretchen's children, her beautiful blonde children. I hope so.

And a long time from now, Gretchen will write to me, and tell me that one day Bosco went out to the water, and he lay down in the sun, and the wind blew his fur around. And it felt so good to the old dog, the sun and the wind, that Bosco never got up.

But that will be okay by Bosco. Everything is okay by Bosco.

He will love her until he dies.

Readers Discussion Guide

1. Who is the main character in this story? Why do you think that?
2. Kathryn's divorce settlement plays a key role throughout this story; it is the reason she wants to rent out the little house in the first place. What does her relationship to this money tell us about Kathryn? What drives her reluctance to spend it?
3. The author of this book believes that sibling relationships and birth order are more important than parental relationships to our overall social development. How does the relationship between Marci and Gretchen change over the course of this novel? Is it stronger or weaker at book's end?
4. If the author's beliefs about siblings and birth order are true, how does this affect an only child like Gentry?
5. How does alcoholism color Marci's daily life? How does it color Gretchen's life? Who is more affected, and why?
6. Why does a smart, beautiful girl like Marci need Garret?
7. We all have the right to pursue happiness. But where do we draw the line? Michael Mumford's decision to start a different family is a selfish one, but he seems happy with it. What happens when our own happiness destroys the lives of people around us?
8. Why do you think Gentry is drawn to teaching as a profession? Is it the right choice for him?
9. Though he is often alone, Gentry rarely seems lonely. Why do you think this is? Explain the role of God, Mel and Bosco in his life.
10. Who in this book cares the most about Gretchen?
11. Why is Kathryn's home furnished as it is? Do you have a strong mental image of Kathryn's home? If so, which is your favorite room?

12. What is your initial impression of Lorrie Gilroy? Does your sense of him change over the book? What are his strengths as a friend and a mentor?

13. Is Kathryn Mumford a good mother or a nightmare mother? Which of her traits are most important?

14. Is it a blessing or a curse for a man to be exceptionally beautiful? How does Gentry's physical beauty affect him? Is he even aware of it?

15. Is Gentry the hero or the villain of this story?

16. Where do these characters go next?

About the Author

After a nomadic childhood that took her to South Dakota, California, Minnesota, Arkansas, Washington and Montana, Karen G. Berry settled in Portland, Oregon. She's stayed put for over thirty years, raising three daughters and walking many dogs. After graduating magna cum laude at age forty with a degree in English, Karen has worked in marketing. Aside from her novel endeavors, she is an extensively published poet, but tries not to let that sneak into her fiction.

Visit her at www.karengberry.mywriting.network/ to learn more.

Made in the USA
San Bernardino, CA
17 June 2018